JAMES KENNEDY PUBLIC LIBRARY

P9-BZD-128

SUSPECT

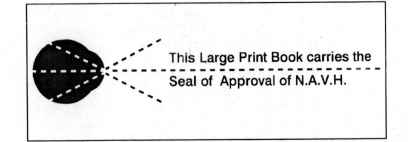

This Large Print Book carries the
Seal of Approval of N.A.V.H.

SUSPECT

ROBERT CRAIS

LARGE PRINT PRESS
A part of Gale, Cengage Learning

JAMES KENNEDY PUBLIC LIBRARY
320 First Avenue East
Dyersville, Iowa 52040

DISCARD

GALE
CENGAGE Learning·

Detroit • New York • San Francisco • New Haven, Conn • Waterville, Maine • London

GALE
CENGAGE Learning

Copyright © 2013 by Robert Crais.
Large Print Press, a part of Gale, Cengage Learning.

ALL RIGHTS RESERVED
This is a work of fiction. Names, characters, places, and incidents either are the product of the author's imagination or are used fictitiously, and any resemblance to actual persons, living or dead, businesses, companies, events, or locales is entirely coincidental.
The text of this Large Print edition is unabridged.
Other aspects of the book may vary from the original edition.
Set in 16 pt. Plantin.

LIBRARY OF CONGRESS CATALOGUING-IN-PUBLICATION DATA

Crais, Robert.
    Suspect / by Robert Crais. — Large Print edition.
        pages cm. — (Wheeler Publishing Large Print Hardcover)
    ISBN 978-1-4104-5513-0 (hardcover) — ISBN 1-4104-5513-0 (hardcover)
    1. Police—California—Los Angeles—Fiction. 2. Los Angeles (Calif.)—Fiction.
    3. Large type books. I. Title.
    PS3553.R264S85 2013b
    813'.54—dc23   2012048831

ISBN 13: 978-1-59413-672-6 (pbk. : alk. paper)
ISBN 10: 1-59413-672-6 (pbk. : alk. paper)

Published in 2014 by arrangement with G. P. Putnam's Sons, a member of Penguin Group (USA) LLC, a Penguin Random House Company.

Printed in the United States of America
2 3 4 5 6   18 17 16 15 14

15:99

Cengage

4/14

for Gregg Hurwitz
friend, dog man, writer.
and his beautiful pack,
Delinah, Rosie, Natalie,
and Simba.

■ ■ ■ ■

PROLOGUE:
THE GREEN BALL

■ ■ ■ ■

Maggie stared at Pete with rapt, undivided focus. His dark face was smiling, his hand was hidden inside the heavy green bulk of his USMC flak jacket, and he cooed to her in the high-pitched, squeaky voice she loved.

"That's a good girl, Maggie. You're the best girl ever. You know that, baby girl Marine?"

Maggie was an eighty-five-pound black-and-tan German shepherd dog. She was three years old, and her full name was Military Working Dog (MWD) Maggie T415, the T415 being tattooed on the inside of her left ear. Corporal Pete Gibbs was her handler. He had been hers and she had been his since they met at Camp Pendleton one and a half years ago. They were now halfway through their second deployment as a patrol and explosives-detection team in the Islamic Republic of Afghanistan.

Pete cooed, "We good to go, baby girl?

You gonna find the bad thing for daddy? You ready to work?"

Maggie's tail thumped the dirt hard. This was a game they played often, so Maggie knew what was coming, and lived for the joy of this moment.

Al-Jabar Province, 0840 hours, the Republic of Afghanistan. It was 109 degrees, and would reach 120.

The desert sun beat hard on Maggie's thick fur as a dozen Marines unassed three Humvees and formed up in a loose column twenty meters behind her. Maggie knew the other Marines, but they meant little to her. Pete was relaxed around them, so Maggie tolerated them, but only when Pete was near. They were familiar, but not pack. Pete was pack. Pete was hers. Maggie and Pete ate together, slept together, and played together 24/7. She loved, adored, protected, defended, and felt lost without him. When the other Marines came too close, Maggie warned them with a low growl. She had been bred to guard and protect what was hers, and Pete was hers. They were pack.

Now, this moment, Maggie was totally focused on Pete. Nothing else mattered or existed. There was only Pete, and Maggie's joyful expectation of the game they were about to play, when a voice called out

behind her.

"Yo, Pete. We're good, bro. Roll out."

Pete glanced at the other humans, then smiled wider at Maggie.

"Wanna see it, girl? Wanna see what I got?"

Pete took a fluorescent green ball from beneath his flak jacket.

Maggie's eyes locked on the ball, and she stood like a shot, up on all fours, whining for Pete to throw it. Maggie lived to chase the green ball. It was their favorite toy and her favorite game. Pete would throw it hard and far, and Maggie would power after it, chasing it down with a feeling of purpose and bliss; catch it, clamp it tight in her jaws, and proudly bring it back, where Pete was always waiting to shower her with love and approval. Chasing the green ball was her absolute favorite game, but now Pete showed her the ball only as a promise of the bliss to come. Maggie knew the routine, and was cool with it. If she found the smells Pete had taught her to find, she would be rewarded with the ball. That was their game. She must find the right smells.

Pete tucked the ball back under his flak, and his voice changed from squeaky to firm. He was alpha, and now he spoke in his alpha voice.

"Show me what you got, Maggie Marine.

11

Find the bad things. Seek, seek, seek."

Seek seek seek.

Maggie was trained as a patrol dog and an explosives-detection dog, making her a dual-purpose dog. She would attack on command, chase and apprehend fleeing persons, and was stellar at crowd control, but her primary job was sniffing out caches of ammunition, artillery ordnance, and roadside bombs. Improvised Explosive Devices. IEDs. The Afghan insurgents' weapon of choice.

Maggie did not know what an IED was, but this was not necessary. She had been taught to recognize the eleven most popular explosive components insurgents used in their bombs, including ammonium nitrate, detonator cord, potassium chlorate, nitrocellulose, C-4, and RDX. She did not know these things could kill her, but this did not matter, either. She sought them for Pete because pleasing Pete meant everything. If Pete was happy, Maggie was happy. They were a pack of two, and Pete was her alpha. He would throw the green ball.

At Pete's command, Maggie trotted to the end of her leash, which was tethered to a metal D-ring on Pete's harness. She knew exactly what Pete expected because Pete had trained her, and they had performed this same mission hundreds of times. Their job was to walk along the road twenty meters ahead of the Marines to find the IEDs. They went first, and their lives and the lives of the Marines behind depended on Maggie's nose.

Maggie swung her head from side to side, checking the high scents first, then dipped her head to taste the smells close to the ground. The humans behind her might be able to identify five or six distinct smells if they concentrated, but Maggie's long shepherd's nose gave her an olfactory picture of the world no human could comprehend: She smelled the dust beneath her feet and the goats that had been herded along the road a few hours earlier and the two young male goatherds who led them. Maggie smelled the infection that one of the goats carried, and knew that two of the female goats were in heat. She smelled Pete's fresh new sweat and the older sweat dried into his gear, his breath, the perfumed letter he kept in his trousers, and the green ball hidden beneath his flak. She smelled the CLP he used to clean his rifle, and the residual gunpowder that clung to his weapon like a fine dust of death. She smelled the small grove of palms not far from the road, and the trace scents of the wild dogs that had slept beneath the palms during the night and defecated and urinated before moving on. Maggie hated the wild dogs. She spent a moment testing the air to see if they were still in the area, decided they were gone, then ignored their scent and concentrated on searching for the scents Pete wanted her to find.

Smells filled her nose as fully as light filled her eyes, all blurred together like the hundreds of colors a person sees without seeing on library bookshelves. But as a person could focus on each individual book to see its colors, Maggie ignored the smells in which she had no interest, and concentrated on finding the smells that would bring the green ball.

Their mission that day was to clear a five-mile dirt road leading to a small village where insurgents were believed to cache arms. The squad of Marines would secure the village, protect Maggie and Pete while they searched, and recover any weapons or explosives that were found.

The miles crept past slowly, and they drew closer to the village without Maggie finding the smells she sought. The heat grew brutal, Maggie's fur became hot to the touch, and she let her tongue hang. She immediately felt a gentle tug on her leash, and Pete approached.

"You hot, baby? Here you go —"

Maggie sat, and thirstily drank from the plastic bottle Pete offered. The Marines stopped in place when she stopped, and one called out.

"She okay?"

"The water's good for now. We reach the vil, I want to get her out of the sun for a while."

"Roger that. Another mile and a half."

"We're good."

A mile later they moved past another palm grove and glimpsed the tops of three stone buildings peeking over the tops of the palms. The same Marine voice called out again.

"Heads up. Vil ahead. We take fire, it'll come from there."

They were rounding the last curve in the road toward the village when Maggie heard the tinkle of bells and bleating. She stopped, pricked her ears, and Pete stopped beside her. The Marines stopped in place, still well behind.

"What is it?"

"She hears something."

"She got an IED?"

"No, she's listening. She hears something."

15

Maggie tested the air with a series of short, fast sniffs, and caught their scent as the first goat appeared through the shimmering heat. Two teenage boys walked near the front and to the right of a small flock, with a taller, older male walking on the left. The taller male raised a hand in greeting.

The Marine behind Maggie shouted a word, and the three oncoming men stopped. The goats continued on, then realized the men had stopped, and milled in a lazy group. They were forty yards away. In the rising, windless air, it took a few seconds for their smells to cover the distance.

Maggie didn't like strangers, and watched them suspiciously. She sampled the air again — sniff sniff sniff — and huffed the air through her mouth.

The taller male raised his hand again, and the molecules that carried their smells finally reached Maggie's nose. She noted their different and complex body odors, the coriander, pomegranate, and onion on their breath, and the first faint taste of a smell Pete taught her to find.

Maggie whined and leaned into the leash. She glanced at Pete, then stared at the men, and Pete knew she was onto something.

"Gunny, we got something."

"Something in the road?"

16

"Negative. She's staring at these guys."

"Maybe she wants the goats."

"The men. She doesn't give a shit about the goats."

"They carrying?"

"We're too far away. She smells something, but the scent cone is too big. These guys might have residue in their clothes, they might be packing guns, I dunno."

"I don't like it we're standing here with the buildings right there. If someone lights us up, it's going to come from the vil."

"Let'm come to us. You guys stay put, and we'll give'm a good sniff."

"Roger that. We got you covered."

The Marines spread to the sides of the road as Pete waved the goatherds forward.

Maggie swung her head from side to side, hunting for the strongest scent, and felt alive with anticipation. The scent grew stronger as the men approached, and she knew Pete would be pleased. He would be happy with her for finding the scent, and reward her with the green ball. Pete happy, Maggie happy, pack happy.

Maggie whined anxiously as the men drew closer and the scent cone narrowed. The older boy wore a loose white shirt and the younger a faded blue T-shirt, and both wore baggy white pants and sandals. The taller man was bearded, and wore a dark loose shirt with baggy long sleeves and faded pants. The sleeves hung in folds, and draped when he raised his arms. His body reeked of days-old sour sweat, but the target scent was strong now. It came from the taller man, and Maggie's certainty flowed up the leash into Pete, who knew what Maggie knew as if they were one creature, not man and dog, but something better. Pack.

Pete shouldered his rifle, and barked at the man to stop.

The man stopped, smiling, and raised his hands as the goats now herded around the boys.

The man spoke to the boys, who stopped, and Maggie smelled their fear, too.

Pete said, "Stay, girl. Stay."

Pete stepped out ahead of her to approach the tall man. Maggie hated when Pete moved away from her. He was alpha, so she obeyed, but she heard his heart beat faster and smelled the sweat pouring from his skin, and knew Pete was afraid. His anxiety coursed through the leash, and poured into Maggie, so she became anxious, too.

Maggie broke position to catch up with him, and shouldered into his leg.

"No, Maggie. Stay."

She stopped at his command, but gave a

low growl. Her job was to protect and defend him. They were pack, and he was alpha. Every DNA strand of her German shepherd breeding screamed for her to put herself between Pete and the men, and warn them off or attack them, but pleasing Pete was also in her DNA. Alpha happy, pack happy.

Maggie broke position again, and once more put herself between Pete and the strangers, and now the smell was so strong Maggie did as Pete had taught her. She sat.

Pete kneed her aside, and raised his rifle as he shouted a warning to the other Marines.

"He's loaded!"

The tall man detonated with a concussion that slammed Maggie backward so hard she was thrown upside down. She lost consciousness briefly, then woke on her side, disoriented and confused as dust and debris fell on her fur. She heard nothing but a high-pitched whine, and her nose burned with the acid stink of an unnatural fire. Her vision was blurred, but slowly cleared as she struggled to rise. The Marines behind her were shouting, but their words had no meaning. Her left front leg collapsed with her weight. She shouldered into the dirt, but immediately stood again, propping herself on three wobbly legs that stung as if being bitten by ants.

The bearded man was a pile of smoking cloth and torn flesh. Goats were down and screaming. The smaller boy was sitting in the dust, crying, and the older boy stumbled in a lazy circle with splashes of red on his shirt and face.

Pete lay crumpled on his side, groaning. They were still joined by the leash, and his pain and fear flowed into her.

He was pack.

He was everything.

Maggie limped to him, and frantically licked his face. She tasted the blood running from his nose and ears and neck, and flushed with the need to soothe and heal him.

Pete rolled over and blinked at her.

"You hurt, baby girl?"

A burst of earth kicked up from the road near Pete's head, and a loud crack snapped through the air.

The Marine voices behind her shouted louder.

"Sniper! Sniper in the vil!"

"Pete's down!"

"We're taking fire —"

The crazy loud chatter of a dozen automatic weapons made Maggie cringe, but she licked Pete's face even harder. She wanted him to get up. She wanted him to be happy.

A heavy crack of thunder so close it shook the ground exploded behind her, and more dirt and hot shards blew through her fur. She cringed again, and wanted to run, but went on with the licking.

Heal him.

Soothe him.

Take care of Pete.

"Mortar!"

"We're gettin' mortared!"

Another puff of dirt kicked up from the road beside them, and Pete slowly unclipped Maggie's lead from his harness.

"Go, Maggie. They're shootin' at us. Go."

His alpha voice was weak, and the weakness scared her. Alpha was strong. Alpha was pack. Pack was everything.

More thunder shook the earth, then more, and suddenly something awful punched her hip and spun her into the air. Maggie screamed as she landed, and snapped and snarled at the pain.

"Sniper shot the dog!"

"Take that fucker out, goddamnit!"

"Ruiz, Johnson, with me!"

Maggie paid no attention as the Marines ran toward the buildings. She snapped at the terrible pain in her hip, then dragged herself back to her pack.

Pete tried to push her away, but his push was weak.

"Go, baby. I can't get up. Get away —"

Pete reached under his flak and took out the green ball.

"Get it, baby girl. Go —"

Pete tried to throw the green ball, but it only rolled a few feet. Pete vomited blood, and shuddered, and everything about him changed in those seconds. His scent, his taste. She heard his heart grow still and the blood slow in his veins. She sensed his spirit leave his body, and felt a mournful loss unlike anything she had ever known.

"PETE! Pete, we're coming, man!"

"Air support comin' in. Hang on!"

Maggie licked him, trying to make Pete laugh. He always laughed when she licked his face.

Another high-pitched snap ripped past her, and another geyser of dust spouted into the air. Then something heavy slammed into Pete's flak so hard Maggie felt punched in the chest, and smelled the bullet's acrid smoke and hot metal. She snapped at the hole in Pete's flak.

"They're shooting at the dog!"

More mortar rounds whumped just off the road, again raining dirt and hot steel.

Maggie snarled and barked, and dragged herself on top of her alpha. Pete was alpha. Pete was pack. Her job was to protect her pack.

She snapped at the raining debris, and barked at the metal birds now circling the distant buildings like terrible wasps. There were more explosions, then a sudden silence filled the desert, and the clatter of running Marines approached.

"Pete!"

"We're comin', man —"

Maggie bared her fangs and growled.

Protect the pack. Protect her alpha.

The fur on her back stood in rage, and her ears cocked forward to scoop in their sounds. Her fangs were fearsome and gleaming as bulky green shapes towered around her.

Protect him, protect the pack, protect her Pete.

"Jesus, Maggie, it's us! Maggie!"

"Is he dead?"

"He's fucked up, man —"

"She's fucked up, too —"

Maggie snapped and ripped at them, and the shapes jumped back.

"She's crazy —"

"Don't hurt her. Shit, she's bleeding —"

Protect the pack. Protect and defend.

Maggie snapped and slashed. She growled and barked, and hopped in circles to face them.

"Doc! Doc, Jesus, Pete's down —"

"Black Hawk's inbound!"

"His dog won't let us —"

"Use your rifle! Don't hurt her! Push her off —"

"She's shot, dude!"

Something reached toward her, and Maggie bit hard. She locked onto it with jaws that brought over seven hundred pounds per square inch of bite pressure to bear. She held tight, growling, but then another long thing reached forward, and another.

Maggie released her grip, lunged at the nearest men, caught meat and tore, then took her place over Pete again.

"She thinks we're gonna hurt him —"

"Push her off! C'mon —"

"Don't hurt her, goddamnit!"

They pushed her again, and someone threw a jacket over her head. She tried to twist away, but now they bore her down with their weight.

Protect Pete. Pete was pack. Her life was the pack.

"Dude, she's hurt. Be careful —"

"I got her —"

"Fuckin' scum shot her —"

24

Maggie twisted and lurched. She was furious with rage and fear, and tried to bite through the jacket, but felt herself lifted. She felt no pain, and did not know she was bleeding. She only knew she needed to be with Pete. She had to protect him. She was lost without him. Her job was to protect him.

"Put her on the Black Hawk."

"I got her —"

"Put her on there with Pete."

"What's with the dog?"

"This is her handler. You gotta get her to the hospital —"

"He's dead —"

"She was trying to protect him —"

"Stop talkin' and fly, motherfucker. You get her to a doctor. This dog's a Marine."

Maggie felt a deep vibration through her body as the thick exhaust of the aviation fuel seeped through the jacket that covered her head. She was scared, but Pete's smell was close. She knew he was only a few feet away, but she also knew he was far away, and growing farther.

She tried to crawl closer to him, but her legs didn't work, and men held her down, and after a while her fierce growls turned to whines.

Pete was hers.

They were pack.

They were a pack of two, but now Pete was gone, and Maggie had no one.

PART I

■ ■ ■ ■

SCOTT AND STEPHANIE

■ ■ ■ ■

1.

Downtown Los Angeles

They were on that particular street at that specific T-intersection at that crazy hour because Scott James was hungry. Stephanie shut off their patrol car to please him. They could have been anywhere else, but he led her there, that night, to that silent intersection. It was so quiet that night, they spoke of it.

Unnaturally quiet.

They stopped three blocks from the Harbor Freeway between rows of crappy four-story buildings everyone said would be torn down to build a new stadium if the Dodgers left Chavez Ravine. The buildings and streets in that part of town were deserted. No homeless people. No traffic. No reason for anyone to be there that night, even an LAPD radio car.

Stephanie frowned.

"You sure you know where you're going?"

"I know where I'm going. Just hang on."

Scott was trying to find an all-night noodle house a Rampart Robbery detective had raved about, one of those pop-up places that takes over an empty storefront for a couple of months, hypes itself on Twitter, then disappears; a place the robbery dick claimed had the most amazing ramen in Los Angeles, Latin-Japanese fusion, flavors you couldn't get anywhere else, cilantro-tripe, abalone-chili, a jalapeño-duck to die for.

Scott was trying to figure out how he had screwed up the directions when he suddenly heard it.

"Listen."

"What?"

"Shh, listen. Turn off the engine."

"You have no idea where this place is, do you?"

"You have to hear this. Listen."

Uniformed LAPD officer Stephanie Anders, a P-III with eleven years on the job, shifted into Park, turned off their Adam car, and stared at him. She had a fine, tanned face with lines at the corners of her eyes, and short, sandy hair.

Scott James, a thirty-two-year-old P-II with seven years on the job, grinned as he touched his ear, telling her to listen. Stephanie seemed lost for a moment, then blossomed with a wide smile.

"It's quiet."

"Crazy, huh? No radio calls. No chatter. I can't even hear the freeway."

It was a beautiful spring night: temp in the mid-sixties, clear; the kind of windows-down, short-sleeve weather Scott enjoyed. Their call log that night showed less than a third their usual number of calls, which made for an easy shift, but left Scott bored. Hence, their search for the unfindable noodle house, which Scott had begun to believe might not exist.

Stephanie reached to start the car, but Scott stopped her.

"Let's sit for a minute. How many times you hear silence like this?"

"Never. This is so cool, it's creeping me out."

"Don't worry. I'll protect you."

Stephanie laughed, and Scott loved how the streetlights gleamed in her eyes. He wanted to touch her hand, but didn't. They had been partners for ten months, but now Scott was leaving, and there were things he wanted to say.

"You've been a good partner."

"Are you going to get all gooey on me?"

"Yeah. Kinda."

"Okay, well, I'm going to miss you."

"I'm going to miss you more."

Their little joke. Everything a competition, even to who would miss the other the most. Again he wanted to touch her hand, but then she reached out and took his hand in hers, and gave him a squeeze.

"No, you're not. You're going to kick ass, take names, and have a blast. It's what you want, man, and I couldn't be happier. You're a stud."

Scott laughed. He had played football for two years at the University of Redlands before blowing his knee, and joined LAPD a couple of years later. He took night classes for the next four years to finish his degree. Scott James had goals. He was young, determined, and competitive, and wanted to run with the big dogs. He had been accepted into LAPD's Metro Division, the elite uniformed division that backed up area-based officers throughout the city. Metro was a highly trained reserve force that rolled out on crime suppression details, barricade situations, and high-conflict security operations. They were the best, and also a necessary assignment for officers who hoped to join LAPD's most elite uniformed assignment — SWAT. The best of the best.

Scott's transfer to Metro would come at the end of the week.

Stephanie was still holding his hand, and Scott was wondering what she meant by it, when an enormous Bentley sedan appeared at the end of the street, as out of place in this neighborhood as a flying carpet, windows up, smoked glass, not a speck of dust on its gleaming skin.

Stephanie said, "Check out the Batmobile."

The Bentley oozed past their nose, barely making twenty miles per hour. Its glass was so dark the driver was invisible.

"Want to light him up?"

"For what, being rich? He's probably lost like us."

"We can't be lost. We're the police."

"Maybe he's looking for the same stupid ramen place."

"You win. Let's forget the ramen and grab some eggs."

Stephanie reached to start their car as the slow-motion Bentley approached the next T-intersection thirty yards past them. At the moment it reached the intersecting street, a deep, throaty growl shattered the perfect silence, and a black Kenworth truck exploded from the cross street. It T-boned the Bentley so hard the six-thousand-pound sedan rolled completely over and came to rest right side up on the opposite side of the street. The Kenworth skidded sideways and stopped, blocking the street.

Stephanie said, "Holy crap!"

Scott slapped on their flashers, and pushed out of their car. The flashers painted the street and surrounding buildings with blue kaleidoscope pulses.

Stephanie keyed her shoulder mike as she got out, searching for a street sign.

"Where are we? What street is this?"

Scott spotted the sign.

"Harmony, three blocks south of the Harbor."

"Two-Adam-twenty-four, we have an injury accident at Harmony, three blocks south of the Harbor Freeway and four north of Wilshire. Request paramedics and fire. Officers assisting."

Scott was three paces ahead, and closer to the Bentley.

"I got the Batmobile. You get the truck."

Stephanie broke into a trot, and the two veered apart. No one and nothing else moved on the street except steam hissing from beneath the Bentley's hood.

They were halfway to the accident when bright yellow bursts flashed within the truck and a hammering chatter echoed between the buildings.

Scott thought something was exploding within the truck's cab, then bullets ripped into their patrol car and the Bentley with the thunder of steel rain. Scott instinctively jumped sideways as Stephanie went down. She screamed once, and wrapped her arms across her chest.

"I'm shot. Oh, crap —"

Scott dropped to the ground and covered his head. Bullets sparked off the concrete around him, and gouged ruts in the street.

Move. Do something.

Scott rolled sideways, drew his pistol, and fired at the flashes as fast as he could. He pushed to his feet, and zigzagged toward his partner as an old, dark gray Gran Torino screamed down the street. It screeched to a stop beside the Bentley, but Scott barely saw it. He fired blindly at the truck as he ran, and zigged hard toward his partner.

Stephanie was clutching herself as if doing stomach crunches. Scott grabbed her arm. He realized the men in the truck had stopped firing, and thought they might make it even as Stephanie screamed.

Two men wearing black masks and bulky jackets boiled out of the sedan with pistols and lit up the Bentley, shattering the glass and punching holes in its body. The driver stayed at the wheel. As they fired, two more masked men climbed from the truck with AK-47 rifles.

Scott dragged Stephanie toward their black-and-white, slipped in her blood, then started backwards again.

The first man out of the truck was tall and thin, and immediately opened fire into the Bentley's windshield. The second man was thick, with a large gut that bulged over his belt. He swung his rifle toward Scott, and the AK-47 bloomed with yellow flowers.

Something punched Scott hard in the thigh, and he lost his grip on Stephanie and his pistol. He sat down hard, and saw blood welling from his leg. Scott picked up his pistol, fired two more shots, and his pistol locked open. Empty. He pushed to his knees, and took Stephanie's arm again.

"I'm dying."

Scott said, "No, you're not. I swear to God you're not."

A second bullet slammed into the top of his shoulder, knocking him down. Scott lost Stephanie and his pistol again, and his left arm went numb.

The big man must have thought Scott was done. He turned to his friends, and when he turned, Scott crabbed toward their patrol car, dragging his useless leg and pushing with his good. The car was their only cover. If he made it to the car, he could use it as a weapon or a shield to reach Stephanie.

Scott keyed his shoulder mike as he scuttled backwards, and whispered as loudly as he dared.

"Officer down! Shots fired, shots fired! Two-Adam-twenty-four, we're dying out here!"

The men from the gray sedan threw open the Bentley's doors and fired inside. Scott glimpsed passengers, but saw only shadows. Then the firing stopped, and Stephanie called out behind him. Her voice bubbled with blood, and cut him like knives.

"Don't leave me! Scotty, don't leave!"

Scott pushed harder, desperate to reach the car. Shotgun in the car. Keys in the ignition.

"DON'T LEAVE ME!"

"I'm not, baby. I'm *not.*"

"COME BACK!"

Scott was five yards from their patrol car when the big man heard Stephanie. He turned, saw Scott, then lifted his rifle and fired.

Scott James felt the third impact as the bullet punched through his vest on the lower right side of his chest. The pain was intense, and quickly grew worse as his abdominal cavity filled with pooling blood.

Scott slowed to a stop. He tried to crawl farther, but his strength was gone. He leaned back on an elbow, and waited for the big man to shoot him again, but the big man turned toward the Bentley.

Sirens were coming.

Black figures were inside the Bentley, but Scott couldn't see what they were doing. The driver of the gray sedan twisted to see the shooters, and pulled up his mask as he turned. Scott saw a flash of white on the man's cheek, and then the men in and around the Bentley ran into the Torino.

The big man was the last. He hesitated by the sedan's open door, once more looked at Scott, and raised his rifle.

Scott screamed.

"NO!"

Scott tried to jump out of the way as the sirens faded into a soothing voice.

"Wake up, Scott."

"NO!"

"Three, two, one —"

Nine months and sixteen days after he was shot that night, nine months and sixteen days after he saw his partner murdered, Scott James screamed when he woke.

2.

Scott threw himself out of the line of fire so violently when he woke, he was always surprised he had not jumped off his shrink's couch. He knew from experience he only made a small lurch. He woke from the enhanced regression the same way each time, jumping from the dream state of his memory as the big man raised the AK-47. Scott took careful, deep breaths, and tried to slow his thundering heart.

Goodman's voice came from across the dim room. Charles Goodman, M.D. Psychiatrist. Goodman did contract work with the Los Angeles Police Department, but was not an LAPD employee.

"Deep breaths, Scott. You feel okay?"

"I'm okay."

His heart pounded, his hands trembled, and cold sweat covered his chest, but as with the violent lunge that Goodman saw as only a tiny lurch, Scott was good at downplaying

41

his feelings.

Goodman was an overweight man in his forties with a pointy beard, a ponytail, sandals, and toenail fungus. His small office was on the second floor of a two-story stucco building in Studio City next to the L.A. River channel. Scott's first shrink had a much nicer office in Chinatown at the LAPD's Behavioral Science Services, but Scott didn't like her. She reminded him of Stephanie.

"Would you like some water?"

"No. No, I'm fine."

Scott swung his feet off the couch, and grimaced at the tightness in his shoulder and side. He grew stiff when he sat for too long, so standing and moving helped ease the pain. He also needed a few seconds to adjust when he left the hypnotic state, like stepping from a sun-bright street into a dark bar. This was his fifth enhanced regression into the events of that night, but something about this regression left him confused and uncertain. Then he remembered, and looked at his shrink.

"Sideburns."

Goodman opened a notebook, ready to write. Goodman constantly wrote.

"Sideburns?"

"The man driving the getaway car. He had

white sideburns. These bushy white side-burns."

Goodman made a quick note in his book, then riffled back through the pages.

"You haven't described sideburns before?"

Scott strained to remember. Had he? Had he recalled the sideburns, but simply not mentioned them? He questioned himself, but already knew the answer.

"I didn't remember them before. Not until now. I remember them now."

Goodman scribbled furiously, but all the fast writing made Scott feel more doubtful.

"You think I really saw them, or am I imagining this?"

Goodman held up a hand to finish his note before speaking.

"Let's not go there yet. I want you to tell me what you remember. Don't second-guess yourself. Just tell me what you recall."

The memory of what he saw was clear.

"When I heard the sirens, he turned toward the shooters. He pulled up his mask when he turned."

"He was wearing the same mask?"

Scott had always described the five shooters in exactly the same way.

"Yeah, the black knit ski mask. He pulled it up partway, and I saw the sideburns. They were long, here below the lobe. Might have been gray, like silver?"

Scott touched the side of his face by his ear, trying to see the image even more clearly — a faraway face in bad light, but there was the flash of white.

"Describe what you saw."

"I only saw part of his jaw. He had these white sideburns."

"Skin tone?"

"I don't know. White, maybe, or Latin or a light-skinned black guy."

"Don't guess. Only describe what you clearly remember."

"I can't say."

"Can you see his ear?"

"I saw part of his ear, but it was so far away."

"Hair?"

"Only the sideburns. He only raised the mask partway, but it was enough to see the sideburns. Jesus, I remember them so clearly now. Am I making this up?"

Scott had read extensively about manufactured memories, and memories recovered while under hypnosis. Such memories were viewed with suspicion, and were never used by L.A. County prosecutors. They were too easily attacked, and created reasonable doubt.

Goodman closed his notebook on the pen.

"Making this up as in imagining you saw something you didn't?"

"Yeah."

"You tell me. Why would you?"

Scott hated when Goodman went all psychiatrist on him, asking Scott to supply his own answers, but Scott had been seeing the man for seven months, so he grudgingly accepted the drill.

Scott had awakened two days after the shooting with a vivid memory of the events that night. During three weeks of intensive questioning by the Homicide Special detectives in charge of the investigation, Scott described the five shooters as best he could, but was unable to provide any more identifying detail than if the men had been featureless silhouettes. All five had been masked, gloved, and clothed from head to foot. None limped or had missing limbs. Scott had heard no voices, and could not provide eye, hair, or skin color, or such identifying information as visible tattoos, jewelry, scars, or affectations. No fingerprints or usable DNA had been found on the cartridge casings, in the Kenworth, or in the Ford Gran Torino found abandoned only eight blocks away. Despite the case being handled by an elite team of detectives from the LAPD's Homicide Special detail, no suspects had been identified, all leads were exhausted, and the investigation had ground to an inevitable, glacial halt.

Nine months and sixteen days after Scott James was shot, the five men who shot him and murdered Stephanie Anders remained free.

They were still out there.

The five men who murdered Stephanie.

The killers.

Scott glanced at Goodman, and felt himself flush.

"Because I want to help. Because I want to feel like I'm doing something to catch these bastards, so I'm making up bullshit descriptions."

Because I'm alive and Stephanie's dead.

Scott was relieved when Goodman wrote none of this down. Instead, Goodman smiled.

"I find this encouraging."

"That I'm manufacturing memories?"

"There's no reason to believe you've manufactured anything. You've described the large elements of that night consistently since the beginning, from your conversation with Stephanie, to the makes and models of the vehicles, to where the shooters were standing when they fired their weapons. Everything you described that *could* be confirmed *has* been confirmed, but so much was happening so quickly that night, and under such incredible stress, it's the tiny things we tend to lose."

Goodman always got into it when he described memory. Memory was his thing. He leaned forward, and pinched his thumb and forefinger together to show Scott what he meant by "tiny."

"Don't forget, you remembered the cartridge casings in our first regression. You didn't remember hearing the Kenworth's engine before you saw the truck until our fourth regression."

Our regressions. As if Goodman had been there with him, getting shot to pieces while Stephanie died. Regardless, Scott had to admit Goodman had a point. It wasn't until Scott's first regression that he recalled the spent casings twinkling like a brass rainbow as they arced from the big man's rifle, and he hadn't recalled hearing the Kenworth rev its engine until the fourth regression.

Goodman leaned so far forward, Scott thought he might fall from his chair. He was totally into it now.

"When the little details begin coming back — the tiny memories forgotten in the stress of the moment — the research suggests you may begin remembering more and more, as each new memory leads to another, the way water trickles through a crack in a dam, faster and faster until the dam breaks, and the water floods through."

Scott frowned.

"Meaning, my brain is falling apart?"

Goodman returned Scott's frown with a smile, and opened his notebook again.

"Meaning, you should feel encouraged. You wanted to examine what happened that night. This is what we're doing."

Scott did not respond. He used to believe he wanted to explore that night, but more and more he wanted to forget, though forgetting seemed beyond him. He relived it, reviewed it, and obsessed about it constantly, hating that night but unable to leave it.

Scott glanced at the time, saw they only had ten minutes remaining, and stood.

"Let's bag it for today, okay? I want to think about this."

Goodman made no move to close his notebook. He cleared his throat, instead, which was his way of changing the subject.

"We still have a few minutes. I want to check in with you about a few things."

Check in. Shrink jargon for asking more questions about things Scott didn't want to talk about.

"Sure. About what?"

"Whether the regressions are helping."

"I remembered the sideburns. You just told me they're helping."

"Not in what you remember, but in helping you cope. Are you having fewer nightmares?"

Nightmares had shattered his sleep four or five times a week since his fourth day in the hospital. Most were like short clips cut from a longer film of that night's events — the big man shooting at him, the big man raising his rifle, Scott slipping in Stephanie's blood, and the impact of bullets punching into his body. But more and more were paranoid nightmares where the masked men were hunting him. They jumped from his closet or hid under his bed or appeared in the back seat of his car. His most recent nightmare had been last night.

Scott said, "A lot less. I haven't had a nightmare in two or three weeks."

Goodman made a note in his book.

"You attribute this to the regressions?"

"What else?"

Goodman made a satisfied nod, along with another note.

"How's your social life?"

"Social life is fine if you mean grabbing a beer with the guys. I'm not seeing anyone."

49

"Are you looking?"

"Is mindless small talk a requirement for mental health?"

"No. Not at all."

"I just want someone I can relate to, you know? Someone who understands what it's like to be me."

Goodman made an encouraging smile.

"In the fullness of time, you'll meet someone. Few things are more healing than falling in love."

Few things would be more healing than forgetting, or catching the bastards who did this, but neither seemed to be in the cards.

Scott glanced at the clock, and was irritated to see they still had six minutes.

"Can we bag it for today? I'm tapped out, and I have to get to work."

"One more thing. Let's touch base about the new job."

Scott glanced at the time again, and his impatience increased.

"What about it?"

"Have you gotten your dog? Last session, you said the dogs were on their way."

"Got here last week. The chief trainer checks them out before he accepts them. He finished yesterday, and says we're good to go. I get my dog this afternoon."

"And then you're back on the street."

Scott knew where this was going and didn't like it. They had been through this before.

"After we're certified, yeah. That's where K-9 officers do their job."

"Face-to-face with the bad guys."

"That's kinda the point."

"You almost died. Are you concerned this might happen again?"

Scott hesitated, but knew better than to pretend he had no fear. Scott had not wanted to be in a patrol car again, or sit behind a desk, but when he learned two slots were opening in the Metro K-9 Unit, he had lobbied hard for the job. He had completed the K-9 dog handler training course nine days ago.

"I think about it, sure, but all officers think about it. This is one of the reasons I want to stay on the job."

"Not all officers are shot three times and lose their partner on the same night."

Scott didn't respond. Since the day he woke in the hospital, Scott had thought about leaving the job a thousand times. Most of his officer friends told him he was crazy not to take the medical, and the LAPD Personnel Division told him, because of the extent of his injuries, he would never be cleared to return, yet Scott pushed to stay on the job. Pushed his physical therapy. Pushed his commanding officers. Pushed his Metro boss hard to let him work with a dog. Scott would lie awake in the middle of the night, making up reasons for all the pushing: Maybe he didn't know what else to do, maybe he had nothing else in his life, maybe he was trying to convince himself he was still the same man he was before the shooting. Meaningless words to fill the empty darkness, like the lies and half-truths he told to Goodman and everyone else, because saying unreal things was easier than saying real things. His unspoken, dead-of-night truth was that he felt as if he had died on the street beside Stephanie, and was now only a ghost pretending to be a man. Even his choice of being a K-9 officer was a pretense — that he could be a cop without a partner.

Scott realized the silence was dragging on, and found Goodman waiting.

Scott said, "If I walk away, the assholes who killed Stephanie win."

"Why are you still seeing me?"

"To make peace with being alive."

"I believe that's true. But not the whole truth."

"Then you tell me."

Goodman glanced at the time again, and

finally closed the notebook.

"Looks like we're a few minutes over. This was a good session, Scott. Same time next week?"

Scott stood, hiding the stitch in his side that came with the sudden movement.

"Same time next week."

Scott was opening the door when Goodman spoke again.

"I'm glad the regressions are helping. I hope you remember enough to find peace and closure."

Scott hesitated, then walked out and down to the parking lot before he spoke again.

"I hope I remember enough to forget."

Stephanie came to him every night, and it was his memories of her that tortured him — Stephanie slipping from his bloody grip, Stephanie begging him not to leave.

Don't leave me!

Scotty, don't leave!

Come back!

In his nightmares, it was her eyes and her pleading voice that filled him with anguish.

Stephanie Anders died believing he had abandoned her, and nothing he did now or in the future could change her final thoughts. She had died believing he had left her to save himself.

I'm here, Steph.

I didn't leave you.

I was trying to save you.

Scott told her these things every night when she came to him, but Stephanie was dead and could not hear. He knew he would never be able to convince her, but he told her anyway, each time she came to him, trying to convince himself.

3.

The narrow parking lot behind Goodman's building was furious with summer heat, and the air was sandpaper dry. Scott's car was so hot, he used his handkerchief to open the door.

Scott bought the blue 1981 Trans Am two months before the shooting. The right rear fender had a nasty dent from the taillight to the door, the blue paint was pocked with corrosion, the radio didn't work, and the odometer showed 126,000 miles. Scott had bought it for twelve hundred dollars as a weekend project, thinking he would rebuild the old car in his spare time, but after the shooting he lost interest. Nine months later, the car remained untouched.

When the air blew cold, Scott made his way to the Ventura Freeway and headed for Glendale.

The K-9 Platoon was headquartered with the Metro Division at the Central Station downtown, but used several sites around the city for training its dogs. The primary training site was in Glendale, which was a spacious facility where Scott and the other two new handlers had been trained as K-9 officers during an eight-week handler school run by the Unit's veteran chief trainer. The student handlers trained with retired patrol dogs who no longer worked in the field due to health or injury issues. They were easy to work with and knew what was expected of them. In many ways, these dogs served as teachers for their baby handlers, but when the school cycle was completed, the training dogs would return to wherever they lived, and the new handlers would be partnered with pre-trained patrol dogs to begin a fourteen-week certification process. This was an exciting moment for the new handlers, as it meant they would begin bonding with their new dogs.

Scott knew he should feel excited, but felt only a dull readiness to work. Once Scott and his dog were certified, he would be alone with the dog in a car, and that's what Scott wanted. The freedom to be alone. He had plenty of company with Stephanie.

Scott was passing the Hollywood split when his phone rang. The Caller ID showed LAPD, so he answered, thinking it was probably his K-9 Platoon Chief Trainer, Dominick Leland.

"This is Scott."

A male voice spoke, but it wasn't Leland.

"Officer James, I'm Bud Orso, here with Robbery-Homicide. I'm calling to introduce myself. I'm the new lead in charge of your case."

Scott drove on without speaking. He had not spoken with his case investigators in more than three months.

"Officer, you still there? Did I lose you?"

"I'm here."

"I'm the new lead in charge of your case."

"I heard you. What happened to Melon?"

"Detective Melon retired last month. Detective Stengler was reassigned. We got a new team in here on this."

Detective Melon was the former lead, and Stengler was his partner. Scott had not spoken with either man since the day Scott gimped into the Police Administration Building with his walker, and unloaded on Melon in front of the entire Homicide Special squad room because they had been unable to name a suspect or develop new leads after a five-month investigation. Melon had tried to walk away, but Scott grabbed him, fell out of his walker, and pulled Melon down with him. It was an ugly scene Scott regretted, and could have derailed Scott's chance to return to the job. After the incident, Scott's Metro boss, a Captain named Jeff Schmidt, cut a deal with the RHD commander, a Lieutenant named Carol Topping, who buried the incident. An act of compassion for an officer who was shot to shit in the street. Melon had not filed a complaint, but shut Scott out of the investigation and stopped returning his calls.

Scott said, "Okay. Thanks for letting me know."

He didn't know what else to say, but wondered why Orso sounded so friendly.

"Did Melon tell you what happened?"

"Yes, he told me. He said you were an ungrateful prick."

"I am."

Fuckit. Scott hadn't cared what Melon thought of him, and didn't care what the new guy thought, either, but he was surprised when Orso laughed.

"Look, I know you had a problem with him, but I'm the new guy. I'd like to meet you, and go over a couple of things in the file."

Scott felt a flare of hope.

"Did Melon turn any new leads?"

"No, I can't say that. This is just me, trying to get up to speed on what happened

58

that night. Could you roll by sometime to-day?"

The flare of hope faded to a bitter ember. Orso sounded like a nice guy, but Scott had just relived what happened that night, and was fed up with talking about it.

"I'm on shift, then I have plans."

Orso paused. This told Scott Orso knew Scott was giving him the brush.

Orso said, "How about tomorrow, or whenever is convenient?"

"Can I give you a call?"

Orso gave him his direct-dial number, and hung up.

Scott dropped his phone on the seat between his legs. The numbness he felt only moments earlier had been replaced with ir-ritation. Scott wondered what Orso wanted to ask about, and if he should have men-tioned the sideburns even though he didn't know if they were real.

Scott cut across lanes and veered toward the city. He punched in Orso's number as he passed Griffith Park.

"Detective Orso, it's Scott James again. If you're there now, I can swing by."

"I'm here. You remember where we are?"

Scott smiled at that, and wondered if this was Orso's idea of a joke.

"I remember."

"Try not to hit anyone when you get here."

Scott didn't laugh, and neither did Orso.

Scott phoned Dominick Leland next, and told him he wouldn't be in to see the new dogs. Leland growled like a German shepherd.

"Why in hell not?"

"I'm on my way to the Boat."

"Fuck the Boat. There is nothing and no one in that damned building more important than these dogs. I did not let you into my K-9 platoon to waste time with those people down there."

Robbery-Homicide housed their special units on the fifth floor of the Police Administration Building. The PAB was a ten-story structure across from City Hall. The side of the PAB facing City Hall was a thin, pointy, triangular glass wedge. This made the PAB look like the prow of a ship, so rank-and-file officers dubbed it the Boat.

"They want me at Robbery-Homicide. It's about the case."

Leland's growl softened.

"Your case?"

"Yes, sir. I'm on my way now."

Leland's voice turned gruff again.

"All right, then, get your ass here as soon as you can."

Scott never wore his uniform to Goodman's office. He kept his uniform in a gym bag and his handgun in a lockbox in the trunk. He dropped off the freeway on First Street, and changed in the Boat's parking garage. He expected more than a few detectives to give him the glare because of his scene with Melon. Scott didn't give a rat's ass, either way. He wanted to remind them he was a police officer.

Scott showed his badge and LAPD ID card to the lobby receptionist, and told her he was there to see Orso. She made a brief call, then gave Scott a different ID card to clip to his shirt.

"He's expecting you. You know where they are?"

"I know."

Scott tried not to limp as he crossed the lobby, which wasn't so easy with all the steel in his leg. The night they wheeled him into the Good Samaritan emergency room, Scott had surgeries on his thigh, shoulder, and lower chest. Three more surgeries followed later that same week, with two additional surgeries six weeks later. The leg wound cost him three pounds of muscle tissue, needed a steel rod and six screws to rebuild his femur, and left him with nerve damage. The shoulder reconstruction required three plates, eight screws, and also left him with

61

nerve damage. The PT after the multiple surgeries had been painful, but he was doing okay. You just had to be tougher than the pain, and eat a few painkillers.

Bud Orso was in his early forties, with a chubby scoutmaster's face topped by a crown of short black hair. He was waiting when Scott stepped off the elevator, which Scott had not expected.

"Bud Orso. Pleasure to meet you, though I'm sorry it's under these circumstances."

Orso had a surprisingly strong grip, but released Scott quickly and led him toward the Homicide Special offices.

"I've been living with this file since they handed me the case. Horrible, what happened that night. How long have you been back on the job?"

"Eleven weeks."

Polite conversation. Scott was already irritated, and wondered what was waiting for him in the Homicide Special squad room.

"I'm surprised they let you."

"Let me what?"

"Come back. You were squared up for a medical."

Scott didn't respond. He was already tired of talking, and sorry he came.

Orso noted the K-9 patch on Scott's shoulder as they walked.

"K-9. That should be interesting."

"Better. They do what you say, don't talk back, and it's only a dog."

Orso finally took the hint and fell silent as he led Scott into Homicide Special. Scott felt himself tense when he stepped through the door, but only five detectives were scattered about the room, and none glanced over or acknowledged him in any way. He followed Orso into a small conference room with a rectangular table and five chairs. A large black file box was on the floor at the head of the table. Scott saw his transcribed statements spread across the table, and statements made by the friends and families of the two men who had been inside the Bentley, a real estate developer named Eric Pahlasian, the driver, who had been shot sixteen times, and his cousin from France, a real estate attorney named Georges Beloit, who had been shot eleven times.

Orso went to the head of the table, and told Scott to sit wherever he liked.

Scott braced himself, then averted his face when he sat so Orso couldn't see his grimace. Taking a seat always caused a painful jolt in his side.

"Want a coffee or some water?"

"I'm good. Thanks."

A large drawing of the crime scene leaned

against the wall on the floor. Someone had sketched in the Kenworth, the Bentley, the Gran Torino, and the Adam car. Someone had sketched in Stephanie and Scott. A manila envelope lay on the floor by the poster board. Scott guessed crime scene photos were in the envelope, and glanced away. When he looked up, Orso was watching, and now Orso didn't look like a scoutmaster. There was a focus to his eyes that hardened them to points.

"I understand talking about this might be difficult."

"No sweat. What did you want to know?"

Orso studied him for a moment, then gave him the question.

"Why didn't the big man finish you?"

Scott had asked himself this ten thousand times, but could only guess at the answer.

"Paramedics, is my guess. The sirens were getting closer."

"Did you see him leave?"

If Orso read the interviews, he already knew the answer.

"No. I saw him lift the rifle. The gun came up, I laid back, and maybe I passed out. I don't know."

Later, in the hospital, they told him he had passed out from blood loss.

"Did you hear them leave?"

"No."

"Doors closing?"

"No."

"Were you awake when the paramedics arrived?"

"What did they say?"

"I'm asking you."

"The rifle came up, I put my head back, and then I was in the hospital."

Scott's shoulder was killing him. A deep ache, as if his muscles were turning to stone. The ache spread across his back as if the scar tissue was splitting apart.

Orso slowly nodded, then made a crooked shrug.

"The sirens are a good bet, but you never know. When you slumped back, maybe he thought you were dead. Maybe he was out of ammo. Gun might have jammed. One day we'll ask him."

Orso picked up a slender report, and leaned back.

"Point is, you were hearing just fine until you passed out. Here in your statements, you mentioned you and Officer Anders were talking about how quiet it was. You stated she turned off the car so you could hear the silence."

Scott felt his face flush, and a stab of guilt up through the center of his chest.

"Yes, sir. That was on me. I asked her to turn off the vehicle."

"You hear anything?"

"It was quiet."

"I get it was quiet, but how quiet? Were there background sounds?"

"I dunno. Maybe the freeway."

"Don't guess. Voices on the next block? Barking? A noise that stood out?"

Scott wondered what Orso was going for. Neither Melon nor Stengler had asked him about background sounds.

"Nothing I recall."

"A door closing? An engine starting?"

"It was quiet. What are you digging at?"

Orso swiveled toward the crime scene poster. He leaned toward it and touched the side street from which the Kenworth had come. A blue X had been drawn on a storefront three doors from the intersection.

"A store here was burglarized the night you were shot. The owner says it happened after eight, which was when he locked up, but before seven the next morning. We have no reason to think the burglary occurred when you and Anders were at the scene, but you never know. I've been wondering about it."

Scott didn't recall Melon or Stengler mentioning the burglary, which would have

66

been a major element in their investigation.

"Melon never asked me about this."

"Melon didn't know. The place is owned by a Nelson Shin. You know that name?"

"No, sir."

"He distributes candy and herbs and crap he imports from Asia — some of which isn't legal to bring into the U.S. He's been ripped off so many times, he didn't bother to file a report. He went shopping for a weapon instead, and got named in an ATF sting six weeks ago. He shit out when the ATF scooped him, and claimed he needed a full-auto M4 because he's been burglarized so many times. He gave the ATF a list of dates to show how many times his store was cracked. Six times in the past year, if you're curious. One of those dates matched with your shooting."

Scott stared at the blue X that marked the store. When Stephanie shut off the engine, they listened to the silence for only ten or fifteen seconds, then began talking. Then the Bentley appeared, but the Bentley was so quiet he remembered thinking it moved like it was floating.

"I heard the Kenworth rev. Before it came out of the side street, I heard the big diesel rev up."

"That's all?"

Scott wondered how much to say, and how to explain.

"It's a new memory. I only remembered hearing it a couple of weeks ago."

Orso frowned, so Scott went on.

"A lot happened that night in a short period. I remembered the big things, but a lot of small things got lost. They're beginning to come back. The doctor says it happens like that."

"Okay."

Scott hesitated, then decided to tell him about the sideburns.

"I caught a glimpse of the getaway driver. You won't find this in the interviews because I just remembered."

Orso tipped forward.

"You saw him?"

"The side of his face. He raised his mask for a second. He had white sideburns."

Orso pulled his chair closer.

"Could you pick him out of a six-pack?"

A six-pack was a grouping of six photographs of suspects who looked similar.

"All I saw were the sideburns."

"Can I put you together with a sketch artist?"

"I didn't see him well enough."

Now Orso was looking irritated.

"Race?"

"All I remember is the sideburns. I might remember more, but I don't know. My doctor says the way it works is, one memory can trigger another. I remembered the Kenworth revving, and now the sideburns, so more things might start coming back to me."

Orso seemed to consider this, and finally settled back in his chair. Everything about him seemed to soften.

"You went through hell, man. I'm sorry this happened."

Scott didn't know what to say. He finally shrugged.

Orso said, "I want you to stay in touch. Anything else you remember, call me. Doesn't matter if you think it's important or not. Don't worry about sounding silly or stupid, okay? I want everything you've got."

Scott nodded. He glanced at the papers spread over the table and the files in the box. It was a larger box and contained more than Scott would have expected, considering the little Melon shared.

Scott studied the box for a moment, then looked back at Orso.

"Could I read through the file?"

Orso followed Scott's eyes to the box.

"You want to go through the file?"

"One memory triggers another. Maybe I'll

see something that helps me remember other things."

Orso considered for a moment, then nodded.

"Not now, but sure. If that's what you want. You'll have to go through it here, but I'm fine with letting you see it. Call in the next couple of days, and we'll set up a time."

Orso stood, and when Scott stood with him, Orso saw his grimace.

"You doing okay?"

"That's scar tissue loosening up. The docs say it'll take about a year for the stiffness to pass."

The same bullshit he told everyone.

Orso said nothing more until they reached the hall and were heading toward the elevator. Then his eyes hardened again.

"One other thing. I'm not Melon. He felt bad for you, but he thought you became a crazy pain in the ass who should've been pushed out on a psycho. You probably think he was a lousy detective. You were both wrong. Whatever you think, those guys busted their asses, but sometimes you can bust your ass and nothing turns up. It sucks, but sometimes that happens."

Scott opened his mouth to say something, but Orso raised a hand, stopping him.

"No one here quits. I'm not going to quit.

I'm going to live out this case one way or another. Are we clear?"

Scott nodded.

"My door is open. Call if you want, but if you call sixteen times a day, I'm not going to return sixteen calls. We clear on that, too?"

"I'm not going to call you sixteen times."

"But if I call *you* sixteen times, you damn well better get back to me asap each and every time, because I will have questions that need answers."

"I'll move in and live with you if it means catching these bastards."

Orso smiled, and looked like the scout-master again.

"You won't have to live with me, but we will catch them."

They said their good-byes at the elevator. Scott waited until Orso returned to his office, then gimped to the men's room. His limp was pronounced when no one was watching.

The pain was so bad he thought he would vomit.

He splashed cold water on his face, and rubbed his temples and eyes. He dried himself, then took two Vicodin from a small plastic bag, swallowed them, then rubbed his face with cold water again.

He patted himself dry, then studied himself in the mirror while he let the pills work. He was fifteen pounds thinner than the night he was shot, and half an inch shorter because of the leg. He was lined, and looked older, and wondered what Stephanie would think if she saw him.

He was thinking about Stephanie when a uniformed officer shoved open the door. The officer was young and in a hurry, so he shoved the door hard. Scott lurched sideways, away from the noise, and spun toward the officer. His heart pounded as if trying to beat its way out of his chest, his face tingled as his blood pressure spiked, and his breath caught in his chest. He stood motionless, staring, as his pulse thundered in his ears.

The young officer said, "Dude, hey, I'm sorry I scared you. I have to pee."

He hurried to the urinal.

Scott stared at his back, then clenched his eyes shut. He clenched his eyes hard, but he could not shut out what he was seeing. He saw the masked man with a large belly coming toward him with the AK-47. He saw the man in his dreams, and when he was awake. He saw the man shoot Stephanie first, then turn his gun toward Scott.

"Sir, are you okay?"

Scott opened his eyes, and found the young officer staring.

Scott pushed past him out of the bathroom. He did not limp when he crossed the lobby, or when he reached the training field to claim his first dog.

4.

The K-9 Platoon's primary training facility was a multi-use site located on the east side of the L.A. River only a few minutes northeast of the Boat, in an area where anonymous industrial buildings gave way to small businesses, cheap restaurants, and parks.

Scott turned through a gate, and parked in a narrow parking lot beside a beige cinder-block building, set at the edge of a large green field big enough for softball games or Knights of Columbus barbeques or training police dogs. An obstacle course for the dogs was set up beside the building. The field was circled by a tall chain-link fence, and hidden from public view by thick green hedges.

Scott parked by the building, and saw several officers working their dogs as he got out of his car. A K-9 Sergeant named Mace Styrik was trotting a German shepherd with odd marks on her hindquarters around the field. Scott did not recognize the dog, and wondered if she was Styrik's pet. On the near end of the field, a handler named Cam Francis and his dog, Tony, were approaching a man who wore a thick padded sleeve covering his right arm and hand. The man was a handler named Al Timmons, who was pretending to be a suspect. Tony was a fifty-five-pound Belgian Malinois, a breed that looked like a smaller, slimmer German shepherd. Timmons suddenly turned and ran. Francis waited until Timmons was forty yards away, then released his dog, who sprinted after Timmons like a cheetah running down an antelope. Timmons turned to meet the dog's charge, waving his padded arm. Tony was still six or eight yards away when he launched himself at Timmons, and clamped onto the padded arm. An unsuspecting man would have gone down with the impact, but Timmons had done this hundreds of times, and knew what to expect. He turned with the impact, and kept spinning, swinging Tony around and around in the air. Tony did not let go, and, Scott knew, was enjoying the ride. The Malinois breed bit so hard and well, and showed such bite commitment, they were jokingly called Maligators. Timmons was still spinning the dog when Scott saw Leland standing against the building, watching the officers work their dogs. Leland was standing with his arms crossed, and a coiled leash clipped to his belt. Scott had never seen the man without the leash at his side.

Dominick Leland was a tall, bony African-American with thirty-two years on the job as a K-9 handler, first in the United States Army, then the L.A. County Sheriffs, and finally the LAPD. He was a living legend in the LAPD K-9 corps.

Bald on top, his head was rimmed with short gray hair, and two fingers were missing from his left hand. The fingers were bitten off by a monstrous Rottweiler-mastiff fighting dog on the day Leland earned the first of the seven Medals of Valor he would earn throughout his career. Leland and his first dog, a German shepherd named Maisie Dobkin, had been deployed to search for an Eight-Deuce Crip murder suspect and known drug dealer named Howard Oskari Walcott. Earlier that day, Walcott fired nine shots into a crowd of high school students waiting at a bus stop, wounding three and killing a fourteen-year-old girl named Tashira Johnson. When LAPD ground and air support units trapped Walcott in a nearby neighborhood, Leland and Maisie Dobkin were called out to locate the suspect, who was believed to be armed, dangerous, and hiding somewhere within a group of four neighboring properties. Leland and Maisie cleared the first property easily enough, then moved into the adjoining backyard of a house then occupied by another Crip gangbanger, Eustis Simpson. Unknown to officers at the time, Simpson kept two enormous male Rottweiler-mastiff mixed-breeds on his property, both of which were scarred and vicious veterans of Simpson's illegal dogfighting business.

When Leland and Maisie Dobkin entered Simpson's backyard that day, both dogs charged from beneath the house and attacked Maisie Dobkin. The first dog, which weighed one hundred forty pounds, hit Maisie so hard she rolled upside down. He buried his teeth into Maisie's neck, pinning her down, as the second dog, which weighed almost as much, grabbed her right hind leg and shook it like a terrier shakes a rat. Maisie screamed. Dominick Leland could have done something silly like run for a garden hose or waste time with pepper spray, but Maisie would be dead in seconds, so Leland waded into the fight. He kneed the dog biting her leg to clear a line of fire, pushed his Beretta into the attacker's back, and pulled the trigger. He then grabbed the other dog's face with his free hand to make the dog release Maisie's neck. The overgrown monster bit Leland's hand, and Leland shot the sonofabitch twice, but not before the big dog took his pinky and ring finger. Leland later said he never felt the bite, and never knew the fingers were missing, until he put Maisie into the ambulance and demanded the paramedics rush her to the closest veterinarian. Both Leland and Maisie Dobkin recovered, and worked together for another six years until Maisie Dobkin retired. Leland still kept the official LAPD picture of himself and Maisie Dobkin on the wall of his office. He kept pictures of himself with all the dogs who had been his partners.

Leland scowled when he saw Scott, but Scott didn't take it personally. Leland scowled at everyone and everything except his dogs.

Leland uncrossed his arms, and entered the building.

"C'mon, now, let's see what we have."

The building was divided into two small offices, a general meeting room, and a kennel. The K-9 Platoon used the facility only for training and evaluations, and did not staff the building on a full-time basis.

Scott followed Leland past the offices and

into the kennel, Leland talking as they walked. Eight chain-link dog runs with chain-link gates lined the left side of the kennel, with a walkway leading past them to a door at the end of the building. The runs were four feet wide and eight feet deep, with floor-to-ceiling sides. The floor was a concrete slab with built-in drains, so the room could be washed and rinsed with hoses. When the training dogs lived here, Scott and his two classmates, Amy Barber and Seymore Perkins, had begun every morning by scooping up dog shit and washing the floor with disinfectant. This gave the kennel a medicinal smell.

Leland said, "Perkins is getting Jimmy Riggs' dog, Spider. I think they will be a good match. That Spider, I'll tell you something, he has a mind of his own, but he and Seymore will come to terms."

Seymore Perkins was Leland's favorite of the three new handlers. Perkins had grown up with hunting dogs, and possessed a calm confidence with the dogs, who instantly trusted him. Amy Barber had shown an intuitive feel for bonding with the dogs, and a command authority that far surpassed her slight build and higher voice.

Leland stopped between the second and third runs, where the two new dogs were waiting. Both dogs stood when Leland entered, and the near dog barked twice. They were skinny male Belgian Malinois.

Leland beamed as if they were his children.

"Aren't these boys gorgeous? Look at these boys. They are handsome young men."

The barker barked again, and both furiously wagged their tails.

Scott knew both dogs had arrived fully trained by the breeder, in accordance with written guidelines supplied by the K-9 Platoon. This meant Leland, who traveled to breeders all over the world in search of the best available dogs. Leland had spent the past three days personally running the dogs through their paces, evaluating their fitness, and learning each dog's personality and peculiarities. Not every dog sent to the K-9 Platoon measured up to Leland's standards. He downchecked those who did not, and returned them to their breeder.

Leland glanced at the dog in the second run.

"This here is Gutman. Why on earth those fools named him Gutman, I do not know, but that's his name."

Purchased dogs were usually around two years old when they arrived, so they had already been named. Donated dogs were

80

often a year older.

"And this here is Quarlo."

Gutman barked again, and went up on his hind legs, trying to lick Leland through the gate.

Leland said, "Gutman here is kinda high-strung, so I'm gonna put him with Amy. Quarlo here is smart as a whip. He's got a good head on his shoulders, and he's easy to work with, so I think you and Mr. Quarlo here are going to make a fine match."

Scott interpreted "easy to work with" and "smart as a whip" as Leland's way of saying the other dog was too much for Scott to handle. Perkins and Barber were the better handlers, so they were getting the more difficult dogs. Scott was the moron.

Scott heard the door open at the far end of the kennel and saw Mace come in with the German shepherd. He put the shepherd into a run, dragged out a large canine crate, and closed the shepherd's gate.

Scott studied Quarlo. He was a beautiful dog with a dark fawn body, black face, and upright black ears. His eyes were warm and intelligent. His steady demeanor was obvious. Where Gutman frittered and fidgeted, Quarlo stood utterly calm. Leland was probably right. This would be the easiest dog for Scott.

Scott glanced at Leland, but Leland wasn't looking at him. Leland was smiling at the dog.

Scott said, "I'll work harder. I'll work as hard as it takes."

Leland glanced up, and studied Scott for a moment. The only time Scott recalled Leland not scowling was when he looked at the dogs, but now he seemed thoughtful. He touched the leash clipped to his belt with his three-fingered hand.

"This isn't steel and nylon. It's a nerve. You clip one end to you, you clip the other to this animal, it ain't for dragging him down the street. You *feel* him through this nerve, and he feels you, and what flows through here flows both ways — anxiety, fear, discipline, approval — right through this nerve without you and your dog ever even having to look at each other, without you ever having to say a word. He can feel it, and you can feel it, too."

Leland let go of his leash, and glanced back at Quarlo.

"You're gonna work, all right, I know you're a worker, but there's things work can't build. I watched you for eight weeks, and you did everything I asked you to do, but I never saw anything flow through your leash. You understand what I'm saying?"

"I'll work harder."

Scott was trying to figure out what else to say when Cam Francis opened the door behind them, and asked Leland to check Tony's foot. Cam looked worried. Leland told Scott he would be right back, and hurried away, scowling. Scott stared at Quarlo for several seconds, then walked to the other end of the kennel where Mace was now hosing out the crate.

Scott said, "Hey."

Mace said, "Watch you don't get splashed."

The shepherd was lying with her head between her paws on a padded mat at the back of the run. She was a classic black-and-tan German shepherd with a black muzzle giving way to light brown cheeks and mask, a black blaze on the top of her head, and enormous black ears. Her eyebrows bunched as she looked from Scott to Mace, and back again. No other part of her moved. A hard rubber toy lay untouched on the newspaper, as did a leather chew and a fresh bowl of water. A name was written on the side of the crate. Scott cocked his head sideways to read it. Maggie.

Scott guessed she had to go eighty or eighty-five pounds. A lot bigger than the Maligators. She was big through the chest and hips the way shepherds were, but it was the hairless gray lines on her hindquarters that drew him. He squeezed past the crate for a better view, and watched her eyes follow him.

"This Maggie?"

"Yeah."

"She ours?"

"Nah. Donation dog. Family down Oceanside thought we could use her, but Leland's sending her back."

Scott studied the pale lines and decided they were scars.

"What happened to her?"

Mace put aside the hose, and joined Scott at the gate.

"She was wounded in Afghanistan. The scars there are from the surgeries."

"No shit. A military working dog?"

"U.S. Marine, this girl. She healed up okay, but Leland says she's unfit."

"What kind of work did she do?"

"Dual-purpose dog. Patrol and explosives detection."

Scott knew almost nothing about military working dogs, except that the training they received was specialized and excellent.

"Bomb get her?"

"Nope. Her handler was blown up by one of those suicide nuts. The dog here stayed with him, and some asshole sniper tried to kill her."

"No shit."

"For real. Shot her twice, Leland says. Parked herself on her boy, and wouldn't leave. Trying to protect him, I guess. Wouldn't even let other Marines get near him."

Scott stared at the German shepherd, but Mace and the kennel faded, and he heard the gunfire that night — the automatic rifle churning its thunder, the chorus of pistols snapping like whips. Then her brown eyes met his, and he was back in the kennel again.

Scott bit the inside of his mouth, and cleared his throat before speaking.

"She didn't leave."

"That's the story."

Scott noted how she watched them. Her nose worked constantly, sucking in their smells. Even though she had not moved from her prone position, Scott knew she was focused on them.

"If she healed up okay, what's Leland's problem?"

"She's bad with noise, for one. See how she lays back there, all kinda timid? Leland thinks she's got a stress disorder. Dogs get PTSD just like people."

Scott felt himself flush, and opened the gate to hide his irritation. He wondered if Mace and the other handlers spoke about him like this behind his back.

Scott said, "Hey, Maggie, how's it going?"

Maggie stayed on her belly with her ears folded back, which was a sign of submission, but she stared into his eyes, which possibly indicated aggression. Scott slowly approached her. She watched as he came, but her ears stayed down and she issued no warning growl. He held the back of his hand toward her.

"You a good girl, Maggie? My name is Scott. I'm a police officer, so don't give me any trouble, okay?"

Scott squatted a couple of feet from her, and watched her nose work.

"Can I pet you, Maggie? How 'bout I pet you?"

He moved his hand slowly closer, and was six inches from her head when she bit him. She moved insanely fast, snarling and snapping, and caught the top of his hand as he jerked to his feet.

Mace shouted, and charged into the run.

"Jesus! She get you?"

Maggie quit her attack as quickly as she bit him, and once more lay on her belly. Scott had jumped back, and now stood three feet away from her.

"Dude, you're bleeding. Lemme see. She get you deep?"

Scott pressed his handkerchief over the cut.

"It's nothing."

He watched Maggie's eyes move from him to Mace and back, as if she had to watch them both because either might attack.

Scott made his voice soothing.

"You got hurt bad, big girl. Yes, you did."

I'll bet I've been shot more times than you.

He squatted again, and held out his hand again, letting her smell his blood. This time she let him touch her. He spread his fingers through the soft fur between her ears, then slowly stepped away. She stayed on her belly, watching him, as he and Mace backed out of her run.

Mace said, "That's why she's going back. Leland says they get fucked up like this, they're never right again."

"Leland said that?"

"Voice of God."

Scott left Mace washing out Maggie's crate, and walked back through the offices, and outside, where he found Leland on his way back.

Leland said, "You and Quarlo ready to get to work?"

"I want the German shepherd."

"You can't have the shepherd. Perkins is gettin' Spider."

"Not Spider. The one you're shipping back. Maggie. Let me work with her. Give me two weeks."

"That dog's no good."

"Give me two weeks to change your mind."

Leland scowled the Leland scowl, then grew thoughtful again and fingered his leash.

"Okay. Two weeks. You got her."

Scott followed Leland back inside to get his new dog.

5.

DOMINICK LELAND

A few minutes later, Leland resumed his position outside in the spare shade cast by the building, crossed his arms, and watched Scott James work with the dog. Mace stood with him for a while, but grew bored, and went inside to get on with his duties. Leland said little. He watched how the man and the dog related to each other.

Inside, before they came out, Leland walked Scott back to the shepherd.

"Take her out back, and introduce yourself. I'm gonna watch."

Leland walked away without another word, and waited outside. After a while, Officer James came around the far side of the building with the dog on his lead. The dog was on James' left, which was the proper position, and did not try to range from him as they walked, but this proved nothing. The dog had been trained by the

United States Marine Corps. Leland did not doubt the excellence of her training, which he had witnessed himself when he evaluated her.

Officer James called over.

"Anything in particular you want me to do?"

Me. Not us. There was your problem, right there.

Leland answered with a scowl. After a while James withered under Leland's scowl, and went on with it. He made a few ninety-degree left and right turns, and trotted in left and right circles. The dog was always in perfect position except when they stopped. When they stopped, the dog lowered her head, tucked her tail, and hunched herself as if she was trying to hide. Officer James seemed not to notice this, even though he glanced at the dog often.

When Leland was sure James was concentrating on the dog, he slipped a black starter pistol from his pocket, and pulled the trigger. The starter pistol fired a .22-caliber blank cartridge, and was used to test new dogs for their tolerance to loud, unexpected sounds. A dog that freaked out when a gun went off was of little use to the police.

The sound cracked sharply across the training field, and caught both the dog and her handler by surprise.

James and the dog lurched at the same time, but the dog tucked her tail, and tried to hide between James' legs. When James looked over, Leland held up the starter pistol.

"Stress reaction. Can't have a police dog that shits out when a gun goes off."

James said nothing for several seconds. Leland was about to ask what in hell he was looking at when James stooped to touch the dog's head.

"No, sir, we can't. We'll work on it."

"Long strokes. Start at her neck and run your hand back to her tail. They like the long strokes. That's the way her mama did it."

James stroked her, long and slow, but he glared at Leland instead of relating to the dog. This set Leland off into one of his tirades.

"Talk to her, goddamnit. She ain't a stick of furniture. She is one of God's creatures, and she will hear you. I see these goddamned people walkin' dogs, yakking on their phones, makes me wanna kick their sissy asses. What they got a dog for, they want to talk on their phones? That dog there will understand you, Officer James. She will understand what's in your heart. Am I just shouting at the grass and dog shit out here, or are you reading what I am telling you?"

"I'm reading you, Sergeant."

Leland watched him stroke the dog, and talk to her, and then he shouted again.

"Obstacles."

The obstacle course was a series of jumping barriers and climbs. Leland had taken her through the course five times, so he knew what to expect. She was fine with the climbs, made the low jumps easily, but when she reached the last and highest barrier, a five-foot wall, she balked. The first time Leland took her through, he assumed her hips hurt because of her wounds or her strength was gone, but he stroked her and spoke with her, and when they tried again, she clawed her way over, and damn near broke his heart for trying so hard. Officer James brought her to the high barrier three times, and all three times she hit the brakes. The third time she splayed her legs, spun toward James, and snarled. To his credit, James did not jerk her lead, raise his voice, or try to force her. He backed off and talked to her until she calmed. Leland knew of a hundred other things Officer James could have done to help her over, but overall he approved of James' response.

Leland called out another instruction.

"Off the line. Voice commands."

James led her away from the obstacle course, unclipped the lead from her collar, and ran through the basic voice commands. He told her to sit, she sat. He told her to stay, she stayed. Stay, sit, come, heel, down. She would still have to learn the LAPD situational commands, which were different from military commands, but she did these well enough. After fifteen minutes of this, Leland called out again.

"She done good. Reward."

Leland had been through this with her, too, and waited to see what would happen. The best dog training was based on the reward system. You did not punish a dog for doing wrong, you rewarded the dog for doing right. The dog did something you wanted, you reinforced the behavior with a reward — pet'm, tell'm they're a good dog, let'm play with a toy. The standard reward for a K-9 working dog was a hard plastic ball with a hole drilled through it where Leland liked to smear a little peanut butter.

Leland watched James dig the hard plastic ball from his pocket, and wave it in front of the dog's face. She showed no interest. James bounced it in front of her, trying to get her excited, but she moved away, and appeared to get nervous. Leland could hear

James talking to her in the squeaky voice dogs associated with approval.

"Here you go, girl. Want it? Want to go get it?"

James tossed the ball past her, watching it bounce along the ground. The dog circled James' legs, and sat down behind him, facing the opposite direction. Leland had made the mistake of throwing the damned ball way out into center field, and had to go get it.

Leland called out.

"That's enough for today. Pack her up. Take her home. You got two weeks."

Leland returned to his office, where he found Mace Styrik drinking a warm Diet Coke.

Mace frowned, just as Leland expected. He knew his men as well as his dogs.

"Why are you wasting his time and ours, giving him a bad dog like that?"

"That dog ain't bad. She's just not fit for duty. If they gave medals to dogs, she'd have so many, a sissy like you couldn't lift'm."

"I heard the shot. She squirrel up again?"

Leland dropped into his chair, leaned back, and put up his feet. He brooded about what he had seen.

"Wasn't just the dog squirreled up."

"Meaning what?"

Leland decided to think about it. He dug a tin of smokeless tobacco from his pocket, pushed a wad of dip behind his lower lip, and worked it around. He lifted a stained Styrofoam cup from the floor beside his chair, spit into it, then put the cup on his desk and arched his eyebrows at Mace.

"Have a sip of that Coke?"

"Not with that nasty stuff in your mouth."

Leland sighed, then answered Mace's original question.

"His heart isn't in it. He can do the work well enough, else I would not have passed him, but they should have made him take the medical. God knows, he earned it."

Mace shrugged, wordless, and had more of the Coke as Leland went on.

"Everyone has been carrying that young man, and, Lord knows, my heart goes out to him, what happened an' all, but you know as well as I, we were pressured to take him. We passed over far better and more deserving applicants to give him this spot."

"That may be, but we gotta take care of our own. We always have, we always will, and that's the way it should be. He paid dear."

"I'm not arguing that point."

"Sounds like you are."

"Goddamnit, you know me better than

that. There are a thousand jobs they could have given him, but we are K-9. We aren't those other jobs. We are dog men."

Mace grudgingly had to agree.

"This is true. We're dog men."

"He is not."

Mace frowned again.

"Then why'd you give him that dog?"

"He said he wanted her."

"I say I want things all the time, you don't give me squat."

Leland worked the dip around again, and spit, thinking he might have to get up for his own Coke to wash down the taste.

"That poor animal is unfit for this job, and I suspect the same about him. I hope to God in His Glory I am wrong, sincerely I do, but there it is. They are suspect. That dog will help him realize he is not right for this job. Then she'll go back to that family, and he'll retire or transfer to a more suitable job, and all of us will be happier for it."

Leland dug the remains of the dip from his lip, dropped it into the cup, then stood to go find a drink of his own.

"See if he needs a hand with her crate. Give him the dog's file to take home, and tell him to read it. I want him to see what a fine animal she was. Tell him to be back here at oh-seven-hundred hours tomorrow."

"You going to help him retrain her?"

Dogs suffering from post-traumatic stress disorder shared similar stress reactions with humans, and could sometimes be retrained, but it was slow work that required great patience on the part of the trainer, and enormous trust on the part of the dog.

"No, I am not. He wanted that German shepherd, he got her. I gave him two weeks, and then I will re-evaluate her."

"Two weeks isn't long enough."

"No, it is not."

Leland walked out to search for a Coke, thinking how some days he loved his job, and others he didn't, and this day was one of the sad ones. He looked forward to going home later, and taking a walk with his own dog, a retired Mal named Ginger. They had long talks when they walked, and she always made Leland feel better. No matter how bad the day, she made him feel better.

6.

Scott held the driver's seat forward, and hipped the door open wide to let the dog out.

"Here we go, dog. We're home."

Maggie stuck her head out a few inches, sniffed the air, then slowly jumped down. Scott's Trans Am wasn't a large car. She filled the back seat, but had seemed to enjoy the ride from Glendale to his place in Studio City. Scott had rolled down the windows, and she lay across the seat with her tongue out and eyes narrowed as the wind riffled her fur, looking content and happy.

Scott wondered if her hips ached when she got out as much as his side and shoulder.

Scott rented a one-bedroom guest house from an elderly widow on a quiet residential street not far from the Studio City park, and parked in her front yard under an elm tree. MaryTru Earle was short, thin, and in her early eighties. She lived in a small California ranch-style home at the front of her property, and rented the guest house in the rear to supplement her income. The guest house had once been a pool house and game room, back in the days when she had a pool and children at home, but when her husband retired twenty-odd years ago, they filled the pool, created a flower garden, and converted the pool house into the guest house. Her husband had been gone now for more than ten years, and Scott was her latest tenant. She liked having a police officer close at hand, as she often told him. Having a police officer in the guest house made her feel safe.

Scott clipped the lead to Maggie's collar, and paused beside the car to let her look around. He thought she might have to pee, so he took her on a short walk. Scott let her set the pace, and sniff trees and plants for as long as she wanted. He talked to her as they walked, and when she stopped to worry a smell, he stroked his hand along her back and sides. These were bonding techniques he learned from Leland. Long strokes were soothing and comforting. The dog knows you're talking to her. Most people who walk their dogs take the dog for a people walk instead of a dog walk, drag the little sonofabitch along until it squeezes out a peanut, as Leland liked to say, then hurry back home. The dog wants to smell. Their nose is our eyes, Leland had said. You want to show the dog a good time, let her smell. It's *her* walk, not yours.

Scott knew almost nothing about dogs when he applied for the slot at K-9. Perkins had grown up training hunting dogs, and Barber had worked for a veterinarian through high school and raised huge white Samoyed show dogs with her mother, and almost all the veteran K-9 handlers had serious lifetime involvements with dogs. Scott had zip, and sensed resentment on the part of the senior K-9 crew when he was shoved down their throats by the Metro commanders and a couple of sympathetic deputy chiefs. So he had paid attention to Leland, and soaked up the older man's knowledge, but he still felt totally stupid.

Maggie peed twice, so Scott turned around and brought her back to the house.

"Let's get you inside, and I'll come back for your stuff. You gotta meet the old lady."

Scott walked Maggie through a locked side gate and back alongside the house, which is how he got to his guest house. He never went to the front door. Whenever he wanted to speak with Mrs. Earle, he went to her back door, and rapped on the wooden jamb.

"Mrs. Earle. It's Scott. Got someone here to meet you."

He heard her shuffling from her Barcalounger in the den, and then the door opened. She was thin and pale, with wispy hair dyed a dark brown. She gave a toothy false-teeth smile to Maggie.

"Oh, she's so pretty. She looks like Rin Tin Tin."

"This is Maggie. Maggie, this is Mrs. Earle."

Maggie seemed perfectly comfortable. She stood calmly, ears back, tail down, tongue out, panting.

"Does she bite?"

"Only bad guys."

Scott wasn't sure what Maggie would do, so he held her collar tight, but Maggie was fine. She smelled and licked Mrs. Earle's hand, and Mrs. Earle ran her hand over Maggie's head, and scratched the soft spot behind her ear.

"She's so soft. How can big strong dogs like this be so soft? We had a cocker spaniel, but he was always matted and filthy, and meaner than spit. He bit all three of the children. We put him to sleep."

Scott wanted to get going.

"Well, I wanted you to meet her."

"Watch when she makes her pee-pee. A girl dog will kill the grass."

"Yes, ma'am. I'll watch."

"What happened to her hiney?"

"She had surgery. She's all better now."

Scott tugged Maggie away before Mrs. Earle could keep going. The guest house had French doors in front that used to face the pool, and a regular door on the side. Scott used the regular door because the French doors stuck, and it was always a wrestling match to open them. He had a spacious living room behind the French doors, with the back half of the guest house being split into a bedroom, bath, and kitchen. A small dining table with two mismatched chairs and Scott's computer was against the wall by the kitchen, opposite a couch and a wooden rocking chair that were set up to face a forty-inch flat screen TV.

Dr. Charles Goodman would not have liked Scott's apartment. A large drawing of the crime scene intersection was tacked to the living room wall, not unlike the map Scott had seen in Orso's office, but covered with tiny notes. Printouts of eight different stories from the L.A. *Times* about the shooting and subsequent investigation were also tacked to the walls, along with sidebar stories about the Bentley victims and Stephanie Anders. The story about Stephanie ran with her official LAPD portrait. Spiral notebooks of different sizes were scattered on the table and couch and the floor around his couch. The notebooks were filled with descriptions and dreams and details he remembered from the night of the shooting. His floor hadn't been vacuumed in three months. He was behind with his dishes, so he used paper plates. He ate mostly takeout and crap out of cans.

Scott unclipped the lead.

"This is it, dog. *Mi casa, su casa.*"

Maggie glanced up at him, then looked at the closed door, then studied the room as if she was disappointed. Her nose sniffed and twitched.

"Make yourself at home. I'll get your stuff."

Getting her stuff took two trips. He brought in her collapsible crate and sleeping pad first, then the metal food and water bowls, and a twenty-pound bag of kibble. These things were provided by the K-9 Platoon, but Scott figured to pick up some toys and treats on his own. When he got back with the first load, she was lying under the dining table as he had seen her in the LAPD run — on her belly, feet out in front, head on the floor between her feet, watching him.

"How're you doing? You like it under there?"

He was hoping for a tail thump, but all she did was watch him.

Orso called as Scott was heading out the door.

"You want to see what we have, can you get in here tomorrow morning?"

Scott thought about Leland's scowl.

"I'm working the dog in the morning. How about late morning, just before lunch? Eleven or eleven-thirty."

"Shoot for eleven. If we get a call-out, I'll text you."

"Great. Thanks."

Scott figured he could leave the dog in Glendale when he split for the Boat.

When he got back with the food and bowls, Maggie was still under the table. He put her bowls in the kitchen, filled one with water, the other with food, but she showed no interest in either.

Scott had figured he would set up her crate in his bedroom, but he put it beside the table. She seemed to be comfortable there, and now he wondered if she had bothered to cruise through his bedroom and bath. Maybe her nose told her everything she needed to know.

As soon as he had the crate up, she slinked from under the table and into the crate.

"I have to put the pad in. C'mon, get out."

Scott stepped back, and gave her the command.

"Come. Come, Maggie. Here."

She stared at him.

"Come."

Didn't move.

Scott knelt at the crate's mouth, let her smell his hand, and slowly reached for her collar. She growled. Scott pulled back and stepped away.

"Okay. Forget the pad."

He dropped the pad on the floor beside the crate, then went into his bedroom to change. He took off his uniform, grabbed a quick shower, then pulled on jeans and a T-shirt from Henry's Tacos. Even pulling the T-shirt over his head hurt like a sonofabitch, and made his eyes water.

When he was hanging his uniform in the closet, he noticed his old tennis stuff in a faded gym bag, and found an unopened can of bright green tennis balls. He popped the tab on the can, and took a ball so fresh and bright it almost glowed.

Scott went to the door and tossed it into the living room. It bounced across the floor, hit the far wall, and rolled to a stop. Maggie charged from her crate, scrambled to the ball, and touched her nose to it. Her ears were cocked forward and her tail was straight up. Scott thought he had found a toy for her, but then her ears went down and her tail dropped. She seemed to shrink. She looked left, then right, as if looking for something, then went back into her crate.

Scott walked to the ball, and studied the dog. Belly down, feet out in front, head between her feet. Watching him.

He toed the ball to the wall hard enough to bounce it back.

Her eyes followed it briefly, but returned to him without interest.

"Hungry? We'll eat, then go for a walk. Sound good?"

He popped a frozen pizza in the microwave, three minutes, good to go. While the microwave was humming, he searched the fridge, and came out with half a pack of baloney, a white container with two leftover Szechuan dumplings, and a container of leftover Yang Chow fried rice. He stopped the microwave, pulled the pie, and smushed the dumplings on top. He covered it with the fried rice, then set a paper plate over it, and put it back into the microwave. Another two minutes.

While Scott's dinner was heating, he put two scoops of kibble into Maggie's bowl. He tore the baloney into pieces, dropped it into the kibble, then added a little hot water to make a nice gravy. He mixed it together with his hand, then took a piece of the baloney to the crate, and held it out in front of Maggie's nose.

Sniff, sniff.

She ate it.

"I hope this stuff doesn't give you the squirts."

She followed him into the kitchen. Scott took his pizza from the microwave, got a Corona from the fridge, and they ate together on the kitchen floor. He stroked her while she ate, like Leland said. Long smooth strokes. She paid him no attention, but didn't seem to mind. When she finished eating, she returned to the living room. Scott thought she was going back to the crate, but she stopped in the center of the room by the tennis ball, head drooping, nose working, her great tall ears swiveling. Scott thought she was staring at the tennis ball, but couldn't be sure. Then she went into his bedroom. Scott followed, and found her with her face in his tennis bag. She backed out of the bag, looked at him, then walked around his bed, sniffing constantly. She briefly returned to the tennis bag before going into the bathroom. He wondered if she was looking for something, but decided she was exploring, then out came the sound of lapping. Scott thought, crap, he would have to keep the seat down. When the lapping stopped, Maggie returned to her crate, and Scott went to his computer. He had been thinking about the robbery Orso described since he left the Boat.

He used Google Maps to find the site of his shooting, then the satellite-view feature to zoom into the street-level view. He had viewed the intersection this way hundreds of times, as well as the location where the getaway car was found. But this time he directed the map along the side street from which the Kenworth emerged. Three storefronts up from the T-intersection, he found Nelson Shin's shop. He recognized the location by the blocky Korean characters painted on the metal shutter covering the windows, with ASIA EXOTICA painted in English below the Korean. The paint was faded, and virtually covered by gang tags and graffiti.

Scott zoomed out enough to see Shin had the bottom of a four-story building, with two storefronts on either side. Scott continued past to the next cross street, then realized it was an alley. The street-level feature wouldn't enter the alley, so Scott zoomed out until he was in satellite view, and looked down from overhead. A small service area branched off the alley behind the row of storefronts. Dumpsters were lined against the building, and Scott saw what appeared to be old fire escapes, though he wasn't sure because of the poor angle. The roofs appeared to be at differing levels. Some were cut with skylights, but others weren't. He zoomed back farther, and saw that if someone had been on the roof that night, they would have had a hawk's view of everything that happened below.

Scott printed the image, and pushpinned it to the wall by his drawing of the crime scene. Orso had given him a good tip, and now he wanted to see the alley himself, and find out if Orso knew anything more about Nelson Shin.

He was still thinking about this at dusk when he took Maggie out. They walked until she pooped. He picked it up with a plastic bag, and brought her home. This time, he beat her to the crate, and arranged the pad. As soon as he backed out of the crate, she went in, turned twice, then eased herself down onto her side, and sighed. The way she had settled, he could see the gray lines of her surgery scars. The gray was her skin, where the fur had not grown back. It looked like a large Y laid on its side.

Scott said, "I have scars, too."

He wondered if the sniper had shot her with an AK-47. He wondered if she understood she had been shot, or if the impact and pain had been a sourceless surprise beyond her understanding. Did she know a man had sent the bullet into her? Did she know he was trying to kill her? Did she know she might have died? Did she know she could die?

Scott said, "We die."

He laid his hand gently on the Y, ready to pull back if she growled, but she remained still and silent. He knew she was not sleeping, but she did not stir. The feel of her was comforting. He had not shared his home with another living creature in a very long time.

"Mi casa, su casa."

Later, he studied the picture of Nelson Shin's roof again, and sat on the couch with one of his spiral notebooks. He wrote everything he remembered from his session with Goodman. As he did every time, he described what he remembered of that night from beginning to end, slowly filling this notebook as he had filled the others, but this time he added the white sideburns. He wrote because sometimes the writing helped focus his thoughts. He was still writing when his eyes grew heavy, the notebook fell, and he slept.

7.

MAGGIE

The man's breathing grew shallow and steady, his heartbeat slowed, and when the surge of his pulse grew no slower, Maggie knew he was sleeping. She lifted her head enough to see him, but seeing him was unnecessary. She could smell his sleep by the change in his scent as his body relaxed and cooled.

She sat up, and turned to peer from her crate. His breathing and heartbeat did not change, so she stepped out into the room. She stood for a moment, watching him. Men came, and men left. She was with some men longer than others, but then they were gone, and she never saw them again. None were her pack.

Pete had stayed with her the longest. They were pack. Then Pete was gone, and the people changed and changed and changed, until Maggie was with a man and a woman.

112

The man and the woman and Maggie had become pack, but one day they closed her crate, and now she was here. Maggie remembered the strong sweet smells of the woman and the sour smell of the disease growing in the man, and would always remember their smells, as she remembered Pete's smell. Her scent memory lasted forever.

She quietly approached the sleeping man. She sniffed the hair on his head, and his ears, and mouth, and the breath he exhaled. Each had its own distinct flavor and taste. She sniffed along the length of his body, noting the smells of his T-shirt and watch and belt and pants and socks, and the different living smells of his man-body parts beneath the clothes. And as she smelled, she heard his heart beat and the blood move through his veins and his breathing, and the sounds of his living body.

When she finished learning the man, she quietly walked along the edge of the room, sniffing the base of the walls, and the windows and along the doors where the cool night air leaked through small openings and the smells from outside were strongest. She smelled rats eating oranges in the trees outside, the pungent scent of withered roses, the bright fresh smells of leaves and grass, and the acidic smell of ants marching along the outer wall.

Maggie's long German shepherd nose had more than two hundred twenty-five million scent receptors. This was as many as a beagle, forty-five times more than the man, and was bettered only by a few of her hound cousins. A full eighth of her brain was devoted to her nose, giving her a sense of smell ten thousand times better than the sleeping man's, and more sensitive than any scientific device. If taught the smell of a particular man's urine, she could recognize and identify that same smell if only a single drop were diluted in a full-sized swimming pool.

Continuing around the room, she smelled the bits of leaves and grass the man carried inside after their walk, and followed the trails left by mice across the floor. She recognized the paths left by living roaches, and knew where the bodies of dead roaches and silverfish and beetles lay hidden.

Her nose led her back to the green ball, where she thought of Pete. The chemical smell of this ball was familiar, but Pete's smell was missing. Pete had not touched this ball, or held it, or thrown it, or carried it hidden from her in his pocket. This ball was not Pete's ball, though it reminded her of him, as did other familiar smells.

Maggie followed those smells into the bedroom again, and found the man's gun. She smelled bullets and oil and gunpowder, but Pete's scent was still absent. Pete was not here, and had never been here.

Maggie smelled water in the bathroom, and returned for a drink, but now the big white water bowl was covered, so she padded back to the kitchen. She drank, then returned to the sleeping man.

Maggie knew this was the man's crate because his smell was part of this place. His smell was not a single smell, but many smells. Hair, ears, breath, underarms, hands, crotch, rectum, feet — each part of him had a different smell, and the scents of his many parts were as different and distinct to Maggie as the colors of a rainbow would be to the man. Together they made up this man's smell, and were distinct from the scent of any other human. His smells were part of the walls, the floor, the paint, the rugs, the bed, the towels in his bathroom, the things in his closet, the gun, the furniture, his clothes and belt and watch and shoes. This was his place, but not her place, yet here she was.

Maggie's crate was her home.

The people and places changed, but the

crate remained the same. This place where the man brought her was strange and meaningless, but her crate was here, and she was here, so here was home.

Maggie was bred to guard and protect, so this was what she did. She stood in the still room near the sleeping man, and looked and listened and smelled. She drew in the world through her ears and her nose, and found no threat. All was good. All was safe.

She returned to her crate, but did not enter. She slipped beneath the table, instead. She turned three times until the space felt right, then lowered herself.

The world was quiet, peaceful, and safe. She closed her eyes, and slept.

Then Maggie began to dream.

8.

— the rifle swung toward him, a tiny thing so far away, but different now. Its barrel was gleaming chrome, as long and thin and sharp as a needle. Its glowing tip found him, looking at him as he looked at it, and then the needle exploded toward him, horribly sharp, dangerously sharp, this terrible sharp point reaching for his eyes —

Scott jerked awake as Stephanie's fading voice echoed.

Scotty, come back back back back.

His heart pounded. His neck and chest were tacky with sweat. His body trembled.

Two-sixteen A.M. He was on the couch. The lights were still on in the kitchen and his bedroom, and the lamp above his head at the end of the couch still burned.

He took deep breaths, calming himself, and noticed the dog was not in her crate. Sometime while he slept, she had left the crate and crawled under the table. She was on her side, sleeping, but her paws twitched and moved as if she was running, and as she ran, she whimpered and whined.

Scott thought, that dog is having a nightmare.

Scott stood, cringing at the sharp pain in his side and the stiffness in his leg, and limped to her. He didn't know if he should wake her.

He eased himself to the floor.

Still sleeping, she growled, and made a woofing sound like a bark, and then her entire body convulsed. She jolted awake, upright, snarling and snapping, but not at Scott. He lurched back anyway, but in that moment she realized where she was, and whatever she had been dreaming was gone. She looked at Scott. Her ears folded back, and she breathed as he had breathed. She lowered her head to the floor.

Scott slowly touched her. He ran his hand over her head. Her eyes closed.

Scott said, "You're okay. We're okay."

She sighed so hard her body shivered.

Scott pulled on his shoes, and gathered together his wallet, and gun, and leash. When he picked up the leash, Maggie stood and shook herself. Maybe she could sleep again that night, but he couldn't. He could never go back to sleep.

Scott clipped the lead to her collar, led her out to the Trans Am, and held the door so she could hop into the back seat. That time of night, almost two-thirty, the driving was easy. He hit the Ventura, slid down the Hollywood, and made it downtown in less than twenty minutes. He had made the same drive many times, at hours like this. When he woke hearing Stephanie call for him, he had no other choice.

He parked in the same place they had parked that night, at the little T-intersection where they had stopped to listen to the silence.

Scott said, "Turn off the engine."

He said those same words every time he came, then turned off the engine.

Maggie stood, and leaned forward between the seats. She was so large she filled the car, her head now higher than his.

Scott stared at the empty street before them, but the street wasn't empty. He saw the Kenworth. He saw the Bentley. He saw the men covered in black.

"Don't worry. I'll protect you."

The same words he spoke that night, this time a whisper.

He glanced at Maggie, then back at the street, only now the street was empty. He listened to Maggie pant. He felt her warmth, and smelled her strong dog smell.

"I got my partner killed. It happened right here."

His eyes filled, and the sob racked him so hard he doubled over. He could not stop. He did not try to stop. The pain came in a torrent of jolting sobs that filled his nose and blurred his eyes. He heaved and gasped, and clenched his eyes, and covered his face. Tears and snot and spit dripped in streamers from his chin, as he heard his own voice.

Turn off the engine.

Don't worry. I'll protect you.

Then Stephanie's voice echoed after his own, haunting him.

Scotty, don't leave me.

Don't leave me.

Don't leave.

He finally pulled himself together. He rubbed the blur from his eyes, and found Maggie watching him.

He said, "I wasn't running away. I swear to God I wasn't, but she doesn't —"

Maggie's ears were back and her rich brown eyes were kind. She whimpered as if she felt his anxiety, then licked his face. Scott felt his tears return, and closed his eyes as Maggie licked the tears from his face.

Don't leave me.

Don't leave.

Scott pulled the dog close, and buried his face in her fur.

"You did better than me, dog. You didn't leave your partner. You didn't fail."

Maggie whimpered and tried to pull away, but Scott held on, and didn't let go.

■ ■ ■ ■

PART II

■ ■ ■ ■

■ ■ ■ ■

MAGGIE AND SCOTT

■ ■ ■ ■

9.

Scott and Maggie were due at the training field at seven that morning, but Scott left early and returned to the scene of his shooting. He wanted to see Shin's building during the light.

He drove the same route he took three hours earlier, only this time when he approached the intersection, Maggie stood with her ears tipped forward.

Scott said, "Good memory."

She whined.

"You'll get used to it. I come here a lot."

Maggie stayed between the two front seats, filling the car as she checked their surroundings.

It was five forty-two that morning, light, but still early. A few pedestrians were making their way along the sidewalks, and the streets were busy with trucks making early deliveries. Scott pushed Maggie out of the way so he could see, turned onto the street where the Kenworth had waited, and parked in front of Shin's store.

Scott clipped on Maggie's leash, let her out onto the sidewalk, and examined Asia Exotica. It looked as it had in the Google picture, only with more graffiti. A security shutter was rolled down over the window like a metal garage door. Padlocks secured the shutter to steel rings set into the sidewalk. The door was barred by a heavy steel throw-bolt locked into the wall. Shin's little store looked like Fort Knox, but wasn't unusual. The other shops along the street were similarly protected. The difference was that Shin's locks, shutter, and door were powdered with undisturbed grime, and appeared not to have been opened in a long time.

Scott walked Maggie toward the alley. She went to his left side as she'd been taught, but walked too close, and let her tail and ears droop. When they passed two Latin women walking in the opposite direction, Maggie edged behind Scott, and would have moved to his right if he let her. She glanced at passing cars and buses as if afraid one might jump the curb.

Scott stopped when they reached the alley, and stooped to stroke her back and sides, hearing Leland's lecturing voice:

These dogs are not machines, goddamnit. They are alive! They are living, feeling, warm-blooded creatures of God, and they will love you with all their hearts! They will love you when your wives and husbands sneak behind your backs. They will love you when your ungrateful misbegotten children piss on your graves! They will see and witness your great-est shame, and will not judge you! These dogs will be the truest and best partners you can ever hope to have, and they will give their lives for you. And all they ask, all they want or need, all it costs YOU to get ALL of that, is a simple word of kindness. Goddamnit to hell, the ten best men I know aren't worth the worst dog here, and neither are any of you, and I am Dominick Goddamned Leland, and I am never wrong!

Three hours earlier, this living, feeling, warm-blooded creature of God had licked the tears from his face, and now she shivered as a garbage truck rumbled past. Scott scratched her head, stroked her back, and whispered in her ear.

"It's okay, dog. It's okay if you're scared. I'm scared, too."

Words he had never spoken to another living being.

Scott's eyes filled as the words came to him, but he said them again as he stroked her back.

"I'll protect you."

Scott pushed to his feet, wiped his eyes clear, and took a plastic Ziploc bag from his pocket. He had sliced the baloney into squares, and brought them along as treats. Food as a reward was frowned upon, but Scott figured he had to go with what worked.

Maggie looked up even before he opened the bag. Her ears stood strong and straight, and her nostrils flickered and danced.

"You're a good girl, baby. You're a brave dog."

She took a square as if she was starving, and whined for more, but this was a good whine. He fed her a second square, put away the bag, and turned down the alley. Maggie stepped livelier now, and snuck glances at his pocket.

The delivery area behind Shin's building was a place for shopkeepers to load and unload their goods, and toss their trash. A pale blue van with its side panel open was currently parked outside a door. A heavyset young Asian man guided a hand dolly stacked with boxes from the store, and loaded the boxes into the van. The boxes were labeled MarleyWorld Island.

Scott led Maggie around the van to the

rear of Shin's store. The door on this side of the building was as bulletproof as the front, but greasy windows were cut into the back of the four-story building, and a rusted fire escape climbed to the roof. The lowest windows were protected by security bars, but the higher windows were not. The fire escape's retractable ladder was too high to reach from the ground, but a person standing on top of the van could reach it, and climb to the higher windows or break into the upper-floor doors.

Scott was wondering how he could reach the roof when a tall thin man with a Jamaican accent came storming around the van.

"Ahr you de wahn gahnna stop dese crime?"

The man strode past the van directly toward Scott, shaking his finger, and speaking in a loud, demanding voice.

Maggie lunged at him so hard Scott almost lost her leash. Her ears were cocked forward like furry black spikes, her tail was straight back, and the fur along her spine bristled with fury as she barked.

The man stumbled backwards, scrambled into the van, and slammed the door.

Scott said, "Out."

This was the command word to break off the attack, but Maggie ignored him. Her

131

claws raked the asphalt as she snarled and barked, straining against the leash.

Then Leland's voice came to Scott, shouting: *Say it like you mean it, goddamnit! You're the alpha here. She will love and protect her alpha, but you are the boss!*

Scott raised and deepened his voice. The command voice. All authority. Alpha.

"Out, Maggie! Maggie, OUT!"

It was like flipping a switch. Maggie broke off her attack, returned to his left side, and sat, though her eyes never left the man in the van.

Scott was shaken by her sudden ferocity. She did not look at Scott, not even a glance. She watched the man in the van, and Scott knew if he released her she would attack the door and try to chew through the metal to reach him.

Scott scratched her ears.

"Good dog. Atta girl, Maggie."

Leland, screaming again: *The praise voice, you goddamned fool! They like it all high and squeaky! Be her. Listen to her. Let her TEACH you!*

Scott made his voice high and squeaky, as if he was talking to a Chihuahua instead of an eighty-five-pound German shepherd who could tear a man's throat out.

"That's my good girl, Maggie. You're my

132

good girl."

Maggie's tail wagged. She stood when he took out the Ziploc. He gave her another piece of baloney, and told her to sit. She sat.

Scott looked at the man in the van, and made a roll-down-the-window gesture. The man rolled down the window halfway.

"Dat dog hab rabies! I not comeeng out."

"I'm sorry, sir. You scared her. You don't have to get out."

"I abide de law an' be good ceetysen. She wahn to bite sahm one, let her bite de bahstards who steal frahm my bizzyness."

Scott glanced past the van into the man's shop. The kid with the hand dolly peeked out, then ducked away.

"Is this your place of business?"

"Yes. I am Elton Joshua Marley. Doan let dat dog bite my helper. He got deeliveries to make."

"She's not going to bite anyone. What were you asking me?"

"Have you catched dese people who did dis?"

"You were robbed?"

Mr. Marley scowled again, and nervously glanced at the dog.

"Dat be now two weeks ago. De officers, dey come, but dey never come back. Hab you caught dese people or no?"

Scott considered this for a moment, then took out his pad.

"I don't know, sir, but I'll find out. How do you spell your name?"

Scott copied the man's info, along with the date of the burglary. By the time he finished making notes, he had coaxed Marley from the van. Marley kept a wary eye on Maggie as he led Scott past the kid loading boxes, and into his shop.

Marley bought cheap Caribbean-style clothes from manufacturers in Mexico, and resold them under his own label in low-end shops throughout Southern California. The shop was filled with boxes of short-sleeved shirts, T-shirts, and cargo shorts. Marley explained that the burglar or burglars had entered and left through a second-floor window, and made off with two desktop computers, a scanner, two telephones, a printer, and a boom box. Not exactly the crime of the century, but Marley's shop had been burgled four times in the past year.

Scott said, "No alarm?"

"De owner, he put in de alarm last year, but dey break, and he no fix, dat cheep bahstard. I put de leetle camerah here, but dey take."

Marley had installed a do-it-yourself

security camera on the ceiling, but the thief or thieves stole the camera and its hard drive two burglaries ago.

Scott thought of Shin as they left Marley's shop. The old building was a burglar's heaven. A mercury-vapor lamp was mounted overhead, but the little delivery area was hidden from the street. With no security cameras in evidence, a thief would have little fear of being discovered.

Marley went on, still complaining.

"I call you two weeks ago. De police, dey cahm, dey go, an' thas last I heer. Every morneeng I come, I wait for more stealeeng. My insurance, he no pay more. He wahnt charge so much, I cannot pay."

Scott glanced at Shin's again.

"Have all the shops along here been broken into?"

"Ehveebody. Dese assholes, dey break in all de time. Dis block, across de street, on de next block."

"How long has this been going on?"

"Two or tree years. I only be heer wahn year, but thees is waht I heer."

"Is there a way up to the roof besides the fire escape?"

Marley led them inside to a common stairwell, and gave Scott a key to the roof. There was no elevator in the old building.

Scott's leg and side ached as he climbed, and the ache grew worse. By the third floor, he stopped, and dry-swallowed a Vicodin. Maggie was engaged and interested as they climbed, but when Scott stopped to let the pain pass, she whimpered. Scott realized she was reading his hurt, and touched her head.

"How about you? Your hips okay?"

He smiled, and she seemed to smile back, so they continued up to the roof and out a metal service door fitted with an industrial security lock. The lock could only be locked and unlocked from the inside. There were no keyholes on the outside, but this hadn't stopped people from trying to break in. The steel frame was scarred with old jimmy marks and dents where people had tried to pry open the door. Most of the marks were painted over or rusted.

Marley's and Shin's building was on the cross street from which the Kenworth appeared. The building next to it overlooked the site of the shooting. The roofs between the two buildings were separated by a low wall.

Marley's roof was poorly maintained like the rest of his building. It was cut with withered tar patches and broken asphalt, and littered with cigarette butts, butane lighters, crushed beer cans, shattered beer bottles, broken crack pipes, and the trash of late-night partiers. Scott figured the partiers probably climbed the fire escape, same as the people who tried to force the door. He wondered if the officers who investigated Marley's burglary had checked out the roof, and what they thought of it.

Careful to avoid the broken glass, Scott led Maggie across Marley's roof to the next building. When they reached the low wall, Maggie stopped. Scott patted the top of the wall.

"Jump. It's only three feet high. Jump."

Maggie looked at him with her tongue hanging out.

Scott swung his legs over the wall, one at a time, wincing at the stitch in his side. He patted his chest.

"I can do it, and I'm a mess. C'mon, dog. You'll have to do better than this for Leland."

Maggie licked her lips, but made no move to follow.

Scott dug out his Ziploc bag, and showed her the baloney.

"Come."

Maggie launched over the wall without hesitation, cleared it easily, and sat at his feet. She stared at the bag. Scott laughed when he saw how easily she cleared the wall.

"You smart ass. You made me beg just to sucker me into a treat. Guess what? I'm a smart ass, too."

He tucked the bag into his pocket without giving her a reward.

"Nothing for you until you jump back."

This building's roof was better maintained, but was also littered with party dregs, a large piece of wall-to-wall carpet, and three cast-off folding lawn chairs. A ripped, dirty sleeping bag was bundled by an air duct, along with several used condoms. Some were only a few days old. Urban romance.

Scott went to the side of the roof that overlooked the kill zone. A short wrought-iron safety fence was bolted to the wall as an extra barrier to keep people from falling. It was so badly rusted, the metal eaten with holes.

Scott peered over the fence, and found an unobstructed view of the crime scene. It was all so easy to see, then and even now. The Bentley floating by on the street below, passing their radio car as the Kenworth roared, the truck and the Bentley spinning to a stop as the Gran Torino raced after them. If someone was partying up here nine months ago, they could have seen everything.

Scott began shaking, and realized he was holding the rusted fence so tight, the rotting metal was cutting into his skin.

"Shit!"

He jumped back, saw his fingers were streaked with rust and blood, and pulled out his handkerchief.

Scott led Maggie back to Shin's building, this time rewarding her when she jumped the wall. He photographed the empties and party debris with his phone, then climbed down the four flights to find Mr. Marley. His helper had finished loading their stock, and the van was now gone. Marley was boxing more shirts in his shop.

When Mr. Marley saw Maggie, he stepped behind his desk, eyeing her nervously.

"You lock de door?"

"Yes, sir."

Scott returned the key.

"One more thing. Do you know Mr. Shin? He has the business two doors down. Asia Exotica."

"He out of bizzyness. He geht robbed too many times."

"How long has he been gone?"

"Months. Eet been a long time."

"You have any idea who's breaking into

139

these places?"

Marley waved a hand in the general direction of everywhere.

"Drug addeeks and assholes."

"Someone you could point out?"

Marley waved his hand again.

"De assholes 'roun here. If I could name who, I would not need you."

Marley was probably right. The small-time burglaries he described were almost certainly committed by neighborhood regulars who knew when the shops were empty and which had no alarms. It was likely that the same person or persons had committed all the robberies. Scott liked this idea, and found himself nodding. If his theory was right, the thief who broke into Marley's shop could be the same person who broke into Shin's.

Scott said, "I'll find out what's going on with your burglary report, and get back to you later this afternoon. That okay?"

"Daht be good. I tank you. Dese other policemen, dey nevehr call back."

Scott checked his watch, and realized he would be late. He copied Marley's phone number, and trotted back to his car. Maggie trotted along with him, and hopped into his car without effort. This time, she didn't stretch out on the back seat. She straddled the console between the front seats.

"You're too big to stand there. Get in back."

She panted, her tongue as long as a necktie.

"Get in back. You're blocking my view."

Scott tried to push her with his forearm, but she leaned into him and didn't move. Scott pushed harder, but Maggie leaned harder, and held her ground.

Scott stopped pushing, and wondered if she thought this was a game. Whatever she thought, she seemed content and comfortable on the console.

Scott watched her pant, remembering how fiercely she lunged for Marley when she thought they were threatened. Scott roughed the fur on her powerful neck.

"Forget it. Stand wherever you want."

She licked his ear, and Scott drove away. Leland would be furious at the way he indulged her, but Leland didn't know everything.

10.

Maggie whined when they pulled into the training facility's parking lot. Scott thought she seemed anxious, and rested a hand on her shoulder.

"Don't sweat it. You don't live here anymore. You live with me."

They were ten minutes late, but Leland's Toyota pickup wasn't in the lot, so Scott took out his phone. He had been brooding since Leland surprised them with the starter pistol.

Can't have a police dog that shits out when a gun goes off.

Or a police officer.

Scott wondered if Leland noticed Scott had jumped, too, though Scott's reaction was small compared to the dog's. Leland would test her again, and reject her again if she reacted the same, and Scott knew Leland was right to do so. She had to be able to do her job, just as Scott had to do his, only Scott could fake it and Maggie couldn't. *Fake it 'til you make it.*

Scott gripped a handful of her fur, and gently pushed her. Maggie's tongue dripped out, and she leaned into his push.

Scott said, "Maggie."

She glanced at him, and went back to watching the building. He liked the way she responded to him — not like a robot obeying a command, but as if she was trying to figure him out. He liked the warm intelligence in her eyes. He wondered what it was like inside her head, and what she thought about. They had been together for only twenty-four hours, but she seemed more comfortable with him, and he was more comfortable with her. It was weird, but he felt calmer having her with him.

"You're my first dog."

She glanced at him, and glanced away. Scott pushed again. She pushed back, and seemed content with the contact.

"I had to interview with these guys when I asked for the job. The LT and Leland asked me all these questions about why I wanted to join K-9, and what kind of dog I had when I was a kid, and all this stuff. I lied my ass off. We had cats."

Maggie's big head swung his way, and she licked his face. Scott let her for a moment, then pushed her away. She went back to watching the building.

"Before the shooting, I never used to lie, not ever, but I lie to everyone now, pretty much about everything. I don't know what else to do."

Maggie ignored him.

"Jesus, now I'm talking to a dog."

An exaggerated startle response was common in people who suffered from PTSD, particularly combat veterans, police officers, and victims of domestic abuse. Anyone will jump if someone sneaks up behind them and shouts boo!, but PTSD can amp up the startle response to crazy levels. An unexpected loud noise or a sudden movement near the face could trigger an over-the-top reaction that varied from person to person — screaming, raging, ducking for cover, and even throwing punches. Scott had an exaggerated startle response since the shooting, but was seeing improvement with Goodman's help. He still had a long way to go, but had made enough progress to fool the review board. Scott wondered if Goodman could help with the dog.

Dr. Goodman often saw clients early before they went to work, so Scott took a chance, and called. Scott expected Goodman's answering machine, but Goodman answered, which meant he wasn't busy with a client.

"Doc, Scott James. You got a fast minute?"

"As fast or as slow as you like. My seven o'clock canceled. Are you doing okay?"

"Doing good. I want to ask you something about my dog."

"Your dog?"

"I got my dog yesterday. A German shepherd."

Goodman sounded uncertain.

"Congratulations. This must be very exciting."

"Yeah. She's a retired Military Working Dog. She was shot in Afghanistan, and I think she has PTSD."

Goodman answered without hesitation.

"If you're asking if this is possible, yes, it is. Animals can show the same symptoms as humans. Dogs, in particular. There's extensive literature on the subject."

"A big truck goes by, she gets nervous. She hears a gunshot, she wants to hide."

"Mm-hm. The startle response."

Scott and Goodman had discussed these things for hours. There were no medicines or "cures" for PTSD, other than talking. Medicines could relieve symptoms like sleeplessness and anxiety, but you killed the PTSD demon by talking it to death. Goodman was the only person with whom Scott had shared his fears and feelings about that night, but there were some things he had not even told Goodman.

"Yeah, her startle response is off the charts. Is there a fast way to help her?"

"Help her do what?"

"Get over it. Is there something I can do, so she won't jump when a gun goes off?"

Goodman hesitated for several seconds before he responded in a careful, measured tone.

"Scott? Are we talking about a dog now, or you? Is there something you're trying to tell me?"

"My dog. I'm asking about my dog. She can't come talk it out with you, Doc."

"If you're having trouble, we can increase the anxiety medicine."

Scott was wishing he had taken a fistful of anxiety meds that morning when he saw Leland's dark blue pickup pull into the lot. Leland saw him as he got out of his truck, and scowled, no doubt pissed off because Scott was still in his car.

Scott said, "I'm asking about my *dog*. She's an eighty-five-pound German shepherd named Maggie. I'd let you talk to her, but she doesn't talk."

"You seem irritated, Scott. Did yesterday's

regression cause an adverse reaction?"

Scott lowered the phone and took a few breaths. Leland hadn't moved. He was standing beside his truck, scowling at Scott.

"I'm talking about this dog. Maybe I need a dog psychiatrist. Do they make anxiety meds for dogs?"

Goodman hesitated for another several seconds, thinking, but this time he sighed before he answered.

"Probably, but I don't know. I *do* know that dogs suffering from PTSD can be retrained. I would guess that, as with people, the results are varied. You and I have the advantage of medicines that can augment or temporarily alter our brain chemistry. You and I are able to discuss what happened over and over until the event loses much of its emotional potency, and becomes something more manageable."

Goodman had gone into lecture mode, which was his way of thinking out loud, so Scott interrupted.

"Yeah, we bore it to death. Is there a short version of this, Doc? My boss is watching me, and he doesn't look happy."

"She was shot. Like you, her subconscious associates the sound of a gunshot, or any surprising noise, with pain and the fear she felt in that moment."

Leland tapped his watch, and crossed his arms. Scott nodded to acknowledge him and held up a finger. One second.

"She can't talk about it like me, so how do we deal with it?"

"I'll find out if there are canine anxiety medicines, but the therapeutic model will be the same. You can't take the bad experience away from her, so you have to reduce its power. Perhaps you could teach her to associate a loud noise with something pleasurable. Then introduce more noises, until she realizes they have no power to harm her."

Leland had gotten tired of waiting, and was now striding toward him.

Scott watched him approach, but was thinking about the possibilities in Goodman's advice.

"This is going to help, Doc. Thanks. I gotta go."

Scott put away his phone, hooked up Maggie, and got out as Leland arrived.

"Guess you and this dog good to go, you got time to yak with your girlfriends."

"That was Detective Orso at Robbery-Homicide. They want me back downtown, but I put them off until lunch so I can work with Maggie."

Leland's scowl softened as Scott expected.

"Why all of a sudden they want you so much?"

"The lead changed. Orso's new. He's trying to get up to speed."

Leland grunted, then glanced at Maggie.

"How'd you and Miss Maggie here get on last night? She pee on your floor?"

"We walked. We had a long talk."

Leland looked up sharply as if he suspected Scott was being smart, but he softened again when he concluded Scott meant it.

"Good. That would be very good. Now let's you go work with this animal, and see what y'all talked about."

Leland turned away.

"Can I borrow your starter pistol?"

Leland turned back.

Scott said, "Can't have a police dog shit out when a gun goes off."

Leland pooched out his lips, and studied Scott some more.

"You think you can fix that?"

"I won't quit on my partner."

Leland stared at Scott for so long Scott squirmed, but then Leland touched Maggie's head.

"Won't do, you shootin' the gun if you're workin' with her. Might hurt her ears, bein' so close. I'll have Mace help you."

"Thanks, Sergeant."

"No thanks are necessary. Keep talkin' to this dog. Maybe you're already learnin' somethin'."

Leland turned away without another word, and Scott looked down at Maggie.

"I need more baloney."

Scott and Maggie went to the training field.

11.

Mace didn't come out with the starter pistol. Leland came out instead, and brought along a short, wiry trainer named Paulie Budress. Scott had met the man twice during his first week of handler school, but didn't know him. Budress was in his mid-thirties, and sported a peeling sunburn because he had spent the past two weeks fishing with three other cops in Montana. He worked with a male German shepherd named Obi.

Leland said, "Forget that business with the starter pistol for now. You know Paulie Budress?"

Budress gave Scott a big grin and firm handshake, but put most of his grin on Maggie.

Leland said, "Paulie here worked K-9 in the Air Force, which is why I want him to talk to you. These Military Working Dogs

151

are taught to do things different than our dogs."

Budress was still smiling at Maggie. He held out his hand to let her sniff, then squatted to scratch behind her ears.

"She was in Afghanistan?"

Scott said, "Dual purpose. Patrol and explosives detection."

Budress was wiry, but Scott felt a super-calm vibe, and knew Maggie sensed it, too. Her ears were back, her tongue hung out, and she was comfortable letting Budress scratch her. Budress opened her left ear and looked at her tattoo as Leland went on. Both Scott and Leland might as well have been invisible. Budress was all about the dog.

Leland went on to Scott.

"As you know, here in the city of Los Angeles, we train our beautiful animals to hold a suspect in place by barking. Heaven help us she bites some shitbird unless he's trying to kill you, coz our spaghetti-spined, unworthy city council is only too willing to pay liability blackmail to any shyster lawyer who oozes out a shitbird's ass. Is that not correct, Officer Budress?"

"Whatever you say, Sergeant."

Budress wasn't paying attention, but Scott knew the Sergeant was describing the find-

and-bark method that more and more police agencies had adopted to stem the tide of liability lawsuits. So long as the suspect stood perfectly still and showed no aggression, the dogs were trained to stand off and bark. They were trained to bite only if the suspect made an aggressive move or fled, which Leland believed risky to both his dogs and their handlers, and which was one of his unending lecture topics.

"Your military patrol dog, however, is taught to hit her target like a runaway truck, and will take his un-American ass down like a bat out of hell on steroids. You put your military dog on a shitbird, she'll rip him a new asshole, and eat his liver when it slides out. Dogs like our Maggie here are trained to mean business. Is this not correct, Officer Budress?"

"Whatever you say, Sergeant."

Leland nodded toward Budress, who was running his hands down Maggie's legs and tracing the scars on her hips.

"The voice of experience, Officer James. So the first thing you have to do is teach this heroic animal not to bite the murderous, genetically inferior shitbags you will ask her to face. Is that clear?"

Scott mimicked Budress.

"Whatever you say, Sergeant."

"As it should be. I will leave you now with Officer Budress, who knows the military command set, and will help you retrain her to work in our sissified civilian city."

Leland walked away without another word. Budress stood, and painted Scott with a big smile.

"Don't sweat it. She was retrained at Lackland to make her less aggressive, and more people-friendly. It's SOP for dogs they adopt out to civilians. The Sarge there thinks her problem will be the opposite — not aggressive enough."

Scott remembered how Maggie lunged at Marley, but decided not to mention it.

Scott said, "She's smart. She'll have find-and-bark in two days."

Budress smiled even wider.

"You've had her now how long? A day?"

"She was smart enough to soak up everything the Marine Corps wanted her to know. She didn't get shot in the head."

"And how is it you know what the Marines wanted her to know?"

Scott felt himself flush.

"I guess that's why you're here."

"I guess it is. Let's get started."

Budress nodded toward the kennel building.

"Go get an arm protector, a twenty-foot

lead, a six-foot lead, and whatever you use to reward her. I'll wait."

Scott started to the kennel, and Maggie fell in on his left side. He had cut and bagged half a pound of baloney, but now worried if it would be enough, and if Budress would object to his using food as a reward. Then he checked his watch, and wondered how much they could accomplish before he left to see Orso. He wanted to share what he learned about the neighborhood burglaries from Marley, and believed Orso would see the potential. Maybe after nine months of nothing, a new lead was beginning to develop.

Scott picked up his pace, and was thinking about Orso when the gunshot cracked the air behind him. Scott ducked into a crouch, and Maggie almost upended him. She tried to wedge herself beneath him, and was wrapped so tightly between his legs he felt her trembling.

Scott's heart hammered and his breathing was fast and shallow, but he knew what had happened even before he looked back at Budress.

Budress was holding the starter pistol loose at his leg. The smile was gone from his peeling face, and now he looked sad.

He said, "Sorry, man. It's a shame. That

155

poor dog has a problem."

Scott's heart slowed. He laid a hand on Maggie's trembling back, and spoke to her softly.

"Hey, baby girl. That's just a noise. You can stay under me long as you like."

He stroked her back and sides, kneaded her ears, and kept talking in the calm voice. He took out the bag of baloney, stroking her the whole time.

"Check it out, Maggie girl. Look what I have."

She raised her head when he offered the square of baloney, and licked it from his fingers.

Scott made the high-pitched squeaky voice, told her what a good girl she was, and offered another piece. She sat up to eat it.

Budress said, "I've seen this before, y'know, with war dogs. It's a long road back."

Scott stood, and teased her by holding another piece high above her head.

"Stand up, girl. Stand tall and get it."

She raised up onto her hind legs, standing tall for the meat. Scott let her have it, then ruffled her fur as he praised her.

He looked at Budress, and his voice wasn't squeaky.

"Another twenty minutes or so, shoot it again."

Budress nodded.

"You won't know it's coming."

"I don't want to know it's coming. Neither does she."

Budress slowly smiled.

"Get the arm protector and the leads. Let's get this war dog back in business."

Two hours and forty-five minutes later, Scott kenneled Maggie and drove downtown to see Orso. She whined when he left, and pawed at the gate.

12.

Twenty minutes later, Orso and a short, attractive brunette wearing a black pantsuit were waiting when the elevator doors opened at the Boat. Orso stuck out his hand, and introduced the woman.

"Scott, this is Joyce Cowly. Detective Cowly has been reviewing the file, and probably knows it better than me."

Scott nodded, but wasn't sure what to say.

"Okay. Thanks. Good to meet you."

Cowly's handshake was firm and strong, but not mannish. She was in her late thirties, with a relaxed manner and the strong build of a woman who might have been one of those sparkplug gymnasts when she was a teenager. She smiled as she shook Scott's hand, and handed him her card as Orso led them toward the RHD office. Scott wondered if Orso would meet him at the elevator every time he arrived.

Cowly said, "You were at Rampart before

Metro, right? I was Rampart Homicide before here."

Scott checked her face again, but didn't recall her.

"Sorry, I don't remember."

"No reason you should. I've been here for three years."

Orso said, "Three and a half. Joyce spent most of her time here on serial cases with me. I told her about our conversation yesterday, and she has a few questions."

Scott followed them to the same conference room, where he saw the cardboard box was now on the table with the files and materials back in their hangers. A large blue three-ring binder sat on the table beside it. Scott knew this was the murder book, which homicide detectives used to organize and record their investigations.

Orso and Cowly dropped into chairs, but Scott rounded the table to Orso's poster-sized diagram of the crime scene.

"Before we get started, I went to Nelson Shin's store this morning, and met a man who has a business two doors down — here."

Scott found Shin's store on the diagram, then pointed out Elton Marley's location.

"Marley was burglarized two weeks ago. He's been hit four or five times in the past year, and he told me a lot of other businesses in the area have been hit, too. Your diagram here doesn't show a delivery area behind the building that opens off this alley —"

Scott drew an invisible box with his finger to illustrate the area behind the buildings where Marley had been loading his van. Orso and Cowly were watching him.

"A fire escape goes to the roof. There's no security except for window bars on the lowest windows, and the area back here is totally hidden from view. I'm thinking the bad guys use the fire escape to reach the higher windows. They dinged Marley for a computer and a scanner this time. Last time, they grabbed a boom box, another computer, and a few bottles of rum."

Orso glanced at Cowly.

"Small-time breaking and entering, easy-to-carry goods."

Cowly nodded.

"Neighborhood locals."

Scott pushed on with his theory.

"Whoever it is, if the same perp is behind all these jobs, he might be the person who broke into Shin's the night I was shot. Also, I went up to the roof. It's a total party hangout —"

Scott took out his cell phone, found a

good picture of the beer cans and debris, and passed the phone to Orso.

"Maybe the guy who hit Shin's store was long gone, but if someone else was up here when the Kenworth hit the Bentley, they could have seen everything."

Cowly leaned toward him.

"Did Marley file a report?"

"Two weeks ago. Someone went out, but Marley hasn't heard back. I told him I'd check the status and get back to him."

Orso glanced at Cowly.

"That's Central Robbery. Ask them for the robbery reports and arrests in this area for the past two years. And whatever they have on Mr. Marley. I'll want to speak with the DIC."

DIC was Detective-in-Charge.

Cowly asked Scott to repeat Marley's full name and the address of his store, and wrote the information on her pad. As she wrote, Orso turned back to Scott.

"This is a good find. Good thinking. I like this."

Scott felt elated, and that something trapped in his heart for nine months was beginning to ease.

Orso said, "Okay, now Joyce has something. Come sit. Joyce —"

Scott took a seat as Cowly picked up a

large manila envelope and took out the contents. She dealt out four sheets of heavy gloss paper in front of Scott like playing cards. Each sheet was printed with six sets of color booking photos. The pictures were in pairs, showing each man's full face and profile. The men were of all ages and races, and all had white or gray sideburns of varying shapes and lengths. Cowly explained as she laid out the pictures.

"Identifiers like hair color, hairstyle, length, et cetera, are part of the database. Anyone look familiar?"

Scott went from elated to nauseous in a heartbeat, and in that moment was once more lying in the street, hearing the gunfire. He closed his eyes, drew a slow breath, and imagined himself on a white sandy beach. He was alone, and naked, and his skin was warm from the sun. He pictured himself on a red beach towel. He imagined the sound of the surf. This was a technique Goodman taught him to deal with the flashbacks. Put himself elsewhere, and create the details. Imagining details took concentration, and helped him relax.

Orso said, "Scott?"

Scott felt a flush of embarrassment, and opened his eyes. He studied the pictures, but none of the men were familiar.

"I didn't see enough. I'm sorry."

Cowly pulled the cap off a black Sharpie and handed it to him, still smiling the relaxed, easy smile. She wore no nail polish.

"Don't sweat it. I didn't expect you to recognize a face. I got three thousand, two hundred, and sixty-one hits for gray or white hair. I pulled these because they have different hair types and sideburn styles. That's the purpose of this exercise. As best you can — *if* you can, and no sweat if you can't — circle the style closest to what you saw, or cross out the styles you can definitely rule out."

One of the men had long thin sideburns as sharp as a stiletto. Another had huge muttonchops that covered most of his cheeks. Scott crossed them out along with the other styles he knew were wrong, and circled five men with thick, rectangular sideburns. The shortest stopped mid-ear, and the longest extended about an inch below the man's lobe. Scott pushed the sheets back to Cowly, wondering again if he had seen the sideburns or only imagined them.

"I don't know. I'm not even sure I saw them."

Cowly and Orso shared a glance as she slipped the sheets back into their envelope, and Orso plucked a thin file from the spread on the table.

"This is the criminalist's report on the Gran Torino. After we spoke, I reread it. Five white hairs from the same individual were found on the driver's side."

Scott stared at Orso, then Cowly. Orso smiled. Cowly didn't. She looked like a woman on the hunt, and picked up where Orso left off.

"We can't affirm they're from the man you saw, but a man with white hair was in that vehicle at some point in time. The DNA from the follicles didn't match anything in the CODIS or DOJ data banks, so we don't know his name, but we know he's a Caucasian male. There's an eighty percent chance his hair was brown before it turned white, and we are one hundred percent positive he has blue eyes."

Orso arched his eyebrows, smiled even wider, and looked like a happy scoutmaster.

"Starts adding up, doesn't it? Thought you'd like to know you aren't crazy."

Then the happy scoutmaster face dropped away, and Orso rested his hand on the file box.

"Okay. The case file here is arranged by subject. The murder book contains the case evidence Melon and Stengler thought was

164

the most important, but isn't as complete as the file. You're the man with the questions. What do you want to know?"

Scott wanted something to trigger more memories, but he didn't know what that thing was or what it might be.

Scott looked at Orso.

"Why don't we have a suspect?"

"A suspect was never identified."

"I knew that much from Melon and Stengler."

Orso patted the file box.

"The long version is in here, which you're free to read, but I'll give you the CliffsNotes version."

Orso sketched out the investigation quickly and professionally. Scott knew most of it from Melon and Stengler, but did not interrupt.

The first person suspected when a homicide occurs is the spouse. Always. This is Rule Number One in the Homicide Handbook. Rule Number Two is "follow the money." Melon and Stengler approached their investigation in this way. Did Pahlasian or Beloit owe money? Did either man cheat a business partner? Was either having an affair with another man's wife? Did Pahlasian's wife jilt a lover, who murdered her husband as retaliation, or did his wife have Eric murdered to be with another man?

Melon and Stengler identified only two persons of interest during their investigation. The first was a Russian pornographer in the Valley who had invested in several projects with Pahlasian. His porno enterprise was financed by a Russian Organized Crime element, which put him on their radar, but the man made better than a twenty percent profit with Pahlasian, so Melon and Stengler eventually cleared him. The second person of interest was tied to Beloit. The Robbery-Homicide Division's Robbery Special group informed Melon that Interpol had named Beloit as a known associate of a French diamond fence. This led to a theory Beloit was smuggling diamonds, but the Robbery Special team eventually cleared him of criminal involvement.

All in all, twenty-seven friends and family members, and one hundred eighteen investors, business associates, and possible witnesses were interviewed and investigated, and all of them checked clean. No viable suspect was identified, and the investigation slowly stalled.

When Orso finished, he checked his watch.

"Anything I've said help your memory?"

"No, sir. I knew most of it."

"Then Melon and Stengler weren't holding out on you."

Scott felt his face flush.

"They missed something."

"Maybe so, but this is what they found —"

Orso tipped his head toward the file box as Cowly interrupted.

"— which means this is where Bud and I begin. Just because Melon and Stengler zeroed out, doesn't mean we will. Just because it's in these pages, doesn't mean we accept it as fact."

Orso studied her for a moment, then looked at Scott.

"I have Shin and his burglar, I have you, and I have a dead police officer. I will break this case."

Joyce Cowly nodded to herself, but did not speak.

Orso stood.

"Joyce and I have work to do. You want to look through the files and reports, here they are. You want to go through the murder book, there it is. Where do you want to begin?"

Scott hadn't thought about where to begin. He thought he might read his own statements to see if he had forgotten anything, but then realized there was only one place to begin.

"The crime scene pictures."

Cowly was clearly uncomfortable.

"Are you sure?"

"Yes."

Scott had never seen the crime scene photographs. He knew they existed, but never thought about them. He saw his own version of them every night in his dreams.

Orso said, "Okay, then, let's get you going."

13.

Orso took a hanging file from the box, and placed it on the table.

"These are the pictures. The murder book has copies of the most important shots, but the master file here has everything."

Scott glanced at the file without opening it.

"Okay."

"The pictures are labeled on the back with the relevant report and page numbers. Criminalist, medical examiner, detective bureau, whatever. You want to see what the criminalist said about a particular picture, you look up the report number, then go to the page."

"Okay. Thanks."

Scott was waiting for Orso to leave, but Orso didn't move. His face was grim, as if he wasn't comfortable with what Scott was about to see.

Scott said, "I'm okay."

Orso nodded silently, and passed Cowly coming in. She had stepped out, but now returned with a bottle of water, a yellow legal pad, and a couple of pens.

"Here. If you have any questions or want to make notes, use these. I thought you might like some water, too."

She was staring at him with the same grim concern he'd seen in Orso when her cell phone buzzed with an incoming text. She glanced at the message.

"Central Robbery. You need anything, I'm at my desk."

Scott waited until she was gone, then opened the hanging file. The individual files were labeled AREA, BENTLEY, KEN-WORTH, TORINO, 2A24, PAHLASIAN, BELOIT, ANDERS, JAMES, and MISC. 2A24 had been Scott and Stephanie's patrol car. It felt strange to see his own name, and he wondered what he would find. Then he considered Stephanie's name, and forced himself to stop thinking.

He opened the AREA file first. The photographs within varied in size, and had been taken in the early hours of dawn, after the bodies had been removed. The Kenworth's front bumper hung at a lifeless angle. The Bentley's passenger side was crumpled, and bullet holes pocked its sides and windows.

Firemen, uniformed officers, criminalists, and newspeople were in the background. The white outline of Stephanie's body held Scott's attention like an empty puzzle begging to be filled with missing pieces.

Scott glanced through the pictures of the Bentley next. Its interior was littered with broken glass. So much blood covered the seats and console it looked as if the interior had been splashed with ruby paint. The floorboard in the driver's well was a deep, congealing pond.

The interior of the Kenworth told a different story, as it was undamaged. Brass shell casings from the AK-47 were scattered over the floorboards and seats, and sprinkled the top of the dashboard. The interior was littered with scraps of paper, a crushed Burger King cup, and several empty plastic water bottles. Scott knew from Melon that these things had been removed, examined, and linked to the truck's owner, a man named Felix Hernandez, who had been in jail for beating his wife when his truck was stolen from Buena Park.

Scott didn't bother to look at the Gran Torino. It had been found eight blocks away beneath a freeway overpass, and, like the Kenworth, had been stolen earlier that day for use in the murders.

Scott quickly turned to Pahlasian and Beloit, examining each closely, as if he might see what it was about one or both that had led to their murders.

These pictures had been taken at night, and reminded Scott of the lurid black-and-white photographs he had seen of mobsters machine-gunned in the thirties. Pahlasian was slumped over the console as if he had been trying to crawl into Beloit's lap. His slacks and sport coat were so saturated with blood Scott was unsure of their color. The broken glass Scott had seen in the daytime picture now glittered from the camera's flash.

Beloit was slumped in the passenger seat as if he had melted. The side of his head was missing, and the arm nearest the camera was hanging by ropy red tissue. As with Pahlasian, he had been shot so many times his clothes were saturated with blood.

Scott spoke aloud to himself.

"Man, somebody wanted you *really* dead."

The next folder contained pictures of Stephanie. Scott hesitated, but knew he must look at them, so he opened the folder.

Her legs were together, bent at the knees, and tipped to the left. Her right arm lay perpendicular to her body, palm down, fingers hooked as if she was trying to hold on to the street. Her left hand rested on her belly. Her body was outlined in the predictable manner, though the pool of blood beneath her was so large the outline was broken. Scott flipped through her pictures quickly, and came to a photograph of a large irregular blood smear labeled B1. B2 showed elongated blood smears as if something had been dragged. Scott realized this was his own blood, and just as suddenly realized he had turned from Stephanie's folder to his own. The amount of blood was amazing. There was so much blood he broke into a prickly sweat. He knew he came very close to dying that night, but seeing the amount of blood on the street made his closeness to death visible. How much more blood could he have lost before he would have been in the picture with a white line around his body? A pint? Half a pint? He flipped back to the first picture of Stephanie. Her pool of blood was larger. When the picture blurred, he wiped his eyes and took a picture of Stephanie's body.

Scott closed the photo files, walked around the table to calm himself, and stretched his side and shoulder. He opened the bottle of water, took a long drink, and studied Orso's poster-sized diagram of the crime scene. He snapped a picture of it, checked his picture for clarity, then returned to the file box, feeling uncertain and stupid. He wondered if he was deluding himself by pretending he might remember something to help catch Stephanie's killers and silence her nightly accusations.

He took out random files and spread them on the table. Auto-theft reports on the Kenworth and the Gran Torino. Statements from people who heard the shooting and phoned 911. Autopsy reports.

Scott saw a file labeled SID — COLLECTED EVIDENCE, and paged through it. The file contained reports analyzing the physical evidence collected at the scene, and began with a list of collected items that went on for pages. The work the SID criminalists put into compiling this amount of detail was stunning, but Scott wasn't interested in endless forensics reports. He knew what happened that night was about Pahlasian and Beloit. Someone had wanted them dead, and Stephanie Anders was collateral damage.

Scott found the stack of reports and interviews concerning Eric Pahlasian. There were so many interviews with family members, employees, investors, and others they stacked almost five inches thick. Scott checked his watch, and realized how long

Maggie had been locked in her run. He felt a stab of guilt, and knew he had to get back to the training facility.

Scott went to the door, and found Cowly on the phone in a cubicle against the far wall. She raised a finger, telling him she'd be off in a second, finished her call, then put down the phone.

"How you doing in there?"

"Good. I really appreciate you and Detective Orso letting me see this stuff."

"No sweat. I was just on with Central Robbery about your Mr. Marley. They're working a line on a crew laying off stolen goods at a swap meet. Some of the goods match up with things stolen in the area."

"Great. I'll let him know. Listen, I have to get back to my dog —"

"Don't mention the swap meet."

"What?"

"If you call Marley. You can call him if you want, but don't mention we're working an investigation at the swap meet. Don't say those words. Swap meet."

"I won't."

"Cool. Someone from Central will call him about his burglary. The swap meet thing isn't his business."

"I get it. My lips are sealed."

"You have a picture?"

Scott was confused again.

"Of what?"

"Your dog. I love dogs."

"I just got her yesterday."

"Oh. Well, you get a picture, I want to see her."

"You think it would be all right if I took a few files with me? I'll sign for them, if you want."

Cowly glanced around as if she was hoping to see Orso, but Orso was gone.

Scott said, "It's the Pahlasian stuff. I'd like to read it, but it's a phone book."

"I can't let you take the murder book, but you can borrow the file copies. We have them on disc."

"Okay. Great. Those are the files I'm talking about."

He followed her back into the conference room. She frowned when she saw the files and folders spread across the table.

"Dude. I hope you weren't planning to leave this mess."

"No way. I'll put them back before I leave."

Scott pointed out the towering Pahlasian file.

"This is what I want. The files Detective Orso took from the box."

She grew thoughtful, and Scott worried

she was going to change her mind, but then she nodded.

"It's okay. Orso won't have a problem unless you lose something. The handwritten notes aren't on the disc."

"When do you want them back?"

"If we need something, I'll call you. Just put the rest of this stuff back before you leave, okay?"

"You got it."

Scott returned the folders to their proper file hangers, and was fingering through the hangers when he saw a small manila envelope in the bottom of the box. It was fastened shut by a metal clasp, and had a handwritten note on front: *return to John Chen.*

Scott opened the clasp and upended the envelope. A sealed plastic evidence bag containing what looked like a short brown leather strap slid out, along with a photograph of the strap, a note card, and an SID document. The strap was smeared with what appeared to be a reddish powder. Melon had written a note on the card: *John, thanks. I agree. You can trash it.*

The SID document identified the strap as half of an inexpensive watchband of no identifiable manufacturer, item #307 on the SID collection list. A note was typed across the bottom of the document:

This was collected on the sidewalk north of the shooting (ref item #307) as part of general recovery. Appears to be half of women's or men's size small leather watchband, broken at hinge. The red smears that appear to be dried blood are common iron rust. No blood evidence found. Location, nature, and condition suggest unrelated to crime, but I wanted to check before I dispose.

Scott tensed when he saw the band had been collected on the north side of the street. The Kenworth had come from the north. Shin's building was on the north.

The photograph showed the leather strap with a white number card (#307) beside it on a sidewalk. Scott went back to the master evidence list in the SID file, looked up its reference number, and found the diagram showing where the watchband was found. When Scott saw the diagram, he felt as if his heart was rolling to a slow stop. Item #307 had been collected directly beneath the roof overlooking the crime scene where Scott had stood that morning and touched the wrought-iron bars that striped his hand with rust.

Scott took out his phone and photographed the diagram. He took a second picture to make sure the image was sharp, then returned the remaining files to their proper hangers.

Scott studied the rusty smears, and thought they looked like the rust he'd gotten on his hands. He wondered why Melon hadn't returned the envelope to Chen, and decided it had fallen between the hangers. Melon had probably forgotten about it. After all, if the broken strap was trash, it wasn't worth thinking about.

Scott put everything back into the file box exactly as he had found it except for the watchband. He slipped it back into the envelope, put the envelope in his pocket, and picked up the Pahlasian files. He thanked Cowly on his way out.

14.

It was late afternoon when Scott returned to the training facility. Almost a dozen personal and LAPD K-9 cars crowded the parking lot. He heard barking and shouted commands behind the building, as dogs and handlers trained.

Scott parked opposite the office end of the building, and let himself into the kennel. Maggie was on her feet in the run, watching for him when he opened the door as if she knew it was him before she saw him. She barked twice, then raised up to place her front paws on the gate. Scott smiled when he saw her tail wag.

"Hey, Maggie girl. You miss me? I sure missed you!"

She dropped to all fours as he approached. He stepped inside, scratched her ears, and grabbed the thick fur on the sides of her face. Her tongue lolled out with pleasure, and she tried to play-bite his arm.

"I'm sorry I was gone so long. You think I left you?"

He stroked her sides and back, and down along her legs.

"No way, dog. I'm here to stay."

Budress came along the runs from the office.

"Got all sulky when you left."

"Yeah?"

Budress rotated his right arm.

"Shit, man, I'm gonna be sore. That dog hits like a linebacker."

"She was into it."

They had worked on bite commands and suspect-aggression earlier that morning, with Budress playing the suspect. Leland had come out to watch. Maggie was hesitant at first, but remembered the military command words, and her USMC training had quickly returned. She would focus on Budress at Scott's command, and watch him without moving unless Scott ordered her to attack or Budress moved toward Scott or herself. Then she would charge for his padded arm like a heat-seeking missile. It was the only part of her exercises she seemed to enjoy.

Budress went on, lowering his voice.

"Leland was impressed. These Mals are fast and all teeth and love to bite, but these

181

big shepherds, man, she's thirty pounds heavier and she'll knock you on your ass."

Scott stroked her a last time, and clipped on her lead.

"I'll work her some more."

"She's worked enough."

Budress now blocked the gate. He lowered his voice even more.

"She was limping. After you left, when she was pacing here in the run. I don't know if Leland saw."

Scott stared at the man for a moment, then led Maggie out of the run, watching her.

"She's walking fine."

"It was small. The back legs. She kinda dragged the right rear."

Scott led her in a tight circle, then down past the runs and back, watching her walk.

"Looks good to me."

Budress nodded, but didn't look convinced.

"Okay, well, maybe she tweaked something what with all the running around."

Scott ran his hands over her back legs and feet, and felt her hips. She showed no discomfort.

"She's fine."

"Wanted to let you know. I didn't tell Leland."

Budress rubbed the top of her head, then glanced at Scott.

"Work on her conditioning. But not here, okay? You're done here today. Take her jogging. Throw the ball. We'll work on her startle response more tomorrow."

"Thanks for not telling Leland."

Budress rubbed the top of her head again.

"She's a good dog."

Scott watched Budress walk away, then led Maggie out to his car, checking her gait for the limp. She hopped in when he opened the door, and filled the back seat. Only two days, and it had become automatic. She jumped into the car without hesitation or signs of discomfort.

"He's right. You probably just tweaked a muscle."

Scott slid in behind the wheel, closed his door, and Maggie immediately took her place on the console, blocking his view out the passenger window.

"You're going to get us killed. I can't see."

Her tongue hung free and she panted. Scott dug his elbow into her shoulder and tried to push her back, but she leaned into him and didn't move.

"C'mon. I can't see. Get in back."

She panted louder, and licked his face.

Scott fired up the Trans Am and pulled

out into the street. He wondered if she had ridden in the Hummers this way, standing between the front seats to see what was coming. A bunch of grunts in an armored Humvee could probably see over her, but he had to push her head out of the way.

Scott picked up the freeway and headed home toward the Valley. He was thinking about the rusty brown strap when he remembered his promise to Elton Marley. He called him, reported what he had learned, and told him that a detective from Central Robbery would be in touch.

Marley said, "Ee already hab call. Two weeks, I heer no-teeng, now dey call. T'ank you for helpeeng dis way."

"No problem, sir. You helped me this morning."

"Dey comin' back, dey say. We see. I geeb you free shirt. You look good in Marley-World shirts. De women, dey lub you."

Scott told Marley he would check back to make sure the robbery detectives followed up, then dropped his phone between his legs. He normally kept it on the console, but the console was filled with dog.

Maggie sniffed the pocket where he stowed the baloney, and licked her lips. This reminded Scott he needed baloney and plastic bags, so he dropped off the freeway in Toluca Lake to find a market. Maggie nosed at his pocket.

"Okay. Soon. I'm looking."

He bogged down in traffic three blocks from the freeway. Yet another apartment building was being framed on a lot intended for a single-family home. A lumber truck was blocking the street as it crept off the site, and a food truck maneuvered to take its place. Locked in the standstill, Scott watched the framers perched in the wood skeleton like spiders, banging away with their nail guns and hammers. A few climbed down to the food truck, but most continued working. The banging ebbed and flowed around periods of silence; sometimes a single hammer, sometimes a dozen hammers at once, sometimes nail guns snapping so fast the construction site sounded like the Police Academy pistol range.

Scott grabbed the fur behind Maggie's ear and ruffled her. It was early for dinner, but Scott had an idea.

"You hungry, big girl? I'm starving."

He parked a block and a half past the construction site, clipped Maggie's lead, and walked her back to the food truck. Maggie grew more anxious the closer they got, so he stopped every few feet to stroke her.

Three workmen were waiting at the food truck, so Scott lined up with them. Maggie twined around his legs, and shifted from side to side. The nail guns and hammers were loud, and every few minutes a power saw screamed. Scott squatted beside her, and offered the last of the baloney. She didn't take it.

"It's okay, baby. I know it's scary."

The man in front of him gave them a friendly smile.

"You a policeman, he must be a police dog."

"She. Yeah, she's a police dog."

Scott continued to stroke her.

The man said, "She's a beauty. We had a shepherd when I was a kid, but now I got this wife hates dogs. Allergic, she says. I'm gettin' allergic to her."

The food truck didn't have baloney, so Scott bought two turkey sandwiches, two ham sandwiches, and two hot dogs, all plain. He led Maggie to a small trailer serving as the construction office, and asked the foreman if they could sit outside to eat.

The foreman said, "You here to arrest someone?"

"Nope. Just want to sit here with my dog."

"Knock yourself out."

Scott sat on the edge of the building's

186

foundation, and took up the slack on the lead to keep Maggie close. Whenever a saw screamed or the nail guns banged, she twisted and turned, trying to get away from the sound. Scott felt guilty and conflicted, but stroked her and talked to her, and offered her food. He kept a hand on her the entire time, so they were always connected. This wasn't something Leland told him to do, but Scott sensed his touch was important.

The workmen occasionally stopped to ask questions, and almost all of them asked if they could pet her. Scott held her collar, told them to move slowly, and let them. After a sniff, Maggie seemed fine with it. The men all told her how beautiful she was.

Scott felt her grow calmer. She stopped fidgeting, her muscles relaxed, and after thirty-five minutes, she finally sat. A few minutes later, she took a piece of hot dog, even with a saw screaming above them. He stroked her, told her how wonderful she was, and broke off more pieces. A noise occasionally startled her, and she would lurch to her feet, but Scott noticed it took her less time to relax. She ate the hot dogs and the turkey, but not the ham. Scott ate the ham.

They sat together for well over an hour, but Scott was in no hurry to leave. He enjoyed sitting with her, talking with the workmen about her, and realized he had not felt this calm in weeks. Then he decided he had not felt so peaceful since the shooting. Scott ruffled her fur.

"It flows both ways."

Scott and Maggie went home.

15.

Scott changed into civilian clothes, took Maggie for a short walk, and told her she had to hang out by herself for a few minutes. He raced to a nearby market, bought three pounds of sliced baloney, five boxes of plastic bags, and a roast chicken. He drove home as if he was rolling Code 3. He worried she was barking or ripping apart his apartment, but when he ran inside, Maggie was in her crate, chin down between her front paws, watching him.

"Hey, dog."

Maggie's tail thumped. She stepped out to greet him, and Scott felt an enormous sense of relief.

He put away the groceries, changed Maggie's water, and printed the pictures he had taken in Orso's office. He did not print the picture of Stephanie's body. He pinned the pictures to the wall by his crime scene diagram, then drew in Marley's shop, Shin's shop, the alley, and the loading area and fire escape behind their building. He drew a small X on the sidewalk where the criminalist found the leather strap.

When Scott finished, he studied his diagram, and felt cowardly for leaving out Stephanie. He printed her picture, and pinned it above the map.

"I'm still here."

Scott took the stack of reports and files to the couch. It was a lot to read.

Adrienne Pahlasian, the wife, had been interviewed seven times. Each interview was thirty or forty pages long, so Scott skipped ahead to skim a few shorter interviews. A homeless man named Nathan Ivers told Melon he witnessed the shooting, and stated that the gunfire came from a glowing blue orb that hovered above the street. A woman named Mildred Bitters told Melon several tall thin men wearing black suits and dark glasses were responsible for the shooting.

Scott put these aside and returned to Adrienne Pahlasian's first interview. He knew this interview was the meat, and set the course the investigation eventually followed.

Melon and Stengler had driven to her home in Beverly Hills, where Melon informed her that her husband had been murdered. Melon noted she appeared genuinely shocked, and required several minutes before they could continue. During this first interview, she agreed to speak without the presence of an attorney and signed a document to that effect. She identified Beloit as her husband's cousin, and described him as a "great guy" who stayed at their home when he visited. She stated her husband told her he was going to pick up Beloit at LAX, take him to dinner at a new downtown restaurant called Tyler's, and drive Beloit past two downtown properties Eric hoped to buy. Melon then allowed her to phone her husband's office, where she spoke with a Michael Nathan to obtain the addresses of the two buildings. She grew so emotional when informing Nathan of the murders that Melon took the phone. Nathan was unable to explain why Pahlasian would show Beloit the two buildings at such an unusual hour. The interview ended shortly thereafter when Mrs. Pahlasian's children returned from school. Melon closed the report by stating both he and Stengler found Mrs. Pahlasian credible, sincere, and believable in her grief.

Scott copied the addresses for the two downtown properties and the restaurants, then stared at the ceiling. He felt drained, as if Adrienne Pahlasian's grief had been added to his own.

Maggie yawned. Scott glanced over, and found her watching him. He swung his feet from the couch, and fought back a grimace.

"Let's take a walk. We'll eat when we get back."

Maggie knew the word "walk." She lurched to her feet, and went to her lead.

Scott bagged two slices of baloney, clipped on her lead, then remembered Budress advising him to work on her conditioning. He stuffed the green tennis ball into his pocket along with a poop bag.

Scott was relieved to find the park deserted except for a man and woman jogging around the perimeter. He unclipped Maggie's lead and told her to sit. She watched him expectantly for the next command. Instead of giving a command, Scott grabbed the sides of her head, rubbed his head on her face, and let her escape. She was in full play mode. She dipped her chest to the ground, stuck her butt in the air, and made play growls. Scott decided this was the time for running. He pulled out the green ball, waved it over her nose, and threw it across the field.

"Get it, girl. Get it!"

Maggie broke after the ball, but abruptly stopped. She watched the ball bounce, then returned to Scott with her head and tail sagging.

Scott considered the situation, then clipped her lead.

"Okay. If we don't chase balls, we jog."

A sharp pain tightened Scott's side when he started off, and his leg lit up with the pinpricks of moving scar tissue.

"Next time I'll take a pill."

He remembered Maggie was loping along with a shattered rear end, and wondered if her wounds hurt the same as his. She wasn't limping and showed no discomfort, but maybe she was tougher than him. Maggie had stuck with her partner. He felt a stab of shame and gritted his teeth.

"Okay. No painkillers for you, then none for me."

They chased the ball another eight times before Maggie's right rear leg began to drag. It was slight, but Scott immediately stopped. He probed her hips and flexed the leg. She showed no discomfort, but Scott headed for home. By the time they reached Mrs. Earle's house, the limp was gone, but Scott was worried.

He fed Maggie first, then showered and ate half the roast chicken. When the remains of the chicken were away, he gave her a series of commands, rolled her onto her back, and held her so she had to struggle to get away. Even with all the rough play, she walked normally, so Scott decided to tell Budress the limp had not recurred. He opened a beer, and resumed reading.

In Adrienne Pahlasian's next two interviews, she answered questions about her husband's family and business, and provided the names of friends, family, and business associates. Scott found these interviews boring, so he skipped ahead.

Tyler's manager was named Emile Tanager. Tanager provided precise arrival and departure information based upon the times orders were placed and the tab was closed. The two men arrived together and placed an order for drinks at 12:41. Pahlasian closed their tab on his American Express card at 1:39. Melon had made a handwritten note on Tanager's interview, saying the manager provided a DVD security video, which was booked into evidence as item #H6218A.

Scott sat back when he read Melon's note. The idea of a security video had not occurred to him. He copied the times, and took the notes to his computer.

Scott printed a map of the downtown

area, then located Tyler's and the two commercial buildings. He marked the three locations with red dots, and added a fourth dot where he and Stephanie were shot.

Scott pinned the map to the wall by his diagram, then sat on the floor to study his notes. Maggie came over, sniffed, and lay down beside him. Scott guessed the drive from Tyler's to either building had taken no more than five or six minutes. The drive from the first building to the second probably added another seven or eight. Scott threw in an extra ten minutes at each building for Pahlasian to make his sales pitch, which added twenty minutes to his total. Scott frowned at the times. No matter which building they visited first, there were almost thirty minutes missing when Pahlasian and Beloit reached the kill zone.

Scott stood to look at his map. Maggie stood with him, and shook off a cloud of fur.

Scott touched her head.

"What do you think, Mags? Would two rich dudes in a Bentley walk around in a crappy neighborhood like this, that time of night?"

The four red dots looked like bugs trapped in a spider web.

Scott eased back to the floor like a creaky

old man, and picked up the plastic bag containing the broken watchband. He re-read Chen's note:

No blood evidence.
Common rust.

Maggie sniffed the bag, but Scott nudged her away.

"Not now, baby."

He took the brown band from the bag, and held it close to examine the rust. Maggie leaned in again, and sniffed the strap. This time he didn't push her away.

Common rust. He wondered if SID could tell whether the rust on the watchband came from the wrought-iron rail on the roof.

Maggie sniff-sniff-sniffed the strap, and this time her curiosity made Scott smile.

"What do you think? Some dude on the roof, or am I losing my mind?"

Maggie tentatively licked Scott's face. With her ears folded back, her warm brown eyes looked sad.

"I know. I'm crazy."

Scott put the watchband back into its bag, sealed it, and stretched out on the floor. His shoulder hurt. His side hurt. His leg hurt. His head hurt. His entire body, his past, and his future all hurt.

He looked up at the diagrams and pictures pinned to the wall, seeing them upside down. He stared at Stephanie's picture. The white line surrounding her body was bright against the blood cloverleaf upon which she lay. He pointed at her.

"I'm coming."

He lowered his hand to Maggie's back. Her warmth and the rise and fall as she breathed were comforting.

Scott felt himself drifting, and soon he was with Stephanie again.

Beside him, Maggie's nose drew in his smells, and tasted his changes. After a while, she whimpered, but Scott was far away and did not hear.

16.

MAGGIE

The man loved to chase his green ball. Pete never chased the green ball, which was Maggie's special treat, but this new man threw his ball, chased it, and Maggie trotted along at his side. When he caught up to the ball, he would throw it again, and off they would go. Maggie enjoyed loping along beside him across the quiet grass field.

Maggie did not enjoy the construction site with the loud, frightening sounds and the smell of burned wood, but the man kept her close and comforted her with touches as if they were pack. His scents were calm and assuring. When other men approached, she sniffed them for rage and fear, and watched for signs of aggression, but the man remained calm, and his calm spread to Maggie, and the man shared good smelling things with her to eat.

Maggie was growing comfortable with the

man. He gave her food, water, and play, and they shared the same crate. She watched him constantly, and studied how he stood and his facial expressions and the tone of his voice, and how these things were re-flected by subtle changes in his scent. Maggie knew the moods and intentions of dogs and men by their body language and smells. Now she was learning the man. She knew he was in pain by the change in his scent and gait, but as they chased the ball, his pain faded, and he was soon filled with play. Maggie was happy the green ball brought him joy.

After a while the man grew tired, and they started back to the crate. Maggie sniffed for new scents as they walked home, and knew three different dogs and their people had followed much the same path. A male cat had crossed the old woman's front yard, and the old woman was inside the house. A female cat had slept for a time beneath a bush in the backyard but was now gone. She knew the female cat was pregnant, and close to giving birth. As they approached the man's crate, Maggie increased her sniff rate, searching for threats. Before the man opened the door, she already knew no one was inside or had been inside since the man and Maggie left earlier that day.

"Okay. Let's get you fed. You're probably thirsty, right, all that running? Jesus, I'm dying."

Maggie followed the man to the kitchen. She watched him fill her water bowl and food bowl, then watched him disappear into his bedroom. She touched her nose to the food, then drank deep from the water. By this time, she heard the man's water running, smelled soap, and knew he was showering. Pete had washed her in the showers when they were in the desert, but she had not liked rain that fell from the ceiling. It beat into her eyes and ears, and confused her nose.

Maggie turned from the food, and walked through the man's crate. She checked the man's bed and the closet and once again circled the living room. Content their crate was as it should be, Maggie returned to the kitchen, ate her food, then curled in her crate. She listened to the man as she drifted near sleep. The running water stopped. She heard him dress, and after a while he came into the living room, but Maggie didn't move. Her eyes were slits, so he probably thought she was sleeping. He moved into the kitchen, where he ate standing up. Chicken. More water ran, then he went to his couch. Maggie was almost asleep when he jumped to his feet, clapping his hands.

"Maggie! C'mon, girl! C'mere!"

He slapped his legs, dropped into a crouch, then sprung tall, smiling and clapping his hands again.

"C'mon, Maggie! Let's play."

She knew the word "play," but the word was unnecessary. His energy, body language, and smile called to her.

Maggie scrambled from her crate, and bounded to him.

He ruffled her fur, pushed her head from side to side, and gave her commands.

She happily obeyed, and felt a rush of pure joy when he squeaked she was a good girl.

He commanded her to sit, she sat, to lay, she dropped to her belly, her eyes intent on his face.

He patted his chest.

"Come up here, girl. Up. Gimme a kiss."

She reared back, front feet on his chest, and licked the taste of chicken from his face.

He wrestled her to the floor, and rolled her over onto her back. She struggled and twisted to escape, but he rolled her onto her back again, where she happily submitted, paws up, belly and throat exposed. His, and happy.

The man released her, smiling, and when

she saw joy in his face, her own joy blossomed. She dropped to her chest, rear in the air, wanting more play, but he stroked her and spoke in his calming voice, and she knew playtime was over.

She nuzzled him as he stroked her, and after a few minutes he lay on the couch. Maggie sniffed a good spot nearby and curled against the wall. She was happy with joy from their play, and sleepy from her long day, but she never fully slept as she sensed a change in the man. Small changes in his scent told her his joy was fading. The scent of fear came with the bright pungent scent of anger as his heart beat faster.

Maggie lifted her head when the man rose, but when he sat at the table she lowered her head and watched him. She took fast, shallow sniffs, noting that the taste of anger left him and was replaced by the sour scent of sadness. Maggie whimpered, and wanted to go to him, but was still learning his ways. She smelled his emotions roll and change like clouds moving across the sky.

After a while he crossed the room, sat on the floor, and picked up a stack of white paper. His tension spiked with the mixed scents of fear and anger and loss. Maggie went to him. She sniffed the man and his paper, and felt him calm with her closeness. She knew this was good. The pack joins together. Closeness brings comfort.

Maggie curled up beside him, and felt a flush of love when he rested his hand upon her. She sighed so deeply she shuddered.

"What do you think, Mags? Would two rich dudes in a Bentley walk around in a crappy neighborhood like this, that time of night?"

She stood at his voice, licked his face, and was rewarded by his smile. She wagged her tail, hungry for more of his attention, but he picked up a plastic bag. Maggie noted the chemical scent of the plastic and the scents of other humans, and how the man focused on it.

He took a piece of brown skin from the plastic, and examined it closely. She watched the man's eyes and the nuanced play of his facial expressions, and sensed the brown skin was important. Maggie leaned closer, nostrils working, sniffing to draw air over a bony shelf in her nose into a special cavity where scent molecules collected. Each sniff drew more molecules until enough collected for Maggie to recognize even the faintest scent.

Dozens of scents registered at once, some more strongly than others — the skin of an animal, organic but lifeless; the vivid strong sweat of a male human, the lesser scents of other male humans; the trace scents of plastic, gasoline, soap, human saliva, chili sauce, vinegar, tar, paint, beer, two different cats, whiskey, vodka, water, orange soda, chocolate, human female sweat, a smear of human semen, human urine — and dozens of scents Maggie could not name, but which were as real and distinct to her as if she was seeing colored blocks laid out on a table.

"What do you think? Some dude on the roof, or am I losing my mind?"

She met the man's eyes, and saw love and approval! The man was pleased with her for sniffing the skin, so Maggie sniffed again.

"I know. I'm crazy."

She filled her nose with the scents. Pleasing the man left her feeling safe and content, so Maggie curled close beside him, and settled for sleep.

A few moments later, he stretched out beside her, and Maggie felt a peace in her heart she had not known in a long while.

The man spoke a final time, then his breath evened, his heart slowed, and he slept.

Maggie listened to the steady beat of his heart, felt his warmth, and took comfort in his closeness. She filled herself with his scent, and sighed. They lived, ate, played, and slept together. They shared comfort and strength and joy.

Maggie slowly pushed to her feet, limped across the room, and picked up the man's green ball. She brought it to him, dropped it, and once more settled for sleep.

The green ball gave the man joy. She wanted to please him.

They were pack.

PART III

■ ■ ■ ■

To Protect
and To Serve

■ ■ ■ ■

17.

Two days later, Scott was dressing for work when Leland called. Leland never phoned him, and seeing his Sergeant's name as an incoming call inspired a twinge of fear.

Leland's voice was as hard as his glare.

"Don't bother coming to work. Those Robbery-Homicide sissies you've been dating want you at the Boat at oh-eight-hundred hours."

Scott glanced at the time. It was a quarter to seven.

"Why?"

"Did I say I know why? The LT got a call from the Metro commander. If the boss knows why, he did not see fit to share. You are to report to a Detective Cowly down there with the geniuses at oh-eight-hundred sharp. Do you have any other questions?"

Scott decided Cowly wanted the files back, and hoped she hadn't gotten in trouble for letting him take them.

"No, sir. This shouldn't take long. We'll see you as soon as we can."

"We."

"Maggie and me."

Leland's voice softened.

"I knew what you meant. Looks like you're learning something, now aren't you?"

Leland hung up, and Scott stared at Maggie. He didn't know what to do with his dog. He didn't want to leave her in the guest house, but he also didn't want to leave her at the training facility. Leland might get it in his head to work with her. If Leland discovered the limp, he wouldn't hesitate to get rid of her.

Scott went to the kitchen, poured a cup of coffee, and sat behind his computer. He tried to think of a friend who could watch her for a few hours, but his friendships had withered since the shooting.

Maggie walked over and put her head on his leg. Scott smiled, and stroked her ears.

"You're going to be fine. Look how screwed up I am, and I made it back."

She closed her eyes, enjoying the ear massage.

Scott wondered if a veterinarian could help with her leg. LAPD had vets under contract to care for their dogs, but they reported to Leland. Scott would have to fly under the radar if he had Maggie checked. If anti-inflammatories or something like cortisone could fix her problem with no one the wiser, Scott would pay for it out of pocket. He had done the same for himself to keep the department from knowing how many painkillers and anti-anxiety meds he took.

He Googled for veterinarians in North Hollywood and Studio City, then skimmed the Yelp, Yahoo!, and Citysearch reviews. He was still reading when he realized it was too late to find someone to dog-sit.

Scott quickly gathered the Pahlasian files, tucked his notes on the missing drive time into his pants, and clipped Maggie's lead.

"Detective Cowly wants to see your picture. We'll do her one better."

The crush-hour drive through the Cahuenga Pass was a forty-five-minute slog, but Scott led Maggie across the PAB lobby with three minutes to spare. They cleared the front desk, and took the elevator to the fifth floor. This time when the doors opened, Cowly was waiting alone. Scott smiled as he led Maggie into the hall.

"I thought the real thing was better than a picture. This is Maggie. Maggie, this is Detective Cowly."

Cowly beamed.

"She's beautiful. Can I pet her?"

Scott ruffled Maggie's head.

"Let her smell the back of your hand first. Tell her she's pretty."

Cowly did as Scott asked, and soon ran her fingers through the soft fur between Maggie's ears.

Scott offered the heavy stack of files.

"I didn't finish. I hope you didn't get into trouble."

Cowly glanced at the files without taking them, and led Scott and Maggie toward her office.

"If you didn't finish, keep them. You didn't have to bring them."

"I thought that's why you wanted to see me."

"Nope, not at all. Some people here want to talk to you."

"People?"

"This thing is developing fast. C'mon. Orso is waiting. He's going to love it you brought your dog."

Scott followed her into the conference room, where Orso was leaning against the wall by his diagram. Two men and a woman were at the table. They turned when Scott and Maggie entered, and Orso pushed away from the wall.

"Scott James, this is Detective Grace Parker from Central Robbery, and Detective Lonnie Parker, Rampart Robbery."

The two Parkers were on the far side of the table, and did not stand. The female Parker made a tight smile, and the male Parker nodded. Grace Parker was tall and wide, with milky skin. She wore a gray dress suit. Lonnie Parker was short, thin, and the color of dark chocolate. He wore an immaculate navy sport coat. Both were in their early forties.

Lonnie Parker said, "Same last name, but we aren't related or married. People get confused."

Grace Parker frowned at him.

"Nobody gets confused. You just like saying it. You say the exact same thing every time."

"People get confused."

Orso cut in to introduce the remaining man. He was large, with a red face, furry forearms, and wiry hair that covered a sun-scorched scalp like cargo netting. He wore a white, short-sleeved shirt with a red-and-blue striped tie, but no sport coat. Scott guessed him to be in his early fifties.

"Detective Ian Mills. Ian's with Robbery Special, down the hall. We've set up a task force to cover these robberies, and Ian's in charge."

Mills was seated on the near side of the table, closest to Scott. He stood and stepped toward Scott to offer his hand, but when he reached out, Maggie growled. Mills jerked back his hand.

"Whoa."

"Maggie, down. Down."

Maggie instantly dropped to her belly, but remained focused on Mills.

"Sorry. It was the sudden move toward me. She's okay."

"Can we try that again? The handshake?"

"Yes, sir. She won't move. Maggie, stay."

Mills slowly offered his hand, this time without standing.

"I'm sorry about your partner. How're you doing?"

Scott felt irritated Mills brought it up, and gave his standard answer.

"Doing great. Thanks."

Orso pointed at an empty chair beside Mills, and took his usual seat beside Cowly.

"Sit. Ian's been involved since the beginning. He and his guys gave us Beloit's French connection, and worked with Interpol. Ian's the reason you're here today."

Mills looked at Scott.

"Not me. You. Bud says you're remembering things."

Scott immediately felt self-conscious, and

216

tried to downplay it.

"A little. Not much."

"You remembered the driver had white hair. That's pretty big."

Scott nodded, but said nothing. He felt as if Mills was watching him.

"Have you remembered anything else?"

"No, sir."

"You sure?"

"I don't know if there's anything else to remember."

"You seeing a shrink?"

Scott felt a rush of discomfort, and decided to lie.

"They make you see someone if you're involved in a shooting, but I didn't get anything out of it."

Mills studied him for a moment, then pushed a manila envelope forward and rested his hand on it. Scott wondered what was inside.

"You know what we do in Robbery Special?"

"You cover the big bank and armored-car scores. Serial robberies. Things like that."

Mills made a satisfied shrug.

"Close enough. The people who shot you and your partner weren't assholes who blew up a couple of rich guys and police officers for kicks. Your boys had skills. The way they worked together to pull this thing off tight. I'm thinking they were a professional crew — the same people who take down big scores."

Scott frowned.

"I thought the robbery idea was ruled out."

"Robbery as the motive, yeah. We chased bad leads for weeks before we ruled that one out, but we didn't rule out the crews who take scores. Any asshole who will blow up bank tellers and rent-a-cops will do murder for hire. We keep tabs on these people."

Mills opened the envelope, and slid out more pictures.

"Crews are made up of specialists. The alarm guy does alarms, the vault man does vaults, the driver drives."

Mills turned the pictures so Scott could see them. Eight Anglo men with white or light gray hair and blue eyes stared up at him.

"These men are drivers. We believe they were in Los Angeles on or about the night you were shot. Anything?"

Scott stared at the pictures. He looked up, and found Mills, Orso, Cowly, and the two Parkers watching him.

"I saw a sideburn when he turned away. I

didn't see his face."

"What about the other four guys? You remember anything new about them?"

"No."

"Was it four or five?"

Scott didn't like the empty expression in Mills' eyes.

"The driver plus four."

"The driver get out?"

"No."

"So that's four plus the driver makes five, altogether. How many got out of that Kenworth?"

"Two. Two got out of the Torino. Two plus two makes four."

Grace Parker rolled her eyes, but if Mills took offense he didn't show it.

"Four people running around, shooting, is a lot of people. Maybe someone pulled off his mask, or called out a name? Remember anything like that?"

"No. I'm sorry."

Mills studied him a few moments longer, then picked up the pictures and slid them into the envelope.

"These aren't the only drivers in town. Maybe you'll remember something else. Maybe you'll even remember someone else. Lonnie?"

Lonnie Parker leaned forward and placed

yet another booking photo on the table. It showed a thin young man with sunken eyes and cheeks, bad skin, and frizzy black hair that haloed his head in a limp 'fro.

Lonnie Parker tapped the picture.

"Seen this dude before?"

Everyone was watching him again.

"No."

"Skinny guy. Six feet. Take your time. Give him a good look."

Scott felt as if he was being tested and didn't like it. Maggie shifted beside his chair. Scott reached down to touch her.

"No, sir. Who is he?"

Mills stood with his envelope before anyone could answer.

"I'm done here. Thanks for coming in, Scott. You remember anything else — I don't care what — let me know asap. Me and Bud."

Mills glanced at Orso.

"You got it from here?"

"I got it."

Mills told the Parkers to come see him when they finished, and left with his pictures.

Grace Parker rolled her eyes.

"They call him the I-Man. Ian 'the I-Man' Mills. Isn't that precious?"

Orso cleared his throat to quiet her, and

looked at Scott.

"Yesterday afternoon, at our request, Rampart and Northeast detectives arrested and questioned fourteen individuals known to resell stolen goods."

Grace Parker said, "Fences."

Orso pushed on.

"Two of these individuals claim to know a thief who laid off Chinese DVDs, Chinese cigarettes, herbs, and the kinds of things Shin carried in his store."

Scott looked from the picture to Orso.

"This man?"

"Marshall Ramon Ishi. Last night, we showed this picture to Mr. Shin. Shin remembers Ishi would loiter in his store, but never buy anything. You put that with the two fences, and, yes, the odds are pretty good Mr. Ishi is the man who burglarized Shin's store the night you were shot."

Scott stared at the picture, and felt a cold prickle over his chest. Maggie sat up, leaned against his legs, and Scott realized Orso was still talking.

"The home he shares with his brother, girlfriend, and two other men is currently under surveillance. Mr. Ishi and the girl are not present. They left —"

Orso checked his watch.

"— forty-two minutes ago. They're being

followed by SIS officers, who tell us Ishi and his friend appear to be selling hits of ice to morning commuters."

Grace Parker said, "Tweakers. They're meth addicts."

Orso nodded happily, and once more resumed.

"They'll go home in a couple of hours. We'll give them a chance to settle in, then arrest them. Joyce will have command. I'd like you to be with her, Scott. Would you go?"

All of them were watching him again.

Scott didn't understand what Orso was asking, then realized he was being handed a ticket into the investigation. He had spent nine months wanting to help catch Stephanie's killers, and now felt unable to breathe.

Maggie rested her chin on his leg and gazed at him. Her ears were folded and her eyes appeared sad.

Grace Parker said, "Damn, that's a big dog. Her poop must be the size of a softball."

Lonnie Parker laughed, and it was the laughter that helped Scott find his voice.

"Yes, sir. Absolutely. I absolutely want to be there. I'll have to clear it with my boss."

"It's cleared. You're mine the rest of the day."

Orso glanced at Maggie.

"Though we only expected one of you."

Cowly said, "He can bring the dog. He's not going to participate."

She grinned at Scott.

"We're management. We watch other people do the work."

Orso stood, ending the meeting, and the other detectives pushed back their chairs and stood with him. Maggie scrambled to her feet, and the two Parkers both stared at her, frowning.

Lonnie said, "What happened to her?"

Scott realized they had not been able to see her hindquarters when they were seated on the other side of the table. Now they saw her scars.

"A sniper shot her. Afghanistan."

"No shit?"

"Twice."

Now Orso and Cowly stared at her, too, and Cowly looked sad.

"You poor baby."

Lonnie's face folded into a grim stack of black plates, and he nudged around the table toward the door.

"I don't wanna hear nuthin' sad 'bout no dog. C'mon. Let's go see the I-Man. We got work to do."

Grace arched her eyebrows at Scott.

"The man has a master's in political science from S.C., and speaks three languages. He puts on the ghetto accent when he gets emotional."

Lonnie looked insulted.

"That's racist and offensive. You know that is not true."

They continued bickering as they left. Scott turned to Orso and Cowly.

"What do you want me to do?"

Cowly answered.

"Stay here or close by. There's a park across the street, if it's easier with Maggie. I'll text you. We have plenty of time. Take the files with you."

When she mentioned the files, Scott remembered the notes in his pocket. He took out his map, showed them the four dots, and pointed out the discrepancy he'd found with Pahlasian's driving time.

"Even if they stopped at both buildings to talk about them, there's no way it should take an hour and ten minutes to get from the restaurant to the kill zone. Seems like there's twenty or thirty minutes missing."

Scott looked up from the map, waiting for their reaction, but Orso only nodded.

"You're missing a stop. Club Red. It's in the files."

Scott had no idea what Orso was talking about.

"I read the interviews with Pahlasian's wife and his office assistant. They didn't mention another stop."

Cowly stepped in with the answer.

"They didn't know about it. Club Red is like a strip club. Melon didn't learn about it until Beloit's credit card charges posted. Beloit picked up the tab."

Scott felt deflated and stupid, and even more stupid when Cowly waved at the heavy stack of files.

"It's in there. Melon interviewed the manager and a couple of waitresses. Use my desk or go to the park. I'll text when we have to roll."

Scott tucked the files under his arm, and looked from Cowly to Orso. He wanted to see the security video, but now felt too embarrassed to ask.

"Thanks for letting me tag along. It means a lot."

Orso smiled the scoutmaster smile.

"Sure."

Scott turned away with Maggie at his side. He felt like an idiot for believing he had discovered a glaring discrepancy when top-cop detectives like Orso and Cowly knew the case inside and out.

Scott wasn't an idiot, but three more days would pass before he understood.

18.

Scott took the files to Cowly's cubicle, saw her tiny, cramped space, and decided Maggie would be happier at the park. Then he noticed the framed pictures beside Cowly's computer, and eased into her chair. Maggie wedged herself under the desk.

The first picture showed a younger, uniformed Cowly at her Police Academy graduation with an older man and woman who were probably her parents. The picture next to it showed Cowly and three other young women all glammed up in satin and sequins for a night on the town. Scott studied the four, and decided Cowly was the only one who looked like a cop. This made Scott smile. Stephanie had looked like a cop, too. The next picture showed Cowly and a good-looking young guy on a beach. Cowly was wearing a red one-piece and her friend was wearing baggy swim trunks that hung to his knees. Scott tried to recall if Cowly wore a wedding ring, but couldn't. The last picture showed Cowly on a couch with three little kids. Christmas decorations were on a table behind them, and the oldest kid was wearing a Santa hat. Scott glanced at the pic of Cowly and the man on the beach, and wondered if these were their kids.

"C'mon, Mags. Let's see the park."

Maggie was too big to turn around in the cramped space, so she backed out from under the desk like a horse backing out of a stall.

Scott led her downstairs and across First Street to the City Hall park. The park was small, but a surrounding grove of California Oaks made the space pleasant and shady.

Scott found an unoccupied bench in the shade, and searched through the file for the Club Red interviews. They were short, and mistakenly attached to a document about Georges Beloit.

The three interviews had been conducted twenty-two days after the shooting. Melon described Club Red as "an upscale after-hours lounge featuring what the management calls 'performance erotica,' where semi-nude models pose on small stages above the bar." Melon and Stengler interviewed Richard Levin, the manager on the night of the shooting, and two bartenders.

None of them remembered Pahlasian or Beloit, or recognized their pictures, but Levin provided the times their tab opened and closed from his electronic transaction records. As he did on the interview with Emile Tanager, Melon had handwritten a note on Levin's interview:

R. Levin — deliv sec vid — 2 discs — EV
 # H6218B

Levin had delivered the Club Red security video on two discs, which were logged into the case file.

When Scott finished the interviews, he entered Club Red's address into his phone's map app to find its location, and added a fifth dot to his map. He stared at the fifth dot for a moment, then checked to be sure he entered the correct address. The address was correct, but now the times and routes seemed even more wrong.

Leaving Club Red, both commercial properties were now several blocks beyond the kill zone. If Pahlasian had driven to either property, he would have passed the kill zone and had no reason to turn back. The freeway was in the other direction.

Scott grew frustrated, and decided to see for himself. The kill zone was less than twenty blocks away, and Tyler's and Club Red were closer.

"C'mon, let's take a ride."

They hurried back to the Boat for his car. Tyler's had been Pahlasian's starting point, so Scott drove to Tyler's.

The restaurant occupied the corner of an older, ornate building at an intersection not far from Bunker Hill. The front was paneled in black glass with its name mounted on the glass in brass letters. Tyler's was closed, but Scott stopped to consider the area. He saw no nearby parking lots, so he assumed valets waited at the corner during business hours. He wondered if the Gran Torino was watching the valet station when Pahlasian arrived, or if it followed him from LAX.

Club Red was only nine blocks away. Scott made the daytime drive in twelve minutes, most of which was spent waiting for pedestrians. At one-thirty in the morning, the travel time would have been four minutes or less.

Club Red was also on the ground floor of an older building. It sat next to a parking lot, and its exposed side bore a faded sign advertising custom machine parts. Jutting from the side of the building into the parking lot was a small vertical neon sign spelling out RED. A red door was cut into the building beneath the sign. Patrons probably passed a couple of oversized bouncers as if entering a clandestine world.

Scott checked his map again. Ignoring Tyler's, the remaining four dots formed a capital Y, with Club Red at the bottom, the kill zone directly above it at the fork, and the two properties Pahlasian wanted to show Beloit at the tips of the arms.

Scott looked at Maggie.

"Everything's wrong."

Maggie sniffed his ear, and blew dog breath in his face. Scott tried to push her off the console, but she held firm.

Two attendants were on duty in the parking lot. Scott parked across their entrance, and got out. The older attendant was a Latin man in his fifties with short black hair and a red vest. He hurried over when he saw Scott block their drive, but pulled up short when he saw Scott's uniform. This was the cop effect.

He said, "You wan' to park?"

Scott let Maggie out. The man saw her, and took a step back. This was the German shepherd effect.

Scott pointed at the building.

"The club here, Club Red? What time do they close?"

"Really late, man. They don't open 'til nine. They close at four."

"Four in the morning."

"Yeah, four in the morning."

Scott thanked the man, let Maggie back into the car, and climbed in behind the wheel. He thought he had it figured.

"There's no mystery here. They were coming back. They saw the buildings, and decided they wanted another drink. That's all there is to it."

Maggie panted, but this time Scott was out of range. Then he glanced at the map again and realized his latest theory was also wrong.

"Shit."

The Bentley's direction.

The Bentley wasn't driving toward Club Red when it passed in front of his radio car. Pahlasian was driving in the opposite direction. Toward the freeway.

Scott was still staring at the map when Cowly texted him.

WE'RE ROLLING. CALL ME

Scott immediately called.

"I'm only a few blocks away. Give me five minutes."

"Take ten, but don't come to the Boat.

232

We're staging at MacArthur Park. Can you be there in ten?"

"Absolutely."

"On the east side between Seventh and Wilshire. You'll see us."

Scott put down his phone, wondering why Pahlasian was going to the freeway when he entered the kill zone. Time was still missing, and it hadn't been filled by looking at buildings.

19.

MacArthur Park was four square blocks split down the middle by Wilshire Boulevard. A soccer field, playgrounds, and a concert pavilion occupied the area north of Wilshire. MacArthur Park Lake took up the south side. The lake was once known for paddleboats until gang violence, drug dealing, and murders drove away the people who rented the boats. Then LAPD and the local business community rolled in, the lake and the park were rebuilt, serious surveillance systems were installed, and the gang-banging drug dealers were rolled out. The paddleboats tried to make a comeback, but the lake's reputation for 'bangers and violence had polluted the water. So had the tools of their trade. When the lake was drained for repair, more than a hundred handguns were found on the bottom.

Scott followed Wilshire to the park, and saw the staging area. Six LAPD radio cars, a SWAT van, and three unmarked but obvious police sedans were parked near the old paddleboat concession. A uniformed police officer blocked the entrance when he saw a Trans Am turning in, but he stepped aside when he saw Scott's uniform. Scott rolled down the window.

"I'm looking for Detective Cowly."

The officer leaned closer to grin at Maggie.

"With the SWAT team. Man, I love having these dogs with us. He's a beauty."

Maybe the officer leaned too close or spoke too loudly. Maggie's ears spiked forward, and Scott knew what was coming even before she growled.

The officer stepped back and laughed.

"Jesus, I love these dogs. Good luck finding a place to park. Maybe put it on the grass over there."

Scott raised the window, and ruffled Maggie's fur as he pushed her out of the way.

"He, my ass. How can he think a beautiful girl like you is a he?"

Maggie licked Scott's ear, and watched the officer until they were parked.

Scott clipped her lead, got out, and watered her with a squirt bottle. After she drank, he let her pee, and spotted Cowly beside the SWAT unit's tactical van. She was huddled with the SWAT commander, a uniformed lieutenant, and three detectives, none of whom Scott recognized. The SWAT team was lounging by the boathouse, as relaxed as if they were on a fishing trip. Scott felt the kiss of a passing dream, then looked down at Maggie, and found her watching him, tongue hanging loose, ears back and happy. He petted her head.

"No limping. Either of us."

Maggie wagged her tail and fell in beside him.

Cowly saw him approaching, and held up a finger, signaling him to wait. She spoke with her group a few minutes longer, then they broke up and went in different directions, and Cowly came over to meet him.

"We'll take my car. Ishi is only five minutes away."

Scott was doubtful.

"You don't mind? She's going to leave hair."

"All I care is she doesn't throw up. She gets carsick, you have to clean it."

"She doesn't get carsick."

"She's never ridden with me."

Cowly led them to an unmarked tan Impala that wasn't in much better shape than Scott's ratty Trans Am. He loaded Maggie in back, and climbed into the shotgun seat as Cowly fired the engine. She popped it in gear, and backed up to leave.

"This won't take long. You see the man-power we got? The I-Man wanted to roll the Bomb Squad, forchrissake. Orso said, these idiots *use* meth, they don't *cook* it."

Scott nodded, not knowing how to respond.

"Thanks again for asking me along. I appreciate it."

"You're doing your part."

"By keeping you company?"

Cowly gave him a glance he couldn't read.

"By eyeballing Ishi. If you see him, maybe you'll remember him."

Scott immediately tensed. Maggie paced from side to side in the back seat, whining. Scott reached back to touch her.

"I didn't see him."

"You don't remember seeing him."

Scott felt as if he was being tested again, and didn't like it. His stomach knotted, and he flashed on the shooting — bright yellow bursts from the rifle, the big man walking closer, the impact as the bullet slammed through his shoulder. Scott closed his eyes, and visualized himself on a beach. Then Cowly and her boyfriend appeared on the sand, and he opened his eyes.

"This is bullshit. I'm not a lab monkey."

"You're what we have. You don't want to be here, I'll let you out."

"We don't even know if this is the guy."

"He laid off Chinese goods three different occasions before Shin closed. He lives fourteen blocks from the kill zone. You see him up close, maybe something will come back to you."

Scott fell silent and stared out the window. He desperately hoped Ishi had witnessed the shootings, but didn't want to believe he had seen the man and forgotten. That was too crazy. Seeing a man and forgetting you've seen him was way more screwed up than recalling white hair. Cowly and Orso seemed to think this was possible, which left Scott feeling they doubted his sanity.

Cowly guided the D-ride onto a narrow residential street past two idling black-and-whites, turned at the first cross street, and stopped in the center of the street. A pale green unmarked sedan exactly like hers faced them at the next cross street. Scott saw no other police presence.

Cowly said, "Fourth house from the corner, left side. See the van covered with graffiti? It's parked in front."

A battered Econoline van covered with Krylon graffiti was parked in front of a pale green house. A broken sidewalk led up a withered yard to a narrow cinder-block porch.

Scott said, "Who's inside?"

Ishi shared the house with two male friends who were also meth addicts, a girlfriend named Estelle "Ganj" Rolley, who worked as a part-time prostitute to support their meth addiction, and his younger brother, Daryl, a nineteen-year-old dropout with several misdemeanor arrests to his credit.

Cowly said, "Ishi, the girl, and one of the males. The other guy left earlier, so we picked him up. The brother hasn't been home since yesterday. You see our guys?"

The street and the houses appeared deserted.

"Nobody."

Cowly nodded.

"A team from Fugitive Section will make the pop. Two guys are on either side of the house right now, and two more have the rear. Plus, we have people from Rampart Robbery to handle the evidence. Watch close. These people are the best."

Cowly lifted her phone and spoke softly.

"Showtime, my lovelies."

The van's driver's-side door popped open. A thin African-American woman slipped out, rounded the van to the sidewalk, and walked toward the house. She wore frayed jean shorts, a white halter top, and cheap flip-flop sandals. Her hair hung in braids dotted with beads.

Cowly said, "Angela Sims. Fugitive detective."

The woman knocked when she reached the door. She waited with the nervous anxiety of an impatient tweaker. When no one opened the door, she knocked again. This time the door opened, but Scott did not see who opened it. Angela Sims stepped into the doorway, and stopped, preventing the door from being closed. Two male Fugitive dicks charged from each side of the house at a dead sprint, converging on the door as Angela Sims shoved her way into the house. The four male officers slammed inside behind her. As the Fugitive detectives made their entry, a male and a female detective jumped from the van and raced up the sidewalk.

Cowly said, "Wallace and Isbecki. Rampart Robbery."

Wallace and Isbecki were still on the sidewalk when two radio cars screeched to a stop behind Cowly's sedan and two more stopped behind the sedan at the far end of the street. Four uniformed officers deployed from each car to seal the street.

Ishi's house was quiet and still, but Scott knew all hell was breaking loose inside. Maggie fidgeted from his anxiety.

Five seconds later, two of the male Fugitive detectives emerged with an Anglo male handcuffed between them. Cowly visibly relaxed.

"That's it, baby. Done deal."

Cowly drove forward, parked alongside the van, and shoved open her door.

"C'mon. Let's see what we've got."

Scott let Maggie out the rear, clipped her lead, and hurried to catch up as Sims and another Fugitive dick brought out Estelle Rolley. Rolley looked like a walking skeleton. Street officers called this "the meth diet."

Cowly motioned Scott to join her in the yard.

The remaining Fugitive Section detective brought out Marshall Ishi last. Ishi's hands were cuffed behind his back. He was maybe five eleven, and had the same hollow eyes and cheeks as in his booking photo. He stared at the ground, and wore baggy cargo shorts, sneakers without socks, and a discolored T-shirt that draped him like a parachute.

Scott studied the man. Nothing about him was familiar, but Scott couldn't turn away.

He felt as if he was falling into the man.

Cowly nudged close.

"What do you think?"

She sounded lost in a tunnel.

The arresting detective steered Ishi off the porch down two short steps to the sidewalk.

Scott saw the Kenworth slam into the Bentley. He saw the Bentley roll, and the flare of the AK-47. He saw Marshall Ishi on the roof, peering down at the carnage, and running away. Scott saw these things as if they were happening in front of him, but he knew this was only a fantasy. He saw Stephanie die, and heard her beg him to come back.

Ishi glanced up, met Scott's eyes, and Maggie growled deep in her chest.

Scott turned away, hating Cowly for dragging him here.

"This was stupid."

"Man, you should've seen your face. Are you okay?"

"I was thinking about that night, is all. Like a flashback. I'm fine."

"Did seeing him help?"

"Does it look like it helped?"

Scott's voice was sharp, and he immediately regretted it.

Cowly showed her palms and took a step back.

"Okay. Just because you didn't see him doesn't mean he wasn't there. He could be our guy. We just have to roll with it."

Scott thought, *Fuck you and your roll with it.*

Scott followed her into a small, dirty house permeated with a burnt-plastic and chemical odor so strong it made his eyes water. Cowly fanned the air, making a face.

"That's the crystal. Soaks into the paint, the floors, everything."

The living room contained a futon piled with rumpled sheets, a threadbare couch, and an elaborate blue glass bong almost three feet tall. Rock pipes dotted the futon and couch, and a square mirror smeared with powder sat on the floor. Maggie strained against her lead. Her nostrils flickered independently as she tested the air, then the floor, then the air again, and her anxiety flowed up the leash. She glanced at Scott as if checking his reaction, and barked.

"Take it easy. We're not here for that."

Scott tightened her lead to keep her close. Maggie had been trained to detect explosives, and explosives-detection dogs were never trained to alert to drugs. Scott decided the combined chemical smells of crystal and rock were confusing her. He tightened her lead even more, and stroked her flanks.

"Settle, baby. Settle. We don't want it."

The male Rampart detective appeared in the hall, and grinned at Cowly.

"We own this dude, boss. Come see."

Cowly introduced Scott to Bill Wallace, who worked Rampart Robbery. Claudia Isbecki was in the first of two tiny bedrooms, photographing dime bags of rock cocaine, a large pill bottle filled with crystal meth, a glass jar filled with weed, and assorted plastic bags containing Adderall, Vyvanse, Dexedrine, and other amphetamines. Wallace then led them to a second bedroom, where he pointed out a tattered black gym bag, and grinned like a man who won the lottery.

"Found this under the bed. Check it out."

The bag contained a pry bar, two screwdrivers, a bolt cutter, a hacksaw, a lock pick set with tension wrenches, a bottle of graphite, and a battery-powered lock pick gun.

Wallace stepped back, beaming.

"We call this a do-it-yourself burglary kit as defined under Penal Code four-forty-six. Also known as a one-way ticket to conviction."

Cowly nodded.

"Pictures. Log everything, and email the

pix to me asap. They'll save time with his lawyer."

Cowly glanced at Scott, then turned away.

"Let's go. We're finished here."

"What happens now?"

"I'll bring you to your car. Then I'm going back to the Boat, and you should probably go wherever you dog guys go."

"I meant with Ishi."

"We'll question him. We'll use the charges we have to press him about Shin. If he didn't rob Shin, maybe he knows who did. We work the case."

Her phone rang when they reached the living room. She glanced at the Caller ID.

"That's Orso. I'll be out in a minute."

She moved away to take the call. Scott wondered if he should wait, then decided to get Maggie out of the stink, and took her outside.

A small crowd of neighborhood residents was gathered across the street and in the surrounding yards to watch the action. Scott was watching them when two senior officers came up the walk with a thin young male in his early twenties. He sported a mop of curly black hair, gaunt cheeks, and nervous eyes. Then Scott saw the resemblance, and realized this was Marshall Ishi's younger brother, Daryl. He was not handcuffed, which meant he was not under arrest.

Scott was stepping off the sidewalk to let them pass when Maggie alerted, and lunged toward Daryl. She caught Scott by surprise, and almost pulled him off his feet. She pulled so hard, she raised up onto her hind legs.

Daryl and the closest officer both lurched sideways, and the officer shouted.

"Jesus Christ!"

Scott reacted immediately.

"Out, Maggie. Out!"

Maggie retreated, but kept barking.

The officer who shouted was bright red with anger.

"Christ, man, control your dog. That thing almost bit me!"

"Maggie, out! Out! Come!"

Maggie followed Scott away. She didn't seem frightened or angry. Her tail wagged, and she glanced from Daryl Ishi to the pocket with the hidden baloney to Daryl Ishi again.

Daryl said, "That dog bites me, I'll sue your ass."

Cowly stepped from the house and came down the steps. The flushed uniform introduced Daryl as Marshall's brother.

"Says he lives here and wants to know what's going on."

Cowly nodded, and seemed to consider Daryl with a remote detachment.

"Your brother has been arrested on suspicion of burglary, theft, possession of stolen goods, possession of narcotics, and possession of narcotics with the intent to distribute."

Daryl waited for her to continue. When she didn't, he leaned sideways, trying to see inside through the open front door.

"Where's Ganj?"

"Everyone within the house has been arrested. Your brother is being processed at the Rampart Community Police Station, and will then be transferred to the Police Administration Building."

"Uh-huh. Okay. I got things in there. Can I go inside?"

"Not at this time. When the officers are finished, you'll be allowed to enter."

"I can leave?"

"Yes."

Daryl Ishi slouched away without looking back. Maggie watched him, whimpering as she looked from Daryl to Scott.

Cowly said, "What's wrong with her?"

"He probably smells like the house. She didn't like that chemical odor."

"Who in their right mind would?"

Cowly watched Daryl disappear down the

street, and shook her head.

"How'd you like Marshall as your resident adult? That boy is following in his brother's footprints right into his brother's shitty life."

She turned to Scott, and her professional face was softer.

"If this was unpleasant for you, I'm sorry. We should have explained why we wanted you here. Bud made it sound like we were doing you a favor."

Scott's head flooded with things to say, but they all sounded like apologies or excuses. He finally managed a shrug.

"Don't sweat it."

Scott said nothing more as they drove back to MacArthur Park. The SWAT van was gone, and only two radio cars and his Trans Am remained.

When Cowly stopped behind his car, he remembered the security videos and asked her about them.

"Melon got the security videos from Tyler's and Club Red. Okay if I see them?"

She seemed surprised.

"Fine by me. All you'll see is whatever the bartenders and waitresses said. They don't show anything else."

Scott tried to figure out how to explain.

"I've never seen Pahlasian and Beloit. Still pictures, yeah, but not alive."

She gave a slow nod.

"Okay. I can make that happen."

"They weren't in the box."

"Physical evidence is in the evidence room. I'll dig them out for you. It probably won't be today. I'll be busy with Ishi."

"I understand. Whenever is fine. Thanks."

Scott got out, and opened the back door for Maggie. He clipped her lead, let her hop out, then looked at Cowly.

"I'm not crazy. It's not like I have big holes in my head."

Cowly looked embarrassed.

"I know you're not crazy."

Scott nodded, but didn't feel any better. He was turning away when she called.

"Scott?"

He waited.

"I'd want to see them, too."

Scott nodded again, and watched as she drove away. He checked the time. It was only ten minutes after eleven. He still had most of the day to work with his dog.

"You don't think I'm crazy, do you?"

Maggie stared up at him and wagged her tail.

Scott scratched her ears, stroked her back, and gave her two pieces of baloney.

"You're a good girl. A really good girl. I

shouldn't have taken you into that damned house."

He drove to the training field, hoping the chemicals in the house hadn't hurt Maggie's nose. A dog man would know. A dog man would keep his dog safe.

20.

The sun beat down hot and hard on the training field, frying the grass and the men and the dogs.

Budress said, "No peeking."

Sweat and sunblock dripped into Scott's eyes.

"No one is peeking."

Scott was crouched beside Maggie behind an orange nylon screen. The screen was pulled taut between two tent poles stuck into the ground. Its purpose was to prevent Maggie from seeing a K-9 officer named Bret Downing hide in one of four orange tents scattered at far points on the field. The tents were tall and narrow like folded beach umbrellas, and big enough to conceal a man. Once Downing was hidden, Maggie would have to use her nose to find him, and alert Scott by barking.

Scott was scratching her chest and praising her when a sharp explosion behind him caught them off guard. Budress had surprised them with the starter pistol.

Scott and Maggie cringed at the shot, but Maggie instantly recovered, licked her lips, and wagged.

Scott rewarded her with a chunk of baloney, squeaked what a good girl she was, and ruffled her fur.

Budress put away the gun.

"Somebody oughta feed you that baloney. You jump pretty good."

"Could you step back a couple of feet next time? I'm going deaf."

Budress surprised them three or four times during each session. He would fire the gun, and Scott would give Maggie a treat. They were trying to teach her to associate unexpected sounds with a positive experience.

Budress waved at Downing to continue.

"Stop whining and get her ready. I like to watch her hunt."

They had already run the exercise eight times, with five different officers posing as "bad guys" to vary the scent. Maggie had been flawless. Scott was relieved to see Maggie's sense of smell was unharmed by the chemical odors in Ishi's house.

Earlier, Leland had watched for almost an hour, and was so impressed he took a turn playing the bad guy. Scott instantly saw why. Leland rubbed himself on all four tents, then climbed a tree at the end of the field. His trick confused her for all of twenty seconds, then she whiffed his track leading from the tents, and narrowed the cone until she found him.

Leland had trotted back from the tree without his usual scowl.

"That dog may be the best air dog I've seen. I do believe she could follow a fly fart in a hurricane."

Air dogs excelled at tracking scent in the air. Ground dogs like bloodhounds and beagles worked best tracking scent particles close to or on the ground.

Scott was pleased with Leland's enthusiasm, but relieved when Leland was called inside for a call. He worried Maggie's limp would return with all the running, and Leland would see.

Now, with Leland gone, Scott felt more at ease, and enjoyed the work. Maggie knew what he expected of her, and Scott was confident with her performance.

When Downing disappeared inside the third tent, which was eighty yards across the field and slightly upwind, Budress gave Scott the nod.

"Turn her loose."

Scott jiggled Downing's old T-shirt in Maggie's face, and released her.

"Smell it, girl. Smell it — seek, seek, seek!"

Maggie charged from behind the screen, head high, tail back, ears up. She slowed to test the air for Downing's scent, then ran in a slow curve downwind of the tents. Thirty yards from the screen, Scott saw her catch the edge of Downing's scent cone. She veered into the breeze, broke his ground scent, and powered hard for the third tent. Watching her dig in and stretch out when she accelerated was like watching a Top Fuel dragster explode off the line.

Scott smiled.

"Got him."

Budress said, "She's a hunter, all right."

Maggie covered the distance to the tent in two seconds, jammed on the brakes, and barked. Downing eased out until he was in full view. Maggie stood her ground, barking, but did not approach him, as Scott and Budress had taught her.

Budress grunted his approval.

"Bring her in."

"Out, Maggie. Out."

Maggie broke away from the tent and loped back, pleased with herself. Her joy showed in her bouncy stride and happy, open-mouth grin. Scott rewarded her with another chunk of baloney and praised her in the high squeaky voice.

Budress shouted for Downing to take five, then turned to Scott.

"Tell you what, dog with her nose, she saved a lot of grunts finding IEDs. That's a masterful fact. You can't fool her."

Scott ran his hand over Maggie's back, and stood to ask Budress a question. Budress had worked with explosives-detection dogs in the Air Force, and knew almost as much about dogs as Leland.

"The house we were in reeked of crystal, that nasty chemical stink?"

Budress grunted, knowing the stink. Leland had the scowl, Budress the grunt.

"We go in, and right away she was whining and trying to search. You think she confused the ether with explosives?"

Budress spit.

"Smells don't confuse these dogs. If she wanted a smell, it was a smell she knew."

"When we were leaving, she alerted on this guy who lives there, same way."

Budress thought for a moment.

"Were they making or using?"

"Does it matter?"

"We taught our dogs to alert to explosives like RDX and Semtex and whatnot, but we also taught'm the main components insur-

255

gents use for homemade explosives. Remember — the 'I' in IED stands for 'improvised.' "

"These people were users. They weren't cooking."

Budress worked his lips as he thought about it some more, then shrugged and shook his head.

"Probably wouldn't matter anyway. A couple of your typical meth lab components could be used to improvise an explosive, but the ingredients are too common. We never taught our dogs to alert to common materials. If we did, we'd have dogs alerting every time we passed a gas station or a hardware store."

"So ether or starter fluid wouldn't confuse her?"

Budress smiled at Maggie, and offered his hand. She sniffed, then lay down at Scott's feet.

"Not this nose. If I asked you to point out the orange tents, would the green hedges or blue sky or the tree bark confuse you?"

" 'Course not."

"She smells like we see. Just laying here, she's picking up thousands of scents, just like we're seeing a thousand shades of green and blue and whatever. I say, show me the orange, you instantly spot the orange, and don't think twice about all those other colors. It's the same way for her with scents. If she was trained to alert to dynamite, you can wrap dynamite in plastic, bury it under two feet of horseshit, and douse the whole thing with whiskey, and she'll still smell the dynamite. Ain't she amazing?"

Scott studied Budress for a moment, and realized how much the man loved these dogs. Budress was a dog man.

Scott said, "Why do you think she alerted?"

"Dunno. Maybe you oughta tell your detective friends to search that house for IEDs."

Budress burst out laughing, pleased with himself, then shouted for Downing to find a new tent.

"She's looking real good. Give her some water, and we'll do one more."

Scott was clipping up Maggie for the tenth run when Leland stormed out of his office.

"Officer James!"

Scott turned, and heard Budress mumble. "Now what?"

Leland covered the ground in long, angry strides.

"Tell me I'm wrong. Tell me you did not DARE to participate in a police action this morning without my permission."

"I watched an arrest with the Robbery-Homicide detectives. I didn't participate."

Leland stomped closer until his nose was in Scott's face.

"I know for a FACT you and your dog took part in an ARREST. My ASS was just reamed for that little FACT."

Maggie growled — a low guttering warning, but Leland did not move.

"Call your dog out."

"Out, Maggie. Down."

Maggie didn't obey. Her eyes were locked on Leland. Her muzzle wrinkled to show her fangs.

"Down."

Maggie growled louder, and Scott knew he was losing more ground with Leland by the second.

Behind him, Budress spoke softly.

"You're the alpha. Be alpha."

Scott made his voice commanding.

"Down. Maggie, down."

Maggie eased to her belly, but did not leave Scott's side. She was totally focused on Leland, who was still totally focused on Scott.

Scott wet his lips.

"We did not take part in the arrest. We were not there as a K-9 team. I didn't know there was going to be an arrest until I got to

258

the Boat. I thought they wanted files back. That's why I took Maggie with me. I assumed I would drop the files off, then come here. That's it, Sergeant."

Scott wondered who complained, and why. He flashed on the senior officer who crapped his pants when Maggie lunged; the officer who turned so red he looked like he was going to stroke.

Scott sensed Leland was trying to decide whether to believe him.

"We were out here for an hour, and you didn't mention it. This makes me think you didn't want me to know."

Scott hesitated.

"The Homicide people thought my seeing the guy they arrested would trigger my memory. It didn't. I don't. It feels like I'm letting my partner down."

Leland was silent for several seconds, but his scowl remained firm.

"It was reported you could not control your dog, and your dog attacked a civilian."

Scott felt himself flush. *As red as the asshole who jumped.*

"I controlled Maggie and the situation, and no one was harmed. Kinda like now. With you."

Budress spoke softly again, but this time to Leland.

"Looks like Scott has Maggie well in hand to me, Top. Even though she's all set to rip out your throat."

Leland's scowl flicked to Budress, and Scott knew Budress had saved him.

Leland's scowling eyes grew thoughtful.

"Do you want to remain in my K-9 platoon, Officer James?"

"You know I do."

"And you still hope to convince me this dog should be approved by me as fit for duty?"

"I'm going to convince you."

"Way it works is, my boss reams me about you, I get your back. I tell him my officer is an outstanding young officer who has surprised the hell out of me by the progress he has made with his dog, and I do not for one goddamn second believe he cannot control his dog, and anyone says otherwise better come over here and say it to my face."

Scott didn't know what to say. This was as close to a compliment as Leland had come.

Leland let it soak in, then continued.

"When all the back-gettin' is done, I then ream you. We clear on this principle?"

"Yes, sir. We're clear."

"Fact is, this dog is not part of my K-9 platoon until I certify her, which I have not. If she had bitten this fool, and the vic's money-chiseling lawyer found out YOU — a member of THIS platoon — exposed the public to an uncertified animal, they could and would sue the blue off our asses. I like my blue ass. Don't you?"

"Yes, sir. I'm liking your blue ass just fine."

"You lock this dog in her crate next time or you leave her with me. We clear?"

"Clear, Sergeant."

A bead of sweat leaked down the side of Leland's face. He wiped it slowly away using the hand with the missing fingers, and let the hand linger. Scott sensed Leland did this on purpose.

"Are you a dog man, Officer James?"

"You bet your blue ass."

"It's not my blue ass on the line."

Leland stared into Scott's eyes a moment longer, then took one step back and looked down at Maggie. She growled, low and deep in her big shepherd's chest.

Leland smiled.

"Good dog. You're a damned good dog."

He looked up at Scott again.

"Dogs do what they do to please us or save us. They don't have anything else. We owe them no less."

He turned and stalked away.

Scott didn't breathe until Leland disappeared into the building, then he turned to Budress.

"Thanks, man. You saved me."

"Maggie saved you. He likes her. Doesn't mean he won't get rid of her, but he likes her. You should've left her here this morning."

"I was scared he'd see her limp."

Budress studied Maggie for a moment.

"She didn't limp. Not once. Has she been limping at home?"

"Not once."

Budress glanced up, and Scott could tell Budress knew he was lying.

"Then let's not press it. Stow the gear. We're done for today."

Budress shouted for Downing to come in, and the two senior officers left Scott to clean up. Scott let Maggie off her leash, and was pleased when she stayed beside him. He broke down the screen, rolled it, and collected the four tents with Maggie beside him.

Scott rolled the last tent, and was carrying them toward the kennel when he glanced down and saw Maggie limping. Same as before, her right rear leg dragged half a heartbeat behind the left.

Scott stopped so Maggie would stop, and looked at the kennel. Leland's window was empty. The door was closed. No one was watching.

Scott put down the tents, clipped Maggie's lead, and hoisted the tents. He made her walk behind him so he was between Maggie and the building.

No one was inside when he stowed the tents. Budress, Downing, and the others were probably in the offices, or gone. Scott made sure the parking lot was empty before he led her to his car. Her limp had grown more and more obvious.

Scott fired the engine and backed away.

Maggie stepped forward on the console. Her tongue was out, her ears were folded, and she looked like the happiest dog in the world.

Scott laced his fingers in her fur. She looked at him and panted, content.

Scott said, "You bet your blue ass."

He pulled out of the lot and headed for home.

21.

An overturned big rig on the northbound 5 turned the freeway into a parking lot. Scott worked his way to an exit when they reached North Hollywood, and found a condo complex being framed in Valley Village. Feeding Maggie at construction sites had become their pattern. He watched her carefully when they left the car. Her leg dragged so slightly now, Scott wasn't sure if she was limping or this was her natural gait, but he was relieved by the improvement.

He bought roast chicken and hot dogs for Maggie, a pork carnitas burrito for himself, and sat with her among snapping nail guns and curious construction workers. Maggie cringed when the first bang surprised her, but Scott decided her startle response was less exaggerated than at the beginning. Once she accepted a piece of hot dog, she focused on Scott and ignored the unpredictable sounds.

They ate and socialized with the construction crew for almost an hour. Scott saved the remains of his baloney stash for a treat, and gave it to her when they returned to the car. By then, her limp was gone.

Twenty minutes later, the sun was behind trees and the sky was purple when Scott parked in MaryTru Earle's front yard. Her shades were down as always, keeping her safe from the outside world.

Scott took Maggie for a short walk to do her business, then through the gate, and along the side of Mrs. Earle's house toward his guest house. The light was gloomy fading to dark, and Mrs. Earle's television provided its usual sound track. Scott had made this same walk hundreds of times, and this time was no different until Maggie stopped. There was no mistaking her expression. She lowered her head, spiked her ears, and stared into the darkness. Her nostrils flickered as she sampled the air.

Scott looked from Maggie to the guest house to the surrounding shrubs and fruit trees.

"Really?"

The light above his side door had been out for months. The drapes covering the French doors were partially open as he had left them, and the kitchen lights were on.

He saw Maggie's crate, the dining table, and part of the kitchen. His guest house looked fine, and nothing appeared different. Scott had never felt unsafe in this neighborhood, but he trusted his dog, and Maggie clearly whiffed something she didn't like. Scott wondered if a cat or a raccoon was in the bushes.

"What do you smell?"

He realized after the fact he had whispered.

Scott considered letting her off the leash, but thought better of it. He didn't want an eighty-five-pound attack dog blindsiding a cat or a kid in the agapanthus. He gave her six feet of lead instead.

" 'kay, baby, let's see what you have."

Maggie hoovered up ground scent as she pulled him forward. She led him directly to the side door, then to the French doors. She returned to the side door, sniffed hard at the lock, then once more rounded the guest house to the French doors, where she pawed at the glass.

Scott opened the French doors, but did not enter. He listened for a moment, heard nothing, then unclipped Maggie and spoke in a loud, clear voice.

"Police. I'm going to release this German

shepherd. Speak up, or this dog will rip you open."

No one answered.

Scott released her.

Maggie did not charge inside, so Scott knew if anyone had been in his home, they were now gone.

Instead, Maggie quickly circled the living room, cruised through the kitchen, then trotted into the bedroom and returned. She crisscrossed the living room, checked her crate and the table and the couch, and again disappeared into the bedroom. When she returned, her anxiety was gone. She wagged her tail, went into the kitchen, and Scott heard her drinking. He stepped inside, and pulled the door closed.

"My turn."

Scott walked through the guest house. He checked the windows and doors first, and found them secure. None were broken or jimmied. His computer, printer, and papers on the table were fine, as were his TV equipment and cordless phone. Its red message light was blinking. The papers on the floor by his couch and the maps and diagrams pinned to his wall seemed undisturbed. His checkbook, his dad's old watch, and the three hundred in cash he kept in an envelope under the clock radio beside his bed were untouched. His gun cleaning kit, two boxes of ammo, and an old .32 snub-nose were still in the LAPD gym bag stowed in his closet. His anxiety meds and pain pills were in their usual places on the bathroom counter.

Scott returned to the living room. Maggie was on the floor beside her crate. She rolled onto her side when she saw him, and lifted her hind leg. Scott smiled.

"Good girl."

Everything appeared normal, but Scott trusted Maggie's nose, and Maggie had smelled something. Mrs. Earle had a key, and would open the guest house for repairmen and the pest service that sprayed for ants. She always warned Scott in advance, but she might have forgotten.

"I'll be right back."

Mrs. Earle answered the door wearing a sweatshirt, shorts, and fluffy pink slippers. The roar of the television was behind her.

"Hey, Mrs. Earle. Did you let anyone in the guest house today?"

She glanced past Scott as if she expected to see the guest house in ruins.

"I didn't let anyone in. You know I always tell you."

"I know, but Maggie smelled something that kinda upset her. I thought maybe you let the plumber or pest people in."

She looked past him again.

"Are you having a problem with that toilet again?"

"No, ma'am. That was just an example."

"Well, I didn't let anyone in. I hope you weren't robbed."

"It's just the way Maggie acted. The windows and doors look okay, so I thought you might have opened the door. She smelled something new. She doesn't like new smells."

Mrs. Earle frowned past him again.

"I hope she didn't smell a rat. You might have a rat in there. I hear them in these trees at night, eating all my fruit. Those nasty things can chew right through a wall."

Scott glanced at the guest house.

Mrs. Earle said, "If you hear it or see poop, you let me know. I'll have the pest people come out."

Scott wondered if she was right, but wasn't convinced.

"I will. Thanks, Mrs. Earle."

"Don't let her pee-pee on the grass. These girl dogs kill a lawn faster than gasoline."

"Yes, ma'am. I know."

Scott went back to the guest house. He locked the French doors, and drew the curtains. Maggie was on her side in front of

269

her crate, halfway to dreamland.

"She thinks we have rats."

Maggie's tail thumped the floor. Thump.

Scott went to his phone, and found a message from Joyce Cowly.

"Scott, Joyce Cowly. I pulled the DVDs. No rush. You can come see them anytime, just call first to make sure one of us is here."

Scott put down the phone.

"Thanks, Cowly."

Scott grabbed a Corona from the fridge, drank some, then took off his uniform. He showered, and pulled on a T-shirt and shorts. He finished the first beer, grabbed a second, and brought it to the pictures on his wall.

He touched Stephanie.

"Still here."

Scott took his beer to the couch. Maggie pushed herself up, gimped over as if she was a hundred years old, and lay on her side by his feet. Her body shuddered when she sighed.

Scott eased onto the floor beside her. He sat with his legs straight out because crossing them hurt. He rested his hand on her side. Maggie's tail thumped the floor. Thump thump thump.

Scott said, "Man, we're a pair, aren't we?"

Thump thump.

"Maybe a doctor can help you. They shot me up with cortisone. It hurt, but it works."

Thump thump thump.

File folders, diagrams, and the mass of newspaper clippings he compiled on the shootings spread from the couch to the wall in neat little stacks. Scott sipped more beer, and decided he looked like a nut case trying to prove aliens worked for the CIA, raving about lost memories, recovered memories, imagined memories, and memories that may not even exist — a flash of white hair, forchrissake — as if some miraculous miracle memory only HE could provide would solve the case and bring Stephanie Anders back to life. And now he even had the best detectives at Robbery-Homicide buying into it, as if he could provide the missing piece to their puzzle.

Scott ran his fingers through Maggie's fur.

Thump thump.

"Maybe it's time to move on. What do you think?"

Thump.

"That's what I thought."

He stared at the stacks with their corners all squared off and neat, and their neatness began to bother him. Scott wasn't neat. His car, his apartment, and his life were a mess. If rats were in his apartment, they had made an effort to make his papers appear undisturbed, and overdid it. If someone had the tools in Marshall Ishi's burglary kit, they wouldn't need Mrs. Earle to get inside without breaking a window.

Scott got his Maglite from the bedroom, and went out. Maggie followed him, sniffing at the French doors as he shined his light on the lock.

"You're in the way. Move."

The lock was weathered and scratched, but Scott found no new scratches on the keyhole or faceplate to indicate the lock had been picked.

He checked the side door next. The French doors had a single lock, but the side door had a knob lock and a deadbolt. Scott knelt close with the light. No fresh cuts showed on either lock, but he noticed a black smudge on the deadbolt's faceplate. It might have been dirt or grease, but it gave a metallic shimmer when he adjusted the light.

Scott touched it with his pinky, and it came away on his skin. The substance appeared to be a silvery powder, and Scott wondered if it was graphite — a dry lubricant used to make locks open more easily. A bottle of graphite had been in Marshall Ishi's burglary kit. Squirt in some graphite, insert a lock pick gun, and the lock would open in seconds. No key was necessary.

Scott suddenly laughed and turned off the light. Nothing had been stolen, and his place hadn't been vandalized. Sometimes a smudge was just a smudge.

"See a burglary kit, and now you're imagining burglars."

Scott went back inside, locked up, and pulled the curtains. He went to Stephanie's picture.

"I'm not moving on, and I'm not going to quit. I did not leave you behind, and I'm not leaving now."

He sat on the floor beneath her picture, and looked over the files and documents. Maggie lay down beside him.

Melon and Stengler had gotten nowhere, but it hadn't been from lack of effort. He now understood their effort had been enormous, but they needed the ATF to bust Shin, and Shin wasn't arrested until they were both off the case. Shin changed everything.

Scott fingered through the clutter, and found the evidence bag containing the cheap leather watchband. Rust, Chen had said. Scott wondered again if the rust on the band had come from the roof. Not that this would prove anything even if it had.

Scott unzipped the bag. Maggie lurched to her feet when he took out the leather strap.

Scott said, "You need to pee?"

She nosed so close she almost stood in his lap. She looked at Scott, wagged her tail, and sniffed the cheap leather. The first time he opened the bag to examine the band, she had been in his face, and now she was trying to reach the strap as if she wanted to play.

She was behaving like she had at Marshall Ishi's house.

Scott moved the band to the right, and she followed the band. He hid it behind his back, and she danced happily from foot to foot as she tried to get behind him.

Play.

Dogs do what they do to please us or save us. They don't have anything else.

Maggie was with him the first time he took the band from the bag. They had been playing a few minutes earlier, and she had nosed at the band when he examined it. She had come so close he pushed her away, so maybe she associated the band with play. He tried thinking about it the way he imagined Maggie would think.

Scott and Maggie play.

Scott picks up the band.

274

The band is a toy.

Maggie wants to play with Scott and his toy.

Find the band when you smell the band, Scott and Maggie will play.

Welcome to Dogland.

Scott dropped the band back into the evidence bag. He originally thought Maggie alerted to the chemicals fumed off the crystal because she confused them with explosives. Budress had convinced him this wasn't the case, which meant there must be another scent on the band she recognized.

Marshall and Daryl would both carry the chemical crystal scent, but Maggie had not alerted to Marshall. She had alerted inside the house, she alerted on Daryl, and now she had alerted on the watchband. Scott stared at Maggie, and slowly smiled.

"Really? I mean, REALLY?"

Thump thump thump.

The thin leather strap had been in the bag for almost nine months. Scott knew scent particles degraded over time, but it seemed logical a person's sweat and skin oils would soak deep into a leather band.

He reached for his phone, and called Budress.

"Hey, man, it's Scott. Hope this isn't too late."

"No, I'm good. What's up?"

Scott heard TV voices in the background.

"How long can a scent last?"

"What kind of scent?"

"Human."

"I need more than that, bro. A ground scent? An air scent? An air scent is gone with the wind. A ground scent, you get maybe twenty-four to forty-eight. Depends on the elements and environment."

"A leather watchband in an evidence bag."

"Shit, that's different. One of those plastic bags?"

"Yeah."

"Why you want to know something like this? You got a sample you want to hunt?"

"One of the detectives asked. It's a piece of evidence from one of their cases."

"Depends. A glass container is best because it's nonporous and non-reactive, but those heavy-duty evidence bags are pretty good. Has the bag been sealed? If it wasn't sealed, you get air migration and the oils break down."

"No, it was sealed. It's been in a box."

"How long?"

Scott felt uneasy with all the questions, but he knew Budress was trying to help.

"They made it sound like a pretty long time. Six months? Call it six months. They were just asking in general."

"Okay. In one of those sealed bags, air-tight, no sunlight, I'm thinking they'd have good scent for three months easy, but I've seen dogs work off clothes sealed for more than a year."

"Okay, man, thanks. I'll pass it along."

Scott was ending the call when Budress stopped him.

"Hey, I forgot. Leland told me he likes the way you're working with Maggie. He thinks we're making progress with her startle response."

"Great."

Scott didn't want to talk about Leland.

"Don't tell him I told you, okay?"

"Never."

Scott hung up, and fingered the band through the bag.

He's following in his brother's footsteps.

Daryl lived in his brother's house, so Daryl's scent was in the house. Maggie alerted on Daryl and on the band. Could the watch have been Daryl's?

Scott touched Maggie's nose. She licked his fingers.

"No effin' way."

Maybe both brothers robbed Shin's store. Maybe Daryl was his brother's lookout, up on the roof to watch for the police. Maybe

Daryl was the witness, and not Marshall.

Scott studied the shabby brown piece of leather in the plastic evidence bag.

Scott put the bag aside, and thought about Daryl as he petted his dog.

22.

Scott woke the next morning, feeling anxious and agitated. He had dreamed about Marshall and Daryl. In the dream, they stood calmly in the street as the shooting unfolded around them. In the dream, Marshall told Orso and Cowly the five men removed their masks after the shooting, and called each other by name. In the dream, Marshall knew their names and addresses, and had close-up photos of each man on his cell phone. Scott just wanted to know if the man had been there.

He took Maggie out, then showered, and ate cereal at the kitchen sink. He brooded over whether to tell Cowly and Orso about the watchband. He decided they already thought he was crazy enough. He didn't want to make things worse by floating a theory based on a dog.

At six-thirty, he was fed up with waiting, and phoned Cowly on her cell.

"Hey, Joyce, it's Scott James. Okay if I pick up the discs?"

"You know it's only six-thirty?"

"I didn't mean now. Whenever you say."

She was silent for a moment, and Scott worried she was still in bed.

"Sorry if I woke you."

"I just finished a five-mile run. Let me think. Can you roll by about eleven?"

"Eleven would be great. Ah, listen, what's happening with Ishi? Did he see anything?"

"As of last night, he wasn't talking. He's got a pretty good P.D. Orso has a D.A. coming down, first thing. They're trying to work out a deal."

Scott reconsidered whether to mention Daryl, but again decided against it.

"Okay, I'll see you around eleven."

Scott worked with Maggie at the training facility from seven-fifteen until ten-thirty, then left her and rolled for the Boat. Her confused expression when he closed her run filled him with guilt. He felt even worse when she barked as he walked away. Her steady bark-bark-bark plea hurt so badly he clenched his eyes. He walked faster when he realized he had heard it before.

Scotty, don't leave me.

The Trans Am felt empty without Maggie beside him. Maggie cut the car in half like a black-and-tan wall when she straddled the console, but now the car felt strange. This was only the second time he had been alone in the car since he brought Maggie home. They were together twenty-four hours a day. They ate together, played together, trained together, and lived together. Having Maggie was like having a three-year-old, only better. When he told her to sit, she sat. Scott glanced at the empty console, and hoped she wasn't still barking.

He pushed on the gas, then realized, here he was, a grown man, a cop, and he was speeding because he was worried his dog was lonely. He laughed at himself.

"Relax, moron. You're all spooled up like she was a human being. She's a dog."

He pushed the gas harder.

"You're talking to yourself way too much. This can't be right."

Scott parked at the Boat twelve minutes later, went up to the fifth floor, and was surprised when he found Orso waiting with Cowly. She held out a manila envelope.

"You can keep them. I burned copies."

Scott felt the discs shift when he took the envelope, but only managed a nod. Orso looked like a funeral director.

"You have a few minutes? Could we see you inside?"

A bitter heat filled Scott's belly.

"Was it Ishi? He was there?"

"Let's talk inside. I'm sorry you didn't bring Maggie. It was fun having her here."

Scott heard only mumbles. He was preparing to relive the shooting through Marshall Ishi's eyes, even as he disappeared in his own nightmare. The Bentley rolling over, the big man raising his rifle, Stephanie reaching out with red hands. Scott was vaguely aware Orso expected a response, but walked on in silence.

None of them spoke again until they were seated in the conference room, and Orso explained.

"Mr. Ishi confessed this morning. He remembered three of the items he stole that night — a set of carved ivory pipes."

Cowly said, "Not ivory. Rhinoceros horn. Inlaid with tiger teeth. Illegal in the United States."

"Whatever. The pipes were among the things Mr. Shin listed stolen."

Scott didn't care what was stolen.

"Did he see the shooters?"

Orso shifted as if he was uncomfortable. His face softened and turned sad.

"No. I'm sorry, Scott. No. He can't help us."

Cowly leaned forward.

"He broke into Shin's almost three hours before the hit. He was back home and loaded by the time you rolled up."

Scott looked from Cowly to Orso.

"That's it?"

"We took our shot. It looked really good, here's this burglary fifty feet from the shooting, on the same night, what are the odds? But he didn't see it. He can't help us."

"He's lying. He saw these guys murder a police officer and two other people. A fucking asshole with a machine gun."

Cowly said, "Scott —"

"He's scared they'll kill him."

Orso shook his head.

"He's telling the truth."

"A meth-addict? A drug-dealing burglar?"

"Between witness testimony and evidence, we had the man cold on nine separate felony and misdemeanor charges. He already has a felony strike, so two more would put him over the three strike mandatory."

"That doesn't mean he told the truth. It means he was scared."

Orso kept going.

"He confessed to four burglaries including Shin's. Everything he told us about time, place, how he got in, what he stole, all the details — everything checked. His statements about the Shin burglary — checked.

283

He was required to take a polygraph. He passed. When we asked him what time he broke into Shin's, and what time he left, and what he saw, he passed."

Orso leaned back and laced his fingers.

"We believe him, Scott. He wasn't lying. He didn't see anything. He can't help us."

Scott felt as if he had lost something. He thought he should ask more questions, but nothing occurred to him, and he didn't know what to say.

"Did you release him?"

Orso looked surprised.

"Ishi? God, no. He's in Men's Central Jail until the sentencing. He's going to prison."

"What about the girl and the roommates?"

"Flipped like three burgers. They helped with our leverage, so we let them walk."

Scott nodded.

"Okay. So now what?"

Orso touched his hair.

"White hair. Ian has sources. Maybe one of them knows of a driver with white hair."

Scott looked at Cowly. She was staring at the table as if she was about to nod out. Scott felt the urge to ask her about the man on the beach, and wondered again if he should mention the watchband.

Cowly suddenly straightened as if she felt his stare, and looked at him.

"This really sucks, man. I'm sorry."

Scott nodded. The connection between the watchband and Daryl was lame. If he tried to explain, they would think he sounded pathetic or crazy. He didn't want Cowly to see him that way.

He absently reached down to touch Maggie, but felt only air. Scott glanced at Cowly, embarrassed, but she seemed not to have noticed. Orso was still talking.

"And we have you, Scott. The investigation didn't end with Marshall Ishi."

Orso stood, ending the meeting.

Scott stood with Cowly. He picked up the manila envelope, shook their hands, and thanked them for their hard work. He respected them the way he now knew he should have respected Melon and Stengler.

Scott believed Orso was right. The investigation didn't end with Marshall Ishi. There was Daryl, only Orso and Cowly didn't know it.

Scott wondered if Maggie was still barking. He was careful not to limp when he hurried out.

23.

Maggie was barking when Scott entered the kennel, but now her bark was pure joy. She jumped onto the gate, standing tall and wagging her tail. Scott let her out and ruffled her fur as he spoke in the squeaky voice.

"Told you I'd be back. Told you I wouldn't be long. I'm happy to see you, too."

Maggie wagged her tail so hard her entire body wiggled.

Paul Budress and his black shepherd, Obi, were at the end of the hall. Dana Flynn was in a run with her Malinois, Gator, checking his razor-sharp teeth. Scott smiled. All these tough K-9 handlers, a lot of them ex-military, and nobody thought twice about grown men and women talking to dogs in a high-pitched, little girl's voice.

Scott clipped Maggie's lead as Leland appeared behind him.

"Good of you to rejoin us, Officer James.

We hope you'll stick around."

Maggie's joy became a soft, low growl. Scott took up the play in her leash and held her close to his leg. If Leland liked the way Scott worked with Maggie and thought they were making progress, then Scott would give him more. But not by sticking around.

"Just coming to see you, Sergeant. I'd like to do some crowd work with her. That okay with you?"

Leland's scowl deepened.

"And what would 'crowd work' be?"

Scott quoted from sessions with Goodman.

"She gets nervous with people because of anxiety that comes with the PTSD. The anxiety makes her think something bad is going to happen, like when she's surprised by a gunshot. It's the same anxiety. I want her to spend time in crowded places so she learns nothing bad will happen. If she gets comfortable with crowds, I think it might help her with gunfire. You see?"

Leland was slow to respond.

"Where'd you get all this?"

"A book."

Leland slowly considered it.

"Crowd work."

"If it's okay with you. They say it's good therapy."

Leland was just as slow to nod.

"I think we should try this, Officer James. Crowd work. All right, then. Go find some crowds."

Scott loaded Maggie into his car, and drove to Marshall Ishi's house. He wanted to put Maggie in a crowd, but not to treat her anxiety. He wanted to test her nose, and his theory about Daryl Ishi.

Scott studied the house. He didn't care if the girl and the two roommates were inside, but he didn't want Maggie to see Daryl. He also didn't want to hang around for hours if no one was home.

Scott drove to the first cross street, turned around, and parked three houses away where grass lined the sidewalk. He let Maggie out, watered her with the squirt bottle, then pointed at the grass.

"Pee."

Maggie sniffed out a spot and peed. A trick she learned in the Marine Corps. Pee on command.

When she finished, Scott dropped her leash.

"Maggie. Down."

Maggie immediately dropped to her belly.
"Stay."

Scott walked away. He did not look back, but he worried. At the park by his house

288

and the training facility, he could drop her, plant her, and she stayed while he crossed the field and back. She even stayed when he walked around the building, and couldn't see him. The Marine K-9 instructors had done an outstanding job with her basic skill set, and she was an outstanding dog.

He went to Ishi's door, and glanced at Maggie. She was rooted in place, watching him, her head high with her ears spiked like two black horns.

Scott faced the door, rang the bell, and knocked. He counted to ten, and knocked harder.

Estelle "Ganj" Rolley opened the door. First thing she did when she saw Scott's uniform was fan the air. Scott wondered how long it had taken her to score crystal once she was released. He ignored the smell, and smiled.

"Ms. Rolley, I'm Officer James. The Los Angeles Police Department wants you to know your rights."

Her face knotted with confusion. She looked even more emaciated, and stood in a hunch as if she wasn't strong enough to stand erect.

"I just got released. Please don't arrest me again."

"No, ma'am, not those rights. We want

289

you to know you have the right to complain. If you feel you were mistreated, or possessions not booked into evidence were illegally taken, you have the right to complain to the city, and possibly recover damages. Do you understand these rights as I have explained them?"

Her face screwed up even more.

"No."

Daryl Ishi walked up behind her. He squinted at Scott, but gave no indication of recognition.

"What's going on?"

Estelle crossed her arms over nonexistent breasts.

"He wants to know if we were arrested okay."

Scott interrupted. He now knew Daryl was home, and that's all he needed. He wanted to leave.

"Are you Mr. Danowski or Mr. Pantelli?"

"Uh-uh. They ain't here."

"They have the right to file a complaint if they feel they were unfairly or illegally treated. It's a new policy we have. Letting people know they can sue us. Will you tell them?"

"No shit? They sent you to tell us we can sue you?"

"No shit. You folks have a good day."

Scott smiled pleasantly, stepped back as if he was going to leave, then stopped and dropped the smile. Estelle Rolley was closing the door, but Scott suddenly stepped close and held it. He stared at Daryl with cold, dangerous street-cop eyes.

"You're Marshall's brother, Daryl. You're the one we didn't arrest."

Daryl fidgeted.

"I didn't do anything."

"Marshall's been saying some things. We'll be back to talk to you. Stay put."

Scott stared at him for another ten seconds, then he stepped back.

"You can close the door now."

Estelle Rolley closed the door.

Scott's heart was pounding as he walked back to his car. His hands trembled as he ruffled Maggie's fur and praised her for staying put.

He loaded Maggie into the car, drove to the next block, parked again, and waited. He didn't wait long.

Daryl left the house eight minutes later, walking fast. He picked up speed until he was trotting, then turned up the next cross street toward Alvarado, which was the nearest and busiest large street.

Scott followed, hoping he wasn't crazy. And hoping he wasn't wrong.

24.

Scott served in two-person, black-and-white Adam cars as a uniformed patrol officer. He had never worked a plainclothes assignment or driven an unmarked car. When Scott followed someone in a black-and-white, he turned on the lights and drove fast. Following Daryl was a pain in the ass.

Scott thought Daryl might catch a bus when he reached Alvarado, but Daryl turned south and kept walking.

The slow pace on a busy street made following Daryl in a car difficult, but following on foot would have been worse. Maggie drew attention, and if Daryl hopped a ride when Scott was on foot, Scott would lose him.

Scott pulled over, watched until Daryl was almost out of sight, then tightened the gap and pulled over again. Maggie didn't mind. She enjoyed straddling the console and checking the sights.

Daryl went into a mini-market, and stayed so long Scott worried he had ducked out the back, but Daryl emerged with a super-size drink and continued hoofing it south. Five minutes later, Daryl crossed Sixth Street and entered MacArthur Park one block from where the arrest team staged to bag Marshall.

"Small world."

Scott frowned into the mirror.

"Stop talking to yourself."

Scott parked at the first open meter across from the park, cracked the door, and stepped out for a better view. Scott liked what he saw.

MacArthur Park above Wilshire contained a soccer field, a bandstand, and bright green lawns dotted with picnic tables, palm trees, and gray, weathered oaks. Paved walkways curved through the grass, inviting women with strollers, skateboard rats, and slow-motion homeless people pushing overloaded shopping carts stolen from local markets. Women with babies clustered at two or three tables, young Latin dudes with nothing to do hung out at two or three more, and homeless people used others as beds. People were catching sun on the grass, sitting in circles with friends, and reading books under trees. Latin and Middle Eastern men raced back and forth on the soccer field, while replacement players waited on the sidelines. Two girls strummed guitars at the base of a palm. Three kids with dyed hair passed a joint. A schizophrenic stumbled wildly across the park, passing three 'bangers with neck ink and teardrops who laughed at his flailing.

Daryl circled the 'bangers and cut across the grass, passed the three stoners, and made his way along the length of the soccer field toward the far side of the park. Scott lost sight of him, but that was the plan.

"C'mon, big girl. Let's see what you got."

Scott clipped Maggie's twenty-foot tracking lead, but held it short as he led her to the spot where Daryl entered the park. Scott knew she was anxious. She brushed his leg as they walked, and nervously glanced at the unfamiliar people and noisy traffic. Her nostrils rippled in triple-time to suck in their surroundings.

"Sit."

She sat, still glancing around, but mostly staring up at him.

He took the watchband from the evidence bag, and held it to her nose.

"Smell it. Smell."

Maggie's nostrils flickered and twitched. Her breathing pattern changed when she sniffed for a scent. Sniffing wasn't breathing. The air she drew for sniffing did not enter her lungs. Sniffs were small sips she took in groups called trains. A train could be from three to seven sniffs, and Maggie always sniffed in threes. Sniff-sniff-sniff, pause, sniff-sniff-sniff. Budress' dog, Obi, sniffed in trains of five. Always five. No one knew why, but each dog was different.

Scott touched her nose with the band, waved it playfully around her head, and let her sniff it some more.

"Find it for me, baby. Do it for me. Let's see if we're right."

Scott stepped back and gave the command.

"Seek, seek, seek."

Maggie surged to her feet with her ears spiked forward and her face black with focus. She turned to her right, checked the air, and dipped to the ground. She hesitated, then trotted a few steps in the opposite direction. She tasted more air scent, and stared into the park. This was her first alert. Scott knew she caught a taste, but did not have the trail. She sniffed the sidewalk from side to side as she moved farther away, then abruptly reversed course. She stared into the park again, and Scott knew she had it. Maggie took off, hit the end of her lead, and pulled like a sled dog. The three 'bangers saw them, and ran.

Maggie followed Daryl's path between the picnic tables and along the north side of the soccer field. The players stopped playing to watch the cop and his German shepherd.

Scott saw Daryl Ishi when they reached the end of the soccer field. He was standing behind the concert pavilion with two young women and a guy about Daryl's age. One of the girls saw Scott first, then the others looked. Daryl stared for maybe a second, then bolted away in the opposite direction. His friend broke past the back of the building and ran for the street.

"Down."

Maggie dropped to her belly. Scott caught up fast, unclipped her lead, and immediately released her.

"Hold'm."

Maggie powered forward in a ground-eating sprint. She ignored the other man and everyone else in the park. Her world was the scent cone, and the cone narrowed to Daryl. Scott knew she saw him, but following his scent to the end of the cone was like following a light that grew brighter as she got closer. Maggie could be blindfolded, and she would still find him.

Scott ran after her, and felt little pain, as

if the knotted scars beneath his skin were in another man's body.

Maggie covered the distance in seconds. Daryl ran past the pavilion into a small stand of trees, glanced over his shoulder, and saw a black-and-tan nightmare. He skidded to a halt at the nearest tree, pressed his back to the trunk, and covered his crotch with his hands. Maggie braked at his feet, sat as Scott taught her, and barked. Find and bark, bark to hold.

When Scott arrived, he stopped ten feet away and took a minute to catch his breath before calling her out.

"Out."

Maggie broke off, trotted to Scott, and sat by his left foot.

"Guard'm."

Marine command. She dropped into a sphinx position, head up and alert, eyes locked on Daryl.

Scott walked over to Daryl.

"Relax. I'm not going to arrest you. Just don't move. You run, she'll take you down."

"I'm not gonna run."

"Cool. Heel."

Maggie trotted up, planted her butt by his left foot, and stared at Daryl. She licked her lips.

Daryl inched to his toes, trying to get as

far from her as possible.

"Dude, what is this? C'mon."

"She's friendly. Look. Maggie, shake hands. Shake."

Maggie raised her right paw, but Daryl didn't move.

"You don't want to shake hands?"

"No fuckin' way. Dude, c'mon."

Scott shook her paw, praised her, and rewarded her with a chunk of baloney. When he put the baloney away, he took out the evidence bag. He studied Daryl for a moment, deciding how to proceed.

"First, what just happened here, I shouldn't have done this. I'm not going to arrest you. I just wanted to talk to you away from Estelle."

"You were at the house when Marsh was busted. You and the dog."

"That's right."

"He tried to bite me."

"She. And, no, she didn't try to bite you, or she would have bitten you. What she did is called an alert."

Scott held up the evidence bag so Daryl could see the broken band. Daryl glanced at it without recognition, then looked again. Scott saw the flash of memory play over Daryl's face as he recognized the familiar band.

"Recognize it?"

"What is it? It looks like a brown Band-Aid."

"It's half your old watchband. It kinda looks like the one you're wearing now, but you caught this one on a fence, the band broke, and this half landed on the sidewalk. You know how I know it's yours?"

"It ain't mine."

"It smells like you. I let her smell it, and she tracked your scent across the park. All these people in the park, and she followed this watchband to you. Isn't she amazing?"

Daryl glanced past Scott, looking for a way out, then glanced at Maggie again. Running was not an option.

"I don't care what it smells like. I never seen it before."

"Your brother confessed to burglarizing a Chinese import store nine months ago. A place called Asia Exotica."

"His lawyer told me. So what?"

"You help him do it?"

"No fucking way."

"That's where you lost the watch. Up on the roof. Were you his lookout?"

Daryl's eyes flickered.

"Are you kidding me?"

"You guys hang out up there after, party a little, kick back?"

"Ask Marshall."

"Daryl, did you and Marshall see the murders?"

Daryl sagged like a leaking balloon. He stared past Scott for a moment, swallowed once, then wet his lips. His answer was slow and deliberate.

"I have no idea what you are talking about."

"Three people were murdered, including a police officer. If you saw anything, or know anything, you can help your brother. Maybe even buy him a get-out-of-jail card."

Daryl wet his lips again.

"I want to talk to my brother's lawyer."

Scott knew he had hit the end of his lead. He couldn't think of anything else, so he stepped back.

"I told you I wasn't going to arrest you. We were just talking."

Daryl glanced at Maggie.

"Is he gonna bite me?"

"She. No, she isn't going to bite you. You can go. But think about what I said, Daryl, okay? You can help Marshall."

Daryl edged away, and walked backwards to keep an eye on Maggie until he was out of the trees. Then he turned, stumbled, and ran.

Scott watched him go, and imagined

Daryl and his brother peering down from the roof, their faces lit by flashes from guns.

"He was there. I know that kid was there."

Scott looked at Maggie. She was staring at him, mouth open in a big grin, tongue hanging out over a ridge of sharp, white enamel.

Scott touched her head.

"You're the best girl ever. You really are."

Maggie yawned.

Scott clipped Maggie's lead and walked back across the park to their car. He texted Joyce Cowly as they walked.

25.

Orso's eyes were flat as a frying pan heating on the stove. Scott had kenneled Maggie with Budress, and now sat at the conference table with Cowly and Orso. His news had not been received in the way he expected.

Orso stared at the evidence bag as if it was filled with dog crap.

"Where was it?"

"Bottom of the box under the files. It was in a manila envelope. One of the small envelopes, not the big size. Melon was sending it back to Chen."

Cowly glanced at her boss.

"SID bagged it because the smears look like blood. Turned out to be rust, so they sent it to Melon for permission to dispose. Melon wrote a card, giving his okay. I guess he didn't get around to sending it."

Orso tossed the bag onto the table.

"I didn't see it. Did you see this envelope when you went through the material?"

"No."

Scott said, "I have it — their notes and the envelope. Down in my car. You want, I'll go get it."

Orso shifted position. He had been shifting and adjusting himself for the past ten minutes.

"Oh, I want, but not now. What made you think you could take *anything* from this office without asking?"

"The note said it was trash. Melon told him to toss it."

Orso closed his eyes, but his face rippled with tension. His voice was calm, but his eyes remained closed.

"Okay. So you gave yourself permission to take it because you thought it was trash, but now you believe it's evidence."

"I took it because of the rust."

Orso opened his eyes. He didn't say anything, so Scott kept going.

"They collected this thing on the sidewalk directly below the roof above the kill zone. This is the roof I told you about. When I was there, I got rust on my hands. I thought there might be a connection. I wanted to think about it."

"So you hoped it was evidence when you took it."

"I don't know what I hoped. I wanted to

think about it."

"I'll take that for a yes. Either way, 'cause I don't give a shit if you thought it was evidence or trash, here's the problem. If it's evidence, by taking it home like you have, you not being an investigating officer on this case, only an asshole we were courteous to, you've broken the chain of custody."

Cowly's voice was soft.

"Boss."

Scott did not respond, and did not care if Orso thought he was an asshole. The cast-off brown leather strip had led to Daryl, and Daryl might lead to the shooters.

Tension played on Orso's face until a tic developed beneath his left eye. Then the ripples settled, and his face softened.

"I apologize, Scott. I should not have said that. I'm sorry."

"I fucked up. I'm sorry, too. But the band was at the scene, and Daryl Ishi was wearing it. Guaranteed. My dog isn't wrong."

Cowly said, "Daryl denies it's his, and denies being at the scene. Okay, we can swab him and comp the DNA. Then we'll know."

Orso considered the evidence bag, then rolled his chair to the door.

"Jerry! Petievich! Would you see if Ian's here? Ask him to come see me."

The I-Man joined them a few minutes later. His face was more red than Scott remembered. A surprised smile split Ian Mills' face when he saw Scott.

"You get a news flash from the memory bank? That white sideburn turn into a big ol' pocked nose?"

The stupid joke was irritating, but Orso got down to business before Scott responded.

"Scott believes Marshall Ishi's younger brother, Daryl, was present when Marshall robbed Shin's store, and may have witnessed the shootings."

Mills frowned.

"I didn't know he had a brother."

"No reason you should. Until now, we had no reason to think he was involved."

Mills crossed his arms. He peered at Scott, then turned to Orso.

"He passed the poly. We established Marshall left before the shootings went down."

"He also claimed he was alone. If Scott's right, maybe Marshall is just a good liar."

The I-Man's gaze clicked back to Scott.

"You remember this kid? He saw the shootings?"

"This isn't a memory. I'm saying he was at the scene, and I believe he was on the roof. I don't know when he was there, and I don't know what he saw."

Orso slid the evidence bag to Mills, who glanced at the bag but did not touch it.

"Scott found this in the case file. It's half a leather watchband SID collected at the scene. Scott believes he's linked it to Daryl Ishi, which would put Daryl at the scene. Before we go further, you need to know we have a chain-of-custody issue."

Orso described Scott's mistake without passion or inflection, but Mills' face grew darker. Scott felt like a twelve-year-old in the principal's office when Mills unloaded.

"Are you fucking kidding me? What the fuck were you thinking?"

"That no one had done a goddamned thing for nine months and the case was still open."

Orso held up a hand for Mills to stop, and glanced at Scott.

"Tell Ian about the dog. Like you explained it to me."

Scott began with Maggie's first exposure to the scent sample, and walked the I-Man through his test at MacArthur Park, where Maggie tracked the scent across the width of the park directly to Daryl Ishi.

Scott gestured at the evidence bag, which was still on the table by Mills.

"This was his. He was there the night we

were shot."

Mills had listened in silence, frowning across his bristling forearms. When Scott finished, his frown deepened.

"This sounds like bullshit."

Orso shrugged.

"Easy enough to find out. The dog might have something."

Scott knew Mills would listen to Orso, so he pressed his case harder.

"She has Daryl Ishi. See these red streaks? There's a rusty iron safety fence on the roof. SID says these little red smears are rust. His watch got caught on the fence, the band broke, and this piece landed on the sidewalk. That's where SID found it."

Orso leaned toward Mills.

"Here's what I'm thinking. We pick the kid up, swab him, run the DNA. Then we'll know if it's his. After that, we can worry about whether he saw anything."

Mills paced to the door, but didn't leave, as if he had needed motion to contain himself.

"I don't know whether to hope the thing is good or garbage. You screwed us, kid. I can't fucking believe you walked out with a piece of evidence, which, by the way, even the stupidest defense attorney will point out you contaminated."

Orso leaned back.

"Ian, it's done. Let it go."

"Really? After nine fucking months with nothing to show?"

"Pray it's good. If we get a match, we'll know he's a liar, we'll know he's hiding something, and we'll find a thousand work-arounds. We've danced this dance before, man."

If a future judge excluded the watchband, he or she might also exclude all downstream evidence derived from the band. The downstream evidence was called "fruits of the poisonous tree," under the principle that evidence derived from bad evidence was also bad. If investigators knew they had a piece of bad fruit, they tried to find a path around the bad fruit by using unrelated evidence to reach the same result. This was called a work-around.

Mills stood in the door, shaking his head.

"I'm too old. The stress is killing me."

He seemed thoughtful for a moment, then turned back to Scott.

"Okay. So when you and the Hound of the Baskervilles ran down this kid, I suppose you questioned him?"

"He denied everything."

"Uh-huh, and you being the trained interrogator you are, did you ask if he saw the shootings?"

"He said he wasn't there."

"Of course he did. So what you actually accomplished here was, you gave the kid a big heads-up that we're coming for him, and what it is we want to know. Now he'll have plenty of time to think up good answers. Way to go, Sherlock."

The I-Man walked out.

Scott looked at Orso and Cowly. He mostly looked at Cowly.

"I know it's worth nothing, but I'm sorry."

Orso shrugged.

"Shit happens."

Orso pushed back from the table and walked away.

Cowly stood last.

"Come on. I'll walk you to the elevator."

Scott followed her, not knowing what to say. When he found the small leather strap in the manila envelope, the sidewalk where it was found and the smears of rust gave him a sense the band and he somehow shared the events of that night. It had been a physical link to Stephanie and the shooting and the memories he could not recall, and he had hoped it would help him see the night more clearly.

When they reached the elevator, Cowly touched his arm. She looked sad.

"These things happen. Nobody died."

"Not today."

Cowly flushed, and Scott realized his comment had made her feel awkward and embarrassed.

"Jesus, I'm batting a thousand. I didn't mean it the way it sounded. You were being nice."

Her flush faded as she relaxed.

"I was being nice, but I meant it. Exclusions aren't automatic. Issues like this are argued every day, so don't sweat it until it's time to start sweating."

Scott was feeling a little better.

"Whatever you say."

"I say. And if the DNA matches Daryl to the band, we have something to chase, which is all thanks to you."

The elevator opened. Scott caught the doors with a hand, but didn't go in.

"The picture of you and a man on the beach. Is he your husband?"

Cowly was so still, Scott thought he had offended her, but she smiled as she turned away.

"Don't even think about it, Officer."

"Too late. I'm thinking."

She kept walking.

"Turn off your brain."

"My dog likes me."

When she reached the Homicide Special door, Cowly stopped.

"He's my brother. The kids are my niece and nephews."

"Thank you, Detective."

"Have a good day, Officer."

Scott boarded the elevator and rode down to his car.

26.

Scott spent the rest of the afternoon working with Maggie on advanced vehicle exercises. These included exiting the car through an open window, entering a car through an open window to engage a suspect, and obeying off-leash commands while outside the vehicle when Scott remained inside the vehicle. Their K-9 vehicle was a standard police patrol sedan with a heavy wire screen separating the front and back seats, and a remote door-release system that opened the rear doors from as far as one hundred feet away. The remote system allowed Scott to release Maggie without exiting the car, or exit the vehicle without her, and release her from a distance by pushing a button on his belt.

Maggie hated the K-9 car. She hopped into the back seat willingly enough, but as soon as Scott got in behind the wheel, she whined and pawed at the screen that kept them apart. She stopped when he gave her commands to lie down or sit, but a few seconds later she would try even harder to reach him. She bit and pulled the mesh so hard, Scott thought her teeth would break. He moved on to other exercises as quickly as possible.

Leland watched them work on and off throughout the afternoon, but was absent most of the time. Scott wasn't sure if this was a good sign, but with Maggie jumping in and out of the car, the less Leland was around, the better. He was relieved when Maggie reached the end of the day without limping.

Scott stowed the training gear, cleaned up, and was leading Maggie out of the kennel when the office door opened behind them and Leland appeared.

"Officer James."

Scott tugged the leash to stop Maggie's growl.

"Hey, Sergeant. Heading for home."

"I won't keep you."

Leland came out, so Scott walked back to meet him.

"I am assigning our beautiful young man, Quarlo, to another handler. Because I first offered Quarlo to you, I thought you should hear this from me."

Scott wasn't sure why Leland was telling him, or what his assigning Quarlo to another handler meant.

"Okay. Thanks for telling me."

"There is one more thing. When we began our work with Miss Maggie here, you asked for two weeks before I re-evaluated her. You may have three. Enjoy your evening, Officer James."

Scott decided a treat was in order. They celebrated at a construction site in Burbank with fried chicken, beef brisket, and two turkey drumsticks. The women who worked in the food truck fell in love with Maggie, and asked if they could take each other's picture, posing with Scott and the dog. Scott said sure, and the construction workers lined up for pictures, too. Maggie growled only once.

Scott walked her when they reached home, then showered and brought the envelope containing the discs to his table. The idea of watching two dead men enjoying themselves creeped him out, but Scott hoped this would help him deal with the crazy, innocent-bystander nature of the shooting and Stephanie's violent loss. He hoped he wasn't deluding himself. Maybe he only wanted a better target for his rage.

Scott found two discs when he opened the

envelope, one labeled Tyler's, the other Club
Red. Something about the number of discs
bothered him, and then he recalled Melon
had logged two discs from Club Red. He
wondered why Cowly gave him only one of
the Club Red discs, but decided it didn't
matter.

Scott fed the Club Red disc into his
computer. While it loaded, Maggie went
into the kitchen, slurped up what sounded
like gallons of water, then curled into a huge
black-and-tan ball at his feet. She did not
sleep in her crate anymore. He reached
down to touch her.

"Good girl."

Thump thump.

The Club Red video had been recorded
using a stationary, black-and-white ceiling
camera. There was no sound. The high angle
covered a room crowded with upscale men
and couples in booths or at tables, watching
costumed women pose while servers moved
between the tables. Thirty seconds into the
video, Beloit and Pahlasian were shown to a
table for two. Scott felt nothing as he
watched them. A couple of minutes later, a
waitress approached to take their order.
Scott grew bored, and hit the fast-forward.
Drinks were delivered by the high-speed,
herky-jerky waitress, Beloit yukked it up,

Pahlasian stared at the dancers. At one point, Beloit stopped a passing waitress, who pointed to the rear of the room. Beloit followed her finger at triple-time speed, and returned just as quickly two minutes later. Pit stop. More fast-forward minutes passed, Beloit paid, they left, off to meet the Wizard, and the image froze.

End of recording.

Other than staff, the two men had interacted with no one. No one approached them. Neither man approached or spoke to another customer. Neither had used his cell phone.

Scott ejected the disc.

Beloit and Pahlasian were no more real now than before — two middle-aged men about to get whacked for reasons unknown. Scott hated them. He wished he had a video of them being shot to death. He wished he had shot them as they left the club, stopped the bastards cold right there before they got Stephanie killed and him shot to pieces, and put Scott James on a path that led to him, here, now, crying.

Thump thump thump.

Maggie was beside him, watching. With her folded ears and caring eyes, she looked as soft and sleek as a seal. He stroked her head.

"I'm okay."

Scott drank some water, took a pee, and loaded the Tyler's disc. The high angle included the reception station, an incomplete view of the bar, and three blurry tables. When Pahlasian and Beloit entered from the bottom left corner of the frame, their faces were hidden by the bad angle.

A host and hostess in dark suits greeted them. After a brief conversation, the woman showed them to their table. This was the last Scott saw of Pahlasian and Beloit until they departed.

Scott ejected the disc.

The Club Red disc was by far the superior, which left Scott wondering what the missing disc showed. He dug out Melon's interview with Richard Levin to make sure he had it right, and reread the handwritten note:

R. Levin — deliv sec vid — 2 discs — EV # H6218B

Scott decided to phone Cowly.

"Joyce? Hey, it's Scott James. Hope you don't mind. I have a question about these discs."

"Sure. What's up?"

"I was wondering why you gave me only

one of the Club Red discs and not both."

Cowly was silent for a moment.

"I gave you two discs."

"Yeah, you did. One from Tyler's and one from Club Red, but there are supposed to be two from Club Red. Melon has a note here saying two discs were logged."

Cowly was silent some more.

"I don't know what to tell you. There was only the one disc from Club Red. We have the LAX stuff, the disc from Tyler's, and the disc from Club Red."

"Melon's note says there were two."

"I hear you. Those things were screened, you know? All we got was a confirmation of arrival and departure times. Nobody saw anything unusual."

"Why is it missing?"

She sounded exasperated.

"Shit happens. Things get lost, misplaced, people take stuff and forget they have it. I'll check, okay? These things happen, Scott. Is there anything else?"

"No. Thanks."

Scott felt miserable. He hung up, put away the discs, and stretched out on the couch.

Maggie came over, sniffed for a spot, and lay down beside the couch. He rested his hand on her back.

"You're the only good part of this."

Thump thump.

27.

MAGGIE

Maggie roamed a drowsy green field, content and at peace. Belly full. Thirst quenched. Scott's hand a warm comfort. The man was Scott. She was Maggie. This place was their crate, and their crate was safe.

Dogs notice everything. Maggie knew Scott was Scott because he looked at other humans when they used the word. This was how she learned Pete was Pete, and she was Maggie. People looked at her when they said it. Maggie understood come, stay, out, crate, walk, ball, pee, bunk, seek, rat, MRE, chow, good girl, drink, sit, down, fucker, roll over, treat, sit up, guard'm, eat up, find'm, get'm, and many other words. She learned words easily if she associated them with food, joy, play, or pleasing her alpha. This was important. Pleasing her alpha made the pack strong.

Maggie opened her eyes when Scott moved his hand. Their crate was quiet and safe, so Maggie did not rise. She listened to Scott move through the crate. She heard him urinating a few seconds before she smelled his urine, which was followed by the familiar rush of water. A moment later, she smelled the sweet green foam Scott made in his mouth. When the water stopped, Scott returned, smelling brightly of the green foam, water, and soap.

He squatted beside her, stroked her, and made words she did not understand. This did not matter. She understood the love and kindness in his tone.

Maggie lifted her hind leg to expose her belly.

Alpha happy, pack happy.

I am yours.

Scott lay down on the couch in the darkness. Maggie smelled the growing cool of his body, and knew when he slept. When Scott slept, she sighed, and let herself drift into sleep.

A sound new to their crate roused her.

Their crate was defined by its scents and sounds — the carpet; the paint; Scott; the scent of the mice in the walls, and the squeak when they mated; the elderly female who lived with only her voice for pack; the rats clawing their way up the orange trees for fruit; the scent of the two cats who hunted them. Maggie began learning their crate when Scott brought her home, and learned more with each breath, like a computer downloading a never-ending file. As the information compiled in her memory, the pattern of scents and sounds grew familiar.

Familiar was good. Unfamiliar was bad.

A soft scuffing came from beyond the old female's crate.

Maggie instantly lifted her head, and cocked her ears toward the sound. She recognized human footsteps, and understood two people were coming up the drive.

Maggie hurried to the French doors and pushed her nose under the curtain. She heard a twig snap, brittle leaves being crushed, and the scuffing grow louder. Tree rats stopped moving to hide in their stillness.

Maggie walked quickly to the side of the curtains, stuck her head under, and sampled more air. The footsteps stopped.

She cocked her head, listening. She sniffed. She heard the soft metal-to-metal clack of the gate latch, caught their scent, and recognized the intruders. The strangers who had entered their crate had returned.

Maggie erupted in a thunder of barking. She lunged against the glass, the fur on her back bristling from her tail to her shoulders.

Crate in danger.

Pack threatened.

Her fury was a warning. She would drive off or kill whatever threatened her pack.

She heard them running.

"Maggie! Mags!"

Scott came off the couch behind her, but she paid him no mind. She drove them harder, warning them.

"What are you barking at?"

The scuffing faded. Car doors slammed. An engine grew softer until it was gone.

Scott pushed aside the curtains, and joined her.

The threat was gone.

Crate safe.

Pack safe.

Alpha safe.

Her job was done.

"Is someone out there?"

Maggie gazed up at Scott with love and joy. She folded her ears and wagged her tail. She knew he was seeking danger in the darkness, but would find nothing.

Maggie trotted to her water, and drank. When she returned, Scott was back on his couch. She was so happy to see him, she laid her face in his lap. He scratched her ears and stroked her, and Maggie wiggled with happiness.

She sniffed the floor, turned until she found exactly the best position, and lay down beside him.

Alpha safe.

Crate safe.

Pack safe.

Her eyes closed, but Maggie lay awake as the man's heart slowed, his breathing evened, and the hundred scents that made him Scott changed with his cooling skin. She heard a living night familiar with squeaking mice and freeway traffic; tasted air rich with the expected scent of rats, oranges, earth, and beetles; and patrolled their world from her place on the floor as if she was an eighty-five-pound spirit with magical eyes. Maggie sighed. When Scott was at peace, she let herself sleep.

28.

The next morning, after he walked Maggie and showered, Scott decided to check on the missing disc himself. Richard Levin's contact information was on the first page of his interview.

Club Red would be deserted at this hour, so he phoned Levin's personal number. The voice mail message was male, but offered no identifying information. Scott identified himself as a detective working on the Pahlasian murder, said he had questions regarding the discs, and asked Levin to phone as soon as possible.

At seven-twenty, Scott was tying his boots while Maggie bounced between the door and her lead. He got a kick out of how she knew the signs. Whenever he tied his boots, she knew they were going out.

Scott said, "You one smart dog."

His phone rang at seven twenty-one. Scott thought he had lucked out, and Levin was returning his call. Then he saw LAPD in the incoming-call window.

"Morning. Scott James."

He tucked the phone under his chin, and finished tying as he listened.

"Detective Anson, Rampart Detectives. I'm in front of your house with my partner, Detective Shankman. We'd like to speak with you."

Scott went to the French doors, wondering why two Rampart detectives had come to his home.

"I'm in the guest house. See the wood gate in front of you? It's not locked. Come through the gate."

"We understand you have a K-9 police dog on the premises. We don't want a problem with the dog. Will you secure her?"

"She won't be a problem."

"Will you secure the dog?"

Scott didn't want to lock her in her crate, and if he put her in the bedroom, she would shred the door trying to get out.

"Hang on. I'll come out."

Scott nudged Maggie aside, and opened the door.

"Do *not* come out. Please secure the dog."

"Listen, man, I don't have anywhere to secure her. So come meet the dog or I'll come to you. Your choice."

"Secure the dog."

Scott tossed the phone onto the couch, slipped past Maggie, and went out to meet them.

A gray Crown Vic was parked in the street across the mouth of the drive. Two men in sport coats and ties had come up partway, and stood in the drive. The taller was in his early fifties, with dusty blond hair and too many lines. The shorter detective was in his late thirties, and broader, with a shiny face and a bald head ringed with brown hair. Neither looked friendly, and neither pretended.

The older man flashed a badge case showing his ID card and gold detective shield.

"Bob Anson. This is Kurt Shankman."

Anson put away the badge.

"I asked you to secure the dog."

"I don't have a place to secure her. So it's out here or inside with the dog. She's harmless. She'll sniff your hands, you'll love her."

Shankman looked at the gate as if he was worried.

"You latch the gate? She can't get out, can she?"

"She's not in the yard. She's in my house. It's fine, Shankman. Really."

Shankman hooked his thumbs in his belt,

opening the sport coat enough to flash a holster.

"You've been warned. That dog comes charging out here, I'll put her down."

The hair on Scott's neck prickled.

"What's wrong with you, man? You pull on my dog, you better pop me first."

Anson calmly interrupted.

"Do you know a Daryl Ishi?"

There it was. Daryl had probably filed a complaint, and these two were here to investigate.

"I know who he is, yes."

"Would Mr. Ishi think your dog is harmless?"

"Ask him."

Shankman smiled without humor.

"We're asking you. When was the last time you saw him?"

Scott hesitated. If Daryl filed a complaint, he would have been asked if there were witnesses. Anson and Shankman might have spoken with Estelle Rolley and Daryl's friends from the park. Scott answered carefully. He wasn't sure where they would take this, but he did not want to be caught in a lie.

"I saw him yesterday. What is this, Anson? You guys work for IAG? Should I call a PPL rep?"

"Rampart Detectives. We're not with Internal Affairs."

Shankman didn't wait for Scott to respond.

"How'd that come about, you seeing him yesterday?"

"Daryl's brother was recently arrested on multiple burglary counts —"

Shankman interrupted.

"His brother being?"

"Marshall Ishi. Marshall copped to four burglaries, but there's evidence Daryl worked with him. I went to his home to speak with him. I was told he was meeting friends at MacArthur Park."

Shankman interrupted again.

"By who?"

"Marshall's girlfriend, a woman named Estelle Rolley. She's a tweaker, hard-core like Marshall. She lives in their house."

Anson gave a vague nod, which seemed to confirm he had gotten a full report, and was now considering the differences between what he had been told and what Scott was telling him.

"Okay. So you went to MacArthur Park."

"Daryl ran when he saw me approaching. My dog stopped him. Neither my dog nor myself touched him at any time, nor was he placed under arrest. I asked for his cooperation. He refused. I told him he was free to leave."

Shankman arched his eyebrows at Anson.

"Listen to this dude, Bobby, out questioning people. When did K-9 officers start carrying detective shields?"

Anson never looked at his partner, nor changed his expression.

"Scott, let me ask you — did Daryl threaten you during this conversation?"

Scott found Anson's question odd, and wondered where he was going.

"No, sir. He didn't threaten me. We talked."

"Did you see Daryl a second time yesterday, after the park?"

Scott found this question even more odd.

"No. Did he say I did?"

Shankman interrupted again.

"You buy drugs from Daryl?"

The drug question came out of nowhere, and caused a sick chill to flash up Scott's spine.

"Oxy? Vicodin?"

Shankman made jazz hands, as if taunting Scott for an answer he already knew.

"No? Yes? Both?"

Both painkillers had been prescribed by Scott's surgeon, and legally purchased from a pharmacy two blocks away. Shankman had used brand names, not generic names. He specifically named the two painkillers prescribed for Scott.

Shankman dropped the hands, and turned serious as death.

"No answer? Are you medicated now, Scott? Do the anxiety meds make it difficult to think?"

The chill spread across his shoulders and out to his fingers. Scott flashed on Maggie's intruder alert when they returned home the other night.

Scott took a step back.

"Until and unless I'm ordered otherwise by my boss, this Q&A is over. You assholes can fuck off."

Anson remained calm and casual, and made no move to leave.

"Do you blame Marshall Ishi for Stephanie's murder?"

The question froze Scott like the click of a shutter.

Anson kept going, voice reasonable and understanding.

"You got shot up, your partner was murdered, these two assholes maybe saw it, and never came forward. You must carry a lot of anger, man. Who could blame you, with the shooters still running around? Marshall and Daryl are letting them skate. I can see how

331

a man would be angry."

Shankman nodded agreeably, his unblinking eyes like tarnished dimes.

"Me, too, Bobby. I'd want to punish them. Oh, yeah. I'd want to get mine."

The two detectives stared at him. Waiting.

Scott's head throbbed. He now understood they were investigating something worse than a harassment complaint.

"Why are you people here?"

Anson seemed genuinely friendly for the first time.

"To ask about Daryl. We did."

Anson turned, and walked to their car.

Shankman said, "Thanks for your cooperation."

Shankman followed his boss.

Scott spoke to their backs.

"What happened? Anson, is Daryl dead?"

Anson climbed into the passenger side.

"If we have further questions, we'll call."

Shankman trotted around the front end, and dropped in behind the wheel.

Scott called out as the Crown Vic started.

"Am I a suspect? Tell me what happened."

Anson glanced back as the car rolled away.

"You have a good day."

Scott watched them leave. His hands trembled. His shirt grew damp with sweat. He told himself to breathe, but he couldn't make it happen.

Barking.

He heard Maggie barking. Him here, Maggie trapped in the guest house, she didn't like it and wanted him back.

Scotty, don't leave me.

"I'm coming."

Maggie bounced up and down when he opened the door, and spun in happy circles.

"I'm here. Hang on, baby. I'm happy, too."

Scott wasn't happy. He was confused and scared, and stood numb by the door as Maggie swirled around him until he noticed the phone's message light was blinking. The counter showed he had received two calls in the minutes he was outside with Anson and Shankman.

Scott touched the playback button.

"Hello, Scott, this is Doctor Charles Goodman. Something rather important has come up. Please call me as soon as possible. This is very important."

This is Doctor Charles Goodman.

As if Scott wouldn't recognize the man's voice after seeing him for seven months.

Scott deleted the message, and moved on. Paul Budress was next.

"Dude, it's Paul. Call me before you come in. Call right now, man. Do *not* come in until we talk."

Scott didn't like the strain in Budress' voice. Paulie Budress was one of the calmest people he'd ever met.

Scott took a deep breath, blew out, and called him.

Budress said, "What the fuck, man? What's going on?"

Scott prayed he wouldn't throw up. He could tell Budress knew something from his tone.

"What are you talking about?"

"Some IAG rats are here waiting for you. Fucking Leland is gonna explode."

Scott took deep breaths, one after another. First Anson and Shankman, and now Internal Affairs.

"What do they want with me?"

"Shit, man, you don't know?"

Fake it 'til you make it.

"Paul, c'mon. What did they say?"

"Mace heard them in there with Leland. They're hauling you downtown, and you won't be coming back here."

Scott felt as if Budress was talking about someone else.

"I'm being suspended?"

"Full on. No badge. No pay. You're going home, pending whatever the fuck investigation."

"This is crazy."

"Call the union. Hook up with a rep and a lawyer before you come in. And for Christ's sake, don't tell them I called you."

"What about Maggie?"

"Dude, you don't own her. I'll find out what I can. I'll call you back."

Budress hung up.

Scott felt woozy and off balance. He clenched his eyes, and imagined himself alone on a beach the way Goodman taught him. Distraction came with focusing on the details. The sand was hot from the sun, and gritty, and smelled of dead seaweed and fish and salt. The sun beat down until his skin crinkled with its terrible heat. Scott's heart slowed as he calmed, and his head cleared. He had to be calm to think clearly. Clarity was everything.

Internal Affairs was investigating, but Anson and Shankman hadn't arrested him. This meant no arrest warrant had been issued. Scott had room to move, but he needed more facts.

He called Joyce Cowly's cell, and prayed his call wouldn't go to her voice mail.

She answered on the third ring.

"It's Scott. Joyce, what's happening? What's going on?"

She didn't answer.

"Joyce?"

"Where are you?"

"Home. Two Rampart detectives just left. They made it sound like Daryl Ishi was dead, and I was the suspect."

She hesitated again as if she was deciding whether to answer, and he grew frightened she would hang up. She didn't.

"The Parkers went to pick him up for a swab last night. They found him shot to death. Daryl, Estelle Rolley, and one of the roommates."

Scott lowered himself to the couch.

"They think I killed three people?"

"Scott —"

"It sounds like a drug killing. These people deal drugs. They're addicts."

"Ruled out. They had a new stash, and they hadn't been robbed."

She paused again.

"There's this talk about you being unstable —"

"Bullshit."

"— the way you blew up at Melon and Stengler, the stress you've been under, all these medications you take."

"The Rampart dicks knew my prescriptions. They specifically knew which meds I take. How could they know, Joyce?"

"I don't know. No one here should know."

"Who's saying this stuff?"

"Everyone's talking about you. Top floor. Division brass. It could have come from anyone."

"But how can they know?"

"It's a big deal. They don't like the way you inserted yourself into the case."

"I didn't kill these people."

"I'm just telling you what's being said. You're a suspect. Lawyer up. I can give you some names."

He went back to the beach. Slow deep breaths in, slow exhales out.

Maggie rested her chin on his knee. He stroked her seal-sleek head and wondered if she would like to run on the beach.

"Why would I kill him? I wanted to know if he saw something. Maybe he didn't. Now we won't know."

"Maybe you tried to make him talk, and got carried away."

"Is that what they're saying?"

"It's been mentioned. I have to go."

"You think I did this?"

Cowly was silent.

"Do you think I killed them?"

"No."

Joyce Cowly was gone.

Scott lowered his phone.

Maggie's soft brown eyes watched him.

He stroked her head, wondering if Daryl

had died with anything worth knowing.

"Now we'll never know."

Nine months was a long time to keep secrets. If Daryl saw something, Scott doubted he could keep quiet, and wondered who Daryl would tell. Marshall might know, but Marshall was currently in Men's Central Jail.

Scott thought for a moment, then went to his computer. He opened the Sheriff's Department website for Marshall's booking number and the phone for the MCJ Liaison Desk.

"This is Detective Bud Orso, LAPD Robbery-Homicide. I need to see a prisoner named Marshall — M, A, R, S, H, A, double-L — Ishi, I, S, H, I."

Scott read off Marshall's booking number, and continued his request.

"I'm coming with information regarding his brother, so this is a courtesy visit. He won't need his attorney."

When the meeting was arranged, Scott clipped up Maggie and left the guest house as quickly as possible. He needed to move, and keep moving, or he wouldn't go through with it.

Scott picked up the freeway in Studio City, and made for downtown Los Angeles and Men's Central Jail. He rolled down the windows. Maggie straddled the console in her usual spot, watching the scenery and enjoying the wind. She looked awkward with the poor footing, but happy and content. Scott leaned into her the way he did when he tried to move her. He felt better when she leaned back.

Once he walked into jail, he hoped they would let him out.

■ ■ ■ ■

PART IV

■ ■ ■ ■

■ ■ ■ ■

PACK

■ ■ ■ ■

29.

Scott was passing Universal Studios at the Hollywood split when his phone rang. He hoped it was Cowly or Budress, with more information, but it was Goodman. The last person he wanted to speak with, but he answered the call.

"This is Charles Goodman, Scott. I've been trying to reach you."

"I was going to call. I have to cancel our session tomorrow."

Scott's regular appointment was the following day.

"I was phoning to cancel, as well. Something happened here at the office. Personally embarrassing for me, and I'm afraid this will be upsetting for you."

Scott had never heard Goodman so strained.

"Are you okay, Doc?"

"The privacy of my clients and their trust is of paramount importance to me —"

"I trust you. What happened?"

"My office was broken into two nights ago. Scott, some things were stolen, your file among them. I'm terribly sorry —"

Scott flashed on Shankman and Anson, and the top-floor brass knowing things about him they had no way to know.

"Doc, wait. My file was stolen? *My* file?"

"Not only yours, but yours was among them. Apparently they grabbed a handful of files at random — current and past clients whose last names begin with the letters G through K. I've been calling to —"

"Did you call the police?"

"Two detectives came out. They sent a man to look for fingerprints. He left black powder on the door and the windows and my cabinet. I don't know whether I'm supposed to leave it or if I can clean it."

"You can clean up, Doc. They're finished. What did the detectives say?"

"They didn't tell me whether to leave it or clean it."

"Not about the fingerprint powder. What about the burglary?"

"Scott, I want you to know I did not give them your name. They asked for a list of the clients whose files were stolen, but that would violate our confidence. The State of California protects you in this. I did not

346

and will not identify you."

Scott had the sick feeling his confidence had already been violated.

"What did they say about the burglary?"

"The door and the windows weren't broken, so whoever broke in apparently had a key. The detectives said burglaries like this are usually committed by someone known to the cleaning crew. They have a key made, and grab the first thing they see."

"What would a janitor want with files?"

"The files have your personal and billing information. The detectives said I should warn you — not you specifically, but all of you — to alert your credit card companies and banks. I can't tell you how sorry I am. These people are out there with my notes on your sessions, and now you have to deal with this credit card nonsense."

Scott's mind raced from Anson and Shankman to Cowly to Goodman's break-in, all of it coming together.

"When did this happen?"

"Two nights ago. I came to the office yesterday morning, and, well, my heart sank when I saw what had happened."

Three nights ago, Maggie alerted to an intruder. Scott recalled a powdery substance on his locks, but had written it off.

Scott steered for the next off-ramp, and

left the freeway in the Cahuenga Pass. He stopped in the first parking lot he saw.

"Doc? Who were the detectives who came out?"

"Ah, well, I have their — yes, here we are. Detective Warren Broder and a Detective Deborah Kurland."

Scott jotted the names, told Goodman he would phone in a few days, and immediately called the North Hollywood Community Police Station. When he reached the Detective Bureau, he identified himself, and asked to speak with Broder or Kurland.

"Kurland's here. Hold on."

A few seconds later, Kurland picked up. Her smart professional voice reminded him of Cowly.

"Detective Kurland speaking."

Scott repeated his name, adding his badge number and station.

Kurland said, "Okey-doke, Officer. How can I help?"

"You and Detective Broder are handling the burglary of a Doctor Charles Goodman. His office in Studio City?"

"You bet. May I ask your interest?"

"Doctor Goodman is a friend. This call is unofficial."

"I get it. Ask whatever you like. I'll answer or I won't."

"How'd the perp get in?"

"Door."

"Funny. You guys told Goodman the guy used a passkey?"

"No, that was me, and what I said was, you see entries this clean, more often than not the perp bought a key from someone who works at the building. My partner thinks the locks were bump-keyed. Personally, I think the dude used a pick gun. Up on that second-floor walkway with your butt in the air, you want the locks open fast. A pick gun is easier."

The ache in Scott's side crept up his back.

"Why either one instead of the passkey?"

"I wanted to check the locks, so I borrowed the doctor's keys. They felt slippery. I wiped them, worked the locks, the keys were slippery again. Both locks were blown full of graphite."

The Trans Am's doors and top bulged toward him, as if the car was being crushed by an outside pressure.

Kurland said, "Anything else?"

Scott started to say no, then remembered.

"The prints?"

"Nothing. Gloves."

Scott thanked her, and lowered his phone. He stared at the passing traffic, and grew more frightened with each passing car.

Someone had invaded his life, and was using his life to frame him for Daryl Ishi's murder. Someone wanted to know what he knew, and thought, and suspected about Stephanie's killers. Someone didn't want Stephanie's killers found.

Scott turned around and drove back to his guest house. He went to his bedroom, and found his old dive bag in his closet. It was a huge nylon duffel, currently packed with fins, a buoyancy compensator, and other diving gear. Scott dumped the contents while Maggie sniffed from the door. He had not opened the bag in almost three years. He wondered if she smelled the ocean and fish, or if time had killed their scent.

Scott filled the bag with his spare pistol and ammo, his dad's old watch, the cash under the clock radio, the shoe box filled with credit card receipts and billing statements, two changes of clothes, and his personal items. He cleaned out his meds from the bathroom. Goodman's name was on the labels, and now Scott had no doubt there was a connection. Three nights ago, someone entered his home, went through his things, and saw Goodman's name. Two nights ago, someone broke into Goodman's office, and made off with Scott's therapeutic history.

Scott carried his bag to the living room. He gathered the material he amassed on the shooting into a single large stack, and packed it into the bag. The empty floor looked larger.

Maggie stuck her head into the bag, looked at Scott as if she was bored, and walked into the kitchen for water.

Scott studied the room, thinking what else should he take? He added his laptop computer, and took down his diagrams and pictures. He considered leaving Stephanie's picture on the wall, but she had been with him at the beginning, and he wanted her with him at the end. Her picture was the last thing he put in the bag.

He clipped Maggie's lead, and braced himself as he slung the dive bag over his shoulder. He expected his side to scream, but he felt almost normal.

"C'mon, big girl. Let's get this done."

Scott told Mrs. Earle he would be away for a few days, stowed the dive bag in his trunk, and headed back to the freeway.

Going to jail.

Driving fast.

30.

JOYCE COWLY

Elton Joshua Marley frowned at their surroundings as she stepped onto the roof.

"Look how fil'ty, all dis mess. You ruin dese nice clothes you hab."

"I'll be fine, Mr. Marley. Thanks."

The roof was littered with wine bottles, broken rock pipes, and condoms, as she had seen in Scott James' pictures. She moved away from the stairwell to get her bearings. She was looking for the roof above the kill zone.

Mr. Marley stayed at the door.

"Leh me do dis, sabe you nice clothes? Come down de stairs. I gib you beach pants an' a beautiful MarleyWorld shirt, de rayahn so soft it keess your skeen."

"Thank you, but I'm good like this."

Cowly determined the direction of the intersection, and picked her way across the roof.

"Watch for de needles. Dey be nahsty tings up here."

His concern was cute, but annoying as hell. Cowly was glad he stayed by the door.

She climbed over a low wall onto the corner building, and moved to the edge of the roof. A low, wrought-iron safety barrier ran along the parapet just as Scott described. It was dirty, rusted, and eaten by corrosion. Cowly was careful not to touch it when she leaned forward to look between the bars. She saw a perfectly normal street four floors below, bustling with normal activity, but nine months ago, three people were murdered here, Scott James was bleeding to death, and the street glittered with cartridge casings.

Cowly walked along the fence. The little remaining black paint had faded to a soft gray. Most of the metal was scabbed with fine, reddish-brown rust. Cowly touched it, and examined the rust on her finger. More brown than red, but enough red to look like dried blood.

She stood on her toes, trying to see the sidewalk, but wasn't tall enough. She was directly above the spot where SID collected the watchband, thinking the red smears were blood.

Cowly took the evidence bag from her

purse. She unsealed the bag and maneuvered the leather strap until it was exposed, being careful not to touch it with her fingers. She held it using the plastic like a glove.

Cowly pressed her free thumb to the fence, and compared the rust on her thumb to the streaks on the leather. They looked alike. Cowly pressed her thumb to the fence again, and grinded it to pick up more rust. The streaks on the band and on her thumb now looked identical. Cowly was encouraged, but knew their appearance proved little or nothing.

She resealed the evidence bag, tucked it into her purse, and took out a white envelope and pen. Using the pen, she scraped a generous amount of rust into the envelope. When she felt she had enough, she sealed the envelope, thanked Mr. Marley for being so helpful, and took her samples to SID.

31.

Men's Central Jail was a low, sleek, concrete building wedged between Chinatown and the Los Angeles River. Built stern and foreboding, it could have passed for the science center at a well-endowed university except for the chain-link fence rimming its perimeter and the five thousand inmates between its walls.

Scott parked in a public parking lot across the street, but stayed in his car, his hand on Maggie's back to keep them both calm. Twenty-five minutes later Maggie sniffed, and her ears went up on alert. Scott clipped her lead and waited. When Paul Budress appeared, they got out.

"She had you forty seconds before I saw you."

Budress was clearly uncomfortable. His mouth was an unhappy line and his eyes were narrowed to slits.

"The rats left. They decided you weren't

coming in."

"I didn't do it."

"Hell, man, I know, else I wouldn't be here."

Scott hadn't been able to figure out what to do with Maggie while he was in jail, so he called Budress from the freeway. Budress thought he was crazy, but here he was.

Scott held out the lead. Budress frowned for a moment, but took it. He let Maggie sniff his hand, and ruffled her head.

"We'll take a walk. Text me when you're out."

"If they take her, find her a good home, okay?"

"She has a home. Go."

Scott walked quickly away and did not look back. They knew Maggie would try to follow him, and she did. In her world, they were a pack, and the pack stayed together.

Maggie whined and barked, and he heard her claws scrape the tarmac like files. Budress had cautioned him not to look back or wave bye-bye or any of the silly things people did. Dogs weren't people. Eye contact would make her struggle harder to reach him. A dog could see your heart in your eyes, Budress told him, and dogs were drawn to our hearts.

Scott dodged cars to cross the street, and

entered the main entrance. During his seven years as a patrol officer, he had visited MCJ less than two dozen times. Most of these had been to transport suspects or prisoners from his area station, and deliveries were made up a ramp in the back.

Scott took a moment to orient himself, then told a Sheriff's Deputy he was scheduled to see a prisoner, and gave Marshall's name. Standing there in his dark navy uniform with his badge pinned to his chest, Scott looked nothing like a Robbery-Homicide detective. He took a breath, and identified himself as Bud Orso.

The dep made a call without comment, and a female deputy appeared a few minutes later.

"You Orso?"

"Yes, ma'am."

"We're bringing him up. I'll take you back."

Scott felt little relief. He followed her past a security station to a room where she asked for his handcuffs and weapon. She gave him a receipt, locked both in a gun safe, and showed him to an interview room. Scott was pleased with the room. Civilian visitors and attorneys were brought to booths where they talked to prisoners on phones while separated by a heavy glass screen. Law-enforcement personnel required an interview environment with greater flexibility. The room contained an ancient Formica-topped table and three plastic chairs. The table jutted from a wall, and was fitted with a steel rod for securing prisoners. Scott took a chair facing the door.

The deputy said, "Here he comes. You need anything?"

"No, thanks. I'm good."

"I'm at the end of the hall when you finish. Out this door, turn right. We'll get you your things."

An athletic young dep fresh from the Academy guided Marshall into the room. Marshall wore a bright blue jumpsuit, sneakers, and manacles on his pencil-thin wrists. He appeared even more frail than Scott remembered, which was probably from the withdrawal. Marshall glanced at Scott, and stared at the floor. Same as when he was led from his house.

The young dep seated Marshall in the chair facing Scott, and hooked the manacles to the steel rod.

Scott said, "You don't need to do that. We're fine."

"Got to. Marshall, you okay?"

"Uh-huh."

358

The deputy closed the door on his way out.

Scott studied Marshall, and realized he didn't have a plan. He didn't know anything about Marshall Ishi other than he was a wasted-away tweaker with a brother and a girlfriend who were murdered the day before. Marshall probably learned about it this morning. The red eyes were probably from crying.

"You love your brother?"

Marshall glanced up before glancing away. Scott caught a flash of anger in the red eyes.

"What kind of question is that?"

"I'm sorry. I don't know what kind of relationship you had. Some brothers, you know how it is, they hate each other. Others . . ."

Scott let it trail. The welling in Marshall's eyes gave the answer.

"I raised him since he was nine."

"I'm sorry. About Daryl, and Estelle, too. I know how it hurts."

Marshall's eyes flashed angry again.

"Oh, that's right, for sure. Spare me, partner, how could you? Let's get down to business here. Who killed my brother?"

Scott pushed his chair back, stood, and unbuttoned his shirt.

Marshall leaned back, clearly surprised.

He didn't understand what was happening, and shook his head.

"No, don't do that. Stop, dude, I'll call the sheriffs."

Scott dropped his shirt on the chair, took off his undershirt, and watched Marshall's expression change when he saw the gray lines across Scott's left shoulder and the large, knobby Y that wrapped around his right side.

Scott let him take a good look.

"This is how I know."

Marshall glanced at Scott, then went back to the scars. He couldn't stop looking at the scars.

"What happened?"

Scott pulled on the undershirt, and buttoned his shirt.

"When you cut your plea, you told detectives about a Chinese import store you hit nine months ago. They asked if you saw a shooting. Three people were murdered. One left for dead."

Marshall nodded as he answered.

"Yes, sir, they asked. I did commit that burglary, but I didn't see the shooting. My understanding is all that happened after I left."

He glanced at Scott's shoulder, but the scars were hidden.

"Was that you, left for dead?"

Marshall was so genuine and natural, Scott knew he was telling the truth. The poly wasn't necessary.

"I lost someone close that night. Last night, you lost your brother. The same people who did this to me killed Daryl."

Marshall sat there, staring, his face pinched as he struggled to get his head around it. His eyes shimmered, and Scott thought, if Budress was right, if a dog saw a person's heart through their eyes, Maggie would see a heart broken in Marshall.

"Help me out here, 'cause —"

"Was Daryl with you that night?"

Marshall leaned back again, and seemed irritated.

"What the fuck? I don't take Daryl with me to do burglary. What are you talkin' about?"

"Up on the roof. Your lookout."

"No fuckin' way."

He meant it. Marshall was telling the truth.

"Daryl was there."

"Bullshit. I'm telling you, he wasn't."

"What if I told you I could prove it?"

"I'd call you a liar."

Scott decided to leave Maggie out of it, and tell Marshall they had a DNA match.

But as he took out his phone for a picture of the watchband, it occurred to him Marshall might remember his brother's watch.

He held out his phone so Marshall could see.

"Did Daryl have a watch with a band like this?"

Marshall slowly sat taller. He reached for the phone, but the manacles stopped him.

"I got that watch for him. I gave it to him."

Scott thought carefully. Marshall was with him now, and Marshall would help. Luck was better than DNA.

"This was found on the sidewalk the morning I was shot. These little smears are from a fence on the roof. I don't know when he was up there that night, or why, or what he saw, but Daryl was there."

Marshall shook his head slow, trying to remember and asking himself questions.

"Are you saying he saw those murders?"

"I don't know. He never mentioned it to you?"

"No, 'course not. Not ever. Jesus, don't you think I'd remember?"

"I don't know if he saw them or not, but I think the shooters were scared he had seen them."

Marshall's gaze shifted, searching the little room for answers.

"Y'all thought I saw the shootings, and I didn't. Maybe Daryl was long gone like me, and didn't see shit."

"Then they killed him for nothing, and he's still dead."

Marshall wiped his eyes on his shoulders, leaving dark spots on the blue.

"Goddamnit, this is bullshit. Fuckin' bullshit."

"I want them, Marshall. For me and my friend, and for Daryl. I need your help to get this done."

"What the fuck, if he saw something, he didn't tell me. Shit, even if he *didn't* see anything, he didn't tell me. Probably scared I'd kick his ass!"

"Something crazy and exciting like this? Let's say he saw it. Let's pretend."

Because if Daryl left the roof having seen nothing, Scott had no place to go.

"It's a big thing to hold. Who would he tell? His best friend. A person he might tell even if he was too scared to tell anyone else."

Marshall's head bobbed.

"Amelia. His baby mama."

"Daryl has a child?"

Marshall's gaze flicked around the room as he sorted through memories.

"Be about two, a girl. Don't *really* know it's Daryl's, but she says it is. He loves her."

Then Marshall realized what he'd said. "Loved."

Her name was Amelia Goyta. The baby's name was Gina. Marshall didn't know the address, but told Scott where to find her building. Marshall hadn't seen the baby in almost a year, and wanted to know if she looked like Daryl.

Scott promised to let Marshall know, and was leaving to find the deputy when Marshall twisted around in his chair and asked a question Scott had been asking himself.

"All this time later, why they all of a sudden get scared Daryl seen'm? How'd they know Daryl was up there?"

Scott thought he knew, but didn't share the answer.

"Marshall, the detectives will probably come see you. Don't tell them about this. Don't tell anyone unless you hear that I'm dead."

Marshall's red eyes grew scared.

"I won't."

"Not even the detectives. Especially not the detectives."

Scott took a right turn out the door, collected his handcuffs and gun, and left the jail as quickly as he could.

He waited on the sidewalk by the parking lot for almost ten minutes before Budress and Maggie rounded the corner. Maggie bounced and yelped and strained at her lead, so Budress let her go. She raced toward Scott with her ears back and tongue out, looking like the happiest dog in the world. Scott opened his arms, and caught her when she plowed into him. Eighty-five pounds of black-and-tan love.

Budress didn't look as happy as Maggie.

"What happened in there?"

"I'm still in the game."

Budress grunted.

"Okay, then. Okay. I'll see you later."

Budress turned to leave.

"Paul. Marshall recognized the watch-band. It was Daryl's. Maggie pinned him, man."

Budress glanced at the dog, then the man. "Never doubt."

"I didn't."

Scott and Maggie climbed into their car.

32.

Scott found Amelia Goyta's prewar apartment house on a shabby run-down street north of the freeway in Echo Park. The old building had three floors, four units per floor, an interior central stair, no air-conditioning, and was pretty much identical to every building on the block except for the Crying Virgin. A towering Virgin Mary crying tears of blood was painted on the front of her building. Marshall told Scott the painting looked more like an anorexic Smurf, but he couldn't miss it. Marshall had told it true. The Virgin Smurf was three stories tall.

Marshall didn't remember which was Amelia's apartment, so Scott checked with the manager. Wearing his uniform helped. Top floor in back, 304.

Scott wondered if news of Daryl's death had reached Amelia. When he and Maggie reached the third floor, he heard crying and knew it had. He paused outside her door to listen, and Maggie sniffed at the floor jamb. Inside, a child wailed between whooping breaths, as a sobbing woman alternated pleas to stop crying with reassurances they were going to be okay.

Scott rapped on the door.

The child kept wailing, but the sobbing stopped. A moment later, the wailing stopped, too, but no one came to the door.

Scott rapped again, and gave her his patrol officer's voice.

"Police officer. Please open the door."

Twenty seconds passed without a response, so Scott knocked again.

"Police officer. Open the door or I'll have the manager let me in."

The wailing began again, and now the woman's sob came from the other side of the door.

"Go away. Go AWAY! You're not the police."

She sounded afraid, so Scott softened his voice.

"Amelia? I'm a police officer. I'm here about Daryl Ishi."

"What's your name? WHAT IS YOUR NAME?"

"Scott James."

Her voice rose to a frantic scream.

"TELL ME YOUR NAME."

"Scott. James. My name is SCOTT. Police officer. Open the door, Amelia. Is Gina safe? I'm not leaving until I see that she's safe."

When he finally heard the deadbolt slide, Scott stepped away to appear less threatening. Maggie automatically stood by his left leg as she'd been trained, and faced the door.

A girl not more than twenty peeked out when the door opened. She had long, straw-colored hair and pale, freckled skin. Her eyes and nose were red, and her lips quivered between gasps, but nothing about her expression suggested a broken heart or mourning.

Scott had seen her expression on the faces of women who were punching bags for their husbands, hookers on the run from pimps out to cut them, and the shell-shocked faces of rape victims. He had seen it on mothers with missing children — an expectation that something worse was coming. Scott knew the face of fear. He saw it on Amelia Goyta, and instantly knew Daryl had witnessed the shooting, and told her he would be killed if the shooters found out.

She wiped away snot, and asked him again.

"What's your name?"

"I'm Scott. This is Maggie. Are you and Gina okay?"

She glanced at Maggie.

"I gotta pack. We're leaving."

"Can I see the baby, please? I want to see she's okay."

Amelia glanced toward the stairs as if someone might be hiding, then threw open the door and hurried to her child. Gina was in a playpen, her face pinched and smeared with snot. She had dark hair, but looked nothing like Daryl. Amelia lifted her, jiggled her, and put her back in the playpen.

"Here, you see? She's fine. Now I gotta pack, I got a friend coming. Rachel."

A faded blue wheelie carry-on was waiting by the door. A Samsonite suitcase older than Scott was open like a giant clam on the floor, half-filled with toys and baby supplies. She ran into the bedroom, and returned dragging a brown garbage bag fat with clothes.

Scott said, "Did Daryl say they would kill you?"

Amelia dropped the bag by the door, and ran back to the bedroom.

"Yes! That dumbass piece of shit. He said they'd kill us, and I ain't waiting."

"Who killed him?"

"The fuckin' killers. You're the policeman.

369

Don't you know?"

She ran back with a wastebasket filled with combs, brushes, hair spray, and toiletries. She upended it into the Samsonite, tossed the basket aside, and pushed a small velvet pouch into Scott's hands.

"Here. Take'm. I told the dumb fuck he was an idiot."

Scott caught her arm as she turned for the bedroom.

"Slow down. Listen to me, Amelia. Nine months ago. What did Daryl tell you?"

She sobbed, and rubbed her eye.

"He saw these masked dudes shoot up a car."

"Tell me exactly what he said."

"He said if they knew he saw, they'd fuckin' kill us and the baby, too. I want to pack."

She tried to twist away, but Scott held her. Maggie edged closer and growled.

"I'm here to stop them, okay? That's why I'm here. So help me. Tell me what Daryl said."

She stopped fighting him, and gazed down at Maggie.

"Is that a guard dog?"

"Yes. A guard dog. What did Daryl tell you?"

Scott felt her relax as she considered the

guard dog, and turned loose her arms.

"He was on some building somewhere, and heard a crash. Stupid Daryl went to see, and here's this truck and the cops and these men were around this Rolls-Royce, shooting the shit out of it."

Scott didn't bother to correct her.

"He said it was crazy. He was, like, fuck, it was Tarantino, these masked guys shootin' the cops and the Rolls. Daryl freaked, and slammed down off the roof, but it was all quiet when he hit the ground, and they were yellin' at each other, so idiot fuckass Daryl goes to see."

"Did he tell you what they were saying?"

"Just bullshit, hurry up, find the damned thing, whatever. They were scared of the sirens. The sirens were coming."

Scott realized he had stopped breathing. His pulse had grown loud in his ears.

"Did Daryl say what they found?"

"This one dude gets in the Rolls, and jumps out with a briefcase. They piled into this car and tore out of there, and stupid Daryl, he's thinking, rich people in this Rolls, he might get a ring or a watch, so he runs to the car."

Scott thought Daryl had embellished his story.

"With the sirens getting closer?"

371

"Is that fuckin' damaged? These two people are shot to shit, blood everywhere, and my moron boyfriend risks his life for eight hundred dollars and this —"

She slapped the velvet pouch.

"I said, you stupid shit, are you crazy? The money had blood on it. Idiot Daryl had blood all over, and he's freaking. He made me promise, we can't tell, we can't even hint, 'cause these maniacs would kill us."

"Did he see their faces?"

"You didn't hear what I just said? They had masks."

"Maybe one of them took off his mask."

"He didn't say."

"How about a tattoo, hair color, a ring or a watch? Did he describe them in any way?"

"All I remember is masks, like ski masks."

Scott thought harder.

"You kept asking my name. Why were you asking my name?"

"I thought you were them."

"Meaning what? He heard their names?"

"Snell. He heard this one guy say, 'Snell, c'mon.' If your name was Snell, I wasn't going to let you in. Listen, man, I gotta pack. Please. Rachel is coming."

Scott looked at the pouch. It was lavender velvet, closed by a drawstring, with a dark discoloration. Scott opened it, and poured

372

seven gray rocks into his palm. Maggie raised her nose, curious about the pouch because Scott was curious. This was something he had learned about her. If he focused on something, she was interested. Scott poured the stones back into the pouch, and slipped the pouch into his pocket.

"When will Rachel be here?"

"Now. Any second."

"Pack. I'll help carry your stuff."

She was ready to go when Rachel arrived. Scott carried the Samsonite and the garbage bag stuffed with clothes. Amelia carried the little girl and a pillow, and Rachel carried everything else. Scott unclipped Maggie, and let her follow off-leash. At Scott's request, Amelia left her apartment unlocked.

When everything was in the car, Scott asked for her and Rachel's cell numbers, and took Amelia aside.

"Don't tell anyone you're with Rachel. Don't tell anyone what you think happened to Daryl, or what Daryl saw that night."

"Can't a policeman stay with me? Like in witness protection?"

Scott ignored the question.

"You hear about Marshall? He's in Men's Central Jail?"

"Uh-uh. I didn't know."

Scott repeated it.

"Men's Central Jail. I'm going to call you in two days, okay? But if you don't hear from me, on the third day, I want you to go see Marshall. Tell him what you told me."

"Marshall don't like me."

"Bring Gina. Tell him what Daryl saw. Tell him everything just like you told me."

She was scared and confused, and Scott thought she might get in the car and tell Rachel to never stop driving, but she looked at Maggie.

"I get a big enough place, I want a dog."

Then she got into Rachel's car and they left.

Scott let Maggie pee, then picked up his dive bag, and lugged it up to Amelia's apartment. He found a large pot in the kitchen, filled it with water, and set the pot on the floor.

"This is yours. We may be here a few days."

Maggie sniffed at the water, and walked away to explore the apartment.

Scott sat with the dive bag on Amelia's couch in Amelia's living room in Amelia's apartment, and stared at the wall. He felt tired, and wished he were living on the far side of the world under an assumed name, with a head that wasn't filled with anger and fear.

Scott opened the velvet pouch and poured out the pebbles. He was pretty sure the seven little rocks were uncut diamonds. Each was about the size of his fingernail, translucent, and gray. They looked like crystal meth, and the irony made him smile.

He poured them back into the pouch, and the smile went with them.

Interpol had supposedly connected Beloit to a French diamond fence, which led Melon and Stengler to speculate that Beloit had smuggled diamonds into the country for delivery, or had come to the U.S. to pick up diamonds the fence purchased. Either way, the bandits learned of the plan, followed Beloit's movements, and murdered Beloit and Pahlasian during the robbery. Melon and Stengler used these assumptions to drive the case until the same person who tipped them to Beloit's diamond connection later told them Beloit had no such involvement.

The I-Man. Ian Mills.

Scott thought it through. Melon and Stengler knew nothing of Beloit's diamond connection until Mills brought it to their attention. Why bring it up, and later discredit it? Either Mills had bad information when he cleared Beloit and made an honest mistake, or he lied to turn the investigation. Scott wondered how Mills knew about the connection, and why he later changed his mind.

Scott searched his dive bag for the clippings he collected during the early weeks of the investigation. Melon still ran the case at that time, and had given Scott a card with his home phone and cell number written on the back, saying Scott could call him anytime. That was before they reached the point Melon stopped returning his calls.

Scott stared at Melon's number, trying to figure out what to say. Some calls were more difficult than others.

Maggie came out of the bedroom. She studied Scott for a moment, then went to the open window. He figured she was charting the scents of their new world.

Scott dialed the number. If his call went to Melon's voice mail, he planned to hang up, but Melon answered on the fourth ring.

"Detective Melon, this is Scott James. I hope you don't mind I called."

There was a long silence before Melon answered.

"Guess it depends. How're you doing?"

"I'd like to come see you, if it's okay?"

"Uh-huh. And why is that?"

"I want to apologize. Face-to-face."

Melon chuckled, and Scott felt a wave of relief.

"I'm retired, partner. If you want to drive all the way out here, come ahead."

Scott copied Melon's address, clipped Maggie's lead, and drove up to the Simi Valley.

33.

Melon tipped his lawn chair back, and gazed up into the leaves.

"You see this tree? This tree wasn't eight feet tall when my wife and I bought this place."

Scott and Melon sat beneath the broad spread of an avocado tree in Melon's backyard, sipping Diet Cokes with lemon wedges. Rotting avocados dotted the ground like poop, drawing clouds of swirling gnats. A few gnats circled Maggie, but she didn't seem to mind.

Scott admired the tree.

"All the guac you can eat, forever. I love it."

"I'll tell you, some years, the best avocados you could want. Other years, they have these little threads all through them. I have to figure that out."

Melon was a big fleshy man with thinning gray hair and wrinkled, sun-dark skin. He and his wife owned a small ranch house on an acre of land in the Santa Susana foothills, so far from Los Angeles they were west of the San Fernando Valley. It was a long commute to downtown L.A., but the affordable home prices and small-town lifestyle more than made up for the drive. A lot of police officers lived there.

Melon had answered the door wearing shorts, flip-flops, and a faded Harley-Davidson T-shirt. He was friendly, and told Scott to take Maggie around the side of the house, and he would meet them in back. When Melon joined them a few minutes later, he brought Diet Cokes and a tennis ball. He showed Scott to the chairs, waved the ball in Maggie's face, and sidearmed it across his yard.

Maggie ignored it.

Scott said, "She doesn't chase balls."

Melon looked disappointed.

"That's a shame. I had a Lab, man, she'd chase balls all day. You like K-9?"

"I like it a lot."

"Good. I know you had your heart set on SWAT. It's good you found something else."

As they settled under the tree, Scott remembered a joke Leland loved to tell.

"There's only one difference between SWAT and K-9. Dogs don't negotiate."

Melon burst out laughing. When his laughter faded, Scott faced him.

"Listen, Detective Melon —"

Melon stopped him.

"I'm retired. Call me Chris or Bwana."

"I was an asshole. I was rude and abusive, and wrong. I'm ashamed of the way I acted. I apologize."

Melon stared for a moment, and tipped his glass.

"Unnecessary, but thank you."

Scott clinked his glass to Melon's, and Melon settled back.

"Just so you know, you were all that and then some, but, hell, man, I get it. Damn, but I wanted to close that case. Despite what you may think, I broke my ass, me and Stengler, shit, everyone involved."

"I know you did. I'm reading the file."

"Bud let you in?"

Scott nodded, and Melon tipped his glass again.

"Bud's a good man."

"I was blown away when I saw all the paperwork you guys generated."

"Too many late nights. I'm surprised I'm still married."

"Can I ask you something?"

"Whatever you like."

"I met Ian Mills —"

Melon's laughter interrupted him.

"The I-Man! Bud tell you why they call him the I-Man?"

Scott found himself enjoying Melon's company. On the job, he had been humorless and distant.

"Because his name is Ian?"

"Not even close, though that's what everyone says to his face. Now don't get me wrong, the man is a fine detective. He truly is, and he's had a scrapbook career, but every time Ian is interviewed, it's always, *I* discovered, *I* located, *I* apprehended, *I* take all the credit. Jesus, the I-Man? The ego."

Melon laughed again, and Scott felt encouraged. Melon enjoyed talking about the I-Man and seemed willing to discuss the case, but Scott cautioned himself to tread carefully.

"Were you pissed at him?"

Melon appeared surprised.

"For what?"

"The business with Beloit. Chasing the diamond connection."

"Him being hooked up with Arnaud Clouzot, the fence? Nah, Ian's the guy who straightened it out. Interpol had a list of Clouzot associates, and Beloit was on the list. It was bogus. Clouzot's business manager invested in a couple of Beloit's projects

381

along with a hundred fifty other people. That's not a connection."

"That's what I mean. Seems he should've checked it out first. Save everyone the trouble."

"Nah, he had to bring it. He had Danzer."

Scott thought for a moment, but didn't recognize the name.

"I don't know it. What's Danzer?"

"You know it. Danzer Armored Cars. Three or four weeks before Pahlasian, a Danzer car on its way from LAX to Beverly Hills was hit. The driver and two guards were killed. Bad guys got twenty-eight million in uncut diamonds, though you didn't hear it on the news. Remember now?"

Scott was quiet for a long time. Pressure built in his temples as he thought about the velvet pouch in his pocket.

"Yeah, vaguely."

"These big heists always end up with Special. Ian heard the rocks were going to France, so he asked Interpol for likely buyers. This was all weeks before Beloit was murdered, so his name meant nothing. But once he gets blown up, if you put Danzer in a world where Beloit is connected to Clouzot, you have to go with it. When you find out they're not connected, Beloit's just

382

another Frenchman who got off the plane that night."

Scott watched gnats circling the avocados. The I-Man was like a gnat circling Beloit. Scott felt the pouch through his pants, and ran his finger over the stones.

Melon swatted the air at a gnat. He checked his hand to see if he had the gnat.

"I hate these damned things."

Scott wanted to ask Melon about the missing disc, but knew he had to be careful. Melon seemed fine with shooting the shit, but if he sensed Scott was investigating the investigation, he might pick up the phone.

"I get it, but I'm curious about something."

"Don't blame you. So am I."

Scott smiled.

"You guys tracked Pahlasian and Beloit from LAX pretty much all the way to the kill zone. Where'd he pick up the diamonds?"

"He didn't."

"I meant before you cleared him. Where did you think he picked them up?"

"I knew what you meant. He didn't. You know what happens when people steal diamonds?"

Melon didn't wait for Scott to answer.

"They find a buyer. Sometimes it's an

insurance company, sometimes a fence like Clouzot. If a fence buys them, you know what the fence has to do? He has to find a buyer, too. We believed Clouzot bought the diamonds earlier, had them in France, and resold them to a buyer here in L.A."

"Meaning Beloit was his delivery boy."

"We had LAX video, baggage claim, parking structure, the restaurant, the bar. Unless somebody tossed him the rocks at a red light — which I considered — it was more likely he carried them in. Not that it mattered. He wasn't in business with Clouzot, so the whole diamond thing was a mirage. You watch. Bud's going to find out one or both of these people borrowed from the wrong guy and couldn't hide behind Chapter Eleven."

Scott felt he had pushed enough. He wanted to learn about Danzer, and decided to wind up his visit with Melon.

"Listen, Chris, thanks for letting me visit. Reading the file is an eye-opener. You did a great job."

Melon nodded, and gave Scott a tiny smile.

"Appreciate it, but all I can say is, if you're reading that file, you must be getting a lot of sleep."

Melon laughed, and Scott laughed with

him, but then Melon sobered and leaned toward him.

"Why are you here?"

Maggie looked up.

Melon's eyes were webbed with lines, but clear and thoughtful. Melon had retired with thirty-four years on the job, and almost twenty in Robbery-Homicide. He had probably interviewed two thousand suspects, and put most of them in prison.

Scott knew he had crossed the line, but he wondered what Melon was thinking.

"What if Beloit had diamonds?"

"I'd find that interesting."

"Danzer unsolved?"

Melon's clear eyes never moved.

"Solved. Case closed."

Scott was surprised, but read nothing in Melon's eyes other than a thoughtful detachment.

"Did you talk to them?"

"Too late."

Scott read something in the unmoving eyes.

"Why?"

"They were found shot to death in Fawnskin thirty-two days after you were shot. They'd been dead at least ten days."

Fawnskin was a small resort town in the

385

San Bernardino Mountains, two hours east of L.A.

"The crew who took Danzer? Positive IDs?"

"Positive. Professional takeover bandits. Long records."

"That isn't positive."

"A gun matching the weapon used to kill the Danzer driver was found. Two uncut rocks were also found. Insurance company confirmed the rocks were part of the Danzer shipment. Positive enough?"

Scott slowly nodded.

"I guess it's supposed to be."

"Regardless, if I had to bet, I would bet they did it."

"Were the diamonds recovered?"

"Not so far as I know."

Scott found this an odd comment.

"Who killed them?"

"They were in a crappy cabin on the side of a mountain with no other cabins near by. The theory is, they hid out up there after the robbery, shopped for a buyer, and got ripped off."

"Two months after the robbery?"

"Two months after the robbery."

"You buy it?"

"Not sure. I'm trying to decide."

Scott searched Melon's eyes, and wondered if the man was giving him permission to ask more.

"Thirty-two days. You blew off Beloit before they were found."

"This is true, but closing Danzer was a nice capper. It put the knife in any lingering doubts."

"Who closed it?"

"San Bernardino Sheriffs."

"Danzer was our case. Who closed it for us?"

"Ian."

Melon pushed slowly to his feet, groaning like an old man.

"Sitting makes me stiff. C'mon, let's get you on your way. It's a longer drive than you think."

Scott once more debated showing the diamonds to Melon as they walked to his car. Melon had obviously been thinking about these things, but only offered cryptic answers requiring Scott to read between the lines. This meant Melon was still on the fence, afraid, or playing Scott to learn what he knew. Scott decided the diamonds would stay in his pocket. He could not reveal the diamonds or Amelia to anyone he didn't trust.

Scott let Maggie hop into the car, and turned back to Melon when a last question

387

occurred to him.

"Did you watch the videos yourself?"

"Ha. Maybe Ian does everything himself, but I'm not the I-Man. A case this size, you delegate."

"Meaning someone else checked them."

"You trust what your people tell you."

"Who checked them?"

"Different people. You might find something in the file or the evidence log."

Scott expected this answer, but Melon also appeared to be giving him a direction. Then Melon added more.

"The I-Man makes out he's a one-man show, but don't you believe it. He has help. And you can bet they are people he trusts."

Scott searched the clear, thoughtful eyes, and realized he would find only what Melon allowed him to find.

"Thanks for letting me come out. The apology was overdue."

Scott slid in behind the wheel, started the engine, and rolled down the window. Melon looked past him to Maggie, who was already perched on the console.

"She doesn't get in your way, riding like that?"

"I'm used to it."

Melon shifted his gaze to Scott.

"I may be retired, but I'd still like to see

this case closed. Take your time driving home. Stay safe."

Scott backed out the long drive, and turned toward the freeway, wondering if Melon meant this as a warning or a threat.

Scott adjusted the mirror until he saw Melon, still on his driveway, watching.

34.

Scott climbed onto the Ronald Reagan Freeway, his stomach knotted and sour. He didn't believe Melon would give him up, but Melon had walked him in circles, giving only enough to get. Melon was good, better than Scott had ever imagined, but Melon had given him Danzer.

The Danzer Armored Car robbery had been just another news story to Scott when it happened, of no more importance than any other, and quickly forgotten. During his weeks in the hospital, Scott had no knowledge of the Danzer case, and had not known an overlapping investigation into an armored-car robbery was having a major impact on his own. He had now read a five-inch stack of reports and interviews about Eric Pahlasian, but Pahlasian had no connection with diamonds, so Danzer had not been mentioned. Danzer Armored Car felt like a secret that had been hiding in the file.

When Scott realized the total case file was four or five feet thick, he wondered how many more secrets were hiding.

The Santa Susana Pass was directly ahead, with the San Fernando Valley beyond it. After a while, Maggie left the console, stretched out across the back seat, and closed her eyes. After all the effort to make her sit in back, he missed having her next to him.

Scott rolled up his window, and checked his cell. His K-9 Platoon Lieutenant, the Metro Commander, and a woman who identified herself as an Internal Affairs Group detective named Nigella Rivers had left messages. Scott deleted them without listening. Budress had not called, and neither had Richard Levin. Joyce Cowly hadn't called, either.

Scott wanted to call her. He wanted to hear her voice, and he wanted her to be on his side, but he didn't know if he could trust her. He wanted to tell her everything, and show her the diamonds, but he could not put Amelia and her baby at risk. He had done this to Daryl. He had painted a target on Daryl's back, and someone had pulled the trigger.

Scott drove on in silence, holding the phone in his lap. He glanced in the mirror.

Maggie still slept. He touched the pouch through his pants to make sure it was real. He didn't know what to do next or where to go, so he drove the lonely miles across the top of the Valley, thinking. He could start with the Internet. Search old news stories about Danzer and the dead men found on the mountain. See if the I-Man was mentioned. Search the stories for someone named Snell.

Sooner or later, he would go back to Cowly, and he needed something to back up Amelia's story. He needed something that would convince her to help him without risking Amelia's life.

Scott's phone rang as he approached the I-5 interchange. He didn't recognize the number, so he let the call go to voice mail. When the phone told him a message was waiting, he played back the message, and heard a bright male voice he didn't recognize.

"Oh, hey, Detective James, this is Rich Levin, returning your call. Sure, whatever you want. I'm happy to answer your questions or help however I can. You have the number, but here it is again."

Scott didn't wait for the number. He hit the call back button. Rich Levin answered on the first ring.

"Hi, this is Rich."

"Scott James. Sorry, I was on another call."

"Oh, hey, no problem. We didn't meet before, did we? I don't remember your name."

"No, sir, we didn't. I've only been with the investigation for a couple of weeks."

"Uh-huh, okay, I see."

"You recall being interviewed by Detectives Melon and Stengler?"

"Oh, for sure. You bet."

"Regarding customers named Pahlasian and Beloit?"

"The men who were murdered. Absolutely. I felt so bad. I mean, here they were enjoying themselves — well, not here, but at the club — and five minutes later this terrible thing happens."

Levin liked to talk, which was good. More importantly, he was one of those people who liked to talk to police officers, which was better. Scott had met many such people. Levin enjoyed the interaction, and he would bend over backwards to help.

"The casebook here indicates you provided two video disc recordings from the night Pahlasian and Beloit were at the club."

"Uh-huh. That's right."

"Did you deliver them personally to

Detective Melon?"

"No, I don't think he was there. I left them with an officer there in the lobby. At that desk. He said that was fine."

"Ah, okay. And this was two discs, not one."

"That's right. Two."

"Two different discs, or two copies of the same disc?"

"No, no, they were different. I explained this to Detective Melon."

"He retired, so he isn't here. I'm trying to make sense of these files and log entries, and between me and you, I'm lost."

Richard Levin laughed.

"Oh, hey, I totally get it. Here's what happened. I burned one disc off the inside camera and one off the outside camera. They feed to separate hard drives, so it was easier that way."

Scott flashed on the parking lot outside Club Red, and felt an adrenaline rush.

"A camera covers the parking lot?"

"Mm-hm. That's right. I clipped the time from their arrival to their departure. That's what Detective Melon said he wanted."

Secret pieces appeared. One by one, they snapped together. A pressure in Scott released like a cracking knuckle.

Maggie sensed something, and stirred

394

behind him. He glanced in the mirror, and saw her stand.

Scott said, "I'm embarrassed to say this, really, but it looks like we lost the outside disc."

"No worries. That isn't a problem."

The man sounded so confident Scott wondered if Levin had walked them to their car, and could describe the entire evening.

"Do you recall what Pahlasian or Beloit did in the parking lot?"

"I can do better than that. I have copies. I'll burn a replacement for you. That way nobody gets in trouble."

Levin laughed when he said it, and the adrenaline burn grew fierce.

"That's great, Mr. Levin. We don't want anyone to get in trouble."

"I can send them or drop them? That same address?"

"I'll pick them up. Now, tonight, tomorrow morning. It's kind of important."

Scott drove on as they worked it out. Maggie climbed onto the console, and rode at his side until they left the freeway.

35.

JOYCE COWLY

At ten-oh-four the next morning, Cowly was in her cubicle. She stood, straightened her pants, and used the opportunity to check the squad room. Orso was in the LT's office, discussing Daryl Ishi's murder with Topping, Ian Mills, two Rampart Homicide detectives, and an IAG rat. The rat was grilling Orso about Scott's access to the case file. They were digging for some sort of administrative violation, and Orso was pissed. Cowly had already been questioned, and expected to be questioned again.

Two-thirds of the squad cubicles were empty, which was typical with detectives out working cases. The remaining cubicles were occupied, including the cubicle next door. Her neighbor was a D-III named Harlan Meeks, but Meeks was on the phone with one of his four girlfriends, flashing his perfect false teeth and shoveling bullshit.

Cowly sat, picked up her phone, and resumed her conversation.

"Okay, keep going. Does it match or not?"

The SID criminalist, John Chen, sounded smug.

"Tell me I'm a genius. I want to hear those words drip over your luscious, beautiful lips."

"You'll hear the sound of a harassment charge. Knock off the crap."

Chen turned sulky.

"I guess we were too busy flirting to pay attention in science class. Only iron and iron alloys rust, and rust, by definition, is iron oxide. Hence, all rust is the same."

"So you can't tell?"

"Of course I can tell. That's why I'm a genius. I didn't look at the rust. I looked at what's *in* the rust. In this case, paint. Both samples contain paint residue showing titanium dioxide, carbon, and lead in identical proportions."

"Meaning, the rust on the watchband came from the fence?"

"That's what I said."

Cowly put down her phone and stared at the picture of her niece and nephews. Her brother was making noise about a family cruise to Alaska. It was one of those ten- or eleven-day voyages where you sail from Vancouver, follow the Canadian coast from port to port, and end up in Alaska. See glaciers, he said. Killer whales. Cowly had her fill of killers on the job.

Orso and the others were still locked in conversation. Cowly got up, and wound her way past Topping's office to the coffeepot. She took her time, trying to eavesdrop. The faces in these meetings changed, but the talk remained the same, and Cowly found it troubling. People who should have no knowledge of such things discussed Scott James' psychiatric and medical history with authoritative detail as they debated a warrant for his arrest. It seemed like a done deal.

The I-Man noticed her lingering at the coffee machine, and closed the door. Cowly dumped the coffee and returned to her cubicle.

The phone rang as she settled into her chair.

"Detective Cowly."

Scott James asked her the damnedest question.

"Can I trust you?"

She straightened enough to glance next door. Meeks was still on with his girlfriend, laughing too hard at something she said. Cowly lowered her voice.

"Excuse me?"

"Are you a bad cop, Joyce? Are you part of this?"

His voice was so strained she grew scared the people in Topping's office were right. She lowered her voice even more.

"Where are you?"

"Someone broke into my home. The next night, someone broke into my shrink's office and stole my file. Dr. Charles Goodman. North Hollywood detectives Broder and Kurland have it. Call. So you know this is real."

"What are you talking about?"

"Call. Whoever stole Goodman's file is feeding the information to someone inside the department, and that someone is trying to frame me."

Cowly checked the squad room. No one was listening or paying attention.

"I don't like where you're going with this."

"I don't like living it."

"Why did you run? You know how bad that looks?"

"I didn't run. I'm getting it done."

"What are you getting done?"

"I have things to show you. I'm not far away."

"What things?"

"Not over the phone."

"Don't be dramatic. I'm on your side. I had SID check the rust on Daryl's watchband. It matches the rust on the roof, okay? He was there."

"I can beat that. I have the missing disc."

She checked Topping's office. The door was still closed. Meeks was still on with his girlfriend.

"The Club Red disc? Where would you get the missing disc?"

"The manager kept copies. You want to see this, Joyce. Know why you want to see it?"

She knew what he thought, and gave him his own answer.

"Someone doesn't want me to."

"Yep. Someone up there with you."

"Who would this be?"

"Ian Mills."

"Are you crazy?"

"That's what they say. Call North Hollywood."

"I don't need to call them. Where are you?"

"Left turn out of the building, walk across Spring Street. If it's safe, I'll pick you up."

"Jesus, Scott, what do you think will happen?"

"I don't know. I don't know who to trust."

"Give me five minutes."

"Come alone."

"I get it."

When Cowly put down the phone, she realized her hands were shaking. She rubbed them together as Topping's door opened, and the sudden surprise made them shake worse. Ian Mills came out, followed by the IAG rat and one of the Rampart dicks. Mills glanced at her, so she snatched up her phone and pretended to talk. He glanced at her again as he passed, but kept going and left the squad room.

Cowly continued her fake conversation, waiting to see if Orso emerged. She waited for thirty seconds, then put down the phone, slung her purse on her shoulder, and quickly left the building.

36.

Scott let the Trans Am idle forward. He watched the Boat's entrance from across City Hall Park. Maggie was on the console, with the AC blowing in her face. The cold air rippled her fur. She seemed to like it.

Scott hoped Cowly would show, but wasn't sure she would. Ten minutes had passed. He grew afraid she was telling Orso or the other dicks about his call, and the passing time meant they were figuring out what to do.

Cowly appeared beneath the Boat's glass prow and walked quickly toward Spring Street. She stopped at the corner for the light to change, and started across. Scott watched the prow, but no one appeared to be following her. He pulled up beside her at the next corner, and rolled down the window.

"Did you tell anyone?"

"No, I didn't tell anyone. Can you get this

dog out of the way?"

Maggie moved to the back seat when Cowly opened the door, almost as if she understood the front seat wasn't large enough.

Cowly dropped into the car, and pulled the door. He could tell she was angry, but it couldn't be helped. He needed her help.

"Jesus, look at this hair. It's going to be all over my suit."

Scott accelerated away, checking his mirror for a tail car.

"I wasn't sure you'd come. Thanks."

"I didn't tell anyone. Nobody's behind us."

Scott took the first turn, and kept an eye on the mirror.

"Suit yourself. Where are we going?"

"Close."

"This better be worth all the drama. I hate drama."

Scott didn't respond. He rounded the block, and a few seconds later badged their way into the Stanley Mosk Courthouse parking lot. Juror parking. They were three blocks from the Boat.

He found a spot in the shade and shut down the engine.

"There's a laptop on the floor by your feet. We'll watch, and you can tell me if I'm being dramatic."

She handed the laptop to him. He opened it to bring it to life, and handed it back. The disc was already loaded. The recording's opening image was frozen in the player's window. It showed a bright, clear, high-angle image of the Club Red parking lot illuminated by infrared light. There were hints of color, though the colors were mostly bleached to grays. The angle included the club's red entrance, the parking attendant's shack on the far side of the entrance, and most of the parking lot. Scott had watched the disc seven times.

Cowly said, "The Club Red parking lot?"

"Outside camera. Before you see this, you need to know a couple of things. I have more than a disc. Daryl saw the shooting. He told a friend about it, and I have the friend."

Cowly looked dubious.

"Is this person credible?"

"Let's watch. Daryl told his friend one of the shooters took a briefcase from the Bentley. I've cued it to the end, when they leave."

Scott leaned close, and touched the Play button. The frozen image immediately snapped to life. Pahlasian and Beloit emerged from the club, and stopped a few paces outside the door. A parking attendant scurried to meet them. Pahlasian gave him a claim check. The attendant ducked into his shack for the keys, then trotted across the parking lot until the camera no longer saw him. Pahlasian and Beloit remained outside the door, talking.

Scott said, "We can fast-forward."

"I'm good."

A minute later, the Bentley heaved into view from the lower right corner of the frame, moving away from the camera. The brake lights flared red, and Pahlasian stepped forward to meet it. The attendant got out, and traded the keys for a tip. Pahlasian got in, but Beloit walked past him to the street in the background. His murky image could be seen on the sidewalk, but he was too far out of the light to be seen clearly. Pahlasian closed his door, and waited.

Scott said, "It goes on like this for twenty-five minutes."

"What?"

"Beloit is waiting for someone. This is the missing time."

"I'm fine."

Two young women as thin as reeds arrived in a Ferrari. A single man left in a Porsche, followed by a middle-aged couple who left in a Jaguar. When the cars entered or left,

405

their headlights flashed over Beloit, who paced back and forth on the sidewalk. Pahlasian remained in the car.

Scott said, "It's coming. Watch."

A car on the street slowly passed Beloit, and stopped. Beloit was lit by its brake lights, and could be seen moving toward the car. Once he passed the brake lights, he could no longer be seen.

Cowly said, "Can you tell what kind of car that is?"

"No. Too dark."

A minute later, Beloit walked from the darkness into the parking lot with a briefcase in his left hand. He got into the Bentley, and Pahlasian pulled away.

Scott stopped the playback, and looked at her.

"Someone in the investigation watched this, right? They told Melon and Stengler there was nothing worth seeing, and then they got rid of the disc."

Cowly slowly nodded. Her eyes seemed lost.

"A briefcase wasn't found in the Bentley."

"No."

"Shit."

"Not yet, but you will. Do you remember the Danzer Armored Car robbery?"

A deep line appeared between her eyebrows.

"Of course. Melon thought Beloit was here for the diamonds."

"Twenty-eight million dollars in uncut, commercial-grade diamonds, right?"

Cowly gave the slow nod again, almost as if she sensed what was coming.

Scott took the velvet pouch with the ugly stain from his pocket, and dangled it between them. Her eyes went to the pouch, and returned to his.

"Daryl didn't only describe what he saw. He gave his friend something he took off one of the bodies after the shooters left. What do you think they are?"

He poured the stones into his hand.

"Holy shit."

"Really? My guess is uncut, commercial-grade diamonds."

She stared at him, not amused.

"You believe the diamonds were in the briefcase?"

"That would be my guess. What's yours?"

"That this stain on the pouch scores a DNA match with Beloit."

"We're on the same page."

Scott poured the stones back into the pouch, and found Cowly still staring at him.

"Who gave these to you?"

"I can't tell you, Joyce. I'm sorry."

"Who did Daryl confess to?"

"I can't tell you. Not yet."

"These things are evidence, Scott. This person has direct knowledge. This is how you build a case."

"This is how you get someone killed. Someone up there murdered Daryl. Someone is trying to frame me for killing three people."

"If this is true, we have to prove it. That's how it's done."

"How, open a case? Go to Orso, and say, hey, what should we do about this? If one person up there knows, everybody knows, and I would be putting a target on this person's back just like I put one on Daryl."

"That's crazy. You didn't kill Daryl."

"I'm glad somebody thinks so."

"You have to trust someone."

Scott glanced at Maggie.

"I do. The dog."

Cowly's face turned hard as glass.

"Fuck. You."

"I trust you, Joyce. You. That's why I called *you.* But I don't know who else is involved."

"Involved in what?"

"Danzer. Everything started with Danzer."

"Danzer closed. Those guys were murdered up in San Bernardino somewhere."

"Fawnskin. One month after the briefcase you saw in this video was stolen from Georges Beloit. The diamonds were never recovered. These diamonds."

Scott dangled the pouch, then pushed it into his pocket.

"The Danzer crew — dead. Beloit and Pahlasian — dead. Daryl Ishi — dead. And the I-Man keeps showing up. West L.A. opened the Danzer case, the I-Man pulled it downtown, and used the West L.A. guys for his task force."

Her mouth was a tight, grim line as Cowly shook her head.

"That's totally normal."

"Fuck normal. Nothing about this is normal. The I-Man shoved Beloit at Melon to convince Melon that Beloit had no connection to the diamonds — the same diamonds Daryl Ishi took off Beloit's body."

"Why would he do that?"

"The same reason someone lied about what they saw on this disc. Because Melon or Stengler or you would eventually find out about Beloit and Clouzot. The I-Man put himself in a position to control what Melon knew. Melon wouldn't question him. Melon had to believe him. He did. Melon told me how it worked."

"You went to Melon?"

"I got a vibe, like he has doubts about Danzer, and how Danzer closed."

Scott could tell she was fitting the pieces together.

"We have to look at the people who opened the case, and see how they're tied with the I-Man. Melon gave me a hint. He told me the I-Man never does anything alone, and only with people he trusts. He wasn't implying they're honest."

"What do you want?"

"A head-shot case. Something so tight they're off the street before they know it, and can't kill anyone else."

"Sooner or later, we'll need Daryl's friend. We need a sworn statement. Whatever this person says has to be checked. We might need a poly."

"When you're ready to lock the cuffs, I'll take you to Daryl's friend."

"We'll need DNA from the pouch, and an order for SID to run it. We'll need the insurance company or some other authority to affirm these diamonds were stolen from Danzer."

"You can have everything."

"Great. Everything. Can I at least have the disc?"

"Why stir the water?"

Cowly sighed, and opened the door.

"I'll walk back. I'll see what I can find out, and let you know."

Scott gave her the last thing.

"Daryl heard a name."

She stopped with one leg out the door, and stared at him.

"One of the shooters called another by name. Snell."

"Are you holding back anything else?"

"No. That's it. Snell."

"Snell."

She got out, closed the door, and started away.

"Stay clear of the I-Man, Joyce. Please. Don't trust anyone."

Cowly stopped, and looked back through the window.

"Too late. I'm trusting you."

Scott watched her walk across the parking lot, and felt his heart breaking.

"You shouldn't."

He had pinned a target on Cowly's back now, and knew he could not protect her.

37.

JOYCE COWLY

Cowly brushed at the last of the dog hair stuck to her pants, and stepped off the elevator. She stared down a hall she had walked for over three years, only now the hall loomed taller and wider and went on forever, and everyone in it watched her. A sharp pain stabbed behind her right eye. She heard her mother's voice, I warned you not to watch so much TV, it must be a brain tumor. If only. Maybe her mother was right, and the tumor had made her as crazy as Scott. Only Scott wasn't crazy. Scott had the disc and the diamonds.

She pushed one foot forward and the next and after a while she entered the squad room. Orso was in his cubicle. Topping's door was open, but now her office was empty. Meeks checked the time like he was anxious to leave. Men and women she had known for three years worked and talked and got coffee.

Are you part of it?

Can I trust you?

Cowly went to the conference room, and sat down with the murder book. She sat facing the door so she could see if someone was coming.

Cowly had spent most of her walk back from the Stanley Mosk Courthouse figuring out how to find out who opened the original Danzer case file at West Los Angeles Robbery. She couldn't ask Ian or anyone who worked with Ian, and she couldn't call West L.A. Robbery. If Scott was right, and these guys were bad, any question about Danzer would be a warning.

Cowly had read the murder book twice and the complete case file once. She had only skimmed the sections referencing Beloit, Arnaud Clouzot, and Danzer. Knowing the Clouzot connection had been discounted by Robbery Special months earlier, she had seen no point in wasting time on a blind alley. She flipped through now, searching for the Danzer case number.

Cowly quickly found the number, and took it back to her cubicle.

She brought up the LAPD File Storage page, and was typing in the number when Orso surprised her.

413

"Have you heard from Scott?"

She swiveled to face him, trying to draw his eye from her computer. He glanced at her screen before he looked at her.

"No. Is he still in the wind?"

Orso's face was pinched.

"Would you mind calling him?"

"Why would I call him?"

"Because I'm asking. I left a message, but nothing. Maybe he'll call you back."

"I don't have his number."

"I'll give it to you. If you reach him, try to talk sense to him. This thing is getting out of hand."

"Okay. Sure."

He glanced at her computer again, and turned away.

"Bud. You think he killed those people?"

Orso made a face.

"Of course not. I'll get his number."

Cowly cleared her screen, and fidgeted until Orso returned. She typed in her file request as soon as he was gone. Officers were only allowed to request materials relevant to a case they were working on, so Cowly provided the number for an unsolved homicide that had been on her table for two years.

Case #WL-166491 appeared as a PDF. The first document was a closure form filled

414

out and signed by Ian Mills, along with a three-page statement describing how Dean Trent, Maxwell Gibbons, and Kim Leon Jones, all deceased, were found and identified as the perpetrators of the Danzer Armored Car robbery. Mills cited and referenced SID and San Bernardino Sheriff's Department reports tying a weapon found as having been a weapon used in the Danzer robbery, as well as Transnational Insurance Corporation documents affirming that the two diamonds found were among those stolen in the robbery. He concluded that the three perpetrators of the robbery were now dead, and as such, the case was rightfully being closed.

Boilerplate bullshit.

Cowly skimmed the documents Ian attached, until she found the beginning of the original West L.A. file. It opened with a couple of form documents filled in and signed by the detectives who caught the case, followed by a scene report describing how the detectives received their orders to report to the scene, and what they found when they arrived. Cowly didn't bother reading it. She skipped to the end. The report was signed by Detective George Evers and Detective David Snell.

Cowly blanked her screen.

Orso was in his cubicle, talking on the phone. Topping's door was closed. She stood, took in the room, then sat and stared at the screen.

She said, "You sonofabitch."

Cowly abruptly stood, and walked down the hall to the Robbery squad room. Same cubicles, same carpet, same everything. A Robbery detective named Amy Linh was in the first cubicle.

"Is Ian here?"

"I think so. I just saw him."

Cowly walked back to Ian's office. The I-Man was scribbling something on a report when Cowly walked in. He looked surprised when he saw her, and maybe a little watchful.

"Ian, you have more names to go with those white sideburns? We gotta bust these low-life, scumbag pieces of shit. We gotta fuck'm up."

She wanted to see him. She wanted to say it.

"I hear ya. I'll get you those names as soon as I can."

Cowly stalked back to her desk.

George Evers.

David Snell.

She wanted to find out everything about them, and she knew how to do it.

38.

IAN MILLS

Robbery Special Section kept extensive files on people who stole for a living, whether they were actively being sought on warrant or not. Not chickenshit perps like teenage car thieves or the clowns who knocked over an occasional gas station, but hard-core professional thieves. Fifty minutes after Cowly left his office, Ian was searching this database for likely white-haired drivers when his email chimed, and he saw the note.

His shoulders tightened when he saw it was an auto-notification from the Storage Bureau. Such notifications were available at the option of the commanding bureau, unit, or closing officer, and Ian had opted to be notified when any of his closed cases were requested. He did this for every case he closed, but he only cared about four. The others were only a cover story.

Ian got up, closed his door, and returned

to his desk. He had only received three notifications since the LAPD adopted the new system. Each time, he was afraid to open them, but all three had turned out to reference meaningless cases. It took him a full thirty seconds to work up his nut before opening it now. Then his belly flushed with acid.

Danzer.

The information provided by the notification was slight. It did not include the name of the requesting officer or agency, only the date and time of request, and the requesting officer's active case number.

The case number told him plenty, and he didn't like what it told him.

The number bore an HSS designator, which meant it was a Homicide Special Section case. Any dick on the Homicide side could walk forty feet, and ask whatever they wanted about Danzer, but someone had chosen to keep him out of the loop. This wasn't good. An active case number was required to process the retrieval, which meant their case file was locked, but Ian had a work-around.

He phoned down the hall, calling Nan Riley. Nan was a civilian employee, and Carol Topping's office assistant.

"Hey, Nanny, it's Ian. Are you as beautiful now as you were ten minutes ago?"

Nan laughed, as she always did. They had flirted for years.

"Only for you, baby. You want the boss?"

"Just a quick answer. You guys have an active down there —"

Ian read off the number.

"Who's on it?"

"Hang on. Let's see here —"

He waited while Nan typed in the number.

"That's Detective Cowly. Joyce Cowly."

"Thanks, babe. You're the best."

Ian put down his phone, and liked this even less. If Cowly was interested in Danzer, he wondered why she didn't mention it when she came to his office. Instead, she had shoveled up some bullshit about nailing the shooters in the Pahlasian case. He mulled over what this might mean, then gathered his things and walked down the hall to Homicide Special.

Cowly was in her cubicle. She was hunched over her computer, and appeared to be on the phone.

He walked up behind her. He tried to see what she was reading, but her head blocked the screen. She spoke so quietly he couldn't hear what she was saying.

"Detective."

She jerked at his voice, and visibly paled

when she turned. She pressed the phone to her chest, and leaned sideways to cover the screen. This wasn't a good sign.

Ian held out the list of names.

"The names you wanted."

She took the page.

"Thanks. I didn't expect it so soon."

He watched shadows move in her eyes. She was afraid. This left him wondering how much the Ishi kid had told Scott James, and how much James told Cowly.

"Happy to help. You going to be here a while?"

"Ah, yeah. Why?"

"I'll try to come up with some others."

Ian returned to his office, closed the door, and used his cell phone to call George Evers.

"We have a problem."

Ian told Evers what he wanted him to do.

39.

Three hours after their earlier meeting, Cowly texted Scott that she had the information about Danzer. They agreed to meet in the Stanley Mosk parking lot, same as before. Scott thought she looked tight and compressed when she got into his car.

"I talked to a friend at Bureau Personnel about Evers and Snell, strictly on the down low. I told her I was thinking about using them on a task force, and needed top people. She understands. This woman was my first supervisor."

"What did you find out?"

"They suck."

Scott wasn't sure what he was supposed to do with that.

"Snell has a rep for smart, efficient case work, but he's sketchy. He likes to take chances and cut corners. He has no history with Ian, but Evers and Ian are hooked through the ass. Jesus, I'm already covered with fur. Look at this."

Maggie was laid out across the back seat.

"I haven't had time to brush. What about Evers?"

Cowly brushed uselessly at her pants, and went on with her report.

"Evers and Ian were partners for four years in Hollenbeck. Evers was the lead, but it was common knowledge Ian carried him. Evers got himself in the tall grass and made a mess of his life. He was drinking, the wife left him, all the usual blue nonsense. Ian covered for him and kept him going, but too many complaints were filed. When Ian jumped to Special, Evers was sent to West L.A."

"What kind of charges are we talking about?"

"Deep-shit charges. You know finders keepers?"

It was cop slang officers joked about, only for bad cops it wasn't a joke. If they found a bag of cash when they made a bust, they left enough to meet the felony statute, and took the rest for themselves. Finders keepers.

"I know. Did any of the dirt stick to the I-Man?"

"Ian came out like a rose. He propped Evers up until Evers got his shit together."

Scott looked at Maggie, and touched her. She opened her eyes.

"It flows both ways."

"What flows?"

"If Ian cleaned up after Evers, there were times Evers cleaned up after Ian."

"Whatever. So now Evers is in West L.A., and his partner is Snell. They had Danzer for all of four days, then Ian sucked it up, and made them his front men. The very next day, that's six days after the robbery, Evers obtained wiretap warrants on Dean Trent and William F. Wu."

Scott had no idea who these people were, but Cowly rolled on like an express train.

"Two months later, Dean Trent, Maxwell Gibbons, and Kim Leon Jones were found murdered in the San Bernardino Mountains."

Scott remembered this from Melon.

"The crew who took Danzer."

"So it's believed, and it's probably true."

Also what Melon said.

"Who's Wu?"

"A fence in San Marino. He deals jewelry and art to rich people in China, but he's hooked up in Europe, too. What makes this telling is Dean Trent and Wu are known to have a long relationship. If Dean Trent steals jewelry or art, you can bet he's going to Wu."

Scott realized where she was going.

"Evers and Snell knew Trent had the diamonds."

"Had to. Maybe one of Ian's informants tipped him. It was only six days after the robbery, and they knew or suspected Dean Trent's crew took the score. So they wired up Trent and Wu, and listened to these guys for the next three weeks. The case file contains no transcripts. None. Zero."

Scott felt numb.

"They heard Wu make the deal with Clouzot. They knew Beloit was arriving, and when and where he would pick up the diamonds. They wanted to steal the diamonds."

Scott looked at Maggie. He touched the tip of her nose, and she play-bit his finger.

"Is this enough to make our case?"

Cowly shook her head.

"No. I wish it was, but it isn't."

"It sounds like enough to me. You can connect the dots from start to finish."

"Here's what Ian would say, we received information from three independent reliable sources Trent was attempting to move the diamonds through Mr. Wu, who we know to have an established history with Mr. Trent. Acting on this reliable information, we obtained the required judicial warrant for wiretap service, but failed in our efforts to obtain incriminating information. We are left to believe Mr. Trent or Mr. Wu communicated only in person or using disposable phones. You see? Nothing here hurts him."

Scott felt himself growing angry.

"Evers, Snell, and Mills make three. Five men hit Beloit."

"No one in what I've seen jumped out at me. Let's focus on who we have. If we can bust these guys, they'll give us the other two."

Scott knew she was right.

"Okay. Are Evers and Snell still on the job?"

"Snell is on the job, but Evers retired six days after the murders."

"That isn't smart."

"I don't know. He had the years. He's older than Ian, so it's not out of line."

"Old enough to have white hair?"

"Jesus. I don't know. I've never seen either one of these people."

Scott thought if Evers was old enough to retire, maybe he was the white-haired, blue-eyed driver, and his DNA would match with the hair follicles recovered from the getaway car.

"Evers is the point man here. You have his

address?"

Cowly leaned back.

"What do you think you'll find, the diamonds? The diamonds are gone. The guns are gone. Every piece of that night is gone."

"We need a direct connection between these people and the robbery, something that puts Evers or Snell or the I-Man there on the scene, right?"

"Yes. If you want this so-called slam-dunk case, that's what we need."

"Okay, I'll nose around. Maybe I'll get lucky."

"Weren't you paying attention when we lectured you about the watchband? Nothing you find will be admissible. Your testimony about whatever you find will not be admissible. It will do us no good."

"I heard you. I won't take anything. If I find something useful, you'll come up with a work-around."

Cowly looked disgusted, but dug through her papers, and found George Evers' address.

"I should have my head examined."

"Have faith."

Cowly rolled her eyes, pushed open the door, and hesitated. She looked concerned.

"You have a safe place to stay?"

"Yeah. Thanks."

"Okay."

Scott watched her get out of the car, and wanted to say more.

"Can I drive you back?"

"I'll walk. It gives me time to pick off the fur."

Scott smiled as she walked away, and pulled out of the parking lot. He went to find George Evers.

40.

JOYCE COWLY

Cowly cut through the Stanley Mosk parking lot, making her way toward the Boat. She picked away dog hair and brushed at her pants as she walked. That German shepherd was a beauty, but she was also a fur machine.

Cowly reached the end of the parking lot, and stepped over a low chain barrier onto the sidewalk. She didn't think they were doing this the right way, and now she worried Scott would contaminate the case. Cowly absolutely believed a conspiracy linked Danzer and the murders of Beloit and Pahlasian, and, by extension, Stephanie Anders, but she and Scott weren't playing it the right way. She knew better, even if he didn't, and she was irritated with herself for going along.

Criminal police conspiracies had always existed, and always would, even within the finest police department in the world. There were protocols for dealing with such investigations, which often had to be conducted in total secrecy until charges were levied. Cowly had a friend who once worked with the Special Operations Division, and planned to ask her advice.

"Detective Cowly! Joyce Cowly!"

She turned to the voice, and saw a nicely dressed man trotting toward her, waving a hand. Tan sport coat over a medium blue shirt and darker blue tie, jeans; he could have trotted off the pages of a Ralph Lauren catalog. His sport coat flapped as he ran, revealing a gold detective shield clipped to his belt.

He slowed to a stop, smiling.

"I hope you don't mind. I saw you at the Mosk."

"Have we met?"

He touched her arm, stepping aside for two women hurrying toward the courthouse.

"I'd like to talk to you about Robbery-Homicide. You going back? I'll walk with you."

He touched her arm again, encouraging her to walk, and fell in beside her. He was relaxed, boyish, and totally charming, but he stood too close. Cowly wondered why he assumed she had come *from* the Boat, and was now going *back*.

A dark blue sedan slid past them and slowed.

Cowly said, "You work Homicide or Robbery?"

"Robbery. I'm good at it, too."

He touched her arm again, as if she should know him, and Cowly felt irritated.

"Now isn't a good time. Give me your card. We can talk another time."

He flashed the boyish smile, and moved so close she teetered on the curb.

"You don't remember me?"

"Not a clue. What's your name?"

The sedan's rear door swung open in front of them.

"David Snell."

He gripped her arm hard, and pushed her into the car.

41.

Sunland was a working-class community in the foothills north of Glendale. Down in the flats, it was arid and dry, and deserving of its name. The neighborhood streets between the freeway and the mountains were lined with small stucco ranch homes, but as the land climbed into Tujunga Canyon, eucalyptus and black walnut trees gave the neighborhoods a rural, country feel. George Evers lived in a clapboard house that might have been a converted barn. He had a large rocky yard, a satellite dish, and a metallic blue powerboat parked on the side of his house. The powerboat was covered, and looked as if it hadn't seen the water in years. Evers had a carport instead of a garage, and the carport was empty.

Scott drove past, turned around, and parked two houses away. Police officers rarely have listed phone numbers, but Scott tried Information, asking for a George Evers in Sunland. Nothing. He studied Evers' house for a while, wondering if anyone was home. The empty carport meant little, but the alternative was to stare at the house forever.

Scott was glad he was wearing civilian clothes. He tucked his pistol under his shirt, let Maggie out, and didn't bother with the leash.

He went to the front door, had Maggie sit to the side out of sight, and rang the bell twice. When no one answered, he walked around the side of the house into the backyard. Scott found no alarms, so he broke the pane from a kitchen window and let himself in. Maggie stretched to reach the window, and whined to follow.

"Sit. Stay."

He opened the kitchen door, called, and Maggie trotted inside. Scott knew she was alerting by her expression. Her head was high, her ears were forward, and her face was furrowed in concentration. She went into a high-speed search, trotting wavy patterns throughout the house as if a scent here concerned her and she was seeking its source.

Scott realized it could only be one thing.

"You got him, don't you? This prick came into our house."

The kitchen, dining room, and family room contained nothing out of the ordinary. Worn, mismatched furniture and paper plates speckled with crumbs. Two framed photos of LAPD officers from the thirties and forties, and a poster from the old TV series *Dragnet,* with Jack Webb and Harry Morgan holding revolvers. It didn't look like the home of a man who banked a five-million-dollar split from the diamonds, but that was the point.

Maggie was calmer when she rejoined him in the family room.

A short hall off the living room led to the bedrooms, but the first room they reached was part storage and part Evers' I-love-me room. Framed photographs of Evers and his LAPD friends dotted the wall. A young, uniformed Evers at his Academy graduation. Evers and another officer posed beside their patrol car. Evers and a blond, sad-eyed woman showing off the gold detective shield he had just received. Evers and a younger Ian Mills at a Hollenbeck crime scene. Scott recognized Evers because Evers appeared in all of the pictures, and as he changed through the years, Scott felt the floor drop from beneath him.

George Evers was bigger than anyone else in the photos. He was a large, thick man with a big belly over his belt, not a soft, flabby belly, but hard.

Scott had no doubt. He knew it in his soul.

George Evers was the big man with the AK-47, and in the moment he realized this he saw the rifle flashing, flashing, flashing.

"Stop."

Scott made himself breathe. Maggie was beside him, whining. He touched her head, and the flashing disappeared.

Nothing on the wall would connect Evers with the crime scene or the diamonds, but Scott couldn't turn away. He glanced from photo to photo until one photo held him. A color shot of Evers and another man on a deep-sea fishing boat. They were smiling, and had their arms across each other's shoulders. The other man was a few years older, and smaller. He was crowned by white hair, and had vivid blue eyes.

Seeing him triggered Scott's memory, which unfolded like a film: The getaway driver lifted his mask as he shouted at the shooters, exposing his white sideburns. The driver faced forward again as the shooters piled into his car, pulled off his mask, and Scott saw his face — this man's face — as the Gran Torino roared away.

Scott was still in the memory when the vibration in his pocket broke the spell. He checked his phone, and found a text message from Cowly.

I FOUND IT

A second message quickly followed the first.

MEET ME

Scott texted back.

FOUND WHAT?

It took several seconds for her answer to arrive.

DIAMONDS. COME

Scott typed back his answer.

WHERE?

He ran to his car, and Maggie ran with him.

42.

MAGGIE

Maggie rode on the console, watching Scott. She noted the nuance of his movements and posture and facial expressions as completely as she noted his scent. She watched his eyes, noting where he looked and for how long and how quickly. She listened to his sounds even when he was not speaking to her. Every gesture and glance and tone was a message, and her way was to read him.

She sipped his changing scent, and tasted a familiar stew — the sour of fear, the bright sweetness of joy, the bitter rose of anger, the burning leaves of tension.

Maggie felt her own anticipation growing. She recalled similar signs in the moments before she and Pete walked the long roads, Pete strapping up, gathering himself, the other Marines doing the same. She remembered their words. Strap up. Strap up. Strap up.

Maggie whined with excitement.

Scott touched her, filling her heart with joy.

They would walk the long road.

Scott was strapped up.

Maggie danced from paw to paw, anxious and ready. The fur on her spine rippled from tail to shoulders as the taste of blood filled her mouth.

Pack would seek.

Pack would hunt.

Maggie and Scott.

War dogs.

43.

Scott left the Hollywood Freeway only a few blocks from the Boat, and crossed the First Street Bridge to the east side of the Los Angeles River. The east side was lined with warehouses, small factories, and processing plants. He drove south between lines of big rig trucks, searching for Cowly's location.

"Take it easy, baby. Settle. Settle."

Maggie was on her feet, nervously moving back and forth between the console and back seat. When she was on the console, she peered through the windshield as if she were searching for something. Scott wondered what.

He turned between two bustling warehouses, and spotted the empty building behind them, the remains of a bankrupt shipping company set well back from the street. It was lined with loading docks built for eighteen-wheel trucks, and marked by a big FOR SALE OR LEASE sign by the entrance.

"There she is."

A light tan D-ride was parked by the loading dock. The big loading door was closed, but a people-sized door beside it was open.

Maggie dipped her head to see, and her nostrils flickered.

Scott pulled up beside the D-ride, and sent a quick text.

HERE

He was getting out when he received Cowly's reply.

INSIDE

Scott let Maggie hop out, and headed for the door. He wondered how Cowly learned about this place, and why the diamonds were here, but didn't much care one way or the other. He wanted this to be the needle that slid into Evers' vein; Evers, the I-Man, and the rest of them.

The warehouse was dim, but lit well enough. The great, empty room was wide enough for four trucks, thirty feet high, and broken only by support pillars as big around as trees. Doors on the far side of the warehouse led to offices. One of the doors was open, and showed light.

Maggie lowered her head, and sniffed.

"Hey, Cowly! You in there?"

Scott stepped inside, and Maggie moved with him. He wondered why Cowly hadn't waited in her car, and why she hadn't come out when he arrived.

Scott called to the open door on the far side of the warehouse.

"Cowly! Where are you?"

Cowly didn't answer. Not even a text.

Scott was moving deeper into the building when Maggie alerted. She froze in place, head down, ears forward, and stared.

Scott followed her gaze, but saw only the empty warehouse and the open door on the far wall.

"Maggie?"

Maggie suddenly looked behind them, and faced the door to the parking lot. She cocked her head and growled, and her growl was a warning.

Scott ran back to the door, and saw two men with pistols coming from the end of the building. One was a man in his thirties wearing a tan sport coat, and the other was George Evers' white-haired fishing buddy. Scott felt sick. His heart pounded. The instant he recognized the white-haired

440

driver, he realized Mills and Evers knew. They had taken Cowly or murdered her, and baited him into a trap.

Then the white-haired man saw Scott, and fired.

Scott shot back, and scrambled away. He thought he hit the older man but he was moving too fast to know.

"Maggie!"

Scott ran through the warehouse toward the far door. The younger man appeared behind him, and fired twice. Scott cut sideways, fired again, and took cover behind the nearest support pillar. He pulled Maggie close.

The man in the tan jacket fired twice more, and a bullet slammed into the pillar.

Scott made himself as small as he could, and held Maggie tight. He glanced at the offices, and prayed Cowly was alive. He shouted as loud as he could.

"COWLY! ARE YOU HERE?"

Stephanie Anders, Daryl Ishi, and now Joyce Cowly.

His personal body count was climbing, and he might be next.

Scott checked the front door, then the door to the offices behind him. He was so scared and angry he trembled. If Evers and the I-Man and the other shooter were there,

they had him boxed. Sooner or later someone with a gun would show in the office
door, and finish what they started nine
months ago. They would kill him, and probably kill Maggie, too.

He pulled her closer.

"No one gets left behind, okay? We're
partners. Cowly, too, if she's here."

Maggie licked his face.

"Yeah, baby. I love you, too."

Scott ran for the office door. Maggie ran
with him, then stretched out and ran ahead.

"Maggie, no! Come back here."

She ran for the door.

"Heel!"

She ran through the door.

"Maggie, out! OUT!"

Maggie was gone.

Maggie

Maggie felt Scott's fear and excitement
when they entered the building, and knew
it as her own. This place was rich with the
scent of threats and danger. Loud noises
like she heard on the long road, the intruder's fresh scent, and the scents of others.
Scott's own rising fear.

Her place was with him.

Please him and protect him.

If Scott wanted to play in this dangerous

442

place, it was her joy to play with him, though each loud noise made her cringe.

Scott ran deeper into the big room and Maggie ran at his side. More loud noises came, and Scott held her close. Approval! Praise!

Alpha happy.

Pack happy.

Her heart was joy and devotion.

Maggie knew the intruder was ahead, as clearly as if she could see through the walls. His fresh, living scent grew brighter as the scent cone narrowed.

Scott ran, Maggie ran, knowing she must protect him. She must drive the intruder away or destroy him.

Maggie lengthened her stride, seeking the threat.

Scott commanded her to stop, but Maggie did not stop. She was strapped up.

Alpha safe.

Pack safe.

Maggie knew nothing else. The air was alive with the scents of intruders and other men, some familiar, some not; she smelled their fear and anxiety. She smelled gun oil and leather and sweat.

They were strapped up, too.

Maggie reached the door well before Scott, and saw another door ahead. The intruder and another man were waiting beyond it.

Ten thousand generations filled her with a guardian's rage.

Scott was hers to care for, and hers to keep.

She would not let him be harmed.

She would rather die.

Maggie ran hard up the cone to save him.

Joyce Cowly

Snell and Evers left Cowly tied and gagged in the I-Man's trunk like a stupid girl victim in an old TV show. Cowly had stayed her own execution with a call-your-bluff play. She told them Orso knew. She identified the captain friend at Bureau Personnel who had given her the background on Evers and Snell, and her story rang true enough to make Ian hesitate. Better for him to check out her story than kill her too quickly. Staying his hand might mean the difference between beating the rap and taking the needle.

But Ian would not stay his hand forever. Cowly could identify four of the five men who murdered Pahlasian, Beloit, and Stephanie Anders. The white-haired driver was George Evers' older brother, Stan. The fifth man was not present, though she had learned his name was Barson.

Cowly knew too much to live. Ian would kill her as soon as he checked her story and came up with a work-around to explain her death.

So now Cowly was in the trunk, furious, and fighting down the pain. She wasn't stupid and didn't intend to be a victim, on this day or any other.

The plasticuffs cut down to the bone. She lost a deep flap of meat on her hand, but she twisted free. She found the trunk release, and let herself out. Blood ran from her hand like water from a faucet.

Ian and Stan had parked behind the warehouse. Her gun and phone were gone, so Cowly tried to get into their cars, but both were locked. She found a lug wrench in Ian's trunk.

Cowly was still blinking at the harsh California light when she heard gunfire within the warehouse. She could have run down the street for help, but she knew Ian had used her phone to text Scott. Ian planned to kill them that day, and he might be killing Scott now.

Cowly ran toward the building, leaving a blood trail in the dust.

Maggie

Maggie sprinted into the dim room and reached the end of the cone. The intruder loomed tall and large, with his scent burning as brightly as if he was on fire. Maggie knew the second man's scent, but ignored him even though he spoke.

"Watch out! The dog!"

The intruder turned, but was slow and heavy.

Maggie snarled as she charged, and the man threw up his arms.

Maggie caught him below the elbow. She bit deep, snarling and growling as she savagely shook her head. The taste of his blood was her reward.

The man stumbled back, screaming.

"Get it off! Get it!"

The other man moved, but was only a shadow.

Maggie twisted, trying to pull down the intruder. He stumbled backwards into a wall, flailing, screaming, but stayed on his feet.

The other man shouted.

"I can't get a shot! Shoot it yourself, damnit! Kill it!"

Their words were meaningless noise, as Maggie fought hard to pull him down.

"Kill it!"

Scott James

Scott ran harder, afraid for his dog. She was trained to enter houses without him, and face danger alone, but she did not understand what she faced. Scott knew, and was scared for both of them.

"Maggie, OUT! Wait for me, damnit!"

Scott heard Maggie snarling as he reached the door, and found himself in a short hall. A man screamed.

A gunshot boomed behind him, and a bullet snapped into the wall. Scott glanced back. The man in the sport coat was chasing him.

Scott steadied his pistol against the door, and squeezed off one shot even as the snarls and screaming grew louder.

The man in the sport coat went down, and Scott turned toward the snarls.

Ian Mills shouted.

"I can't get a shot! Shoot it yourself, damnit! Kill it!"

Scott thought, *I'm coming.* He ran toward the voice.

The hall opened into a large, barren utility room with dirty windows. Ian Mills was on the far side of the room, waving a gun. George Evers was stumbling sideways along the wall with Maggie hanging from his arm. Evers was big, a big strong man with a big

447

belly, maybe even bigger than Scott remembered, but he couldn't escape her. Then Scott saw his pistol, and the pistol swung toward Maggie.

The muzzle kissed her shoulder.

A voice in Scott's head screamed, or maybe the voice was his own, or maybe Stephanie's.

I won't leave you.

I'll protect you.

A man does not let his partner die.

Scott slammed into the gun, and felt it go off. He did not feel the bullet, or his ribs break when the bullet punched through him. He felt only the pressure of hot gas blow into his skin.

Scott shot George Evers as he fell. He saw Evers wince, and clutch at his side. Scott bounced on the concrete floor as Evers stumbled sideways. The I-Man was in the shadows, but was swept by light when an outside door opened. Joyce Cowly may have come in, but Scott was not sure. Maggie stood over him, and begged him not to die.

He said, "You're a good girl, baby. The best dog ever."

She was the last thing he saw as the world faded to black.

Joyce Cowly

The gunshots were loud, so loud Cowly knew they were on the other side of the door. She pushed into the warehouse, and found Ian Mills in front of her. Scott was on the floor, Evers was down on a knee, and the dog was going crazy.

Mills turned at the sound of the door, and looked surprised to see her. He was holding a gun, but it was pointed the wrong way.

Cowly swung hard, and split his forehead with the lug wrench. He staggered sideways and dropped the gun. Cowly hit him again, above the right ear, and this time he fell. She scooped up his gun, checked him for other weapons, and scored his cell phone.

The dog stood over Scott, barking and snapping in a frenzy as Evers crabbed past, trying to reach the far door.

Cowly pointed her gun at him, but the damned dog was in the way.

"Evers! Put it down. Lower it, man. You're done."

"Fuck you."

The dog was acting like she wanted to gut Evers, but she wouldn't leave Scott to do it.

"You're shot. I'll get an ambulance."

"Fuck you."

Evers fired a single wide shot and scrambled into the warehouse.

Cowly called the Central Station's emergency number, recited her name and badge number, told them she had an officer down, and requested assistance.

She checked Mills again, then ran to help Scott, but the dog lunged at her and stopped Cowly cold.

Maggie's eyes were crazy and wild. She barked and snarled, showing her fangs, but Scott lay in a pool of blood, and the red pool was growing.

"Maggie? You know me. That's a good girl, Maggie. He's bleeding to death. Let me help him."

Cowly edged closer, but Maggie lunged again. She ripped Cowly's sleeve, and once more stood over Scott. Her paws were wet with his blood.

Cowly gripped the gun, and felt her eyes fill.

"You gotta move, dog. He's going to die if you don't move."

The dog kept barking, snarling, snapping. She was wild with an insane fury.

Cowly checked the pistol. She made sure the safety was off as tears spilled from her eyes.

"Don't make me do this, dog, okay? Please don't."

The dog didn't move. She wouldn't get

450

off him. She wouldn't leave.

"Dog, please. He's dying."

Maggie lunged at her again.

Cowly aimed, crying harder, but that's when Scott raised a hand.

Scott James

Scott was floating in darkness when he heard her call.

Scotty, come back.

Don't leave me, Scotty.

Scott drifted toward her voice.

I won't leave you.

I never left.

I won't leave you now.

He drifted closer, and the darkness grew light.

The voice became barking.

Scott opened his eyes, and reached up.

Maggie

Maggie attacked the intruder with primal ferocity, and fought to bring him down. Her fangs had been designed for this. They were long, sharp, and curved inward. They sank deep, and when he tried to pull away, his own struggles forced them deeper, making his escape even less likely. Her fangs, as was her bone-crushing jaw, were gifts from her wild ancestors before her kind were tamed.

451

The tools for killing were in her DNA.

Scott safe.

Pack safe.

She had ranged ahead to protect him, but now her heart soared when Scott entered the room.

They were pack.

A pack of two, they were one.

Scott attacked, fighting beside her and for her, fighting as pack, and Maggie's soaring heart filled with bliss.

A loud, sharp crack ended it.

Scott fell, and his changing scents confused her. His pain and fear washed through her as if they were her own. The smell of his blood filled her with fire.

Alpha hurt.

Alpha dying.

Maggie's world shrank to Scott.

Protect. Protect and defend.

Maggie released the intruder, and turned to Scott. She frantically licked his face, whined, cried, and snarled her rage at the intruder as he crawled past them. She stood over Scott, and snapped her jaws as a warning.

Protect.

Guard.

The intruder ran away, but the woman approached. Maggie knew her, but the woman was not pack.

Maggie snarled, warning the woman. She barked and snapped. Maggie slashed the woman's arm and held her at bay. Then she felt Scott's calming touch.

Maggie's heart leaped with happiness. She licked his face, healing him with her heart, as his heart now healed her.

Scott opened his eyes.

"Maggie."

She was instantly alert.

Maggie looked into his eyes, watching, waiting, wanting his command.

Scott glanced toward the big room beyond the door.

"Get'm."

Maggie leaped over Scott without hesitation and sprinted after the intruder. His fresh blood scent was easy to follow.

She powered up the scent cone, stretching and pulling, and closed on him in seconds. She flashed through the warehouse, outside into the sun, and saw the man who hurt Scott stumbling toward a car.

Maggie ran harder, joy in her heart, for this was what Scott wanted.

She will get'm.

The man saw her coming, and raised a gun. Maggie knew this was an act of aggression, but this was all she understood.

His aggression fueled her rage, and darkened her purpose.

She stared at his throat.

She will get'm.

Scott safe.

Pack safe.

Maggie launched herself into the air, baring her fangs, jaws open wide, her heart filled with a terrible, perfect bliss.

She saw the flash.

44.

Eleven Hours Later
Keck/USC Hospital
Emma Wilson, ICU/Recovery Nurse

Three female nurses and two female surgeons told her the waiting room was filled with hunky young cops. Emma was dying to see, even though they also warned her about the nasty old Sergeant who scowled and shouted. He'll be on you like an attack dog, they told her.

Emma was curious about him most of all, and she wasn't afraid. She had been a head floor nurse for almost twenty years, and damn few doctors had the balls to stand up to her.

She put away Officer James' chart, told her staff she would be back in a minute, and pushed through the double doors into the hall.

Emma Wilson had seen this kind of thing before when officers were brought in, but

455

the sight always moved her.

Dark blue uniforms spilled from the waiting room, and crowded the hall. Male officers, female officers, officers in civilian clothes with their badges clipped to their belts.

"What in hell is going on in there?"

His voice cut through the hall, and every officer turned.

Emma wheeled around, and thought, yep, you're him.

A tall thin uniformed Sergeant pushed through the crowd. Bald on top, hair short and gray on the sides, and the nastiest scowl she had ever seen.

Emma held up a hand, motioning for him to stop, but he stalked right up to her until his chest touched her hand. He scowled down his nose.

"I am Sergeant Dominick Leland, and Officer James is *mine.* How is my officer doing?"

Emma stared up at him, and lowered her voice.

"Take one step back."

"Goddamnit, if I have to go back there to —"

"One. Step. Back."

His eyes bulged so wide she thought they would pop from his head.

"Please."

Leland stepped back.

"The surgeon will be out to give you more details, but I can tell you he came through the surgery well. He woke a few minutes ago, but now he's sleeping again. This is normal."

A murmur swept through the officers filling the hall.

Leland said, "He's okay?"

"The surgeon will answer your questions, but, yes, he appears to be doing fine."

The fierce scowl softened and the Sergeant sagged with relief. Emma thought he seemed older, and tired, and not nearly so fearsome.

"All right then. Thank you —"

He glanced at her name tag.

"Nurse Wilson. Thank you for helping him."

"Is Maggie here?"

Leland stood taller, and the edge returned to his eyes.

"Officer James is in my K-9 Platoon. Maggie is his police service dog."

Emma didn't expect Maggie to be a dog, but she was touched by the idea, and nodded.

"When he woke, he asked if Maggie was safe."

The Sergeant stared, and seemed unable to speak. His eyes filled, and he blinked hard to fight the tears.

"He asked after his dog?"

"Yes, Sergeant. I was with him. He said, 'Is Maggie safe?' He didn't say anything else. What should I tell him when he wakes?"

Leland wiped his eyes before he answered, and Emma saw two of his fingers were missing.

"You tell him Maggie is safe. Tell him Sergeant Leland will look after her, and keep her safe until he returns."

"I'll tell him, Sergeant. Now, as I said earlier, the surgeon will be out shortly. All of you rest easy."

Emma turned for the double doors, but Leland stopped her.

"Nurse Wilson, one more thing."

When she turned back, Leland's eyes were filled again.

"Yes, Sergeant?"

"Tell him I will continue to pretend I have not seen that dog limp. Please tell him. He will understand."

Emma assumed this was a private joke, so she didn't ask for an explanation.

"I'll tell him, Sergeant. I'm sure he will be happy to hear it."

Emma Wilson stepped through the double doors, thinking how wrong the others were about the scowling Sergeant. He was a sweetheart, once you got past the fierce scowl, and stood up to him.

All bark and no bite.

45.

Sixteen Weeks Later

Scott James jogged slowly across the field at the K-9 training facility. His side hurt more now, after the second shooting, than it had after the first. A full bottle of painkillers was back at his guest house. He told himself he should stop being stubborn and take them, but he didn't. Being stubborn was good. He was stubborn about being stubborn.

Dominick Leland scowled as Scott lurched to a stop.

"I see my dog here is responding to her injections. I have not seen her limp in almost two months."

"She's my dog, not yours."

Leland puffed himself up, and swapped a glare for the scowl.

"The hell you say! Every one of these outstanding animals is my dog, and best you not forget it."

Maggie gave him a low, menacing growl.

Scott touched her ear, and smiled when her tail wagged.

"Whatever you say, Sergeant."

"You may be the toughest, most stubborn sonofabitch I've ever met."

"Thank you, Sergeant."

Leland glanced at Maggie.

"The vet tells me her hearing is better."

After the warehouse, Leland and Budress noticed that Maggie didn't hear so well with her left ear. The vets tested her, looked in her ears, and determined she had suffered a partial hearing loss. Something about nerve trauma, but the loss was temporary. They prescribed drops. One drop in the morning, one every night.

Leland and Budress decided it happened when she ran down George Evers in the parking lot. He tried to shoot her at point-blank range. He missed, but she was only inches from the gun when he fired. Evers survived, and was currently serving three consecutive life sentences, as were Ian Mills, David Snell, and the fifth member of their crew, Michael Barson. These were the terms of a sentencing agreement they accepted to avoid the needle. Scott was disappointed. He wanted to testify at their trials. Stan Evers died at the warehouse.

Scott touched Maggie's head. It was a

close call.

"She hears fine, Sergeant. Comes when I call her."

"She gettin' those drops?"

"One in the morning, one at night. We never miss."

Leland grunted approvingly.

"As it should be. Now, they tell me you are still refusing to accept a medical retirement."

"Yes, sir. That would be true."

"Good. You stay stubborn and tough, Officer James, and I will be with you every step of the way. I will back you one hundred percent."

"Gettin' my back?"

"If you choose to see it that way. And when all the back-gettin' is done, and you can move faster than an old man like me, you and this beautiful dog will still be here. You are a dog man. This is where you belong."

"Thank you, Sergeant. Maggie thanks you, too."

"No thanks are necessary, son."

Scott offered his hand, and Leland shook.

Maggie made the growl again, and Leland broke into a wide, beaming smile.

"Would you look at yourself, growling like that? You lived in my house for damn near two months, and you were my lapdog! Now you are back with our friend here, and you got nothin' but growls!"

Maggie growled again.

Leland burst into a great booming laugh, and headed back to his office.

"My God, I love these dogs. I do so love these fine animals."

"Sergeant —"

Leland kept walking.

"Thanks for pretending. And everything else."

Leland raised a hand, and called over his shoulder.

"No thanks are necessary."

Scott watched him walk away, and bent to stroke Maggie's head. Bending hurt, but Scott didn't mind. The hurt was part of the healing.

"Want to jog a little more?"

Maggie wagged her tail.

Scott set off at a slow lurch. He jogged so slowly, Maggie kept up fine by walking.

"You like Joyce?"

Maggie wagged her tail.

"Me, too, but I want you to remember, you're my best girl. You always will be."

Scott smiled when she nuzzled his hand.

They were pack, and both of them knew it.

OF NOTE

Readers knowledgeable about the LAPD K-9 Platoon or PTSD will note several differences between the facts of these subjects and their portrayal in this novel. These differences are not mistakes of research. They are choices made to increase drama or facilitate the telling of this story.

Post-traumatic stress disorder in humans and canines is real. Symptoms such as exaggerated startle response are difficult to treat, and the timeline for improvement is longer than is presented here.

LAPD K-9 Platoon is an elite organization of superbly trained individuals and police service dogs. My thanks to Lt. Gerardo Lopez, Officer in Charge, for his help and cooperation. The training time needed for Scott to become a certified K-9 dog handler was compressed for this story. The actual LAPD training facility, also known as "the K-9 field" or "the mesa," is located in

Elysian Park near the Police Academy. The facility depicted in this novel does not exist. Rules governing canine care, feeding, and housing are stated in the LAPD's *K-9 Platoon Procedures and Guidelines Handbook*. The approved K-9 diet does not include baloney. Additional thanks to Deputy Chief Michael Downing and Capt. John Incontro, Commanding Officer of Metro Division.

Acknowledgments and thanks once again go to Meredith Dros and her production team, Linda Rosenberg (Director of Copyediting) and Rob Sternitzky (proofreader), whose efforts at the wire are heroic. Copy editor Patricia Crais has the most difficult c/e job in publishing, with the lost sleep to prove it. Neil Nyren and Ivan Held could not have been more supportive; they almost certainly believe I am disordered. Not without reason. Aaron Priest remains my hero. Thanks go to Diane Barshop for sharing her knowledge about German shepherds. Also to Joanie Fryman. Kate Stark, Michael Barson, and Kim Dower — thanks for believing.

Any and all mistakes in this book are my responsibility.

ABOUT THE AUTHOR

Robert Crais is the author of many *New York Times* bestsellers, most recently *The First Rule, The Sentry,* and the #1 bestseller *Taken.* He lives in Los Angeles.

CPSIA information can be obtained
at www.ICGtesting.com
Printed in the USA
FFOW03n0204190314
4363FF

Having a
Mary Heart
in a
Martha World

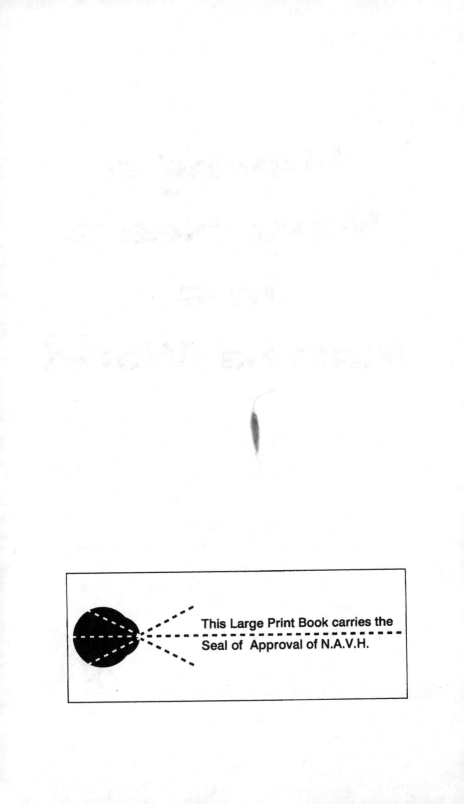

This Large Print Book carries the
Seal of Approval of N.A.V.H.

Having a Mary Heart in a Martha World

FINDING INTIMACY WITH GOD IN THE BUSYNESS OF LIFE

Joanna Weaver

Walker Large Print • Waterville, Maine

Copyright © 2000, 2002 by Joanna Weaver
Additional copyright information on page 469

All rights reserved.

Published in 2004 by arrangement with Waterbrook Press,
a division of Random House, Inc.

The text of this Large Print edition is unabridged.
Other aspects of the book may vary from the original edition.

Set in 16 pt. Plantin by Warren S. Doersam.

Printed in the United States on permanent paper.

Library of Congress Cataloging-in-Publication Data

Weaver, Joanna.
    Having a Mary heart in a Martha world : finding intimacy
with God in the busyness of life / Joanna Weaver.
       p. cm.
    Includes bibliographical references.
    ISBN 1-59415-009-5 (lg. print : sc : alk. paper)
    1. Christian women — Religious life. I. Title.
BV4527.W43 2004
  248.8′43—dc21   2003056390

*To my Mary-hearted mother, Annette Gustafson,
and my Mary-hearted mentor, Teri Myers*

The beauty and balanced grace
of your lives
continue to challenge and inspire me.
Thank you for making the path to the
Master's feet so clear
I couldn't help but follow.

National Association for Visually Handicapped
-------------------------- *serving the partially seeing*

As the Founder/CEO of NAVH, the only national health agency solely devoted to those who, although not totally blind, have an eye disease which could lead to serious visual impairment, I am pleased to recognize Thorndike Press★ as one of the leading publishers in the large print field.

Founded in 1954 in San Francisco to prepare large print textbooks for partially seeing children, NAVH became the pioneer and standard setting agency in the preparation of large type.

Today, those publishers who meet our standards carry the prestigious "Seal of Approval" indicating high quality large print. We are delighted that Thorndike Press is one of the publishers whose titles meet these standards. We are also pleased to recognize the significant contribution Thorndike Press is making in this important and growing field.

Lorraine H. Marchi, L.H.D.
Founder/CEO
NAVH

★ Thorndike Press encompasses the following imprints: Thorndike, Wheeler, Walker and Large Print Press.

Contents

Acknowledgments

One   *A Tale of Two Sisters* · · · · 11

Two   *"Lord, Don't You Care?"* · · 34

Three   *The Diagnosis* · · · · · · · 67

Four   *The Cure* · · · · · · · · · 102

Five   *Living Room Intimacy* · · 133

Six   *Kitchen Service* · · · · · 166

Seven   *The Better Part* · · · · · 201

Eight   *Lessons from Lazarus* · · 236

Nine   *Martha's Teachable Heart* 274

Ten   *Mary's Extravagant Love* 311

Eleven   *Balancing Work and Worship* 346

Twelve   *Having a Mary Heart in a Martha World* · · · · · 383

Resources for a Mary Heart in a Martha World

Appendix A *Study Guide* 411

Appendix B *Resources for Living Room
                Intimacy* 439

Appendix C *Resources for Kitchen
                Service* 442

Appendix D *Journal the Journey*. . . 445

Appendix E *A Simple Plan for a
                Half-Day of Prayer* · · 447

Appendix F *Christian Rights in the
                Workplace* 449

        Notes · · · · · · · · · · 452

Acknowledgments

I've been blessed to have many friends walk with me on this journey called "writing a book." Friends who've read manuscripts, dropped off home-cooked meals, prayed me out of tight spots, and told me to "go for it!" when I felt I couldn't go on. Looking back on the journey, I can't imagine how one could walk it all alone.

Though I can't thank everyone by name, I must thank Erica Faraone and Tricia Goyer for their gifts of perspective and encouragement, as well as the women of my church, FaithBuilders, and One Heart/ Blessed Hope for their faithful intercession. Special thanks to my friend, Rosemarie Kowalski, who allowed me to use her story in chapter 4 to illustrate the freedom of grace, capturing the very essence of this book.

To my editor, Anne Buchanan, my heartfelt thanks. Truly "two are better than one." Thank you, Anne, for helping me find the right words to convey the message that has so filled my heart and for all the laughter we've shared along the way.

To the great people at WaterBrook — Carol Bartley and Liz Heaney, to name two — my deepest gratitude as well.

I am especially grateful to my agent and friend, Janet Kobobel Grant. Thank you for all the wonderful things you are.

And finally, to my husband, John, and my two incredible kids, John Michael and Jessica. Your loving support and patience have been precious and costly gifts, treasures I've not taken for granted. John, thank you for believing in me. Kids, thank you for all the chuckles and for letting me share you with the world. You're the best!

But most of all, Lord Jesus, thank you for making it possible for each one of us to know you — really know you! — Marys and Marthas alike. Go beyond these inadequate human words, and by your Spirit, lead each one of us into your presence. Help us discover the joy and the secret of *Having a Mary Heart in a Martha World*.

Soli Deo Gloria. To you alone.

1

A Tale of Two Sisters

As Jesus and his disciples were on their way,
he came to a village where a woman named
Martha opened her home to him.
She had a sister called Mary,
who sat at the Lord's feet listening
to what he said.
LUKE 10:38-39

~

Have you ever tried to do it all?

I have, I do, and I probably always will. It's not only in my nature; it's also in my job description — and yours, too. Being a woman requires more stamina, more creativity, and more wisdom than I ever dreamed as a young girl. And that's not just true for today's busy women. It has always been the case.

In 1814, Martha Forman was married to

11

a wealthy Maryland plantation owner. You might expect she spent her days sipping tea, being fitted for lovely gowns, and giving orders to her servants as she chatted with important guests. Instead, Martha worked right beside her servants from four in the morning to eleven o'clock at night. Among her daily activities were the following:

> Making thirty to thirty-four pounds of old tallow into candles; cutting out fourteen shirts, jackets or trousers for the slaves (whom she always called "the people" or "our family"); knitting stockings; washing; dyeing and spinning wool; baking mince pies and potato puddings; sowing wheat or reaping it; killing farm animals and salting the meat; planting or picking fruits and vegetables; making jams, jellies, and preserves with her fruit; helping whitewash or paint walls; ironing; preparing for large parties; caring for sick family and slaves.[1]

So, what did you do today? You may not have slaughtered a hog or harvested wheat, but I know you were busy. Whether you were out selling real estate or at home kissing boo-boos (or both), your day passed just as quickly. And your mind and body are probably as tired as poor Martha Forman's as you steal a few moments to spend with this book.

Having a Mary Heart in a Martha World. The thought intrigues you. Deep inside of you there is a hunger, a calling, to know and love God. To truly know Jesus Christ and the fellowship of the Spirit. You're not after more head knowledge — it's heart-to-heart intimacy you long for.

Yet a part of you hangs back. Exhausted, you wonder how to find the strength or time. Nurturing your spiritual life seems like one more duty — one more thing to add to a life that is spilling over with responsibilities.

It's almost as if you're standing on the bottom rung of a ladder that stretches up to heaven. Eager but daunted, you name the rungs with spiritual things you know you should do: study the Bible, pray, fellowship . . .

"He's up there somewhere," you say, swaying slightly as you peer upward, uncertain how to begin or if you even want to attempt the long, dizzy climb. But to do nothing means you will miss what your heart already knows: There is more to this

Christian walk than you've experienced. And you're just hungry enough — just desperate enough — to want it all.

A Tale of Two Sisters

Perhaps no passage of Scripture better describes the conflict we feel as women than the one we find in the gospel of Luke. Just mention the names Mary and Martha around a group of Christian women and you'll get knowing looks and nervous giggles. We've all felt the struggle. We want to worship like Mary, but the Martha inside keeps bossing us around.

Here's a refresher course in case you've forgotten the story. It's found in Luke. It's the tale of two sisters. It's the tale of you and me.

As Jesus and his disciples were on their way, he came to a village where a woman named Martha opened her home to him. She had a sister called Mary, who sat at the Lord's feet listening to what he said. But Martha was distracted by all the preparations that had to be made. She came to him and asked, "Lord, don't you care that my sister has left me to do the work by myself? Tell her to help me!"

"Martha, Martha," the Lord answered, "you are worried and upset about many things, but only one thing is needed. Mary has chosen what is better, and it will not be taken away from her." (10:38-42)

A Martha World

When I read the first part of Mary and Martha's story, I must admit I find myself cheering for Martha. I know we tend to sing Mary's praises in Bible studies. But Martha, to be honest, appeals more to my perfectionist tendencies.

What a woman! She opens her home to a band of thirteen hungry men, possibly more. What a hostess! She doesn't whip up an impromptu casserole of Kraft macaroni and cheese and Ballpark franks as I've been known to do on occasion. Not her! She is the original Martha Stewart, the New Testament's Proverbs 31 woman, and Israel's answer to Betty Crocker. Or at least that's the way I imagine her. She's the Queen of the Kitchen — and the rest of the house as well.

And Luke's story starts with Martha in her glory. After all, this is Jesus. She scraps her ordinary everyday menu of soup and bread and pulls out all her cookbooks. This, she decides, will be a banquet fit for a messiah. For *the* Messiah. Martha sends one servant to the field to slaughter a lamb, another to the market to pick up a few of those luscious pomegranates she saw yesterday. Like a military general, she barks commands to her kitchen staff. Soak the lentils! Pound the grain! Knead the dough!

So many things to do and so little time. She must make sure the centerpiece and the napkins match, that the servant pours the wine from the right and not the left. Martha's mind is as busy as a room filled with kindergartners. What would be just right for dessert? A little goat cheese with a tray of fresh fruit? Will Jesus and his followers stay overnight? Someone must change the sheets and fold some towels.

"Where's Mary? Has anyone seen Mary?" she asks a servant scurrying by. If Mary changed the sheets, Martha might have time to fashion an ark from the cheese and carve the fruit into little animals marching two by two. Productions of this magnitude require the skill of a master planner. And Martha's an administrator extraordinaire — a whirling dervish of efficiency, with a touch of Tasmanian she-devil thrown in to motivate the servants.

I happen to be the oldest in my family. Perhaps that's why I understand how frustrated Martha must have felt when she finally found Mary. The entire household is in an uproar, busy making ready to entertain the most famous teacher of their day, the man most likely to become the next king of Israel. I can relate to the anger that boils up inside of Martha at the sight of her lazy sibling sitting at the Master's feet in the living room.

It's simply too much. With everything still left to do, there sits little Mary, being quite contrary, crashing a party meant only for men. But worse, she seems oblivious to all of Martha's gesturing from the hall.

Martha tries clearing her throat. She even resorts to her most effective tool: the "evil eye," famous for stopping grown men in their tracks. But nothing she does has any effect on her baby sister. Mary only has eyes for Jesus.

Pushed to the limit, Martha does something unprecedented. She interrupts the boys' club, certain that Jesus will take her side. After all, a woman's place is in the kitchen. Her sister, Mary, should be helping prepare the meal.

Martha realizes there is a cutting edge to

her voice, but Jesus will understand. He, of all people, knows what it's like to carry the weight of the world.

Now of course, you won't find all that in the Bible. Luke tends to downplay the whole story, dedicating only four verses to an event that was destined to change Martha's life forever. And mine as well. And yours, if you will let the simple truth of this passage soak deep into your heart.

Instead of applauding Martha, Jesus gently rebukes her, telling her Mary has chosen "what is better." Or, as another translation puts it, "Mary has chosen the better part" (NRSV).

"The better part?" Martha must have echoed incredulously.

"The better part!" I say to God in the midst of my own whirl of activity. "You mean there's more? I have to do more?"

No, no, comes the answer to my tired heart. Jesus' words in Luke 10 are incredibly freeing to those of us on the performance treadmill of life.

It isn't "more" he requires of us.

In fact, it may be less.

The Bible doesn't tell us a lot about Mary and Martha. They are mentioned by name only three times in Scripture: Luke 10:38-42, John 11:1-44, and John 12:1-11. But from these brief accounts, a fascinating picture develops of what life must have been like at the house in Bethany — and what life is often like for us.

They say variety is the spice of life. Perhaps that's why God so often puts people of such different personalities in the same family. (Either that, or he's trying to prepare us for marriage!) Mary was the sunlight to Martha's thunder. She was the caboose to Martha's locomotive. Mary's bent was to meander through life, pausing to smell the roses. Martha was more likely to pick the roses, quickly cut the stems at an angle, and arrange them in a vase with baby's breath and ferns.

That is not to say one is right and one is wrong. We are all different, and that is just as God made us to be. Each gifting and personality has its own strengths and weaknesses, its glories and temptations.

I find it interesting that when Jesus corrected Martha, he didn't say, "Why can't you be more like your sister, Mary?" He knew Martha would never be Mary, and Mary would never be Martha. But when the two were faced with the same choice — to work or to worship — Jesus said, "Mary has chosen the better part."

To me, this implies the Better Part was available to both Mary and Martha. And it's available to each one of us, regardless of our gifting or personality. It's a choice we each can make.

It is true that, personality-wise, the choice may have come easier to Mary than it did to Martha. Mary does seem more mellow by nature, more prone to walk in the dew of the morning than to get caught up in the "dos" of the day.

I'm sure when Jesus dropped by unexpectedly that afternoon, Mary probably began the visit by serving, just as she had many times before. I can see her taking walking staffs and sleeping rolls as the disciples spill into her sister's well-ordered home. Buried beneath cloaks and backpacks, she watches the man who has taken the heart of Israel captive by his words. There is such joy and winsomeness about him, she can't help but be drawn to this man.

Could Jesus be the Messiah the people say he is? Mary wonders. She knows he's a great teacher, but could this actually be the Son of God admiring the tapestry she wove, drawing her out of her shyness and into the circle of his closest friends?

She drops the disciples' belongings in a corner and hurries to pour wine for the thirsty crew. There is an ease about them, a true camaraderie. The men laugh at each other's jokes as they wash down the dust of the road with the liquid she provides. Then they settle on low couches around the room, and Jesus begins to teach.

He speaks as none she ever heard before. There is a magnetism about his words, as though they contain breath and life — breath and life Mary hasn't known she needed until this day. She creeps closer and stands in a dark corner listening to Jesus, her arms wrapped around the empty pitcher.

She's aware of movement around her. Several servants busy themselves washing dirty feet, while another sets the table at the other end of the room for the meal to come. Mary knows there is plenty to do. And yet she is unable to move — except closer.

It isn't customary for a woman to sit with a group of men, but his words welcome her. Despite her natural reticence, she gradually moves forward until she's kneeling at his feet. His teaching envelops her, revealing truth to her hungry heart.

The Bible isn't clear whether or not this was Jesus' first visit to the home in Bethany. Martha's openness with Christ seems to indicate a prior acquaintance, but whatever the case, this day Mary chose to let someone else do the serving so she could do some listening. It isn't every day God visits your house. So she ignores tradition, she breaks social etiquette, and she presses closer. As close to Jesus as possible.

It doesn't matter that she might be misunderstood. She cares little that the disciples look at her strangely. Somewhere in the distance she hears her name, but it is drowned by the call of her Master. The call to come. The call to listen.

And listen she does.

A Tale of Every Woman

Against this Bethany backdrop of unexpected guests, I see the struggle I face every day when work and worship collide.

Part of me is Mary. I want to worship extravagantly. I want to sit at his feet.

But part of me is Martha — and there's

just so much to do!

So many legitimate needs surround me, compelling me to work. I hear God's tender call to come away, and I respond, "Yes, Lord, I will come." But then the phone rings, or I'm reminded of the check I was supposed to deposit — yesterday. Suddenly all of my good intentions about worship disappear, swallowed up by what Charles Hummel calls "the tyranny of the urgent."

"We live in constant tension between the urgent and the important," Hummel writes. "The problem is that the important task rarely must be done today or even this week. Extra hours of prayer and Bible study can wait. But the urgent tasks call for instant action — endless demands pressure every hour and day."[2]

Does that sound familiar? It does to me. The twenty-four hours allotted to each day rarely stretch far enough to meet all the obligations I face. I have a household to run, a husband to love, children to care for, and a dog to feed. I have church commitments, writing deadlines, lunch engagements to keep. And very little of this is what I would call deadwood. Long ago I tried to cut out what I thought was extraneous. This is my life — and the hours are packed full.

Not long ago, *Today's Christian Woman* magazine sponsored a survey of more than a thousand Christian women. Over 60 percent indicated they work full time outside the home.[3] Add housework and errands to a forty-hour-a-week career, and you have a recipe for weariness. Women who choose to stay at home find their lives just as full. Chasing toddlers, carpooling to soccer, volunteering at school, baby-sitting the neighbor kids — life seems hectic at every level.

So where do we find the time to follow Mary to the feet of Jesus? Where do we find the energy to serve him?

How do we choose the Better Part and still get done what really has to get done?

Jesus is our supreme example. He was never in a hurry. He knew who he was and where he was going. He wasn't held hostage to the world's demands or even its desperate needs. "I only do what the Father tells me to do," Jesus told his disciples.

Someone has said that Jesus went from place of prayer to place of prayer and did miracles in between. How incredible to be so in tune with God that not one action is wasted, not one word falls to the ground!

That is the intimacy that Jesus invites us to share. He invites us to know him, to see him so clearly that when we look upon him, we see the face of God as well.

Just as he welcomed Mary to sit at his feet in the living room, just as he invited Martha to leave the kitchen for a while and share in the Better Part, Jesus bids us to come.

In obedience to his invitation, we find the key to our longings, the secret to living beyond the daily pressures that would otherwise tear us apart. For as we learn what it means to choose the Better Part of intimacy with Christ, we begin to be changed.

This is no cookie-cutter conversion. This is a Savior who accepts us just the way we are — Mary or Martha or a combination of both — but loves us too much to leave us that way. He is the one who can give us a Mary heart in a Martha world.

This transformation is exactly what we see in the continuing stories of Mary and Martha in the Gospels. Martha, as we will discover, doesn't lay aside her personality, give up her hobbies, and burn her cookbooks in order to worship Jesus. She doesn't try to mimic Mary the Little Lamb; she simply obeys. She receives Jesus' rebuke and learns that while there is a time for work, there is also a time for worship. The Martha we see later in the Gospels is no longer frantic and resentful, but full of faith and trust. The kind of faith and trust that come only from spending time at Jesus' feet.

Mary does some changing too. For although her contemplative nature makes her a natural worshiper, it also leaves her vulnerable to despair, as we'll see later in the Gospels. When disaster strikes, Mary's tendency is to be swamped with sorrow and paralyzed with questions. But in the end, when she realizes Jesus' time is short, Mary puts into action what she has learned in worship. She steps forward and seizes the opportunity to serve both beautifully and sacrificially.

That's what I see in the biblical portraits of the two sisters of Bethany. Two completely different women undergo a transformation right before our eyes: a holy makeover. The bold one becomes meek, the mild one courageous. For it is impossible to be in the presence of Jesus and not be changed.

As you read the following chapters, I pray you will allow the Holy Spirit access to all the hidden corners of your life. Whether you tend to be a bit driven, like

Martha, or more contemplative, like Mary, God is calling you to intimacy with him through Jesus Christ.

The choice he offered to these two very different sisters — and the transformation they experienced — is exactly what he offers to each of us as well.

First Things First

The Living Room Intimacy Mary enjoyed with Jesus will never come out of the busyness of Martha's Kitchen. Busyness, by itself, breeds distraction. Luke 10:38 shows us a woman with the gift of hospitality. Martha opened her home to Jesus, but that doesn't automatically mean she opened her heart. In her eagerness to serve Jesus, she almost missed the opportunity to *know* Jesus.

Luke tells us that "Martha was distracted by all the preparations that had to be made." Key word: *had.* In Martha's mind, nothing less than the very best would do. She *had* to go all out for Jesus.

We can get caught in the same performance trap, feeling as though we must prove our love for God by doing great things for him. So we rush past the intimacy of the Living Room to get busy for him in the Kitchen — implementing great ministries and wonderful projects, all in an effort to spread the good news. We do all our works in his name. We call him "Lord, Lord." But in the end, will he know us? Will we know him?

The kingdom of God, you see, is a paradox. While the world applauds achievement, God desires companionship. The world clamors, "Do more! Be all that you can be!" But our Father whispers, "Be still and know that I am God." He isn't looking as much for workers as he is looking for sons and daughters — a people to pour his life into.

Because we are his children, Kitchen Service will be the natural result of Living Room Intimacy with God. Like Jesus, we must be about our Father's business. The closer we draw to the heart of the Father, the more we see his heart for the world. And so we serve, we minister, and we love, knowing that when we do it to "the least of these," we have done it unto Christ.

When we put work *before* worship, we put the cart before the horse. The cart is important; so is the horse. But the horse must come first, or we end up pulling the cart ourselves. Frustrated and weary, we can nearly break under the pressure of service, for there is always something that needs to be done.

When we first spend time in his presence — when we take time to hear his voice — God provides the horsepower we need to pull the heaviest load. He saddles up Grace and invites us to take a ride.

The Call

I'll never forget crying in the darkness one night many years ago. My husband was an associate pastor at a large church, and our lives were incredibly busy. Carrying a double portfolio of music and Christian education meant we worked long hours on project after project, and the size of the church meant there were always people in need. I would go to bed at night worried about the people who had slipped through the cracks — the marriages in trouble, the children in crisis. I worried about all the things I didn't accomplish and should have, about all the things I'd accomplished, but not very well.

I remember clinging to my husband that night and sobbing as he tried to comfort me. "What's wrong, honey?" he asked, caressing my hair. But I couldn't explain. I was completely overwhelmed.

The only thing that came out between sobs was a broken plea, "Tell me the good news," I begged him. "I honestly can't remember . . . Tell me the good news."

Perhaps you have felt the same way. You've known the Lord your whole life, and yet you haven't found the peace and fulfillment you've always longed for. So you've stepped up the pace, hoping that in offering more service, somehow you will merit more love. You volunteer for everything: you sing in the choir, you teach Sunday school, you host Backyard Bible Club, you visit the nursing home weekly. And yet you find yourself staring into the night and wondering if this is all there is.

Or perhaps you've withdrawn from service. You've gone the route I've described above and, frankly, you've had it. You've stopped volunteering, stopped saying yes. No one calls anymore. No one asks anymore. You're out of the loop and glad for it. And yet the peace and quiet holds no peace and quiet. The stillness hasn't led to the closer walk with God you'd hoped for, just a sense of resentment. Your heart feels leaden and cold. You go to church; you go through the motions of worship, then leave and go home the same. And at night, sometimes you wonder, "What is the good news? Can someone tell me? I can't remember."

The Good News

The good news is woven through the New Testament in a grace-filled strand that shines especially bright in the Gospel stories of Mary and Martha. The message is this: Salvation isn't about what I do; it's about what Jesus did.

The Cross did more than pay for my sins; it set me free from the bondage of the "shoulds" and "if onlys" and "what might have beens." And Jesus' words to Martha are the words he wants to speak to your heart and mine: "You are worried and upset about many things, but only one thing is needed."

The "one thing" is not found in doing more.

It's found by sitting at his feet.

Catch that: Mary sat at his feet. She didn't move a muscle. She listened. She didn't come up with clever responses or a doctrinal thesis. Her gift was availability. (In the end, I believe that was

Martha's gift as well.)

The only requirement for a deeper friendship with God is showing up with a heart open and ready to receive. Jesus said: "Come to me, all you who are weary and burdened, and I will give you rest. Take my yoke upon you and learn from me, for I am gentle and humble in heart, and you will find rest for your souls" (Matthew 11:28-29).

Jesus invites us to come and rest, to spend time with him in this incredible Living Room Intimacy. Intimacy that allows us to be honest in our complaints, bold in our approach, and lavish in our love. Intimacy that allows us to hear our Father's voice and discern our Father's will. Intimacy that so fills us with his love and his nature that it spills out to our dry, thirsty world in Kitchen Service.

In the Living Room. That's where it all begins. Down at his feet.

An Invitation

Perhaps, like Martha, you never knew you could enter into Living Room Intimacy with God. But that is exactly what Jesus Christ came to do. His death and resurrection made a way for each

---

of us to be reconciled to God. But the gift of salvation he offers is just that — a gift. And a gift must be received.

You can receive this marvelous gift by praying this simple prayer:

Dear Lord Jesus,

I do believe you are the Son of God and that you died on the cross to pay the penalty for my sin.

Please come into my life, forgive my sin, and make me a member of your family. I now turn from going my own way. I want you to be the center of my life.

Thank you for your gift of eternal life and for your Holy Spirit, who has now come to live in me.

I ask this in your name. Amen.[4]

Jesus answered, "I am the way and the truth and the life. No one comes to the Father except through me."
JOHN 14:6

2

"Lord, Don't You Care?"

Martha was distracted by all the preparations that had to be made. She came to him and asked, "Lord, don't you care that my sister has left me to do the work by myself? Tell her to help me!"
LUKE 10:40

It had been a busy day. I'd dragged my kids through a morning of errands and grocery shopping, and now it was an hour past lunchtime. We were all hungry and a little bit grumpy, but the day brightened as I pulled the car into our favorite pizza place.

"Pizza, pizza, pizza!" my four-year-old son, Michael, chanted as he bounced up and down in the backseat. Jessica, two, clapped her hands at the thought of the merry-go-round in the kiddy playland. But our joy was cut short when I opened my checkbook and discovered I didn't have enough money in my checking account.

"It just isn't fair!" Michael informed me defiantly from the backseat as we drove toward home and plain old peanut-butter-and-jelly sandwiches. "You promised we could have pizza."

He was right. The pizza bribe had bought good behavior all morning. I sighed as I looked in the rearview mirror. It's difficult explaining to a child that even though you have checks in the checkbook, you may not have enough money in the bank. I have a hard time understanding it myself sometimes.

So we were at a standstill. All my explanations fell on deaf ears. Michael sat scrunched against the car door, arms folded tightly across his chest, a scowl so fierce his eyebrows and angry pout nearly met.

Then from the other side of the backseat, little Jessica piped up, "Life's hard, Miko!"

It Just Isn't Fair

Life *is* hard and rarely fair. Even when we work diligently and do what is expected, the daily duties of life often seem to provide few rewards. When was the last time you received a standing ovation at the dinner table? "Great tuna casserole, Mom! The best!" Your family applauds, their smiling faces flushed with admiration. Your picky teenager gives you a high-five and calls, "Encore! Encore!"

Or when was the last time your boss and coworkers applauded the fact that you got to work on time, did your job with a smile, and stayed late to finish an assignment? "Great job on the Anderson account," your boss says, poking his head around the door. "Take the next week off with pay! Hey, why not make it two?"

Doesn't happen, does it? The last time I checked, they don't hand out awards for sparkling toilet bowls, and the extra hours and effort we give outside the home often go unnoticed and unrewarded.

Sorry. No pizza for you.

While Martha may have been the first person to ask Jesus the question, "Lord, don't you care?" she definitely wasn't the last. We've all felt the loneliness, the frustration, the left-out-ness and resentment she experienced in the kitchen that Bethany afternoon — doing all that work for others when no one seems to notice and no one seems to care.

We've all echoed my son's complaint. "It just isn't fair!"

In Luke 10:40, we get a clear picture of Martha's struggles. Surprise visitors appear on her doorstep. We don't know how many. If the beginning of Luke 10 is any indication, it could be as many as seventy people descending upon this quiet home. And Martha responds with open arms and a wide smile. But somewhere between the kitchen and the living room, a seed of resentment starts growing. Before long, it sprouts into a question that echoes in women's hearts today: "Lord, don't you care?"

The problem is obvious. Martha is doing all the work while Mary basks in all the glory. It just isn't right. At least Martha doesn't think so, and I know how she feels. A part of me wishes Jesus had said, "So sorry, Martha — terribly insensitive of us. Come on, Mary! Come on, guys, let's all pitch in and give Martha a hand."

After all, that's what Martha wanted.

That's what I want when I'm feeling overwhelmed: soft, soothing words and plenty of helpful action. I want everyone to carry his own weight. But most of all, I want life to be fair.

The Scales of Justice

I grew up playing with my mother's decorative scales. Made of ornate brass, the set of balances stood proudly on the piano with several pieces of artificial fruit on either side, dispersed creatively so one side was slightly higher than the other.

Now and then, instead of practicing my piano lesson, I'd adjust the fruit. The exercise was quite educational. One plastic orange equaled two plums. The banana and apple weighed roughly the same, and together they balanced nicely with the grapefruit. If I went about it right, I could take up quite a lot of practice time rearranging fruit on those scales.

Warning Signs of a Martha Overload

You may be prone to the kind of perfectionist overload Martha experienced in Bethany. Carol Travilla, in her book

Caring Without Wearing, lists five unrealistic expectations that can contribute to servant burnout. Can you see yourself in the following false beliefs?

- There should not be any limits to what I can do.
- I have the capacity to help everyone.
- I am the only person available to help.
- I must never make a mistake.
- I have the ability to change another person.

> *What you are doing is not good. . . .*
> *You will only wear yourselves out.*
> *The work is too heavy for you;*
> *you cannot handle it alone.*
> EXODUS 18:17-18

Then one day I decided to take my little experiment a step further. After arranging all the plastic fruit in a huge pyramid on one side, I looked around for a counterbalance. Ah. Grandma's glass grapes.

Remember the kind? I loved to look through the big round balls of colored glass wired tightly to a piece of twisted wood. Their purple depths made everything appear wavy and distorted and otherworldly. A perfect distraction for a bored piano student — almost as much fun as playing with the scales.

Almost.

You can guess what happened, of course, when I placed the grapes on the other side of the scale. They dropped like a brick on the mahogany surface of my mother's treasured piano, sending the brass rattling and the plastic fruit flying. Mom came running, and I started playing the "Indian War Song," hoping she'd think it was the pounding bass and not my goofing around that had caused the disturbance.

It didn't work. I deserved everything I got. That time.

But my mother's brass scales are not the only set of balances I've paid undue attention to in my life. I suspect that's true for you, too. Since childhood, we've all had an invisible set that weighs what happens to us against what others experience.

Growing up, for instance, we weighed how our parents treated us by the way they treated our siblings. "Julie has two more Ju-Ju Fruits than I do!" "Daddy, it's my turn to sit in the front seat."

That's just a part of childhood, of course. But many of us have carried the scales into adulthood, unaware, and we waste surprising amounts of time trying to get those scales to balance.

Fair or not fair. Equal or unequal. Just or unjust. We weigh it all. And if we're not careful, our view of the world can become distorted. Every little word can take on a hidden meaning. Each action can turn into a personal attack.

"I do all the work," we mutter to ourselves. "Why do they get all the glory?"

"How dare they treat me like that!"

Like grandma's glass grapes, these "sour grapes" can easily outweigh everything good in our lives, tipping the scale against us. Because when we look for injustice, we usually find it. And when we expect life to always be fair, we inevitably set ourselves up for a big disappointment.

The Three Deadly Ds

The story is told of a priest who served a small parish in an obscure countryside. He loved his people, and they loved him, and he was doing God's work quite effectively — so effectively, in fact, that two demons were assigned by Satan to pester him and somehow derail his ministry. They tried every method in their bag of tricks, but to no avail. The placid priest seemed beyond their reach. Finally, they called for a conference with the devil himself.

"We've tried everything," the demons explained, listing their efforts. Satan listened, then offered this advice. "It's quite easy," he hissed. "Bring him news that his brother has been made bishop."

The demons looked at one another. It seemed too simple. They had expected something more diabolical. But it was worth a try. Nothing else had worked.

Several weeks later they returned gleefully. The old priest hadn't taken the happy news of his brother's promotion well at all. The man's former joy had been turned to moping. His encouraging words had been replaced with grumbling and gloom. In a short time, the man's vibrant ministry had been destroyed by the green worm of envy and the black cloud of disappointment — the bitter conclusion that "it just wasn't fair."

Satan's never been terribly creative. The tools he uses today are the same tools he's always used — and no wonder, for they've been quite effective. From the Garden of Eden to Martha's Bethany kitchen to our own everyday world, Satan still plans his attacks around what I call the "Three Deadly Ds of Destruction."

They are
- Distraction
- Discouragement
- Doubt

Throughout time, Satan has resorted to these tactics to bring down God's best and brightest. The underlying strategy is fairly simple: Get people's eyes off God and on their circumstances. Make them believe that their "happiness" lies in the "happenings" that surround them. Or send them good news — about somebody else. When they're thoroughly discouraged, tell them God doesn't care. Then sit back and let doubt do its work.

It's really a brilliant strategy, when you think of it. Plant the Deadly Ds deep in human hearts, and sooner or later people will destroy themselves.

Unless, of course, someone intervenes — which is exactly what Jesus came to do.

A Distracted Heart

When Jesus met Martha that day in Bethany, she was "distracted." That's where Satan usually begins. He knows if we're overly worried and bogged down by duties, chances are good our hearts will not hear the Savior's call to come. While distraction may not win the battle for our soul, getting our eyes off of what is important will certainly make us more vulnerable to attack.

The *King James Version* tells us that "Martha was cumbered about much serving." Which is really just another way of saying *distracted*. The *Oxford English Dictionary* defines the word *cumber:* "(1) to overwhelm, overthrow, rout, destroy, (2) to harass, distress, bother, (3) to trouble, confound, perplex." Felt any of those lately? I certainly have.

The original Greek word used in this passage is *perispao* — "to be overoccupied about a thing; to draw away." That sounds eerily familiar to me as well.

Strong's concordance adds another dimension to the word *cumber,* defining it as "to drag all around." Can't you see Martha — all of her responsibilities snapping at her skirt like angry Chihuahuas; all her expectations dragging behind her like balls and chains?

Martha's pursuits were far from trivial. That's important to recognize. In fact, the "preparations" Martha pursued were described by Luke as *diakonia* — the New Testament word for ministry. "But even pure ministry for Jesus can become a weight we drag around," says pastor and author Dutch Sheets. "It's called the 'treadmill anointing,' and it isn't from God."[1]

I've experienced the treadmill anointing in ministry far more than I'd like to admit. Even on those days when I have the best of motives, my heart can be pulled away from doing things "as unto the Lord" and settle for simply getting things done. And when that happens, I can tell you, this Martha isn't very merry.

Neither, of course, was the original Martha. Like the rabbit in *Alice's Adventures in Wonderland*, she had a schedule to keep, but no one seemed to sense the importance of her mission. In fact, they seemed quite oblivious to her need. It wasn't long before the gracious hostess in Martha collapsed and the Queen of Hearts took over, pointing fingers and screaming, "Off with their heads! Off with everyone's head!"

I'm familiar with the Queen of Hearts. She raises her regal head around our house every once in a while. Just let the housework pile up, my schedule run wild, and obligations go unmet, and I have the makings of a royal temper tantrum. The Queen in me stalks the kitchen, slamming cupboards and rattling pans, making wild statements to no one in particular.

Pity the child who crosses the Queen on a rampage. Especially after her highness has made a sweep through the house for laundry, only to find half of it clean and lying on the floor. "Clean socks?" I bellow. "You want clean socks? Try under your bed where you keep the rest of your clothes!"

And by the way, off with your head! I don't say it, but sometimes I feel it.

I'm overwhelmed and distracted. I feel incredibly alone, just like Martha felt. And though you might never know it from my Queen-of-Hearts facade, the weight of discouragement is already tugging at my heart.

A Discouraged Heart

When we're distracted, discouragement is just around the corner. Weariness creeps in as life overpowers us. It causes us to say and do things we would never consider saying or doing otherwise. Discouragement breaks down our perspective and our defenses. Though we may have just completed great things for God, weary discouragement tells us we're useless, hopeless, and abandoned.

Elijah felt that kind of discouragement. Having just won a mighty victory over the prophets of Baal (1 Kings 18), Elijah had been flying high. But when Jezebel took out a contract on Elijah's life, the wicked queen's haughty words brought the mighty prophet back to earth with a thud. Less than a day after holy fire fell from heaven — proving once and for all that God was God — Elijah was running for his life.

Distraction made him fear.

Discouragement made him hide.

"Don't you care?" Elijah asked God as he sat trembling under the broom tree in the desert. "I have had enough, LORD," he whimpered in 1 Kings 19:4. "Take my life." Just let me die.

Have you spent much time under the broom tree of self-pity? I have. It's easy to find a shady spot and feel sorry for ourselves when we're distracted and discouraged. Especially when we run up against unexpected opposition. Especially when it feels like we're running for our lives.

In the dictionary you'll find *self-pity* stuck between *self-perpetuating* and *self-pollinating*. I had to laugh when I saw it, because it's so true. I happen to be an expert on the subject. Being quite the hostess myself, I throw pity parties fairly regularly. Trouble is, no one wants to come. Self-pity is a lonely occupation.

Or perhaps you're more familiar with the broom closet of isolation. Failure seems imminent, and it's easier to hide than face life head-on. So we pull our shredded confidence around trembling shoulders, cover our heads, and beg to be excused from the regular business of life. We're downhearted and downright depressed — and all because of discouragement.

Discouragement can drain us of all hope, of all vision, of all our tomorrows and dreams. It certainly did that for Elijah.

But I love the tender picture of 1 Kings 19:5-7, for it hints at the tenderness available to us in our own discouragement. Remember what happened? God sent an angel to bring food to his downhearted prophet. "Get up and eat," the angel told Elijah, "for the journey is too much for you." Then the angel stood guard as Elijah fell back asleep.

When we're distracted and discouraged, tired and overwhelmed, there is no better place to go than to our Father. He alone has what we need. Don't snivel under a broom tree. Don't hide in a broom closet.

Go to the Lord and let him sweep away your discouragement.

As you do, you'll find healing for your hurting heart.

Even when it can't help but doubt.

A Doubtful Heart

Throughout history, Satan has found that trying to make humanity question God's existence is futile. As Paul writes in Romans 1:19-20, God's existence is written upon man's heart. Time and time again, over the course of history, agnosticism and atheism have fallen before the bedrock belief: *God is.* In our lifetime, we've seen a century of atheistic unbelief crumble along with the Soviet Union and the Berlin Wall. Contrary to Communist prediction, belief in God has definitely not died. In fact, the rise of atheistic states in the twentieth century did little except spur the growth of religion.

Five Strategies for Fighting Discouragement

We all dip down now and then into discouragement. The secret is not to stay there. Here are several ways you can beat the downward spiral of the Deadly Ds in your life.

1. *Allow for rest stops.* Discouragement is often our body's way of saying, "Stop! I need rest." Try taking a nap or getting to bed a little earlier. It's amazing how different things will look in the light of morning (Exodus 34:21).

2. *Get a new point of view.* Take a few steps back and ask God to help you see his perspective on your situation. Often what seems to be an impassable mountain in our eyes is only a steppingstone in his (Isaiah 33:17).

3. *Have patience.* It's easy to get discouraged when things don't go the way you planned. But if you've committed your concerns to the Lord, you can be sure he is at work, even when you don't see his hand (Romans 8:28).

4. *Mingle.* Discouragement feeds off isolation. Get out of the house! Go visit some friends. It's amazing how good, old-fashioned fellowship can lift our spirits and chase away the blues (Psalm 133:1).

5. *Set the timer.* Okay. So things aren't

so good. I've found it helpful to set the oven timer and allow ten minutes for a good cry. But when the buzzer sounds, I blow my nose, wipe my eyes, and surrender my situation to the Lord so I can move on (Ecclesiastes 3:4).

The LORD himself goes before you and will be with you; he will never leave you nor forsake you. Do not be afraid; do not be discouraged.
DEUTERONOMY 31:8

Since atheism has been less than effective, Satan has returned to another lie in his bag of tricks. If he can't make us doubt God's existence, Satan will do his best to make us doubt God's love. After he has distracted us . . . after he has discouraged us . . . Satan's final tactic is disillusionment and doubt.

"You're on your own, baby," he whispers to our loneliness. "See? God doesn't really care, or he would have shown up by now."

Nothing could be further from the truth, of course. And yet, Satan continues to use this deception with great success. Even against God's own children.

I'm ashamed to say my heart has sometimes listened to Satan's siren song. The words of doubt and notes of disillusionment echo the frustration and confusion I feel inside. A countermelody to faith, the mournful tune arises during those times when God neither acts the way I think he should nor loves me the way I want to be loved. Like two songs being played in different keys, the dissonance of what I *feel* clashes with what I *know* and threatens to drown out the anthem of God's eternal love.

Lord, Don't You Care?

It began one spring as the crocuses pushed their way through hard-crusted soil and the tight buds of trees slowly unfurled toward the sun. All around me the world was waking, but the warmth of the changing season never reached my soul. While I still loved God, he seemed distant and preoccupied with someone other than me. It was, I suppose, my first true spiritual crisis.[2]

Having been raised in a Christian home, I'd eagerly accepted Jesus at the age of four. I loved God with a childlike totality and knew he loved me, though sometimes

I wondered why. Yet slowly over the years, mostly without my knowledge, little strands of uncertainty had been spun in my soul, and gradually they had knit themselves together into a dark veil. That spring, after fifteen years of full-time ministry, I began struggling with doubt. Especially in the area of prayer.

God didn't seem to be answering my prayers as he should. "Ask what you will and it shall be given you," he had promised, but I felt as if someone at the pearly gates was marking my prayer mail "return to sender." My friend wasn't healed of terminal cancer, and my mother continued to struggle after open-heart surgery. Even small requests were left unanswered. My van, for instance, still made a frustrating squeal, impervious to the efforts of the mechanics and their lube jobs — the heater wouldn't work right. Other little things kept going wrong. Nothing major, just enough to keep me worried and, yes, distracted.

The van proved to be the final showdown — my spiritual Alamo. Winter returned to Montana, and I drove down to see my mother, who was battling depression. A year had passed since her surgery, and despite a strict vegetarian diet, her cholesterol level had soared. The medication caused terrible mood swings and chest pains. She was ready to give up.

"I'd rather go be with the Lord," she said. "If the quality of my life is diminished, there's no sense in living."

We cried and prayed together. I wanted to be understanding and supportive, but I felt so frustrated. My mother was ready to end it all because she felt winded after pulling weeds and cleaning house!

"Mom, it isn't what you do that makes you who you are," I told her through my tears. "It's never been that. I love you for you. I need you — please don't give up."

She looked so small and fragile as she leaned in my van to hug me the next evening. I'd come to encourage, to build up, to somehow fix the emotional short circuit that left my normally positive mother negative and hopeless. But the short visit had ended bittersweet with an impasse.

"Did you get the window up?" she asked. A day before, she had lowered my van's power window and there it had stayed, refusing all our creative attempts to close it.

"No, but I'll be okay." I gave her one last hug, glancing at the sky. Snow had begun to fall, and the clouds looked stormy dark.

A gas-station mechanic offered no solutions, so I closed the door on the top of a towel and drove out of town angry. Angry at the window that still wouldn't budge. Angry at my mother, who seemed to be giving up. But most of all, angry at God, who didn't seem to be paying any attention at all.

"Okay, God," I prayed. "You said I have not because I ask not, so here goes. Please Lord, please make the window go up. I've tried everything, You're the only one who can help."

I worked up a reasonable amount of faith and pressed the button on the armrest. Nothing. Wind whipped through the window, tearing the towel from its place as I joined the traffic on the interstate. Icy snow swirled around the flapping towel and into the cab.

"Lord, you know my heater doesn't work and it's 150 miles home." Tears spilled over as I groped, trying to zip my coat with one hand. "You say you'll provide all our needs according to your riches in glory. I just need one little miracle."

"Please." I paused a moment, as if giving my petition time to make it to heaven. My eyes closed for a split second as I pressed the little black lever.

Nothing. Frustrated, I pulled over to the shoulder of the road and slammed on the brakes.

"Fine." I got out of the car and slammed the door. The wind sliced across the valley floor, burying the highway in a flurry of snow. I removed the towel and pulled a flimsy bedspread from the backseat. "If you won't take care of me, I will."

Hostility burned high in my throat, choking me as I spit out the words with an anger that had built over the long, spiritually frigid summer and fall.

"How can I know you're real if you won't answer one little prayer? I'm desperate, but you're silent. I'm angry, but you don't seem to care."

Earlier that month, I'd driven fifteen miles with the window down in subzero weather. It'd taken hours to feel warm again. I climbed back into the van, wrapping the bedspread around my shoulders, preparing for a miserable trip.

I finally shut off the faulty heater, as the lukewarm air only aggravated the cold. We fell into an uneasy silence. My traitorous Friend didn't seem interested in talking, so I spent the rest of the blizzard alone, struggling beneath the shroud of angry darkness.

I turned on the Christian radio station and listened as people talked about God's love. But for the first time in my life, I doubted its reality. Did they ever question? Did doubt about the Father's sovereignty ever shake their faith? It was all new to me, this cold, hard cynicism.

The radio's clock glowed 10:59 P.M. when I finally arrived home. I'd driven slowly most of the trip, staring through the blinding snow for any sign of the center-line. But somewhere along those fearful, frigid miles I'd lost the anger.

The last remnant of rage melted when I realized, twenty-five miles from home, that I was warm. Truly warm. Though my nose felt chafed by the wind and my cheeks tingled to the touch, the rest of my body was extraordinarily comfortable. Miraculously so.

The Father had heard. The Father had answered. Not in the way I'd asked, and certainly not in the way I'd planned. He hadn't rolled up the window. But he *had* wrapped me in his arms.

I began to cry again. This time the tears weren't those of a demanding child, but those of a chastened daughter.

Trust me, my child. I have your ultimate good in mind.

Doubting God's Goodness

I wonder how the Father feels when we assume the worst about him rather than the best. Does his heart hurt like mine when we question his love?

"You don't love me," my thirteen-year-old son said with the same pout he'd used that pizza-deprived afternoon many years ago. He was teasing (more or less) and he said it with the hint of a grin, but he still wanted the remark to sting. And it did.

"What do you mean?" I wanted to scream. "I clothe you. I feed you. I make sure you have cleats for football. I have a forever-ugly zipper on my lower belly where the doctor ripped me open so you could live, ungrateful child — and now, I don't love you?"

But none of that counted at the moment. I had told him he couldn't stay up and watch the NFL playoffs on a school night, and suddenly all my love had been erased.

Doubting God's love doesn't require tragedy. It can creep into the everyday just as insidiously, just as dangerously. It happens when our will is crossed, when our needs are ignored, or when we, like Martha, are stuck doing the dirty work while everyone else is having fun.

Now, such doubt in itself is not a sin. It's simply a thought or feeling that springs up almost involuntarily. But when we let it lodge in our heart long enough, wedged tightly like a poppy seed between our teeth, that little doubt can become a big problem. For doubt, left unchecked, can fester into unbelief. And unbelief, my friend, is not only sin — it's deep trouble. When we no longer believe in God's goodness, when we no longer trust in his care, we end up running away from the very Love we need to live.

Unbelief brought down Judas — he refused to trust God's timing. Unbelief hardened Saul's heart — he closed his eyes to the rightness of God's ways. Unbelief kept the Israelites in the wilderness for forty years because they questioned God's ability to lead them. And it was unbelief way back at the beginning of time that opened a doorway of darkness in a world designed for pure light.

The Garden of Eden must have been wonderful. Just think: no house to clean, no meals to cook, no clothes to iron! Eve had it made. A gorgeous hunk of a husband. Paradise for a living room. God for a playmate. But somehow, in the midst of all these blessings, the marvelous grew mundane, the remarkable ho-hum. And a nagging sense of discontentment sent Eve wandering toward the only thing God had withheld: the Tree of the Knowledge of Good and Evil.

What is it about us women that creates such a desperate need in us to always "know," to always "understand"? We want an itinerary for our life, and when God doesn't immediately produce one, we set out to write our own.

"I need to know," we tell ourselves.

"No," God answers softly, "you need to trust."

But like the original first lady, we push aside his tender voice and head straight for the tree. Not the sacrificial tree of the cross, but the proud, towering beauty called Knowledge. Because, after all, knowledge is power. And power is what we secretly crave.

I believe Eve's eventual sin began with a tiny thought — a small, itching fear she was somehow missing something and that God didn't have her best interest at heart. What could be wrong with something so lovely, so desirable as the forbidden fruit? Perhaps a hidden resentment had worked down into her spirit. Adam got to name the animals while *she* got to pick papayas.

60

Whatever the identity of the tiny irritation, it sent her looking for more.

And Satan was ready and waiting, willing to give her more than she'd ever bargained for. He filled her mind with questions. "Did God really say . . . ?" Satan encouraged Eve to doubt God's word and God's goodness until the continual question marks finally obliterated her trust in God's love.

Humanity has questioned God's love ever since.

Asking Questions

"Lord, don't you care?" Like Martha, we have our questions. Like Martha, we have our doubts. I'm so glad God isn't threatened by our doubts and questions, our fears or even our frustration. He wants us to trust his love enough to tell him what we are thinking and feeling. David did that. He is a marvelous example of a heart honest and open before God. The shepherd-boy-turned-king poured out his complaint before the Lord all through the psalms. In Psalm 62:8, he invites us to do the same: "Trust in him at all times, O people; pour out your hearts to him, for

God is our refuge."

Our friend Martha was on the right track that day in Bethany. Instead of allowing her doubtful questions to fester, she took her worries and her fears and voiced them to Jesus. While her bristling, abrasive approach is hardly the best model, there are still several important lessons we can learn from her gutsy encounter with Christ.

First, *we can bring our needs to Jesus anytime and anywhere.* "Ask and it will be given to you," Jesus said in Matthew 7:7. In the Greek, the form of the word for *ask* implies "keep on asking." We can't wear our Savior out. He's never too busy to hear our hearts' cries. Martha took full advantage of his availability, even in the midst of her busyness and party preparations.

Second, *Jesus really cares about what concerns us.* "Cast all your anxiety on him," 1 Peter 5:7 tells us, "because he cares for you." Jesus didn't laugh off Martha's concerns. He didn't become angry. Instead, he spoke to her with infinite gentleness and tenderness, recognizing the pain behind her whining words.

Finally, *Jesus loves us enough to confront us when our attitude is wrong.* "Those whom I love," says the Lord, "I rebuke and discipline" (Revelation 3:19). And that is what the Savior did with Martha. He intuitively understood Martha's pain, but that didn't stop him from telling her what she needed to hear.

And Martha, to her credit, listened.

Too often, I think, we hold on to doubt and confusion until our questions explode as accusations. We shake our fists at God, raging from all the hurt. Then human nature makes us want to run and hide, nursing our perceived injustice and licking our wounds.

But Martha didn't do this. She stated her case, yes, but then she stuck around to hear Jesus' ruling. Though she accused him of neglect, she was willing to listen to his response. She was willing to leave the outcome in his hands.

I love the compassion of Jesus in this story. He saw Martha's situation. He understood her complaint. But he loved her too much to give her what she wanted. Instead, Jesus gave her what she needed — an invitation to draw close to him. With open arms, he invited the troubled woman to leave her worries and cares and find refuge in him alone.

Because when you have questions, there is no better place to go than to the One who has the answers.

The Answer to the Question

"Lord, don't you care?"

Of course he cares. That's why he came.

If I were God, wanting to touch base with man, I'd drop by for a visit. Maybe a week or two with plenty of advance advertising, hitting the major cities before returning to my comfy celestial throne. Just long enough to get people's attention and straighten things out, then, "Beam me up, Scotty!" I'd be out of there.

Who in their right mind would leave heaven to actually live on earth? Why that would be like a farmer selling his cozy farmhouse so he could live in his pigsty. Like Bill Gates giving up Microsoft's billions so he could run a hot-dog stand for minimum wage. Unthinkable. But that is exactly what Jesus did.

God became one of us so that when we ask, "Lord, don't you care?" we can know without a doubt that he does. Instead of paying a house call or a flashy extraterrestrial visit, he took up residence among us. Through Jesus Christ incarnate, God entered the world through the same doorway we do. Then he stuck around as long as we'd let him, until we sent him, dying, out the same painful exit we will go.

Does he care? You'd better believe it!

You'd *better* believe it. Because until you settle that question once and for all, you will never get past doubt to true belief. You'll forever be faced with a shiny apple and the hiss of temptation to take matters into your own hands.

The fact is, until we stop doubting God's goodness, we can't experience God's love.

Martha spoke her secret fear aloud, and we can too. But, like Martha, we must stick around long enough to hear the sweet reassurance of his answer.

Don't expect any explanations or apologies. After all, God is God. If righteous Job couldn't force God to give an account for his actions, then we shouldn't expect to always understand his mysterious ways.

But rest assured, God will answer. He longs to reveal his love to you. But you won't find it by shaking your fist in his face. You won't find it by barging into his presence and demanding to be treated fairly. You'll find it by sitting at his feet and remembering who he is.

Emmanuel. God *with* us.

He knows the journey is difficult. He knows life is rarely fair. Jesus fought the same frigid winds of distraction, discouragement, and doubt that keep us from knowing God's love. But like the Father, he longs to gather us in his arms. He longs to trade the flimsy blankets of our own self-sufficiency for his all-sufficiency. The Lord Jesus invites us to cast our doubts, our fears and anxiety upon him, to discover how much he really does care.

Trust me, my child, he whispers. *I have your ultimate good in mind.*

3

The Diagnosis

"Martha, Martha," the Lord answered,
"you are worried and upset
about many things."
Luke 10:41

Far out in the Aegean Sea, in the Cycladic chain, lies a Greek island called Naxos. Largely untouched by the march of technology and the information age, Naxos has remained the same for centuries. Olive trees line the island's rocky shores as turquoise waters shimmer in the harbor. Mount Za looms above; its lush meadows and cool streams rush down to meet the sea. The pace of life is unhurried, the people willing to talk to passersby.

One of the first things you notice when you step on this island is the strings of beads worn by many people. Rich and poor. Tall and short. Both the young and the old — but especially the old men, for this is a very old Greek custom. The islanders finger and manipulate the beads around their necks all day long. They say the beads bring comfort, that the process of handling them cuts down on anxiety. They call them *komboloi* — "worry beads."[1]

A quaint custom, we may say. Yet we have worry rituals ourselves. While we may not wear anxiety around our necks, it certainly affects our lives. We bite our fingernails. We pace the floor. We lie awake at night. And all because of worry. Hour after hour, our mental fingers twist around a problem, turning it this way, then that, like a Rubik's Cube. We manipulate and postulate, desperate to solve the puzzle. And yet we seem to find few answers.

The sad fact is, we are an anxious people. We are a nation of worriers.

"I think there's an epidemic of worry," confirms Dr. Edward Hallowell in his book *Worry*. The best-selling author and psychiatrist estimates that one in four of us — about sixty-five million Americans — will meet the criteria for anxiety disorder at some point in our lifetime.[2] Over half of us are what he calls chronic worriers.

But worry is hardly a modern phenomenon. Jesus described precisely the same condition two thousand years ago. He didn't write a book or establish a clinic. He had no medical degree, but he knew the human heart and soul. Out of the vast knowledge known only to a creator concerning the created, Jesus spoke truth to a woman caught in chronic worry.

"Martha, Martha," Jesus observed gently, "you are worried and upset about many things."

The Curse of Anxiety

Those words must have stopped Martha in her tracks. I know they stop me.

"Now wait a minute, Lord!" Martha must have wanted to say. "I'm just trying to serve you."

But his tender words cut through her excuses and pretense. In one short sentence, Jesus diagnosed the problem that has plagued humankind since the beginning of time. We can trace its roots back to a Garden, a Tree, and the Fall of mankind.

It is the curse of anxiety. The ongoing burden of worry and fear.

It wasn't supposed to happen to us. The Tree of the Knowledge of Good and Evil was off-limits for good reason — our own protection. God had created the man and the woman to enjoy a mutual love relationship with him, the same relationship we were created to enjoy. He would take care of us and provide all of our needs. We, in return, would "enjoy God and worship him forever," as the Westminster Creed so beautifully puts it.

But rather than viewing the boundaries as evidence of God's mercy, Adam and Eve interpreted the command as a power play on God's part — a desire to withhold something good. So they took and they ate. Their eyes were opened. And what they saw was far more than they expected. Instead of receiving godlike power, they were terrified to behold their nakedness and utter helplessness. But instead of running back to God, they hid from him.

Why? Genesis 3:10 tells us they were afraid. But I think it was more than simple fear of God's wrath that sent them diving for cover.

For the very first time, the man and the woman saw themselves apart from God. Like two children lost and alone, they suddenly saw Eden as a frightening place rather than a beautiful paradise. Suddenly, with the knowledge of good and evil, came shadows and dark corners, strange sounds and frightening noises. No longer were God's children innocent and unaware. No longer were they safe under God's protection.

With the bite of the apple came the stark, terrible truth: Adam and Eve were on their own. So like naughty little kids, they ran and hid, trying to buy enough time to figure a way out of this snake-induced mess. Cut off by their own disobedience from the very God they needed, they grew chronically fearful and anxious.

And so it has gone, all the way down to Martha of Bethany. All the way down to you and me.

A Born Worrier

I come from a long line of Swedish worriers.

"Käre mej," my Grandma Anna used to say over and over. "Dear me, dear me." Too high, too fast. Too much, too little. With all the potential danger in the world, there seemed to be only one response — worry.

I remember lying in bed at night going over my list of fears. Somehow, as a young teenager, I had determined that the secret for avoiding trouble was to worry about it. In fact, I worried if I forgot to worry about something.

When Mom and Dad went to Hawaii for their fifteenth anniversary, I spent most of the week trying to think of everything that might go wrong. What if the plane crashed? What if a tidal wave wiped out Waikiki? Anything could happen. Rotten pineapples. Bad sushi. Salmonella poisoning from coconut milk left out overnight. I'd be left an orphan, sob. I'd be left to raise my little brother and sister alone. Big, big sobs.

Of course, my parents returned home safe and sound, healthy and tan. But in some twisted way, this merely confirmed my thesis: Worry so it won't happen. And so, little by little, worry became my mode of operation.

What about you? Has worry become a dominating factor in your life? Dr. Hallowell, who describes himself as a born worrier as well, provides a checklist to help you decide — you'll find it in the sidebar on the following page. If you recognize yourself in these descriptions, chances are you have a problem with worry.

And make no mistake — worry is indeed a problem.

Ten Signs of a Big Worrier

Is worry a problem in your life? Dr. Hallowell says it might be if these worry signs are true about you:

1. You find you spend much more time in useless, nonconstructive worry than other people you know.
2. People around you comment on how much of a worrier you are.
3. You feel that it is bad luck or tempting fate not to worry.
4. Worry interferes with your work — you miss opportunities, fail to make decisions, perform at lower than optimal level.
5. Worry interferes with your close relationships — your spouse and/ or friends sometimes complain that your worrying is a drain on their energy and patience.
6. You know that many of your worries are unrealistic or exaggerated, yet you cannot seem to control them.
7. Sometimes you feel overwhelmed

by worry and even experience physical symptoms such as rapid heart rate, rapid breathing, shortness of breath, sweating, dizziness, or trembling.

8. You feel a chronic need for reassurance even when everything is fine.

9. You feel an exaggerated fear of certain situations that other people seem to handle with little difficulty.

10. Your parents or grandparents were known as great worriers, or they suffered from an anxiety disorder.[3]

Search me, O God, and know my heart; test me and know my anxious thoughts.
See if there is any offensive way in me, and lead me in the way everlasting.
PSALM 139:23-24

Worthless Worry

"An anxious heart weighs a man down," Proverbs 12:25 tells us. And yet the heavy burden of anxiety offers no real benefits. Jesus highlighted this basic futility when he reminded us, "Who of you by worrying can add a single hour to his life?" (Matthew 6:27).

It's been said that worry is like a rocking chair — it gives you something to do, but it doesn't get you anywhere. One interesting set of statistics indicates that there is nothing we can do about 70 percent of our worries:

What We Worry About

40% are things that will never happen.
30% are about the past — which can't be changed.
12% are about criticism by others, mostly untrue.
10% are about health, which gets worse with stress.
8% are about real problems that can be solved.[4]

When it comes down to it, worry is really a waste of time. But it's also more than that. Worry is not only futile. It's actually bad for us.

The physical and emotional damage caused by chronic anxiety is well known and well documented. Years ago Dr. Charles H. Mayo of the Mayo Clinic pointed out that worry affects circulation, the glands, the whole nervous system, and profoundly affects the heart. "I have never known a man who died from overwork," he said, "but many who died from doubt." In the years since then, researchers have established connections between chronic worry and weakened immune systems, cardiovascular disease, neurological imbalances, clinical depression, and other physical and psychological dysfunctions — not to mention specific anxiety-related illnesses such as panic attacks, agoraphobia, and obsessive-compulsive disorders.[5]

All that from worry. No wonder Jesus warned Martha about her anxiety. No wonder the Bible tells us more than 350 times to "fear not."

The truth is, we were simply not wired for worry. We were not fashioned for fear. And if we want to live healthy lives, we have to find a way to leave our chronic anxiety behind.

But beyond our physical well-being, there lies a more pressing spiritual reason not to worry. If anxiety caused God's closest friends, Adam and Eve, to hide from his face, just imagine what worry must do to you and to me.

Why the Bible Tells Us Not to Worry

When God tells us in the Bible not to worry, it isn't a suggestion. It's a command. Worry and/or anxiety is specifically mentioned twenty-five times in the New Testament alone as something we should avoid.

The words used most often for worry and anxiety in the New Testament come from the same Greek word, *meridzoe,* which means "to be divided, to be pulled in opposite directions, to choke." (Perhaps we wear anxiety around our necks after all.)

In the parable of the sower, Jesus tells us: "The seed that fell among thorns stands for those who hear, but as they go on their way they are *choked by life's worries,* riches and pleasures" (Luke 8:14, emphasis mine). These people have accepted the Word of God, Jesus says, but "they do not mature." Gasping for spiritual breath, worry-bound, thorny-ground Christians may survive, but they never truly thrive.

The Old English word for worry meant "to gnaw." Like a dog with a bone, a worrier chews on his problem all day long. Jesus warned us specifically against this kind of chronic anxiety when he said, "Therefore I tell you, stop being perpetually uneasy (anxious and worried) about your life" (Matthew 6:25, AMP).

Why is the Bible so adamant about our avoiding fear and worry? Because God knows worry short-circuits our relationship with him. It fixes our eyes on our situation rather than on our Savior.

It works a little like a thick London fog — the kind of fog that is legendary. Why, it wouldn't be a Sherlock Holmes story without fog to obscure the villain and allow him to get away. "Thick as pea soup," Londoners describe it. "Can't see your hand in front of your face," they say.

However, while physical fog may seem dense and almost solid, scientists tell us that a fog bank a hundred feet deep and covering seven city blocks is composed of less than one glass of water. Divided into billions of droplets, it hasn't much substance. Yet it has the power to bring an entire city to a standstill.[6]

So it is with anxiety. Our mind disperses the problem into billions of fear droplets, obscuring God's face. Taking our anxiety to the Lord is often the last thing we think of when we are spiritually fogged in. And yet only the "Son" has the power to disperse it. Without him, one fear leads to another, and our lives slow to a painful crawl.

Worry As a Way of Life

In her book *Bring Back the Joy*, Sheila Walsh writes about a group of women she spoke to about fear and the place it occupies in our lives. One woman said, "Fear is what's holding me together. Without it I'd be like a sweater. I'd unravel." The women all laughed, Sheila writes, "but we knew there was some truth to her words. Fear was half the structure of her life, and she was afraid (there's that word again) of what would hold her together if it were gone."[7]

Worry can become a habit, even a way of life — and it's not easy to let go of it. After all, sometimes it actually seems to work.

We may be slightly neurotic, but our kids never get hurt. (We don't allow them to climb on anything higher than the sofa.) Our husband always has clean, freshly ironed undershorts. (In case of an accident, the paramedics will know he has a wife who really cares.) We don't get out much, but our house sparkles. (We'd like to invite someone over, but what if they said no? What if they said *yes?*)

Unfortunately, the belief that worry actually helps us is just an illusion — and a dangerous illusion at that. Worry doesn't prevent bad things from happening. In fact, it may prevent us from leading the full lives God intends us to live. Instead of helping us solve life's problems, anxiety creates new ones, including a tendency to unhealthy introspection. For many of us, our worries can be like Lay's potato chips — you can't stop with just one.

Dr. Hallowell tells of one patient who described her worry like this: "It's like a pattern of frost that shoots across a cold pane of glass. In seconds I am fighting with an enormous net of dangerous, intricate detail. You can't believe how quickly I go from dealing with one worry to having a jumbled mess of them."[8]

My friend Penny agrees. "I can be sitting on the couch, when suddenly one of my thoughts takes on a life of its own." Soon she finds herself crying, downright sobbing. "In a matter of seconds, my children have died, my husband's divorced me, and I'm living on the street!"

Hallowell says it is common for worriers to let their imaginations get the best of them. Rather than relying on facts, they let one worry stack against another until the domino effect sets in — one fear gets the next one moving and so on and so on. This is why truth can be such a powerful antidote to worry. "Get the facts," Hallowell suggests, "because so much of toxic worry is based upon exaggeration or misinformation."9

Toxic worry. That's quite a description — but it rings true to me. I've tasted its stomach-churning effects many times.

Unchecked, worry seeps into our thoughts, poisoning our joy, convincing us to give up on solutions before we've even tried them. Like Eeyore the donkey in *Winnie the Pooh*, we can let our lives be consumed by negativity. "What's the use? It will never work." Instead of looking for the best, we assume the worst. And we're not in the least surprised when the worst finds us.

What a terrible way to live! No wonder Jesus commanded us to set our worries aside, to "fear not."

Worry Versus Concern

Don't misunderstand. When Jesus told us not to worry, he wasn't asking us to live in denial, a sugarcoated fairy tale. He wasn't telling us there's nothing to be concerned about.

The truth is, we live surrounded by opportunities for fear, anxiety, and worry. Because our world is filled with struggles and real pain, we face legitimate concerns every day. Bad things do happen to good people — and not-so-good people as well. Real problems do occur, usually on a daily basis. People don't act the way they ought to. Relationships falter and sometimes fail. There is potential for pain all around us. And there are certainly things that require concern and action on our part.

Jesus knew this better than anybody. He spent most of his life being harassed and pursued by his enemies. So why did he tell us not to worry? Jesus knew that a life filled with fear has little room left for faith. And without faith, we can neither please God nor draw close to him for the comfort and guidance we need to face the cares and affairs of everyday life.

So what is the difference between healthy concern and toxic worry? Here are a few things I've discovered in my own battle against fear:

Concern	Worry
• Involves a legitimate threat	• Is often unfounded
• Is specific (one thing)	• Is generalized (spreads to many things)
• Addresses the problem	• Obsesses about the problem
• Solves problems	• Creates more problems
• Looks to God for answer	• Looks to self or other people for answers

Pastor and teacher Gary E. Gilley sums up the difference like this: "Worry is allowing problems and distress to come between us and the heart of God. It is the view that God has somehow lost control of the situation and we cannot trust Him. A legitimate concern presses us closer to the heart of God and causes us to lean and trust on Him all the more."[10]

Concern draws us to God. Worry pulls us from him. I think this distinction is especially helpful for those of us who tend to spiritualize worry, convincing ourselves that it's our duty to fret about such things as the state of the world, our finances, or our futures. Oswald Chambers puts it this way in *My Utmost for His Highest*:

> Fussing always ends in sin. We imagine that a little anxiety and worry are an indication of how really wise we are; it is much more an indication of how really wicked we are. Fretting springs from a determination to get our own way. Our Lord never worried and He was never anxious, because He was not "out" to realize His own idea; He was "out" to realize God's ideas. Fretting is wicked if you are a child of God. . . . All our fret and worry is caused by calculating without God.[11]

That's something we all need to remember when it comes to this issue of worry. We face legitimate concerns every day of our lives. But instead of fretting, instead of worrying, we need to focus on discerning what *we* can do (with God's help) and what should be left entirely up to God.

Even more important, we need to keep our focus on who God is and what God can do.

The bills won't pay themselves. But we serve *Jehovah Jireh* — the God who provides. The mole on our arm may indeed need to be checked and may even turn out to be cancerous. But we serve *Jehovah-Rapha* — the God who heals. There is plenty in this world to be concerned about. But we serve *El-Shaddai* — an almighty God.

Jesus warned us, "In this world you will have trouble" (John 16:33). Catch that! He said, "you *will*," not "you might." Troubles come with this earthly territory.

"But take heart!" Jesus says. "I have overcome the world."

If we have Jesus Christ as our Lord and Savior, we are not alone. We are *never* alone. When life comes blustering down the street, threatening to huff and puff and blow our house down, we can rest in ease. Because we live within a mighty fortress. Because we are hidden beneath almighty wings. Because we have a strong older Brother right there beside us. And he's rolling up his sleeves.

That's the reason we *can* leave our worry behind — not because there's nothing to be concerned about, but because we have Someone who can handle them a lot better than we can.

Three Steps to Victory

Paul had all kinds of reasons to worry as he sat in a Roman prison awaiting a possible death sentence. But instead of writing the Philippians a sob story, Paul wrote an incredible epistle of joy. And that epistle includes a passage that has been helpful to me as I've tried to learn not to worry.

"Do not be anxious about anything," Paul wrote in Philippians 4:6-7, "but in everything, by prayer and petition, with thanksgiving, present your requests to God. And the peace of God, which transcends all understanding, will guard your hearts and your minds in Christ Jesus."

In this short passage, we find three concise and practical steps to victory over worry.

1. Be *anxious* about *nothing*.
2. Be *prayerful* about *everything*.
3. Be *thankful* for *all things*.

When Paul wrote the words, "Do not be anxious about anything," he literally meant "not even one thing!" Nothing. Not our families nor our finances, not our future nor our past. Not even one thing. That's important for someone like me to hear this because worry is such a treacherous habit. Allow one little worry in, and another is sure to follow, then another. It's better to cut it all off at the source. To be anxious about nothing.

But of course, the only way to carry off that first order is to carry out the second — to "pray about everything." And Paul literally meant "every single thing!" There is nothing too big, nothing too small, that we cannot bring to the heart of our Father. Corrie Ten Boom put it this way: "Any concern too small to be turned into a prayer is too small to be made into a burden."[12]

Realizing that has been enormously helpful to me. One of the ways God brought me out of my worried way of life was just that: prayer. Novel idea, eh? Especially for someone who'd lived most of her life by the axiom: "Why pray when you can worry?"

Here's what I did: Instead of mentally obsessing about my problems, I began consciously turning my worry into prayer.

Instead of worrying, "What if my husband has a wreck while he's on the road," I'd pray, "Dear Jesus, be with John as he drives today . . ."

Instead of telling myself, "If I don't finish this costume, Jessica will really be disappointed," I'd tell Jesus, "Lord, you know how much this means to Jessica . . ."

That may sound trite and overly simplistic, but something in this tiny act broke the bondage. Rather than nursing and rehearsing my concerns, I began giving them over to the Lord. And gradually as I did, I found that chronic anxiety had lost its grip on me.

You see, fretting magnifies the *problem,* but prayer magnifies *God.* "The reasons our problems often seem overwhelming is [that] we allow the things of time to loom larger in our gaze than the things of eternity," writes Selwyn Hughes in *Every Day Light.* "The tiniest of coins, when held close to the eyes, can blot out the sun."[13]

Perhaps that's why Paul finishes his prescription for worry with one last piece of crucial advice: "Be thankful for all things!" Look at everything God has done. In the words of the old hymn, "Count your blessings, name them one by one!" If we aren't grateful for what God has done in the past and in the present, we won't have the faith to believe God for things in the future.

Gratitude is important because it has the power to change our attitude. When we are willing to give thanks to God in *all* things, not just some things — to consciously thank him even when we don't feel very grateful — something in us begins to shift. We begin to see life as Christ sees it, full of opportunities rather than obstacles. And when we view life through eyes of faith, fear just has to flee.

The Choice That Leads to Peace

So much depends on our perspective. If my God isn't bigger than life, then my life is bigger than God — and that's when anxiety takes over.

"It's an interesting thing, the human mind," say authors Bill and Kathy Peel in their book *Discover Your Destiny*. "It can only focus on a couple of things at a time. When we're preoccupied with a problem and focus on our own inadequacy to handle it, there's really no room to add God to the picture. The ability to think rationally returns only when we refocus on God's adequacy."[14]

And when we do that, Paul says, "The peace of God, which transcends all understanding, will guard your hearts and your minds in Christ Jesus" (Philippians 4:7). When we decide to pray instead of worry — when we choose to have a grateful heart in not-so-great circumstances — then the peace of God comes and takes us into "protective custody." It stands guard at the door of our heart, transcending, surpassing, and confounding our own human understanding, bringing us peace.

Relieved of duty, we can take off our worry beads and pick up our shield of faith. And then we can stand back and watch God move.

Speaking of worry beads, the use of *komboloi* had declined significantly in Greece over the past three or four decades as young Greeks tried to adopt more modern ways. But now, it seems, these ancient stress reducers are making a big comeback. Even in cosmopolitan Athens, they're everywhere. You can pick up plastic worry beads cheaply at newsstands or fork out as much as a thousand dollars at a jewelry store for something more ornate. Executives in Armani suits flick their fingers over ivory beads and smooth black stones. Old men click wooden ones. Hip young Greeks twirl their strings of beads, comparing styles and price tags. It's a tradition that still brings a form of comfort.

I wonder how many of them know where the *komboloi* originated? I wonder if they would trade in their clicking and clacking for the original purpose these strings represented? *Komboloi,* you see, were first used in other cultures for the sole purpose of counting prayers. Bead by bead, prayer by prayer, the *komboloi* were an outward expression of a godward heart.

It is the same choice we are offered today. Will we pray? Or will we worry? We really can't do both.

The Battlefield of the Mind

"Finally, brothers, whatever is true, whatever is noble, whatever is right, whatever is pure, whatever is lovely, whatever is admirable — if anything is excellent or praiseworthy — think about such things" (Philippians 4:8). Paul closes his advice on worry with a checklist of things to think about. Will our thoughts center on things *true* or false? *Noble* or nasty? *Right* or wrong? *Pure* or putrid? *Lovely* or lewd? *Admirable* or abominable? *Excellent* and *praiseworthy?* Or sordid and contemptible?

"Garbage in, garbage out." We've all heard the saying. What we put in our minds affects our hearts. And out of the abundance of our hearts, our mouths speak. Our minds churn. Our lust burns. And lives overturn.

We cannot underestimate the effect of what we think about. The war of worry, as well as the trial of temptation, is won and lost on the battlefield of our minds.

The young woman's gray eyes darted nervously behind wire-rimmed glasses as she looked around the crowded library. For a moment, I thought she might turn and leave. Instead, she stepped up to the librarian's desk and waited her turn.

"Do you have any books on fear and worry?" she asked the man behind the desk, her voice soft and low. I recognized the pain that laced her every word. I, too, had lived in her anxious world.

But God had done so much in my life in the area of anxiety. I had been a fixer, trying to make everyone happy, trying to make everything okay, while somehow impressing God with all my works. Like Martha, I had been continually upset and worried about many things. I had wanted to grow in Christ, but every time I came up against an obstacle, I had balked in fear. Rather than leaping over the road-block "through Christ who strengthens me," I'd skid to a stop. Then I'd back up for a good look and try to figure a way around it on my own.

Now, as I stood there in the library, I

wondered if I would have a chance to share what God had done for me. The young woman came toward me, her arms stacked with books on overcoming fear. *Should I stop her, Lord?* my heart whispered. But she and the librarian were still talking, so I waited.

"By the way," I heard the young woman ask, "do you have the latest Stephen King novel?"

A New Mind

I'm embarrassed to admit I didn't talk to the young woman. The moment to speak seemed lost in irony and awkwardness. I wandered back to my work, feeling my advice would have been unwelcome at that point.

It's been my experience that God won't usually take away our "friends," those things we look to for comfort — even if those friends aren't good for us. We must be willing to release them ourselves. And until we do, the battle for the mind will rage on.

So many of us, even Christians, complain about our struggle against sin, but then we secretly supply Satan with all the ammunition he needs. We *know* we shouldn't be reading that book. We *know* the telephone conversation we had yesterday was less than glorifying to the Lord. We *know* the unforgiveness we've harbored for so long is hardening into rage. But still we cling to it — and then we wonder why we have such a hard time making positive changes in our lives.

We must be willing to take an active role in the battle against anxiety. For too long I'd allowed Satan total access to my thought life, and by doing so, I'd given him free rein.

But as I began to "take captive every thought to make it obedient to Christ" (2 Corinthians 10:5), anxiety began to lose its hold. Instead of being led astray by fear, I took a second look at each thought as it came. Many were incognito, disguised to look like ordinary emotions. But instead of entertaining them, I handcuffed the intruding thoughts that triggered fear and took them to Jesus. Together we interrogated them, asking two questions:

- *Where did you come from?* (What is the source of this fear? Is it real or imagined?)
- *Where are you going?* (Will this thought draw me to God or into fear?

94

Can I do anything about this problem, or should I turn it over to God?)

For so long, I had let thoughts come and go without realizing that if Satan controls my thought life, he controls me. Before that time, I'd carelessly let my emotions lead me down the treacherous paths of self-reliance rather than trusting in God. I'd allowed my worry to lead me by the poisoned waters of doubt. My fears had made me lie down in green pastures of self-pity.

But no longer. A note in the margin of the old British *Revised Version* translates Isaiah 26:3, "Thou wilt keep him in perfect peace whose *imagination* is stayed on Thee."[15]

The Word leapt to life for me the day I read that particular translation. It was the diagnosis I'd needed to hear. My imagination had controlled my life for so long that it had grown into a giant sheepdog, loping unrestrained across the meadows of my mind. My emotions trailed behind my imagination like frolicking puppies, never certain where they were being led, but quite happy to go along for the ride.

"Here, Imagination! Here, boy." Sometimes I said it out loud. So strong was the pull to fear that it took a living word picture to pull me back to center. Back to faith. I'd point to the ground beside me and instruct both my imagination and any stray emotions to "Stay."

Crazy? Yes, maybe. But it worked for me. Nothing could be crazier than the anxious way I had lived before.

I began to search the Scriptures for verses on fear and worry and the mind. When I found a verse that fit, I memorized it. Then, when the temptation to fear came, I could answer it with the Word of God: "For God hath not given us the spirit of fear; but of power, and of love, and of a sound mind" (2 Timothy 1:7, KJV).

Like King David in Psalm 1:2, I began to meditate on God's Word day and night. The word for *meditate* has been likened to a cow chewing on its cud. Instead of gnawing on my problem, I trained my mind to chew on the promises of God. And as the Holy Spirit and I brought back the Word to remembrance, something exciting happened. Anxiety fled in the face of truth, and peace — the kind of peace that quieted the disciples' raging storm — came to take its place.

The kind of peace only Jesus can give. *Peace, be still.*

Perfect Peace

"Perfect love casteth out fear," 1 John 4:18 (KJV) tells us. I love the way J. B. Phillips translates this verse: "Love contains no fear — indeed fully developed love expels every particle of fear, for fear always contains some of the torture of feeling guilty. This means that the man who lives in fear has not yet had his love perfected."

That particular verse is helpful to me because it speaks to the root of my worry habit. I was anxious for the same reason the first man and woman became anxious: I was not secure in God's love.

Oh, I knew that I was saved and that if I died, I'd go to heaven. But somewhere along the way, I had twisted God's love into something I had to earn. If I could just be good enough, then God had to love me. But of course I stumbled again and again. Each time it took me weeks to work up enough spiritual brownie points to feel like I was back on God's good side.

No wonder I worried. No wonder I was afraid. I was constantly sewing fig leaves, trying to cover up my inadequacy.

When Jesus said, "Martha, Martha . . ." so gently that frantic day in Bethany, he was speaking to you and me as well. Lovingly, if we'll listen, he whispers his diagnosis concerning the state of our souls: "You're worried," he points out. "You're anxious. It isn't just about this meal; it's about everything."

And with the diagnosis comes a choice.

Come find love, Jesus invites us. Come find a love so perfect that it covers all your faults and pronounces you "not guilty." Come find a love that chases fear out the door! Come find everything you've ever longed for. Come find peace for your soul.

"Joanna, Joanna . . . ," the Lord speaks to my life today. Listen closely. You'll hear him calling your name as well. "Do not let your hearts be troubled," he's saying. "Trust in God; trust also in me" (John 14:1).

He's urging us all to lay aside our worry beads, to give up fiddling with things we can never hope to fix and to seek his face instead.

He's calling us to the Great Exchange — the one where we can never lose. As we trade the "many things" that make us anxious, he gives us the "one thing" that calms our hearts. Himself.

For he is the Prince of Peace.

10. *Separate toxic worry from genuine concern.* Determine if you can do anything about your situation. If so, sketch a plan to handle it (Proverbs 16:3).

9. *Don't worry alone.* Share your concerns with a friend or a counselor. You may receive helpful advice. Talking your fears out with someone often reveals solutions that were invisible before (Proverbs 27:9).

8. *Take care of your physical body.* Regular exercise and adequate rest can defuse a lot of worry. When our bodies are healthy, our minds can handle stress better and react more appropriately (1 Corinthians 6:19-20).

7. *Do what is right.* A guilty conscience can cause more anxiety than a world of problems. Do your best to live above reproach. Take care of mistakes quickly by confessing and seeking forgiveness (Acts 24:16).

6. *Look on the bright side.* Consciously focus on what is good around you.

Don't let yourself speak negatively, even about yourself (Ephesians 4:29).

5. *Control your imagination.* Be realistic about the problems you face. Try to live in the "here and now" not in the "what might be" (Isaiah 35:3-4).

4. *Prepare for the unexpected.* Put aside a cash reserve and take sensible measures so you'll be ready if difficulties arise (Proverbs 21:20).

3. *Trust God.* Keep reminding yourself to put God in your equation. Then, when fear knocks, you can send faith to answer the door (Psalm 112:7).

2. *Meditate on God's promises.* Scripture has the power to transform our minds. Look for scriptures that deal with your particular areas of anxiety. Answer life's difficulties with God's Word (2 Peter 1:4).

1. And the number one way to tame a worry habit? *Pray!* Joseph M. Scriven's hymn says it all: "O what peace we often forfeit, / O what needless pain we bear, / All because we do not carry / everything to God in prayer"[16] (Colossians 4:2).

I sought the LORD, and he answered me; he delivered me from all my fears.
Those who look to him are radiant; their faces are never covered with shame.
PSALM 34:4-5

4

The Cure

You are worried and upset about many things,
but only one thing is needed.
LUKE 10:41-42

The story is told of a man who met God in a lovely valley one day.[1]

"How are you this morning?" God asked the fellow.

"I'm fine, thank you," the man replied. "Is there anything I can do for you today?"

"Yes, there is," God said. "I have a wagon with three stones in it, and I need someone to pull it up the hill for me. Are you willing?"

1. Adapted from a story by Rosemarie Kowalski. Used by permission.

"Yes, I'd love to do something for you. Those stones don't look very heavy, and the wagon's in good shape. I'd be happy to do that. Where would you like me to take it?"

God gave the man specific instructions, sketching a map in the dust at the side of the road. "Go through the woods and up the road that winds up the side of the hill. Once you get to the top, just leave the wagon there. Thank you for your willingness to help me today."

"No problem!" the man replied and set off cheerfully. The wagon pulled a bit behind him, but the burden was an easy one. He began to whistle as he walked quickly through the forest. The sun peeked through the trees and warmed his back. What a joy to be able to help the Lord, he thought, enjoying the beautiful day.

Just around the third bend, he walked into a small village. People smiled and greeted him. Then, at the last house, a man stopped him and asked, "How are you this morning? What a nice wagon you have. Where are you off to?"

"Well, God gave me a job this morning. I'm delivering these three stones to the top of the hill."

"My goodness! Can you believe it? I was just praying this morning about how I was going to get this rock I have up to the top of the mountain," the man told him with great excitement. "You don't suppose you could take it up there for me? It would be such an answer to prayer."

The man with the wagon smiled and said, "Of course. I don't suppose God would mind. Just put it behind the other three stones." Then he set off with three stones and a rock rolling behind him.

The wagon seemed a bit heavier. He could feel the jolt of each bump, and the wagon seemed to pull to one side a bit. The man stopped to adjust the load as he sang a hymn of praise, pleased to be helping out a brother as he served God. Then he set off again and soon reached another small village at the side of the road. A good friend lived there and offered him a glass of cider.

"You're going to the top of the hill?" his oldest friend asked.

"Yes! I am so excited. Can you imagine, God gave me something to do!"

"Hey!" said his friend. "I need this bag of pebbles taken up. I've been so worried that it might not get taken care of since I haven't any time to do it myself. But you could fit it in right between the three stones here in the middle." With that, he placed his burden in the wagon.

"Shouldn't be a problem," the man said. "I think I can handle it." He finished the cider, then stood up and brushed his hands on his overalls before gripping the handle of the wagon. He waved good-bye and began to pull the wagon back onto the road.

The wagon was definitely tugging on his arm now, but it wasn't uncomfortable. As he started up the incline, he began to feel the weight of the three stones, the rock, and the pebbles. Still, it felt good to help a friend. Surely God would be proud of how energetic and helpful he'd been.

One little stop followed another, and the wagon grew fuller and fuller. The sun was hot above the man pulling it, and his shoulders ached with the strain. The songs of praise and thanksgiving that had filled his heart had long since left his lips as resentment began to build inside. Surely this wasn't what he had signed up for that morning. God had given him a burden heavier than he could bear.

The wagon felt huge and awkward as it lumbered and swayed over the ruts in the road. Frustrated, the man was beginning to have visions of giving up and letting the wagon roll backward. God was playing a cruel game with him. The wagon lurched, and the load of obligations collided with the back of his legs, leaving bruises. "This is it!" he fumed. "God can't expect me to haul this all the way up the mountain."

"Oh God," he wailed. "This is too hard for me! I thought you were behind this trip, but I am overcome by the heaviness of it. You'll have to get someone else to do it. I'm just not strong enough."

As he prayed, God came to his side. "Sounds like you're having a hard time. What's the problem?"

"You gave me a job that is too hard for me," the man sobbed. "I'm just not up to it!" God walked over to where the wagon was braced with a stone. "What is this?" He held up the bag of pebbles.

"That belongs to John, my good friend. He didn't have time to bring it up himself. I thought I would help."

"And this?" God tumbled two pieces of shale over the side of the wagon as the man tried to explain.

God continued to unload the wagon, removing both light and heavy items. They dropped to the ground, the dust swirling up around them. The man who had hoped to help God grew silent. "If you will be content to let others take their own burdens," God told him, "I will help you with your task."

"But I promised I would help! I can't leave these things lying here."

"Let others shoulder their own belongings," God said gently. "I know you were trying to help, but when you are weighted down with all these cares, you cannot do what I have asked of you."

The man jumped to his feet, suddenly realizing the freedom God was offering. "You mean I only have to take the three stones after all?" he asked.

"That is what I asked you to do." God smiled. "My yoke is easy, and my burden is light. I will never ask you to carry more than you can bear."

"I can do that!" said the man, grinning from ear to ear. He grabbed the wagon handle and set off once again, leaving the rest of the burdens beside the road. The wagon still lurched and jolted lightly, but he hardly noticed.

A new song filled his lips, and he noticed a fragrant breeze wafting over the path. With great joy he reached the top of the hill. It had been a wonderful day, for he had done what the Lord had asked.

An Overloaded Wagon

I've felt like the man hauling rocks — overburdened, overworked, and overwhelmed. What started as a joy became drudgery, and I felt like giving up.

Nothing is harder to bear than a burden we're not called to carry. While God does ask us to bear one another's burdens, he has not asked us to step in and do what people are not willing to do themselves. And while there are many needs, God has not asked us to meet every one.

In fact, we, like Martha, may be surprised by how little God actually requires.

The Jews, eager to please God, were big on rules and regulations. God had given the law, and because they loved him, they were determined to live it out to the fullest. If a little law was good, then surely more law was even better. At least that was the opinion of the Pharisees, one of the two religious sects who most influenced the common people of Jesus' day.

In their desire to be a perfect nation, the Pharisees took the basic precepts God had laid out to Moses and began creating ways to apply them to everyday life. Eventually they created the *Mishnah*, a collection of over six hundred rules and regulations designed to help Jews live out the Law to the last jot and tittle. The mandates ranged from the sublime to the ridiculous. Especially those surrounding the Sabbath.

God's law required a weekly day of rest, a ceasing from labor and a laying down of burdens. From the appearance of the first evening star on Friday night until the setting sun on Saturday, Jews were required to cease all work — and the rules about what constituted work were quite exacting. The Pharisees interpreted this to mean that a man who carried a needle in his cloak on the Sabbath was sewing. If he dragged a chair across a sandy floor, he was plowing. If he carried his mattress, he was bearing a burden. If he plucked corn and rubbed it in his hands, he was reaping. In all of these things, he was considered to be breaking the Law.[2]

The Pharisees even argued that it was wrong to eat an egg laid on a Sabbath because the *hen* had been working. The "official" Sabbath burden that one could legally carry was the weight of one dried fig.[3]

But instead of drawing the nation of Israel closer to God, the pharisaic law became a stumbling block. It was impossible to keep every petty particular of what Jesus called "heavy loads" (Matthew 23:2-4).

It is in this legalistic setting that we find Martha. The Jewish religion was patriarchal by nature. Only men were allowed to sit on the Sanhedrin ruling council. Only men were allowed in the synagogue; the women sat outside. Only men were allowed to wear scripture-filled phylacteries upon their foreheads or left arms to remind them to obey God's Law. The outward trappings of godly devotion were largely a male domain.

Women who wanted to show their love for God were encouraged to do it through good works — but that was about their only option. They were allowed to enter the Women's Court of the Temple to worship, but no farther. In the wilderness, they had only been allowed as far as the tabernacle door. Even Solomon, in his description of the perfect woman, mentioned little of her spiritual walk with God — only the duties she fulfilled.

And Jewish women had duties by the dozens. Even keeping the Sabbath meant a lot of work for the women of Jesus' day. Though the Sabbath was mandated as a day of rest for women as well as men, the day *before* the Sabbath was filled with frantic preparation. There were three kosher meals to prepare, lamps to be filled with olive oil, and jugs to be filled to the brim with water for ceremonial washing. The house had to be cleaned, and the whole family needed freshly laundered tunics to wear the next day.[4]

And that was for an "ordinary" Sabbath. Feast days and special events required extra preparations.

The day Jesus visited Martha and Mary was probably busier than usual. The Feast of the Tabernacles was near, and the house was filled with cooking and activity. This pilgrimage feast was held early in the fall and was one of three feasts every adult male Jew within a fifteen-mile radius was required to come to Jerusalem to celebrate.

The Feast of Tabernacles lasted seven days, followed by a special Sabbath. Held just after harvest, it was a time of great celebration and joy. The people left their homes to live in booths or small tents in memory of their time in the wilderness. William Barclay, in his commentary on John, describes it like this:

> The law laid it down that the booths must not be permanent structures but built specially for the occasion. Their

walls were made of branches and fronds, and had to be such that they would give protection from the weather but not shut out the sun. The roof had to be thatched, but the thatching had to be wide enough for the stars to be seen at night. The historical significance of all this was to remind the people in unforgettable fashion that once they had been homeless wanderers in the desert without a roof over their heads.[5]

Bethany sat at the eastern edge of the Mount of Olives, just two miles away from Jerusalem. At the time of Jesus' visit, the town's gentle slopes were probably filled with pilgrims' booths. In order to make room for worshipers during the great feasts, the boundaries of Jerusalem were usually extended to include Bethany.

So when Martha invited Jesus and his disciples to stay at her home on their way to Jerusalem, they accepted her kind hospitality. Martha continued with her expected tasks — making everything comfortable so everyone else could worship.

The thought of joining Jesus never occurred to her because it simply wasn't allowed. But she loved Jesus. I think she knew she was entertaining the Messiah. And so Martha showed her devotion by giving the gift she knew best. The gift of service.

But even welcome wagons can grow heavy, as Martha quickly discovered. Especially when they're laden with the extra weight of our human agendas and expectations.

Dumping Rocks

Jesus came to earth and immediately tipped the Jewish wagonload of rules and regulations. He hit the religious leadership right where it hurt — smack dab in the middle of their spiritual pride. "Woe to you, because you load people down with burdens they can hardly carry, and you yourselves will not lift one finger to help them" (Luke 11:46).

To those helpless under the weight of Law, Christ became a Burden Bearer: "Come unto me, all ye that labour and are heavy laden, and I will give you rest" (Matthew 11:28, KJV). But to those who put faith in their religious accomplishments, he added yet another load: "One thing you lack," Jesus told the rich young ruler. "Go,

113

sell everything you have and give to the poor. . . . Then come, follow me" (Mark 10:21). Jesus knew that sooner or later, the legalistic load would grow too heavy to bear alone and the religious would cry out for relief. And he would be there.

Jesus stripped away all the "traditions of men," the layers of dos and don'ts that had obscured the face of God. "This is who God is," he declared to the world. "Look and see! He loves you. He sent me so you could have life and fellowship with him. It isn't outward appearance that concerns the Father. It's your inner person."

That's what Jesus told Martha that busy afternoon. "You're worried and upset about many things, but only one thing is needed." And what was that one thing? Not cooking or cleaning or doing good works, but knowing God. Listening to him. Leaving the Kitchen long enough to experience the intimate fellowship of the Living Room.

"Only one thing is needed." With those words, Christ swept away centuries of chauvinism and bias, tradition and ritual. Women were no longer to be on the outside looking in when it came to spiritual matters. Just as surely as Christ's death would bridge the gap between God and humankind, so Jesus' words this day removed the gender barrier that separated women from their Maker.

Scripture doesn't tell us Martha's response to Jesus' astounding statement. But I can see Jesus offering his hand, welcoming her to join Mary down at his feet.

What did Martha do then, I wonder? Perhaps she sputtered excuses: the dinner, her apron, her hair. Perhaps she just withdrew, chastened. Or perhaps — as she stood there looking into her Master's eyes — Martha simply sank to her knees and began to listen.

The point is, we just don't know. While negative responses to Jesus' invitations in the Bible are usually mentioned — the rich man left downcast, and the keepers of the Law left angry — this particular story is left unfinished. Perhaps it is to leave us room to determine our own response.

What will we do when told we've missed out on the best God has for us? Will we bow our knees, or will we run back to what is familiar? Will we sputter excuses or humble our hearts?

It's hard to ignore the love of Jesus. The sweet wooing of the Holy Spirit calms our fears and shatters our defenses. Based on her subsequent encounters with Jesus, which we will discuss in later chapters, I believe that's exactly what happened to Martha. I believe she followed her Master's leading. She bent her knees and found his feet. She let God dump her wagon, so loaded with care, then allowed him to fill it with his presence.

Only then, as Martha let go of her lengthy list of to-dos and began doing the one thing that was needed, did she begin to give God what he really wants.

Dumping Rocks

When my friend Tricia started feeling overwhelmed by her too-busy life, she and her husband, John, decided to dump some rocks from their overloaded wagons. Here's the simple process they followed. Maybe you'll find it helpful too.

1. They made a list of all the activities they were involved in (children, work, church, etc.).
2. They prayed over and prioritized the activities as to importance, assigning each one a number from one to four.
3. Then they eliminated all the fours.

While this process may sound overly

---

simplistic, it really helped John and Tricia lighten their load. "It was hard to see things we enjoyed go out the door!" Tricia says. "But the freedom and the peace we've gained have been more than worth it."

Now this is what the LORD Almighty says: "Give careful thought to your ways."
HAGGAI 1:5

Giving the Gift God Desires

My husband and I had been married less than a year when my birthday rolled around. He was so secretive about his plans to celebrate, I was certain this birthday would be something wonderful. And it was. I came home to find candlelight and roses, the table set with our new china, and a homemade birthday cake on the counter. John had gone over to see Mrs. Chapman, our next-door neighbor, and she'd shown him how to make it — from scratch!

I was terribly impressed. But what intrigued me most was the huge box in the center of the table. What could it be? Lingerie? A new dress? Chocolate? John seemed just as excited as I, insisting that I open his gift before we sat down to dinner.

"I hope you like it," John said, his eyes as bright as a little boy's. "You said you needed it."

"Needed it." That should have been my first clue. But being young and naive when it came to men, I assumed the gift would be even more wonderful than I'd first believed. It just had to be that expensive food processor I'd been admiring downtown.

I carefully removed the bow and began peeling the tape off one end. "Open it!" John urged. "Just rip it open!" We laughed as I tore the beautiful wrapping off in big strips. Neither of us could wait for my reaction.

And there it was, beneath Hallmark's most expensive foil — my birthday gift in all its glory. The love of my life had given me not one, but two (because he is a generous man!) Rubbermaid organizers. One to hang my iron and ironing board on. The other to organize my mop and broom.

I was speechless to say the least. John was so excited, he insisted on hanging them right away. "You said you needed them," he chattered as he searched for a screwdriver.

"I did, didn't I?" I replied weakly, following him to the laundry room.

Fortunately, we were still newlyweds. I managed to bite my lip before offering a thank-you kiss, and for several years John thought he had made gift-giving history. Boy, did he.

So often we give God the gift we think he needs rather than take time to find out what he desires.

We make promises and New Year's resolutions to be more heavenly minded. This year we'll read the Bible through. This year we'll join a prayer group — or start a new one ourselves. This year we'll try that forty-day fast everyone's talking about.

We make goals to be more loving and less selfish. We look for opportunities to serve. We visit a shut-in on Monday, man the crisis pregnancy line on Tuesday, volunteer at school on Wednesday, work at the food bank on Thursday, type the church bulletin on Friday, play with our kids on Saturday, and go to church on Sunday. And everything we do is important. All of it is good.

The problem is, contrary to popular belief, we can't do it all. We're not even supposed to try.

Paul explained just that in Romans 12. He said that the body of Christ has many members, and each of them has a different gifting — which means each has a different job to do. The fact that 20 percent of the church does 80 percent of the work is not at all what God intended.

Jesus' words to Martha are words to those of us who are overextended in service as well: "Only one thing is needed." We must take time to sit at Jesus' feet, to worship him, to get to know him better. When we put that first thing first, then he delights to reveal his will and our part in fulfilling it.

Sometimes I think I struggle to discern God's will because I'm surrounded by the obvious. Someone obviously needs to care for the toddlers during church service. Someone obviously needs to visit Kathleen, who's bedridden with a difficult pregnancy. Someone obviously needs to cut out blocks for missionary quilts — and tell my neighbor about Jesus. I'm surrounded by legitimate needs, and I want to do them all. And so I try. But midway through a blustery day of service, I find myself cross and frustrated, not at all aglow with the saintly aura I'd expected when I'd set out that morning.

That's exactly what happened a few years ago when our church in Oregon scheduled a missions banquet. Someone — *obviously* — needed to head it up, so I cheerfully volunteered, certain I was doing God a favor. I was bursting with creativity and energy for the project. "Oh Lord," I told him, "you are going to love what I have planned for you!" Then I set off, certain he was walking beside me.

Unfortunately, everything about the event was a struggle. There were interpersonal rumblings and my own amount of grumbling. But after it was through, I felt quite satisfied. The banquet was beautiful, the food delicious, and the decorating exquisite. People were touched by the missionary message, and money was raised for crucial needs.

I remember sighing with pride, "Wasn't that wonderful, God?" But I heard no reply

---

The Practical Power of "One Thing"

The one thing that Jesus said was needed in Martha's life was fellowship with him — and that's true for us, too. But the principle of "one thing" can also have smaller, practical implications

---

that can help when life feels over-whelming. Here are some ways to practice one-thing thinking when your wagon feels overloaded.

1. *Invite Jesus to rule and reign.* Each morning before you get out of bed, invite the Lord to come take the throne of your life, to be your "one thing." Present your day to him and ask him for wisdom and guidance.

2. *Ask God to reveal the next step.* As you go through your day, keep asking the Lord, "What is the one thing I need to do next?" Don't let the big picture overwhelm you. Just take the next step as he reveals it — wash one dish, make one phone call, put on your jogging clothes. Then take the next step . . . and the next.

3. *Have faith that what needs to get done will get done.* Since you have dedicated your day to the Lord, trust that he'll show you the one thing or many things that must be done. Do what you can do in the time allotted. Then trust that what wasn't accomplished was either unnecessary or is being taken care of by God.

4. *Be open to the Spirit's leading.* You may find your day interrupted by divine appointments. Instead of resisting the interruptions, flow with the one thing as God brings it across your path. You'll be amazed at the joy and freedom that comes from surrendering your agenda and cooperating with his.

Commit to the LORD whatever you do,
and your plans will succeed.
PROVERBS 16:3

in my spirit. It was as if I'd turned to speak to the Lord, only to find him missing.

"God," I cried in my heart, "where are you?"

His voice answered in the distance, "Over here, Joanna." There he stood, patiently waiting on the path where I'd first told him of my glorious plan.

"I thought you were in this, Lord," I said as I walked back to where he was. "I thought you'd be pleased."

He gently took my hand, then wiped away my tears. "It was good. Perhaps it was even important. But it wasn't my plan for you."

I realized then that, while there are many

things that need to be done, things I'm capable of doing and want to do, I am not always the one to do them. Even if I have a burden for a certain need or project, my interest or concern is not a surefire sign that I need to be in charge. God may only be calling me to pray that the right person will rise up to accomplish it. What's more, I may be stealing someone else's blessing when I assume I must do it all.

How I wish I would have learned earlier in ministry to wait upon the Lord. Much of my energy and joy has been swallowed up by jobs and obligations that were not my own. I still tend to rush in, presuming to know his will rather than waiting to hear what he desires.

It is a costly mistake, for often, when the Holy Spirit does ask something of me, I'm either knee deep in another project or too exhausted from my latest exercise in futility to do what God wants of me.

What Does God Desire?

Which brings us back to the crucial question — what is it God desires?

If we could just get a handle on what God expects, the overachiever in us surmises, then it would be easy to please him. But that was the downfall of the Pharisees. They had reduced their relationship with God to a series of dos and don'ts, entirely missing the purpose for which God had set them apart. They put on religious work clothes, not realizing God wasn't looking for maids and valets — he was looking for a people to call his own.

Now that's not to say that service for God is unimportant. The Bible tells us, "Whatever your hand finds to do, do it with all your might" (Ecclesiastes 9:10). "Faith by itself, if it is not accompanied by action, is dead," according to James 2:17. As we will see in chapter 6, serving God and others really is important. Hard work is often part of what we are called to do.

But service was never supposed to be our first priority. Work is not our first order of business — even working for the Lord. In fact, our own efforts are so far down the line when it comes to what God wants that they didn't even register in Jesus' conversation with Martha.

Only *one* thing is needed — and it was happening, not in the Kitchen, but right there in the Living Room.

Notice, however, Jesus didn't rebuke Martha because she was fixing supper, thus instituting the eleventh commandment: "Thou shalt not cook" — although that would be a handy excuse when I don't feel like fixing dinner. Jesus wasn't concerned about Martha's external abilities at all. It was her internal disabilities that he probed — the dark corners of pride and prejudice, the spiritual handicap of busyness that left her unable to enjoy the intimacy of his presence.

After all, intimacy can be threatening. Getting close to Jesus means we can no longer hide our inadequacies. His light illuminates everything that is wrong and ugly about our lives. Unconsciously, therefore, we may flee God's presence rather than pursue it. And Satan spurs on our retreat by telling us we're not good enough to earn God's favor. He tells us that when we get our act together — that's when we can enter the Living Room.

But the truth is, we can't get our spiritual act together unless we go to the Living Room *first*.

It's not always easy to get there. Intimacy with God may require leaving our comfort zones. Some people feel uneasy in the presence of God. They dismiss the act of worship as too emotional, preferring the intellectual pursuit of Bible study or doctrine. Or they simply have trouble being still, because that's their personality. But regardless of our temperament, regardless of our emotional preference, we are all called to intimacy with God. The one thing Martha needed is the one thing we need as well.

If you struggle to stay at his feet, ask the Lord to reveal what is hindering you. There is no need to lay aside your intellect or your personality when you enter the Living Room. Just come as you are.

As a child of God.

Children, after all, love intimacy. "Hug me, Mommy!" With arms stretched upward, they beg, "Daddy, hold me!" From infancy, when frightened or ill, the first place our children long to be is as close to our heart as they can get. They cuddle in, pressing themselves into our arms.

That is the intimacy our Father desires to share with us. Not because we've earned it, but because he hungers for it. And so do we, whether we're aware of it or not.

Longing for Fellowship

I didn't realize how much I longed for God until that dark night I cried out to hear the good news. Although I had served him since I was a child, there was a devastating emptiness about my relationship with my heavenly Father. I had worked and worked to please him, yet I couldn't feel his love.

The Galatians knew that same kind of emptiness. They had accepted Christ as Savior and thrived under Paul's teaching and care. But when Paul left Galatia, the Judaizers moved in, telling them they still had a long way to go before they could enjoy true closeness to God. These were Jewish Christians who believed that the ceremonial practices of the Old Testament — including circumcision — were still binding upon the New Testament church. Paul, they said, had inappropriately removed legal requirements from the gospel in order to make it more appealing to the Gentiles.

Just as the scribes and Pharisees added rules and regulations to the Law, so the Judaizers attempted to mix a new form of legalism in with the gospel of grace. They wanted an outward manifestation of what could only be an inward work.

That's why Paul sent a wake-up letter to his beloved church in Galatia. He called the Judaizers' gospel slavery, and he added, "You foolish Galatians! Who has bewitched you? . . . After beginning with the Spirit, are you now trying to attain your goal by human effort?" (Galatians 3:1,3).

If we aren't careful, we can fall prey to the same kind of lies the Galatians fell for — lies that tell us that we must perform in order to earn God's love. We can add so many requirements to our faith that the "one thing" is swallowed by the "many," and the "best" is obliterated by the "good."

The thing we must understand is that God did not choose us to "use" us.

We are not spiritual Oompa-Loompas in some cosmic chocolate factory, working night and day to churn out a smoother, better-tasting Christianity.

We were not created to fill some egotistical need God has for praise — the angels forever encircle his throne with worship.

We are not some celestial science project; laboratory mice let loose in a maze to see how they interact.

No, the Bible makes it clear that God created us because he longs to have fellowship with us. Our Father longs to pour his very life into us, to give us an inheritance and a share in his divine nature.

What does God desire? It is actually very simple.

He wants you. All of you.

One Thing Is Needed

When Jesus told Martha that only one thing was needed in her life, the context of the verse clearly points to a spiritual call. The Better Part that Mary discovered was to be found not on the table, but at his feet.

However, the Greek phrase for "only one thing is needed" may also refer to food portions. Perhaps in a subtle turn of word, Jesus was issuing two invitations:

- First, to know him — to put worship before work
- But also, not to overdo — even in our efforts on his behalf

Instead of partaking from a sideboard of fancy entrées, Jews usually ate out of a large common bowl placed in the middle of the table. Guests would break off pieces of bread and dip them in the soup or broth. Jesus may have gently reminded Martha that her overdone effort in preparing multiple dishes was keeping her so busy in the kitchen that she was missing out on the real "food," the real "life" of the party.

"Her fault was not that she served," Charles Spurgeon writes of Martha in his devotional classic *Morning and Evening.*

"The condition of a servant well becomes every Christian. Her fault was that she grew 'cumbered with much serving,' so that she forgot him and only remembered the service."[6]

How easy it is to confuse duty with devotion; the common with communion. That was Martha's downfall, and it can be mine as well. For in her effort to set a table worthy of the Son of God, she nearly missed the real banquet. And I, too, can get so overwhelmed that my worship becomes work rather than delight, and devotion becomes just another duty.

If I am not careful, the spiritual disciplines of prayer, Bible study, and praise can become little more than items to be checked off my to-do list or rocks I'm tempted to dump off my wagon because they slow me down. And so I need to hear Jesus' cure for *all* my worry and distress.

"Only one thing is needed" — and that is found in true fellowship with him.

For he, after all, is the Bread of Life, the Living Water, the only "dish" we need. He wants to change our hearts and empower our lives. He wants us to find the great freedom of Luke 10:42.

I cannot do everything, but I can do "one thing."

I cannot meet every need, but I can respond in obedience to the need the Spirit lays on my heart.

I cannot carry every load, but I can carry the load God has for me.

For his yoke, indeed, is easy, and his burden is truly light.

5

Living Room Intimacy

Here I am!
I stand at the door and knock.
If anyone hears my voice and
opens the door,
I will come in and eat with him,
and he with me.
REVELATION 3:20

❧

Simeon was probably like most boys his age in A.D. 403. The thirteen-year-old spent much of his time caring for his father's flocks on the hillsides of Cilicia.

But one day, while listening to a sermon on the Beatitudes, Simeon's heart was stirred and changed. He left his home and family and began a lifelong pursuit of God that took him from a monastery to the Syrian desert to three decades of sitting upon a pole.

Yes. A pole.

Simeon the Stylite began a spiritual fad that would last more than a thousand years. He was the very first "pillar hermit."

Spiritual zeal has always taken a variety of forms, but the first thousand years of Christianity saw more than its share of the bizarre. As the church grew during the first centuries, so did worldliness. In reaction, many Christians withdrew to a life of poverty, chastity, and separation. Hungry for holiness, monks gathered in communities, often competing with one another in their quest for self-denial.

Simeon, I'd say, won the contest hands down.

"Simeon moved to the Syrian desert and lived with an iron chain on his feet before having himself buried up to the neck for several months," writes Robert J. Morgan in his book *On This Day.* . . . "When crowds flocked to view his acts of perceived holiness, Simeon determined to escape the distractions by living atop a pillar. His first column was six feet high, but soon he built higher ones until his permanent abode towered sixty feet above ground."[1]

There he lived for thirty years, exposed to every element, tied to his perch with a rope to keep from falling while he slept. By ladder, his followers brought him food each day and removed his waste. Thousands came to gawk at this strange man on the pillar. Hundreds listened daily as Simeon preached on the importance of prayer, selflessness, and justice.

But the question that occurs to me, as I'm sure it occurred to some of those who came to listen, is this: Did Simeon's life on a pillar really bring him any closer to God?

The Burden of Spirituality

Intimacy with God. What does it mean to you — and how do you achieve it? Does it require sitting on a pillar like Simeon or being buried up to your neck in sand? Is it some mystical level of consciousness attainable only by the deeply devout?

Some religions say that it is. According to Hinduism, a religion based on the karma of good works, one lifetime isn't enough for the soul to achieve spiritual enlightenment. Hindu mathematicians calculate it takes 6.8 million rotations through reincarnation for the good and evil in us to finally balance out so that we can receive the ultimate spiritual level of nirvana.[2]

In the Far East, during religious festivals, men often have hooks inserted under the skin of their backs. These hooks are then tied to wagonloads of rocks, which the men drag through the streets, hoping to obtain forgiveness for their sins. In certain areas of Mexico, the devout crawl miles on their knees in pilgrimage.

All over the world, people go to unimaginable lengths to find God — which is sad when you consider the unimaginable lengths God has already gone to find *us*.

We don't need millions of lifetimes in order to be pure enough to see God. We don't need to stick hooks in our backs or tear the flesh off our knees in order to earn God's favor.

All we really need is Jesus. For he is all the evidence we need. The Father actually *wants* us close and is willing to do whatever is necessary to make sure it happens.

It's hard to imagine the Creator of the universe wanting to know us. We feel so unworthy. That's why many of us persist in thinking that we must earn our way to heaven, that only the superspiritual — only the Simeons of this world — can really know God. Burdened with the weight of our own spirituality, we struggle beneath a load of self-imposed obligations: "I have to do this . . ." or "I can't really know God until I do that . . ." We can spend so much of our lives getting ready to know God or backing away out of fear of displeasing God that we never get around to enjoying the Living Room Intimacy Jesus came to provide.

And yet intimacy with God was indeed the very point of Jesus' coming and of his dying. "You who once were far away have been brought near through the blood of Christ," Paul writes in Ephesians 2:13. For when Jesus died, his cross bridged the great chasm of sin that separated us from God. With his last breath, Jesus blew aside the curtain that had kept sinful humans from touching a holy God. Now we could come into God's very presence, clean and approved, not by our works, but by his grace. Jesus "destroyed the barrier, the dividing wall of hostility" (verse 14) that had separated humanity from God.

When we couldn't reach up to heaven, heaven came down to us and welcomed us into the Living Room through the doorway of Jesus Christ.

That is the good news of the gospel.

The way has been made. The price has been paid. All we need to do is come.

The Price Has Been Paid

The story is told of a young man who left the Old Country and sailed to America to make a new life in the New World. Before he left, his father pressed some money in his hand. It wasn't much, but it was all he had. He hoped it would tide the boy over until he found a job. His mother handed him a box of food for the journey, then they kissed and hugged and tearfully said good-bye.

On the boat, the young man gave his ticket to the porter and found his way to the tiny cabin he'd share with several others during the month-long voyage to New York. That evening at mealtime, the young man went topside and unwrapped a sandwich his mother had made. He ate silently as he watched the other passengers file into a large room crowded with tables. He listened to their chatty laughter and watched as waiters brought plates filled with hot, steaming food. But he just smiled, enjoying his mother's fresh home-made bread and the crisp apple his brother had picked that morning. *Bless my family,* he prayed.

The days went by slowly, and the young man's box of food quickly dwindled. But meals such as they offered in the dining room were certain to cost a lot. He'd need that money later.

He ate alone in his cabin now. The smell from the dining hall made his stomach wrench with hunger. He allowed himself a few crackers and some cheese each day, whispering a prayer of thanks before scraping the mold off the hard lump. A shriveled apple and the tepid rainwater he'd collected in a can completed his meager meal.

Three days out of New York, the last of the food was gone except for a wormy apple. The young man could take no more. Pale and weak, he asked the porter in broken English, "How much?" The porter looked confused. "Food," the young man said as he held out some coins and pointed to the dining room. "How much?"

Finally the ship steward understood. He smiled and shook his head. "It costs nothing," he said, closing the immigrant's hand back around his money. "You are free to eat! The cost of food was included in the price of passage."

This story means a lot to me. For years I lived like a pauper instead of a princess. I'd settled for stale cheese and shriveled apples instead of enjoying the rich table

God had prepared for me. I kept waiting for the day I'd be worthy to sit at his table, never realizing that the cost of such fellowship was included in the price Christ paid for my passage.

The price has been paid. Please hear this simple truth. If you have accepted Jesus Christ as your Savior, the price has been paid for you.

And that means there is nothing keeping any of us away from Living Room Intimacy. The "dividing wall of hostility" has been torn down, at least on God's side. But there may need to be a bit of demolition work on your end, because the enemy of our souls keeps quite busy building barriers to block spiritual intimacy.

Barriers to Intimacy

Before salvation, Satan tells us we're just fine. We don't need a savior.

But after we're saved, the Accuser points his bony finger at us and tells us we're no good. We don't deserve a savior.

He's lying, of course. Jesus says so in John 8:44. Satan is "the father of lies." In fact, lying is what he does best — it's "his native language." The word for *lie* in the

Greek is *pseudos,* which means falsehood or "an attempt to deceive." We attach the prefix *pseudo* in the English language to convey the thought of a counterfeit, a false look-alike.

And that's exactly what we get when we listen to Satan's lies and settle for less than God's best: pseudo-Christianity, pseudo-grace. Satan usually doesn't try to make us swallow a blatant lie — he's too smart for that. Instead, he just doctors the truth for his own purpose, which is to keep us as far away from God as possible.

"Look at what you've done," he w*hiss*pers. "How could God ever forgive you?" He twists the truth of sin into a bludgeon of guilt and shame and beats us with it. "You're no good, you're no good, you're no good . . . baby, you're no good."

If we let him, he's gonna sing it again. Because every time we listen to his lying lyrics, we take another step backward, away from the Living Room. Away from the closeness our hearts yearn for.

Now you may not struggle with the lies I've described above. Perhaps you've never experienced the lonely alienation of such doubt and guilt. In fact, your basic relationship and standing with God may be secure and unshakable. But beware! Satan can use other circumstances just as effectively to keep you from drawing close to God.

Take busyness, for example.

Anne Wilson Schaef tells about a flier advertising new twelve-step meetings forming in the San Francisco Bay area. The meetings were especially for workaholics. At the bottom of the flier was this blurb: "If you are too busy to attend these meetings, we'll understand."[3]

I wonder if God understands when we're too busy to attend to his presence in our lives. Or too tired. Or too embarrassed to admit we've done something he would disapprove of.

Make no mistake. Satan enjoys using our hectic schedules, stressed bodies, and emotional upsets in his efforts to put up barriers to our intimacy with God. That's why we need to take a close look at any thought, feeling, or activity that diminishes our appetite for intimacy with God.

Spiritual Snickers Bars

Teri Myers was my pastor's wife when my family lived in Grants Pass, Oregon. She was, and still is, a dear friend and a spiritual mentor, a true picture of a Mary heart in a Martha world. As I've watched her walk with God over the years, I've grown more eager for a deeper walk of my own. But Teri's the first to admit that it isn't always easy to stay close to the Lord.

She tells the story of having company over for dinner one night. She'd worked hard all day on a beautiful meal — four courses and a fancy dessert. It was going to be wonderful. But somewhere around the middle of the afternoon, Teri realized she was hungry.

"I'd been so busy cooking and cleaning," she says, "I had completely missed lunch." But it was only four o'clock and the guests weren't due until six. "I always kept a hidden stash of Snickers bars," she says with a grin. So she grabbed a couple of candy bars and sat down to rest, enjoying her clean living room and beautifully set table.

"It did the trick! My stomach wasn't growling anymore. I was able to take my shower, do my hair, and get dressed with plenty of time to spare."

It wasn't until Teri sat down to dinner that she discovered the problem. "There I was with that wonderful dinner I'd worked all day to prepare, but my appetite was gone!" The midafternoon snack had taken the edge off her hunger. She ended up picking at her plate as she watched everyone else dig in, enjoying their meal.

"The Lord spoke to me at that moment," Teri says. "He showed me that we often fill our lives with spiritual Snickers bars — things like friends, books, and shopping. They may be good things, completely innocent things — but not when they take the edge off our hunger for God."

Teri's illustration has stayed with me for years because it applies so aptly to my own life. I constantly fight the tendency to fill the God-shaped hole he created in me with fluffy stuff. I don't like loneliness, so I fill the space with phone calls and social events and trips to the mall — but loneliness, as my friend Jeanne Mayo puts it, can be "God's call to fellowship with him." I don't like quietness, so I fill up the silence with sitcoms and talk shows, Christian music and CNN — but it was in the quiet of the night that Samuel heard God's voice.

We were designed to be close to God. Just as our bodies hunger and thirst for food and drink, our spirits hunger and thirst for his presence. But just as it's possible to bloat our bodies with empty calories, we can find ways to pacify our spiritual cravings without really getting the nourishment we need. We can fill up with spiritual Snickers bars while all the time our spirits are withering for want of real food.

If you're having a little trouble feeling close to God — or even wanting to draw close — you might want to consider what activities you are using to fill the empty places of your life. What's taking the edge off of your hunger for him?

Then again, it could be that you just need to start "eating" the good things of the Lord to find out how spiritually hungry you really are. You see, spiritual hunger and thirst don't work the same way as our physical needs. When our physical body feels hunger pains, we eat and our hunger is satisfied. But spiritually speaking, it isn't until we "eat" that we realize how famished we are. As we feast at God's table, something strange happens. We get hungrier. Thirstier. We want more! We have to have more.

"Our souls are elastic," Kent Hughes writes in his book *Liberating Ministry from the Success Syndrome*. "There are no limits to possible capacity. We can always open ourselves to hold more and more of his fullness. The walls can always stretch further; the roof can always rise higher; the floor can always hold more. The more we receive of his fullness, the more we can receive!"[4]

Once you've tasted the Living Room Intimacy Jesus offers, you'll find nothing else will satisfy. For even Snickers bars taste flat in comparison to the sweetness of the Lord's presence. When you've sampled the best of the best, you'll be willing to skip the junk food this world offers in order to have a real sit-down meal with the Savior.

"Taste," as the psalmist says, "and see that the LORD is good!" (Psalm 34:8).

Making Room for the Savior

Few things have whetted my hunger for God like the discipleship course I took back in 1987. While other people may struggle with worldly temptations, my struggle has always been in the area of spiritual disciplines. My devotional life has been haphazard at best. Because I hadn't developed the habit of a quiet time as a child, when the busyness of adulthood came, I found it difficult to find time alone with the Lord.

Some of you may be aghast at such a thought. Your devotional life runs like clockwork. You find it impossible to make it through the day without time alone with God.

If that is true for you, may I tell you how blessed you are? It has taken me nearly twenty years to come to this discipline, and even then, it has been a gift of grace, not an accomplishment of my own making.

Until I took the Navigator's 2:7 Course, I didn't even know what I was missing. There are many wonderful discipleship programs available, and I don't highlight this one for any reason except that it happened to be the one our church used. It gave me the discipleship tools I needed and some necessary accountability as well.

The class was wonderful. My spirit began to grow and thrive as the soil of my heart was tilled deep and fed by the Word of God. But then my Martha-like perfectionist tendencies kicked in, causing me to approach my devotional time as another duty to perform. I loved the feeling I got as I checked off chapters in my Bible reading and conquered another memory verse. To be honest, much of my motivation came from my competitive nature. I wanted to be the star pupil, one of those disgusting teacher's pets.

Robert Boyd Munger's article "My Heart Christ's Home" changed all that. Through the simple analogy he suggested, I discovered what it meant to have a Mary heart toward God. Suddenly my eyes were open to what true devotion is.

It is not a duty. It is a delight.

It is not an exercise in piety. It is a privilege.

And it is not so much a visit as it is a homecoming.

"Without question one of the most remarkable Christian doctrines is that Jesus Christ Himself through the presence of the Holy Spirit will actually enter a heart, settle down and be at home there," Munger says. "[Jesus] came into the darkness of my heart and turned on the light. He built a fire in the cold hearth and banished the chill. He started music where there had been stillness and He filled the emptiness with His own loving, wonderful fellowship."

Munger goes on to tell how he showed Christ around the house of his heart, inviting him to "settle down here and be perfectly at home," welcoming him room by room. Together they visited the library of his mind — "a very small room with very thick walls." They peered into the dining room of his appetites and desires. They spent a little time in the workshop where his talents and skills were kept, and the rumpus room of "certain associations and friendships, activities and amusements." They even poked their heads into the hall closet filled with dead, rotting things he had managed to hoard.

As Munger described each room, they reflected my heart as well. But it was his depiction of the drawing room that would forever change the way I viewed my time with the Lord.

> We walked next into the drawing room. This room was rather intimate and comfortable. I liked it. It had a fireplace, overstuffed chairs, a bookcase, sofa, and a quiet atmosphere.
>
> He also seemed pleased with it. He said, "This is indeed a delightful room. Let us come here often. It is secluded and quiet and we can have fellowship together."
>
> Well, naturally, as a young Christian I was thrilled. I could not think of anything I would rather do than have a

few minutes apart with Christ in intimate comradeship.

He promised, "I will be here every morning early. Meet with Me here and we will start the day together." So, morning after morning, I would come downstairs to the drawing room and He would take a book of the Bible . . . open it and then we would read together. He would tell me of its riches and unfold to me its truths. . . . They were wonderful hours together. In fact, we called the drawing room the "withdrawing room." It was a period when we had our quiet time together.

But little by little, under the pressure of many responsibilities, this time began to be shortened. . . . I began to miss a day now and then. . . . I would miss it two days in a row and often more.

I remember one morning when I was in a hurry. . . . As I passed the drawing room, the door was ajar. Looking in I saw a fire in the fireplace and the Lord sitting there. . . . "Blessed Master, forgive me. Have You been here all these mornings?"

"Yes," He said, "I told you I would be here every morning to meet with you." Then I was even more ashamed. He had been faithful in spite of my faithlessness. I asked His forgiveness and He readily forgave me. . . .

He said, "The trouble with you is this: You have been thinking of the quiet time, of the Bible study and prayer time, as a factor in your own spiritual progress, but you have forgotten that this hour means something to Me also."[5]

What an amazing thought — that Christ wants to spend quality time with me. That he looks forward to our time together and misses me when I don't show up. Once that message started sinking into my heart, I started looking at my devotional time in a whole new way — not as a ritual, but as a relationship.

And a relationship doesn't just happen. It has to be nurtured, protected, and loved.

The Comforts of Home

The place Mary found at Jesus' feet is the same place available to you and me. It's a place where we can be comfortable, where we can kick off our shoes and let down our hair. It's a place of transparency and vulnerability; a place where we are completely known yet completely loved. It is truly a place called home.

If we love him and obey his teachings, Jesus says in John 14:23, God will actually come and live with us. "My Father will love him," he said of those who follow him, "and we will come to him and *make our home* with him" (emphasis mine).

And it goes both ways. Jesus not only wants to be at home in us; he also wants us

---

Creating a With-Drawing Room

There is something special about a sacred space consecrated to God — a prayer closet set aside especially for your quiet times. But if you don't have a lot of extra room at home, consider the following ideas for creating a prayer closet wherever you are:

- *Emilie Barnes,* a writer and speaker who has inspired thousands of Christian women toward beautiful living, keeps a special prayer basket on hand to help with her devotions. In it she keeps (1) her Bible, (2) a daily devotional or other inspirational reading, (3) a small box of tissues "for the days I cry in joy or pain," (4) a pen for journaling or writing notes, and (5) a few pretty cards in case she feels moved to write a note to someone she's praying for. For Emilie, seeing the basket is both an invitation and a reminder to spend time with the Lord. And because it's portable, she can take it anywhere.[6]

- *Robin Jones Gunn,* a popular Christian novelist, began lighting a candle to set apart her prayer times after a friend made her feel especially welcome by lighting a candle for their visit. "Sometimes the house is still dark and quiet when I sit down and light the candle for my quiet time. Other times life is in full swing around me, but my corner becomes a quiet place of intimate conversation. When my family sees the candle lit, they know to leave mom alone for however long I sit there, opening my heart to the Lord and listening to Him. I've noticed that after I blow out the candle and enter the frenzy of the rest of the day, a sweet fragrance lingers in my house and in my soul."[7]

- For years, *Gwen Shamblin,* a Christian weight-loss advisor, has wakened in the middle of the night to spend her quiet time. To "preplan for these rendezvous with God," she keeps a heating pad tucked under the couch cushion, with a blanket and her Bible on top. "I get all snuggled up, then open my Bible and converse with God. They are times I look forward to."[8]

When you pray, go into your room,
close the door and pray to your Father,
who is unseen. Then your Father,
who sees what is done in secret,
will reward you.
MATTHEW 6:6

to make our home in him. "God wants to be your dwelling place," Max Lucado writes in *The Great House of God.*

He has no interest in being a weekend getaway or a Sunday bungalow or a summer cottage. Don't consider using God as a vacation cabin or an eventual retirement home. He wants you under his roof now and always. He wants to be your mailing address, your point of reference; he wants to be your home.9

What a beautiful, gracious offer from the Lord of hosts. It's hard to imagine saying no to the opportunity to live in God and rest in him. But we can — and so often we do. Isaiah 28 gives a vivid picture of what happens when we refuse. "This is the resting place, let the weary rest," God told the Israelites through his prophet Isaiah (28:12). "This is the place of repose," he said, inviting them to be at home with him.

But the Israelites would not listen, according to Isaiah. Instead of making God their dwelling place, they insisted on a more independent living arrangement. And what happened then is the very picture of what happens to us when we refuse the Father's offer of at-home intimacy. Isaiah says in verse 13:

So then, the word of the LORD to
   them will become:
      Do and do, do and do,
      rule on rule, rule on rule;
      a little here, a little there.

Matthew Henry, writing about these

verses, says that the Israelites "would not heed . . . they went on in a road of external performances. . . . The prophet's preaching was continually sounding in their ears, but that was all; it made no impression upon them; they had the letter of the precept, but no experience of the power and spirit of it; *it was continually beating upon them, but it beat nothing into them*"[10] (emphasis mine).

Sound familiar, Martha? It does to me. When we refuse God's offer of grace-filled rest in the Living Room, the only alternative is the tyranny of works — which, as we have seen, doesn't work! We will be driven to do more and more — more service projects, more committee chairmanships, more spiritual extracurricular activities — trying to win God's approval. And still we will fail, because what the Father really wants is for us to find our identity — our "mailing address" as Lucado puts it — in him and him alone.

How to Live Together

Jesus came to show us the way to the Father's house. Instead of making a once-a-year visit to the Holy of Holies, we're invited to dwell there. To make our home in God's throne room — or, if you prefer, his Living Room.

But practically speaking, how is that possible? Jesus gives us a hint in John's gospel.

"Remain in me," Jesus says in John 15:4, "and I will remain in you."

The *King James* translation of that verse makes the relationship even clearer. "Abide in me," Jesus says. And *abide* means to live or dwell.

Dwell in me, he promises. And I will dwell in you.

Then, to give us an even better idea of what being at home with God really means, Jesus uses a word picture so simple a child can grasp it, though it may take a lifetime to implement.

"See this vine?" I can hear Jesus ask, holding one up for inspection. "See this branch? See where they are connected? Well, that's the way it is with you and me."

"I am the vine" was what he actually said. "You are the branches. If a man remains in me and I in him, he will bear much fruit; apart from me you can do nothing" (John 15:5).

All our "do and do," our "rules on rules," will never accomplish what Jesus can when we let him have his way in our life. But in order for that to happen we must be *connected* to him. It's not enough simply to be associated. To be acquainted. We have to be spiritually grafted on — to draw our life from him, to be so closely attached that we would wither and die if we were cut off.

I missed that point for a long time. I had spent so much of my life concentrating on the "fruit" of my own personal holiness, that I missed out on the connection, the sweet intimacy of being attached to the Vine. And as a result, what I tried to do was as ludicrous as an apple tree branch trying to produce apples by its own effort.

"Be good, be good. Do good, do good," the broken branch chants as it lies on the orchard grass.

"That apple should be popping out anytime," says the helpless, lifeless stick.

But that isn't how it works. It's the tree, not the branch, that determines the fruit. The tree is the life source. The branch has no power of its own. But once it gets connected, once that sap gets flowing and those leaves start growing, that insignificant little twig will find itself loaded with fruit. And it didn't have to do anything — except abide.

My relationship with God works the same way. My sole responsibility is keeping my connection to Jesus Christ solid and secure. How is that done? It's really not that complicated. As trite as it may sound, the formula for intimacy with God remains the same today as it has always been:

PRAYER + the WORD + TIME = INTIMACY with GOD

We'll talk further in chapter 7 about developing a quiet time, but for now let's take a moment to look at these necessary components of a close relationship with God.

First of all, what is *prayer?* There are entire books written on the subject, but when it comes down to this essential first factor, prayer is simply talking to God. Prayer is my heart crying out to the Lord for guidance and wisdom, for my own needs as well as the needs of others. As I focus my heart on him, prayer allows me to express my love through praise, to declare my absolute dependence on him alone. Then, as I wait before the Lord, he reveals his heart to me.

One of the most precious ways God

expresses his love for us is through his Word, the Bible, which is the second essential factor in intimacy. The Hebrew word for *Bible* is *mikra,* which means "the calling out of God."[11]

Isn't that wonderful? We don't have to wonder what God thinks, what he feels about certain topics, because to a large extent he has already told us through Scripture. Better yet, we don't have to wonder whether he loves us or not. According to my dictionary, the Old English word for *gospel* is *godspell.* God spells out his love for the whole world to see. It's right there in his Word.

"Fear not, for I have redeemed you," the Lord tells us in Isaiah 43:1,4. "I have summoned you by name. . . . You are precious and honored in my sight . . . because I love you." We are a chosen people. Made holy. Deeply and dearly loved by God. How do I know that? I hear God's voice telling me, "calling out" to me, every time I open his Word.

Time is an essential factor in Living Room Intimacy for a purely practical reason. If I don't take time to pray, there will be no real communication in our relationship. If I don't take time to read God's Word, I won't hear his loving call. And if I

Finding God's Will

Have you ever wondered how other people have learned to discern God's will? George Mueller, a nineteenth-century English pastor who was known for his life of prayer and his close walk with God, once shared this simple method for determining God's will through prayer and the Word:

1. "I seek at the beginning to get my heart into such a state that it has no will of its own in regard to a given matter. . . .

2. "Having done this, I do not leave the result to feeling or simple impression. If so, I make myself liable to great delusions.

3. "I seek the Will of the Spirit of God through, or in connection with, the Word of God. . . . If the Holy Ghost guides us at all, He will do it according to the Scriptures and never contrary to them.

4. "Next I take into account providential circumstances. These often plainly indicate God's Will in connection with His Word and Spirit.

5. "I ask God in prayer to reveal His Will to me aright.

> 6. "Thus, (1) through prayer to God, (2) the study of the Word, and (3) reflection, I come to a deliberate judgment according to the best of my ability and knowledge, and if my mind is thus at peace, and continues so after two or three more petitions, I proceed accordingly."[12]

> *Whether you turn to the right or to the left, your ears will hear a voice behind you, saying, "This is the way; walk in it."*
> ISAIAH 30:21

don't make time to be alone with Jesus, our relationship will suffer, because time is integral to any relationship.

I love the way Kent Hughes describes the intimate impact of spending time with God. "Think of it this way," Hughes writes. "Our lives are like photographic plates, and prayer is like a time exposure to God. As we expose ourselves to God for a half hour, an hour, perhaps two hours a day, his image is imprinted more and more upon us. More and more we absorb the image of his character, his love, his wisdom, his way of dealing with life and people."[13]

That's what I want. That's what I need.

And that's what I receive when I spend time in God's Word and in prayer. I get more of Jesus and, in the process, a little less of me.

Maintaining Intimacy

God longs to make his home in us. And he longs for us to make our home in him. Think of it. Christ "in us" (1 John 4:13). Our lives "hidden with Christ in God" (Colossians 3:3). What an incredible, intimate entangling of humanity and divinity!

There is only one thing that can stop such Living Room Intimacy, and that is our own sin. For though there is nothing we can do to attain our salvation, there is much to be done to maintain our connection to the Vine. Because sin interrupts the life-flow we need to grow, we must do all we can to maintain a pure heart before God.

Here's something I'm learning to do on a regular basis — something I've found that makes a big difference in the level of intimacy I enjoy with Christ.

I call it "spiritual housekeeping."

We tend to suffer from dropsy around our house. You know the affliction? We

163

come in the door and drop whatever we have on the floor. On the next trip, we drop some more. This makes for a quite messy house and a very frustrated housekeeper. Which is me.

But spiritually speaking, I tend to do the same thing. I'll drop an unkind word here, spill a negative attitude there, let a resentment lie where it fell in a corner. It isn't long before the clutter of sin is knee high and my heart is paralyzed, not knowing where to start cleaning up the mess and feeling far away from God.

Not a great way to live, I'm sure you'll agree — either in a house or in a heart.

But I'm learning. I'm getting better.

Now, instead of letting sin pile up, I try to do my housekeeping every day. My goal is obedience — avoiding sin by following God's commands. But when I mess up, I try to choose repentance. I tell God I'm sorry and look for ways to make amends for any damage I've caused. I consciously give the Lord those things I just can't fix and resolve to do better, depending on God to make it possible.

Conscious repentance leads to unconscious holiness. That phrase, gleaned from the writings of Oswald Chambers, has done incredible things in my walk with God. It has lifted me from the orchard floor and grafted me to the tree.

Before, I'd tried to produce the fruit of holiness on my own, with little result except failure and self-condemnation. But when I realized that holiness was a work of the Spirit in my life, that my responsibility was to live connected to the Vine, I was able to abandon my own fruitless trying and focus on staying close to the One who gives me life.

Intimacy with God? It's pretty simple, really.

It's not a pillar we sit on; it's a house we live in.

It's not a list of dos and don'ts; it's a branch staying connected to the Vine.

It's not striving to know God, but realizing that our Father longs to know us. And it's free for the taking — at least for you and me.

But we must never forget — it cost Jesus his very life.

6

Kitchen Service

Whatever your hand finds to do,
do it with all your might.
ECCLESIASTES 9:10

"I know who you are."

The Chinese president's eyes were calm and unflustered as he spoke in careful English. His comment interrupted the flow of conversation that had carried the room for most of the afternoon.

Don Argue looked at the man, uncertain what he meant.

The year was 1998. As president of the National Association of Evangelicals, Dr. Argue had been invited to meet with the president of the People's Republic of China, Jiang Zemin, to discuss China's stance on religious freedom. Tens of thousands of Christians were being persecuted for their faith, with thousands more in prison or already executed. Dr. Argue had earlier presented the logic of allowing Christians to practice their faith. "They will be your best workers," he had told the president. "They are honest and trust-worthy." But the conversation had moved on from there, swallowed up in political posturing and diplomatic niceties.

"I know who you are," President Jiang now repeated, his voice low as he bent toward Dr. Argue. With the help of an interpreter he shared this story: "When I was a youth, I was very sick and in a hos-pital. One of your people, a Christian nurse, cared for me. Even at the end of a long and busy day, she would not leave until all of our needs were met."

President Jiang smiled and nodded.

"I know who you are."[1]

Templates of Christianity

Of all the identifying marks of a Chris-tian, Jesus said love would be the thing that gives us away. "By this all men will know that you are my disciples," he said, "if you love one another" (John 13:35). *Agape* is to be our signature — the unconditional, never-ending love of God flowing through and out of our lives. A feel-good *phileo* kind of love isn't enough. We need a love that loves "in spite of" and "because of." In spite of rejection, hardship, or persecution, we love. Because of the great compassion God lavished upon us, we share it with our world — both in words and in sacrificial service.

We've been filled with great treasure for one purpose: to be spilled.

Christ illustrated this *agape* love to his disciples by washing their feet. "As I have loved you, so you must love one another," Jesus told the group of men in John 13:34, their freshly laundered toes a gentle witness to his words.

What Jesus did must have shocked the disciples. The *Midrash* taught that no Hebrew, even a slave, could be commanded to wash feet. The streets and roads of Palestine were rugged back then, unsurfaced and unclean. William Barclay says, "In dry weather they were inches deep in dust and in wet they were liquid mud."[2] Add the fact that most people wore sandals, a simple flap of leather fastened to the foot by a few straps, and foot washing was a dirty job, to say the least.

Though disciples, by tradition, attended to their favorite rabbi's many needs, they never considered such a filthy task. Nor was it expected. It simply wasn't done.

So when Jesus bent his knee to serve his followers, it was a graphic display of humility. Their Teacher became the lowest of the low. Then he invited — no, commanded — them to do the same. "It is noteworthy that only once did Jesus say that he was leaving his disciples an example, and that was when he washed their feet," says J. Oswald Sanders.[3]

Kitchen Service, you see, isn't optional for Christians. We're supposed to spend a good part of our time following our Lord's example. We're supposed to serve others and show love to them — and, in the process, to represent Jesus to the world around us. Unfortunately, as the world well knows, it's easy for Christians to forget what we're here for. It's easy to fall into the hypocrisy of talking one way and living another way — or to get so involved with our religious activities that we neglect to reach out to those around us.

Mahatma Gandhi once said, "If Christians lived according to their faith, there would be no more Hindus left in India."[4] This great leader of the Indian nation was fascinated at the thought of knowing Christ. But when he met Christians, he felt let down. Unfortunately, the world is filled with people who feel the same. They are intrigued by the claims of Christ, but they shrink back because of disappointment with his offspring.

"Don't look at people," we might protest. "Look at Jesus." But while that may be true, the sobering truth remains: Whether we like it or not, we're the only Jesus some will ever see. Dwight L. Moody put it this way: "Of one hundred men, one will read the Bible; the ninety-nine will read the Christian."5

The apostle Paul understood the responsibility of representing Christ to others. More than nine times in the New Testament, Paul wrote something to the effect of "Follow me as I follow Christ." Here are a few:

- "I urge you to imitate me" (1 Corinthians 4:16).
- "Whatever you have learned or received or heard from me, or seen in me — put it into practice" (Philippians 4:9).
- "Follow my example, as I follow the example of Christ" (1 Corinthians 11:1).

In verses such as these, Paul was not only encouraging people to replicate *his* life, but to live life in such a way that they themselves became templates of Christianity. Paul says in 1 Thessalonians 1:6-7: "You became imitators of us and of the Lord. . . . And so *you* became a model to all the believers" (emphasis mine).

There were no Gideon Bibles in the New Testament church. There were no Bibles at all, except for the Hebrew scriptures. The only evidence of this new and living way came in the form of the walking, breathing, living epistles that filled the young church's meeting rooms and spilled out into the street.

"You are a letter from Christ . . . ," Paul reminded the Christians at Corinth, "written not with ink but with the Spirit of the living God, not on tablets of stones but on tablets of human hearts" (2 Corinthians 3:3).

You are a letter that is known and read by everyone, Paul said.

The same is true of us today. We are God's love letter to the world. We were set apart for a purpose — to communicate his glory to a lost and dying world.

Fruitful Living

I once heard of a man who loved experimenting in his garden. He was always coming up with a hybrid this and a hybrid that. His crowning achievement was a tree he'd pieced together. Part plum, part apricot, part peach, and part prune — it was the craziest mixed-up tree you ever saw. But that tree had a major problem.

Oh, it was alive. It grew fine. The leaves were there. Every once in a while in the spring he would even get a blossom. But it never did bear any fruit.

John the Baptist noticed the same problem in the lives of many of his Jewish followers. He didn't mince words in warning them about the lack of fruit in their lives. He didn't mix pears and kumquats either.

You identify a tree by the fruit it produces, John said — and a tree that doesn't produce is worth nothing at all. "Therefore bear fruits worthy of repentance, and do not begin to say to yourselves, 'We have Abraham as our father.' For I say to you that God is able to raise up children to Abraham from these stones" (Luke 3:8, NKJV).

John was chastising the Jews for

believing their DNA — their "root stock" was enough to please God. It wasn't enough to be sons of Abraham, he said. They also needed to live like chosen people — to bear fruit worthy of their lineage. If they wouldn't do it, God was prepared to find people who would. "The ax is already at the root of the trees, and every tree that does not produce good fruit will be cut down and thrown into the fire" (Luke 3:9).

In the same respect, it isn't enough to call ourselves Christians. We must *live* like Christians. "Not everyone who says to me, 'Lord, Lord,' will enter the kingdom of heaven," Jesus once said, speaking of the barren lives of many, "but only he who does the will of my Father who is in heaven" (Matthew 7:21).

Apple trees bear apples. Plum trees bear plums. If we call ourselves Christians, then our lives should be unmistakably and obviously Christlike.

Fruit Happens

Throughout the Word of God, the analogy of fruit is used. All four Gospels include Christ's picture of the Vine and the branches. Out of the twenty-seven books in the New Testament, fifteen mention the kinds of fruit we are to have in our lives, including:

- *The fruit of our lips:* "Let us continually offer to God a sacrifice of praise — the fruit of lips that confess his name" (Hebrews 13:15).
- *The fruit of our deeds:* "That you may live a life worthy of the Lord and may please him in every way: bearing fruit in every good work, growing in the knowledge of God" (Colossians 1:10).
- *The fruit of our attitudes:* "But the fruit of the Spirit is love, joy, peace, patience, kindness, goodness, faithfulness, gentleness and self-control" (Galatians 5:22-23).

So how can I make sure my life is producing this kind of fruit?

It's not really that difficult. You see, fruit isn't something you can sit down and manufacture in your life. Fruit *happens.* You get connected to the Vine and pretty soon you've got zucchini — tons and tons of zucchini.

So much zucchini you just have to share!

As we "abide" in the intimate relationship with Christ that we talked about in chapter 5, something incredible happens. We begin loving as we never loved before. Our lives change, and we become examples worth imitating.

We begin producing fruit. Juicy, lusciously lovely, lip-smacking-delicious fruit. Fruit in our lives that tells the world who we are and what our God is like. Even when we're stuck doing dishes in the Kitchen.

Joy in the Kitchen

Nicholas Herman was born in the Lorraine region of France in the middle of the seventeenth century. Largely uneducated, he worked briefly as a footman, then a soldier. At the age of eighteen, Nicholas experienced a spiritual awakening, and from that moment on his life had one goal: "to walk as in God's presence."

In 1666, Nicholas joined a Carmelite monastery in Paris. There he served as a lay brother until he died at eighty years of age, "full of love and years and honored by all who knew him."

Perhaps you'd recognize Nicholas by his Carmelite name: Brother Lawrence. A group of letters he wrote during his lifetime were collected into a book called *The Practice of the Presence of God*. Though Brother Lawrence never meant his correspondence to be published, this tiny book has sold millions, challenging centuries of Christians to a closer walk with God.

It is a picture of a life devoted to God — a truly fruitful life. A picture of a Mary heart in a Martha world.

More particularly, Brother Lawrence's influential book beautifully illustrates how the fruit-making process is supposed to operate in our lives. In uncomplicated but striking detail he shows that it's not just what we do for Christ that matters, but how we go about it. He didn't learn the secret of fruitfulness sitting high upon a pole like Simeon the Stylite. He learned it in a kitchen. Yeah. A kitchen.

When Brother Lawrence joined the monastery, he had fully expected to spend his days in prayer and meditation. Instead, he was assigned to cooking and cleanup, a position for which he admitted a "great aversion."

Yet once Brother Lawrence decided to "do everything there for the love of God, and with prayer . . . for his grace to do his work well," he found his own Kitchen Service a joy and an avenue to a closer walk with God. He wrote:

> The time of business does not with me differ from the time of prayer, and in the noise and clatter of my kitchen, while several persons are at the same time calling for different things, I possess God in as great tranquillity as if I were upon my knees at the blessed sacrament.[6]

What a goal! To be so in tune with the presence of God that washing dishes becomes an act of worship. That the moments of our lives, no matter how mundane, become aflame with the divine.

When Jesus rebuked Martha, remember, he wasn't rebuking her act. He was rebuking her attitude. "He blamed Martha, not for her attentive service of love," author Charles Grierson says, "but for allowing that service to irritate, agitate, and absorb her."[7]

Service without spirituality is exhausting and hopeless. But in the same respect, spirituality without service is barren and selfish. We need to unite the two and do it all "as unto the Lord."

When we do that, something wonderful happens to our work in the Kitchen. Sinks turn into sanctuaries. Mops swab holy ground. And daily chores that used to bore us or wear us down become opportunities to express our gratitude — selfless avenues for his grace.

Serving Like Jesus

Our sanctification, as Brother Lawrence once said, "does not depend upon *changing* our works, but in doing that for God's sake which we commonly do for our own."[8]

For three and a half years, Jesus of Nazareth did just that. He ministered out of everyday life. Instead of renting a coliseum or building a synagogue, then waiting for people to come to him, Jesus went to them.

God's Kitchen Patrol

Do you want to be in service for the Lord but aren't sure what to do? Maybe the following tips will spark an idea in your own heart for ways you can serve God as you serve his children. Once you get started, you'll find the opportunities are endless.

- *Join God's Secret Service.* Find ways to serve anonymously — send an

---

encouraging note, leave a plate of cookies on a doorstep, sponsor a kid to camp, pay someone's electric bill.

- *Give a cup of cold water in his name.* Volunteer for drink crew at the Special Olympics. Hand out Popsicles in the park on hot days. Sponsor a refreshment stand for thirsty travelers at a nearby rest stop.

- *Look for your "angel unaware."* God often puts a needy person in our lives he wants us to serve. Instead of resisting, accept that person as a "divine assignment" and love him or her as unto the Lord.

- *Comfort with the comfort you've received.* Often we serve best in an area where we've experienced pain. If you're a cancer survivor, you can offer hope and support to someone newly diagnosed. If you've been bereaved, you have words the grieving need to hear.

Whatever your hand finds to do,
do it with all your might.
ECCLESIASTES 9:10

He took time to meet the needs of people. Our Savior stopped midstride to heal the woman with a bleeding disorder. He cleared his afternoon and made room on his lap for little kids. Jesus confronted religious hypocrites and comforted lost souls — each one as the opportunity arose.

And it is exactly this kind of spontaneous ministry that God entrusts to you and me. "He seems to do nothing of Himself which He can possibly delegate to His creatures," C. S. Lewis writes. "He commands us to do slowly and blunderingly what He could do perfectly and in the twinkling of an eye."9

To trembling, inadequate saints like you and me, God gives the ministry of reconciliation — bringing humanity back home to God. A mighty task, yes. But it's not impossible when we take it one day at a time and follow the example that Jesus set — the example Brother Lawrence himself imitated.

I see three simple principles of ministry in the life of Christ that can show us how to live our lives in fruitful Kitchen Service.

- Jesus ministered as he *went on his way.*
- Jesus ministered as he *went out of his way.*
- Jesus ministered in *all kinds of ways.*

On Our Way

First of all, Jesus was available. He ministered as he was needed — *as he went on his way.* He delivered the demon-possessed man as he passed through the Gadarenes (Matthew 8:28-34). On the walk to Capernaum, he used the time to teach his disciples (Mark 9:33-37). While he was returning from Decapolis, he took advantage of opportunities to heal the sick and raise the dead (Luke 8:40-56).

Even the incident that forms the centerpiece of this book — the story of Mary and Martha told in Luke 10:38-42 — took place while Jesus was "on the way." Instead of pressing on to Jerusalem, where he was headed, Jesus apparently made an unscheduled stop in Bethany when, as verse 38 tells us, "a woman named Martha opened her home to him."

This is a God who comes to us. When we open our lives, he enters our hearts and dwells within us. Then he invites us to join him on his journey — for that's what serving God is all about. God doesn't come to sign our guest book. He comes to make us his own.

"Jesus watched to see where the Father was at work and joined Him,"[10] Henry

Blackaby reminds us in *Experiencing God.* Jesus did nothing of his own initiative, according to John 5:19. Instead the Son did "only what he [saw] his Father doing."

That is the secret of holy Kitchen Service. Instead of expecting God to acquiesce to our plans, dreams, and schemes — or frantically trying to impress him with our efforts on his behalf — we simply need to "watch to see where God is working and join Him!"[11]

When we do that, Kitchen Service becomes a delight rather than a distraction. It becomes a natural outflow of our relationship with God rather than one more duty to keep us from what we really want to do. When we minister *on the way,* every day can become an adventure!

I'll never forget driving home one winter from a youth pastor's retreat. Driving across eastern Montana, we encountered a detour that took us off the rural highway and onto a snow-packed dirt road. Mile after mile we drove, the only car on the vast Montana plain, with only a barbed-wire fence to outline the way.

"I think we're lost," I said.

"We're not lost," John said. "Go back to sleep."

So being the obedient wife I am, I did. I

don't know how much farther we went, but I awoke when the car finally slowed and turned into a driveway — the only driveway, I learned later, that John had seen in the last fifty miles.

I rubbed my eyes and sat up in time to see a small, pink-and-white-oxidized single-wide trailer leaning slightly into the wind. I looked over at John as he pulled the car to a stop.

"We're lost," he admitted.

But we weren't lost at all.

The old man who came out to greet us looked a bit disappointed when John crawled out of the car. It was his birthday, you see. And he'd hoped against hope that the car he'd heard in the driveway was his son coming to visit from Minnesota.

But he seemed to cheer up as we stayed and chatted for a while, giving him as a birthday present a small, stuffed animal I'd bought on the trip. There was a tear in his eye but a smile on his face when he shook John's hand and pointed the way back to the main road.

I've found that when we're willing to serve like Jesus did — while we're *on the way* — divine appointments like that start popping up everywhere. And if we'll take the time to stop and listen, we may find our destination, even when we thought we were lost.

Going Out of Our Way

In the book *Love Adds a Little Chocolate*, Linda Andersen writes:

> Duty can pack an adequate sack lunch, but love may decide to enclose a little love note inside. . . . Obligation sends the children to bed on time, but love tucks the covers in around their necks and passes out kisses and hugs (even to teenagers!). . . . Duty gets offended quickly if it isn't appreciated, but love learns to laugh a lot and to work for the sheer joy of doing it. Obligation can pour a glass of milk, but quite often, love adds a little chocolate.[12]

That description of love is a beautiful description of the way Jesus led his life. Again and again, he went beyond the call of duty and acted out of love. He *went out of his way* to minister — and I believe he wants us to do the same.

Jesus must have been exhausted that

long-ago evening we see sketched in Matthew 14. All day long, the crowds had pressed in with their needs. I have a feeling Jesus didn't mind that. He could still see the sparkling eyes of the little lame girl as she took her first step. He could still hear the joyful cries of the crowd as she grabbed his hand and began to dance. He could still feel the squeeze of the old knotted hand as an elderly man thanked him for making him see. It was the very thing he had come to do — "to heal the brokenhearted, to proclaim liberty to the captives" (Isaiah 61:1, NKJV).

But who would heal Jesus' broken heart? His cousin John had been executed just days before, and Jesus grieved. The sparkling city of Tiberius glowed that evening across Galilee. Torches lit the early dusk, illuminating King Herod's palace. Within its walls was a platter, Jesus had been told. A platter holding his dear friend's head.

Now, as the evening came on, Jesus wanted to be alone. He needed to be alone. Only the Father could comfort this overwhelming sadness and soothe this bone-weary exhaustion.

"There he is!" Voices echoed across the water as a long stream of people made their way around the lake. The disciples groaned. They had seen the pain in their Master's eyes. They, too, were weary from the demands of the day. Surely they deserved a little rest.

"Let's send them away," one of the disciples suggested to Jesus.

But Jesus said no.

Instead of sending the people away, Jesus "had compassion on them and healed their sick" (Matthew 14:14). He moved past his own neediness and loved them. He did what he could do to help them. And then, if that wasn't enough, he provided dinner for the hungry crowd. Fish and chips for five thousand.

The word Matthew uses for *compassion* in this passage is *splagchnizomai*. It means that Jesus didn't respond to the people out of duty; he ministered to them because he felt their distress. So deep, so profound was his compassion, his *splagchnizomai*, Jesus literally felt it in his gut. He laid aside his hurt so he could pick up their pain. He laid aside his wishes so he could become their one Desire. He laid aside his agenda so he could meet all of their needs.

And that is the essence of ministry that goes out of its way. It puts self aside and reaches out in true compassion.

"True love hurts," Mother Teresa once said. "It always has to hurt." And elsewhere she has written pointedly, "If you really love one another, you will not be able to avoid making sacrifices."[13] For many years, this tiny nun and her followers went out of their way to minister to the dying — first in Calcutta, India, and later around the world. Their ministry went far beyond simply holding hands and praying. They physically carried broken bodies in off the streets. They sponged out foul-smelling wounds. They got down on their knees to mop up accidents. They tenderly spooned warm food into toothless mouths.

Now that Mother Teresa is gone from this earth, her Missionaries of Charity still continue the work she began — work that again and again goes out of its way to love and serve.

Why do they do it?

If you ask them, their answer is clear and confident: "We do it because Jesus did."

And so must we.

Serving in All Kinds of Ways

When Brother Lawrence gave himself to service for God, he didn't get to choose his job. If you were to go to Calcutta and volunteer with the Missionaries of Charity, you wouldn't get to pick and choose either. Everyone starts at the same place — at the most humble point of service. But when you're truly a servant, a job title and a position are completely secondary. You're willing to do whatever needs to be done.

Jesus didn't have a luxurious corner office on Jerusalem's east side with a brass doorplate that said "Messiah." He didn't have a multiacre campus to base his ministry. He just ministered as he went along. On his way. As he went out of his way. *In all kinds of ways.*

I think this is an important thing to note when we speak of Kitchen Service — especially in this age of motivational "giftedness" studies. The last two decades have brought a surge of books, seminars, and other educational opportunities designed to help us become aware of our natural and spiritual gifts. These offerings, ranging from the classic *Discovering Your Spiritual Gifts* to the *Wagner-Modified Houts Spiritual Gifts Questionnaire,*[14] have helped Christians by the thousands become aware of the special gifts God has placed within them for building up the church.

The purpose of such offerings was to

equip the saints for the work of the ministry. And the principle was sound: Working from our God-given gifts releases ministry potential in greater measure and helps the various members of the body work harmoniously.

I'm afraid, however, that instead of mobilizing the body of Christ, this emphasis on gifts may have provided many of us with a handy excuse. Now when churches call for workers, we have a spiritual reason why we can't help.

"It just isn't my gift," we can say piously, pointing to the twelfth chapters of Romans and 1 Corinthians.

"Sure would like to help, Pastor, but I don't do babies."

"I don't do junior highers."

"I don't do rest homes."

"I'm an exhorter, you know — I don't do toilets!"

When the verbal smoke screen finally clears, a question still remains: What exactly *do* we do?

I don't want to minimize the importance of understanding our strengths and our weaknesses. There is much to be learned about the ministry gifts God gives to the church and our part in the body of Christ as outlined in Romans 12. Besides, as we've discussed before, a need is not necessarily a call — and no one is called to do *everything*. That is why we always must start in the Living Room, spending time waiting before the Lord and asking him what he'd have us do.

But as far as I can tell, the biblical description of gifts and the reminders to serve wisely were never intended as excuses to pick the kind of service that feels comfortable and convenient and ignore all the others!

After all, the same chapter of Romans that lists spiritual gifts also makes it clear that we are *all* called to serve regardless of our specific gifts. We may or may not have the *gift* of servant hospitality (Romans 12:7), but we are *all* called to "practice" hospitality (verse 13). We may or may not have the *gift* of giving (verse 8), but we are *all* called to "share with God's people who are in need" (verse 13).

"Rather than picking and choosing ministry opportunities based solely on our talents and interests," Jack Hoey writes in *Discipleship Journal*, "we are directed, 'Always give yourselves fully to the work of the Lord.'"[15]

That's what our Savior did. He ministered everywhere he went in all kinds of ways. He stopped to chat with a lonely woman. He told stories to children and cooked fish for his disciples. He had dinner with publicans and sinners, even calling one down from his hiding place in a tree so they could share a little *koinonia* fellowship.

Instead of guarding his life, Jesus gave it away — and he beckons his followers to do the same. When we surrender ourselves to be used by God, we don't always get to pick the time, the method, or the place of ministry. In fact, sometimes, we may find ourselves doing nothing at all — except praying and waiting for God's leading.

"He also serves who only stands and waits," the great English poet John Milton once wrote.[16] Frustrated by the limitations of becoming blind, Milton had struggled with feelings of worthlessness — feelings that God couldn't use him. But as the poet discovered, the key is not in our activity, but in our receptivity to God's voice — and in our willingness to be used in whatever ways he brings to our attention.

When we bring to him our willingness to serve, he'll always, eventually, point us toward something we can do for him. And that task will always have something to do with love.

Passion, Compassion, and Power

A true passion for God will naturally result in compassion for people. We can't love the Father without also being willing to love his kids — even when they're less than lovable.

In his beautiful book *Love Beyond Reason*, John Ortberg tells the story of his sister's rag doll, Pandy. "She had lost a good deal of her hair, one of her arms was missing, and, generally speaking, she'd had the stuffing knocked out of her." But she was his sister's favorite doll.

Checking Your Motives

Kitchen Service is a vital part of any Christian life, but we must never forget that *why* we serve is as important as *how* we serve — the motives of our heart really make a difference. Jan Johnson, author of *Living a Purpose-Full Life*, suggests a series of helpful questions that can help us "do the work of Christ with the heart of Christ."

- Am I serving to impress anyone?
- Am I serving to receive external rewards?
- Is my service affected by moods

---

and whims [my own as well as others']?

- Am I using this service to feel good about myself?
- Am I using my service to muffle God's voice demanding I change?[17]

The LORD does not look at the things man looks at. Man looks at the outward appearance, but the LORD looks at the heart.
1 SAMUEL 16:7

So when Pandy turned up missing on the way home from family vacation, Ortberg's dad turned the car around and drove all the way back to Canada to find her. "We were a devoted family," Ortberg writes. "Not a particularly bright family, perhaps, but devoted." They found Pandy at the hotel, wrapped in sheets and down in the laundry, "about to be washed to death."

What made Pandy so valuable to that family? It wasn't her beauty. It was the fact Ortberg's little sister loved her so much. "If you loved [my sister], you just naturally loved Pandy too."

And so it is with our heavenly Father. As his children, we are flawed and wounded, broken and often bent. "We are all of us rag dolls," Ortberg says. "But we are God's rag dolls." And Jesus made it clear that serving him also involves serving the ones he loves.

" 'Love me, love my rag dolls,' God says," writes Ortberg. "It's a package deal."[18]

I think that's why, in Acts 3, Peter and John couldn't just walk by the lame man sitting at the temple gate called Beautiful. When they looked at the crumpled rag doll of a man they didn't see a cripple, they saw a child of God. So they loved him. They wanted to help. Their passion for God spread out naturally into compassion for one in need. But instead of offering the man money, they gave him something far more valuable — something we all need to remember when we offer compassionate service.

"Silver and gold have I none," Peter said. Then, with all the passion and power of the Holy Spirit within him, Peter continued, "but such as I have give I thee: In the name of Jesus Christ of Nazareth rise up and walk" (Acts 3:6, KJV).

Compassion, you see, is just the beginning of what we have to offer the people Jesus loves. After all, the world is filled with charitable works, people, and foundations that give money and time and do incredible things on behalf of the poor. And I know such compassion pleases the heart of God — even when it comes from non-Christians.

But it wasn't Peter's charity the lame man needed that day. He needed something not found in pockets or purses or even in other people's sympathy. That man needed healing. He needed the power of God to transform his life.

And power was exactly what he got. By the empowerment of the Spirit, Peter took the man by the right hand and helped him up. "Instantly the man's feet and ankles became strong. He jumped to his feet and began to walk . . . walking and jumping, and praising God!"(3:7-8).

What We Have to Offer

And that, more than anything, is what the world needs from us today. They've heard the TV sermons; they've seen our church buildings and read our ads. What they're hungry for is the manifest glory of God. Something bigger than they are. Something bigger than we are. They want to see God.

It's always been that way. Paul referred to the same reality when he wrote in 1 Corinthians 2:4-5, "My message and my preaching were not with wise and persuasive words, but with a demonstration of the Spirit's power." Why was that important? "So that your faith might not rest on men's wisdom, but on God's power."

The world has had enough of man's wisdom. If a little extra know-how was all your neighbor needed, she'd find the answers to all life's questions on *Oprah*. If all your brother-in-law needed was advice, he could get it from coworkers or on the Internet, but what he can't get there is what he needs — a new life. If human wisdom were enough to solve the world's problems, we'd have already gotten rid of war, famine, and disease. And we'd have no need of God.

Obviously, that hasn't happened. The world is still embroiled in strife, still wasting away from physical and spiritual emptiness, still hurting and dying. Still desperate for the kind of healing only God can offer.

It might be a good idea, then, for each of us to stop ourselves periodically in the midst of serving and ask, "What am I relying on? Whom am I pointing people to?"

Because if our Kitchen Service doesn't point people to Jesus, we risk becoming surrogate messiahs. If we, not God, end up being their source of hope, we are setting them up for profound disappointment and ourselves for profound burnout — because we, in ourselves, are simply not up to the task of saving the world. In ourselves, like Peter and John at the gate called Beautiful, we have nothing to offer. But in Christ, we are given the power to give people what they most desperately need.

Only God, you see, can make rag dolls whole. Only God can put Humpty Dumpty together again. Our job is just to be his rag-doll emissaries, formed in his likeness, filled with his love, and endued with his power. And gifted with the privilege of sharing a loving Father with our orphan world.

Sticking Out All Over

The story is told of a young boy who approached an evangelist after a revival tent meeting. "Excuse me, sir?" the little boy said politely. "You said everyone should ask Jesus into their hearts, right?"

"That's right, son." The evangelist

squatted down so he could look the boy in the eye. "Did you ask him in?"

"Well, I'd like to," the boy said, shuffling dirt with the toe of his shoe before returning his gaze to the evangelist. "But I got to figurin' . . . I'm so little and Jesus is so big — he's just gonna stick out all over!"

"That's the point, son," the evangelist said with a smile. "That's the point."

I don't know about you, but I want Jesus to be so evident in my life that people don't just consider me a nice moral person, full of good works. I want my relationship with God to be so real and vital, so like that of the apostles Peter and John, that people can't help but sit up and take notice.

Wouldn't it be wonderful to have words said of us like those Acts 4:13 records? "When they saw the courage of Peter and John and realized that they were unschooled, ordinary men, they were astonished and they took note that these men had been with Jesus."

I think that's what President Jiang Zemin was saying when he told Don Argue the story at the beginning of this chapter. He'd "taken note" of the difference in an obscure Christian's life. It remained etched upon his memory.

Unfortunately, unlike Paul Harvey, I have no "rest of the story" for this particular tale. Chinese Christians are still being persecuted for their faith every day. Chinese officials give no appearance of softening their stance.

But who knows? It may be the tender compassion of one woman — a Christian nurse who, while she was *on her way, went out of her way, in all kinds of ways* — that ultimately changes the heart of a president and his country.

One thing is certain. The cause of Christ is alive and well in China because of Christians like her. Christians who dared to love. Christians who dared to serve. Christians who dared to let Jesus stick out all over.

Instead of fighting the government during the last forty years of communist rule, "Chinese Christians devoted themselves to worship and evangelism, the original mission of the church," Philip Yancey writes in *What's So Amazing About Grace?* "They concentrated on changing lives, not changing laws." And something incredible has been happening in those forty years.

"There were 750,000 Christians when I left China," one elderly missionary, an expert on China, told Yancey. And now?

"You hear all sorts of numbers," the man says. "But I think a safe figure would be 35 million."[19]

One life truly can make a difference. Your life plus my life makes two.

Let's get connected to the Vine so that we start bearing fruit. Let's start living in such a way that Jesus sticks out all over. Let's start loving in such a way people can point at our lives and say, "I know who you are!"

Or better yet, "I know *whose* you are" — because they see our Lord and his love in us.

7

The Better Part

There is need of only one thing.
Mary has chosen the better part,
which will not be taken away from her.
LUKE 10:42, NRSV

Sometimes a picture is worth a thousand words.

My thirty-something birthday had dawned bright and busy. Tucked into a pile of bills and credit-card applications I found a card sent from my friend Janet McHenry. The message inside wished me a "hoopy birthday," and that made me smile, but the picture on the front was what really grabbed my attention. It illustrated everything I'd been feeling that dreary, getting-older day.

"That's me," I said to my husband,

poking at the black-and-white glossy.

Taken back in the early 1950s, the photo showed a young woman in Greta Garbo shorts with eight or nine Hula-Hoops swinging madly around her waist. "How does she do that?" I wanted to know.

It had been a frustrating day of too many responsibilities and not enough of me to go around. One by one, I named the Hula-Hoops I had been trying to keep in motion: wife, mother, pastor's wife, friend, writer, piano instructor, cook, cleaning lady, and the big one — Little League mother. If we weren't racing to baseball games, we were rushing to church; if I wasn't folding laundry, I was stealing a few moments to write.

"That's me!" I laughed. I made exaggerated motions with my hips, trying to keep my invisible hoops afloat. My eyes darted from the photo to my husband's concerned face then back again. "That's me!"

After a few cups of chamomile tea and some chocolate-chip sedatives — I mean, cookies — I calmed down and read my friend's letter while my husband ran our kids to yet another ball game. Chatty and full of humor, Janet shared her hectic schedule and the things the Lord had been teaching her.

I finished the letter, then closed the card and looked once more at the girl on the front. There were so many hoops, but she appeared calm. Her upper body seemed to be perfectly still, her arms outstretched slightly, as the hoops raced around her waist in synchronized chaos.

Her face captured me. Looking straight into the camera, she smiled peacefully as though she hadn't a care in the world.

Then it dawned on me — I saw her secret. "She found a rhythm," I whispered to myself. "She established her center, then let everything move around that."

That's exactly what I *wasn't* doing in my life. All the things I'd been trying to accomplish were important, but I had lost my center. Busy being busy, I'd forgotten to tend to my inner self, the spiritual me. Like a wheel without an axle, I'd careened through life, bouncing off one duty and onto another.

If there was an adequate pause, I'd spend some time with the Lord. But lately, more often than not, my busy days had slipped by without a quiet time. And my life was revealing what my spirit had missed.

"Teach me, Lord. Show me the rhythm of life," I found myself praying.

"Be my center."

Hula-Hoops and Holiness

Life is filled with Hula-Hoops. We all have responsibilities, important things that need our attention. If we're not careful, however, our hearts and our minds can be consumed with the task of keeping them in the air. Rather than centering ourselves in Christ and letting the other elements of our lives take their rightful place around that center, we end up shifting our attention from one important to-do item to another, frantically trying to keep them all in motion.

It's easy to forget that while there is a time to work, there is also a time to worship — and it's the worship, the time we spend with God, that provides the serene center to a busy, complex life.

Mary of Bethany didn't fall for that. She knew the difference between work and worship. Martha didn't. That is why she nearly missed the Better Part.

I can almost see Martha as she greeted Jesus on his way through Bethany. I don't suppose the Hula-Hoops were actually visible as she came out to meet him, but I wouldn't be surprised if there was a slight movement around Martha's hips. "Come in! Come in!" she probably said. "Mi casa, su casa! Now, if you'll excuse me, I need to check the soup."

I, too, have been guilty of giving my Lord a breathless hello and a quick hug. I've welcomed him into my life and gotten him situated, but then moved on like Martha, gyrating frantically as I pursued other duties.

Mary didn't do that. She dropped her Hula-Hoops and sat at his feet. Who has time for recess games when you're in the presence of the wisest Teacher who ever lived?

Now it's been argued that Mary probably didn't have any hoops (the lazy thing!) "That's why *she* had *time* to sit at his feet," we Marthas like to emphasize. But we have no proof of that, and I believe Scripture is vague for a purpose.

Stereotypes keep us from embracing truth. The story of Mary and Martha was never meant to be a psychological profile or a role play in which we choose the character with whom we most identify. This is the story of two different responses to one singular occasion. In it, we should find not our personality type, but the kind of heart Christ longs for us to have.

A heart centered in him alone.

Keeping a Focus

As I read the birthday card in my hand that day, I couldn't help but marvel at the work God had done in my friend. A mother of four and married to a farmer-lawyer, Janet had a full-time job teaching high school English and wrote books and articles in moments found here and there. Her life was busy. Hula-Hoops galore.

A year earlier, Janet had sent out an SOS to the e-mail fellowship we both belong to. A number of painful crises, including an unjust lawsuit, had slammed into her family's lives without warning. "Pray for me," she wrote. "I'm going under."

Melancholy in personality, yet driven to excel, Janet found herself swamped by despair. She couldn't fix her situation. She couldn't change it. But in the middle of it all, God was calling her to himself.

"I'm getting up an hour early and prayer walking," she had written us several months later. Each morning before work, Janet donned her sweats and spent an hour walking around her small California town, praying for people and situations as they came to mind. "I can't believe the change getting alone with God is making in my life," she wrote in the birthday card. "I actually caught myself singing the other day!"[1]

Hudson Taylor once said, "We will all have trials. The question is not when the pressure will come, but where the pressure will lie. Will it come between us and the Lord? Or will it press us ever closer to His breast?"[2] Rather than let her circumstances drag her away from God, Janet chose to let them draw her closer.

My friend was experiencing the truth Selwyn Hughes writes about: "Life works better when we know how to glance at things but gaze at God. Seeing Him clearly will enable us to see all other things clearly."[3]

It is so easy to lose focus in life, to lose our center. Life conspires to drag our eyes away from the face of the Savior, hypnotizing us with the unending sway of our problems.

"I can't spend time with God today," I may rationalize. "I haven't the time." But the truth of the matter is this: The rougher the day, the *more* time I need to spend with my Savior. The more hoops I have to handle, the more I need to keep my center.

I think it's important to remember that if Mary hadn't chosen to take time out of her busy Martha-run schedule to sit at Jesus' feet, the whole encounter wouldn't have happened. The Gospels would have moved right along without recording this intimate pause between a woman and her Savior. And we wouldn't have seen the difference Living Room Intimacy can make in a life — in a family — surrendered to God.

Making Room

I've found I need solitude, a daily quiet time alone with God, if I am to have any hope of keeping my center. Left to my own devices, I am fickle and ever-changing. One day I'm hot: "O Lord, I love you! Be glorified in me." The next day I'm luke-warm: "Sorry, God, have to run." I have found the words of the hymnist so true:

Prone to wander, Lord I feel it,
Prone to leave the God I love.[4]

The only way I've found to fight this wandering tendency in my life is to keep my heart centered on Christ, to keep my gaze fixed on him. But that takes time and an act of my will. I have to be willing to make room in my life if I want to experience the Better Part.

In his book *First Things First*, Stephen Covey tells the story of a man teaching a time-management seminar. In order to make a point, the man pulled a wide-mouthed gallon jar from under the counter that served as his podium. He picked up some fist-size rocks and put them in the jar. Then he looked out at the class and asked, "Is the jar full?"

Some of the students, not knowing where he was going, blurted out, "Yes." The teacher laughed gently and said, "No, it's not." He pulled out a bucket of pea gravel and began to pour it in the jar. The class watched as the pea gravel filtered down between the rocks, filling the spaces until it reached the top.

"Now, is the jar full?"

The class was a bit reticent to answer. After all, they'd been wrong before. Instead of waiting for their response, the man poured a bucket of sand down among the pea gravel and the large rocks. He shook the jar gently to let the sand settle, then added more, until finally the sand reached the mouth of the jar. Then he asked again, "Is the jar full?" And they said, "Probably not."

Now the teacher reached for a pitcher of water and slowly poured the water in the jar. It filtered down until it was running out of the jar at the top. "Is the jar full?" the time-management consultant asked. The class answered, "We think it is."

"Okay, class," he said. "What is the lesson in this visual aid?"

Somebody in the back raised his hand and said, "No matter how busy your life is, there is always room for more!"

"No," the teacher said as the class broke into laughter. "That's not it!"

"The lesson is, class," he said when the chuckles subsided, "if you don't put the big rocks in first you'll never get them in later."[5]

What a powerful picture of a powerful truth! It sounds like the same point Jesus made when he said, "Seek first his kingdom and his righteousness, and all these things will be given to you as well" (Matthew 6:33).

First things first, the Lord was saying. Take care of my business, and I'll take care of yours. Make room in your heart for me, and I'll make room for everything else.

Too Full for Comfort

You see, we were created for fullness. According to Ephesians 3:17-19, when we come to know Jesus as our Lord through faith, we begin to understand the incredible love of our Savior. And as we come to know this love better, we are "filled to the measure of all the *fullness* of God" (v. 19, emphasis mine).

We were created for the fullness of God, not an ounce or liter less. But are we ready for that? After all, being filled to the measure with all the fullness of God will most likely require our being stretched. At the very least, it is sure to disturb our comfort.

Are we willing to let God explode our comfort zone and expand our capacity for him? Or do we want a God we can manage?

Unfortunately, a lot of the time that is exactly what we want — enough of God to make us happy, but not enough to make us change. We'd never say it, but our attitude is just what Wilbur Rees had in mind when he wrote:

I would like to buy $3 worth of God, please, not enough to explode my soul or disturb my sleep, but just enough to equal a cup of warm milk or a snooze in the sunshine. I don't want enough of Him to make me love a black man or pick beets with a migrant. I want ecstasy, not transformation; I want the warmth of the womb, not a new birth. I want a pound of the Eternal in a paper sack. I would like to buy $3 worth of God, please.[6]

The trouble, of course, is that God doesn't work that way. He's not on the market in manageable, bargain-size portions. He's not on the market in the first place. And he's not looking for buyers; he's looking to *buy* — you and me. He wants a people who are sold out to him. All the way. Total liquidation. He's not willing to barter. He's not looking to please. He has already paid the price. His Son died on the cross to pay our debt and ransom our souls.

But the transaction is never a forced sale — and that's crucial to realize. God is a gentleman, not a robber baron. He will court us and pursue us, but he'll never push himself on us. We can actually say no to the Maker of the Universe. We can choose to keep him in a corner of our lives.

Author and teacher Cynthia Heald puts

it this way, "We are as intimate with God as we choose to be."[7] The only limitations of God's presence in our lives are the limits we ourselves set — the excuses we set up to avoid being filled to the measure with God.

Martha's excuse was duty. She had cleaning and cooking to do. She didn't think she had time to sit at Jesus' feet.

Perhaps your excuse is children or work. Or maybe like me, the only excuse you really have for devotional delinquency is sheer laziness. But whatever it is — whatever keeps us from spending regular time with God — it is sin.

Does it sound harsh to say that cooking or cleaning or taking care of children or doing your job might be sinful? But think about it. The very *definition* of sin is separation from God. So no matter how important the activity, no matter how good it seems, if I use it as an excuse to hold God at arm's length, it is sin. I need to confess and repent of it so that I can draw close to the Lord once more.

Because the longer I go without being filled with God's presence, the drier and emptier and more frustrated I'm going to become.

There's Got to Be More

When my husband and I left Montana so he could serve as music pastor in Grants Pass, we were exhausted. The oil boom of the late 1970s had gone bust in eastern Montana, leaving a trail of bankruptcies, foreclosures, and hopelessness. In one month alone, fifty families in our church had left town looking for work. It had been a hard time for us both, emotionally and financially. But I had no idea it had drained me so much spiritually.

Someone commented recently, "I didn't know I was 'dry,' until I got around people who were 'wet.'" I knew what she meant, because that's exactly what happened to me when we got to Oregon. The people in Grants Pass were "all wet"! Soaking wet, drenched with God. The presence of the Lord was so sweet in our services, the people so mature in their faith, that all I could do was weep.

I'd known the Lord for years. I'd been a pastor's wife for nearly a decade. But I was spiritually dry. Dry-bone dry.

Who were these people? I wondered. How could they be so happy? What did they have that I didn't have? How could they sit there enjoying the presence of the

Lord when I always felt compelled to be in a state of constant motion, busy but exhausted from the effort of keeping my Hula-Hoops in the air?

Sometimes we have to slow down in order to take spiritual inventory and see where we stand with God. Sometimes we have to realize how empty we are before we're willing to be filled. During that first year in Grants Pass, I did both.

As I looked back at my life, I could see a series of mountaintop experiences where the rain had fallen rich and deep, but there were quite a few dry valleys as well. Famine times when I was so dry and so low emotionally that I barely felt alive. I had the classic sanguine personality when it came to my walk with God. Big, big highs. Big, big lows. And now, more recently, I felt lost in a barren, featureless desert.

"Tear down the mountaintops if you have to, Lord," I cried one night. "But fill in my valleys! Bring a steadfastness to my life so I can walk faithfully in the good times as well as the bad. I want to know you! I want to be filled with you — and stay filled."

What was wrong with me? When I stopped to think about it, I knew part of the answer. My personal times of devotion were erratic at best. My prayer life was quirky, my reading of the word sporadic. And because I was not spending regular quiet time with God, I was not putting myself in a position to be filled and refilled.

No wonder I was running on empty!

What it really came down to was I only met with God when I felt like it. And that, I was learning, just wasn't enough. If I wanted to be filled with God on a more consistent basis, I had to determine to let myself be stretched, to make room for the Better Part on a daily basis in my life. And that would mean learning to abandon my emotions as a compass and start exercising my will.

An Act of the Will

Making room for the Better Part in our lives isn't easy. Many great men and women of God have struggled to hammer out time alone with their Savior. I love the candor and the humor of J. Sidlow Baxter as he describes his battle to reestablish a regular devotional time after a "velvety little voice told him to be practical . . . that he wasn't of the spiritual sort, that only a few people could be like that."

That did it. Baxter was horrified to think he could rationalize away the very thing he needed most, so he set about to make some definite changes. He writes:

As never before, my will and I stood face to face. I asked my will the straight question, "Will, are you ready for an hour of prayer?" Will answered, "Here I am, and I'm quite ready, if you are." So Will and I linked arms and turned to go for our time of prayer. At once all the emotions began pulling the other way and protesting, "We're not coming." I saw Will stagger just a bit, so I asked, "Can you stick it out, Will?" and Will replied, "Yes, if you can." So Will went, and we got down to prayer. . . . It was a struggle all the way through. At one point . . . one of those traitorous emotions had snared my imagination and had run off to the golf course; and it was all I could do to drag the wicked rascal back. . . .

At the end of that hour, if you had asked me, "Have you had a 'good time'?" I would have had to reply,

"No, it has been a wearying wrestle with contrary emotions and a truant imagination from beginning to end." What is more, that battle with the emotions continued for between two and three weeks, and if you had asked me at the end of that period, "Have you had a 'good time' in your daily praying?" I would have had to confess, "No, at times it has seemed as though the heavens were brass, and God too distant to hear, and the Lord Jesus strangely aloof, and prayer accomplishing nothing."

Yet something *was* happening. For one thing, Will and I really taught the emotions that we were completely independent of them. Also, one morning, about two weeks after the contest began, just when Will and I were going for another time of prayer, I overheard one of the emotions whisper to the other, "Come on, you guys, it's no use wasting any more time resisting: they'll go just the same." . . .

Then, another couple of weeks later, what do you think happened? During one of our prayer times, when Will and I were no more thinking of the emotions than of the man in the moon, one of the most vigorous of the emotions unexpectedly sprang up and shouted, "Hallelujah!" at which all the other emotions exclaimed, "Amen!" And for the first time the whole of my being — intellect, will, and emotions — was united in one coordinated prayer-operation. All at once, God was real, heaven was open, the Lord Jesus was luminously present, the Holy Spirit was indeed moving through my longings, and prayer was surprisingly vital. Moreover, in that instant there came a sudden realization that heaven had been watching and listening all the way through those days of struggle against chilling moods and mutinous emotions; also that I had been undergoing necessary tutoring by my heavenly Teacher.[8]

When I first read Baxter's words, they unlocked something deep within my soul. So I wasn't alone! Other people struggled as well. Suddenly I felt hope — hope that I, too, could experience the joy of the Better Part. I didn't have to wait until I felt spiritual to spend time with God. I just had to make a decision of the will, and the spiritual feelings would eventually come around.

So I began to try it, but it wasn't easy. Sometimes I had to struggle like J. Sidlow Baxter. Sometimes God seemed far away and my heart like cold steel. Sometimes I just felt irritable and impatient. But I persisted, and gradually things began to change. Like a patient waking from a long coma, I began to experience a hunger for God like I'd never known before — a kind of "unsatisfiable satisfaction" that grew and grew.

Amazing Grace

As I began to understand grace — God's marvelous, amazing, abundant grace — in a brand-new way, I began to recognize the Holy Spirit at work within me, giving me the power and the desire to do God's will as never before.

I found myself at the altar praying after the services had ended — seeking the Lord. I found myself waking in the middle of the night to spend time in his Word — seeking the Lord. I found myself turning to books and tuning in religious broadcasts in the middle of the day — seeking the Lord.

I wanted everything that Jesus Christ had to offer. And as I sought his face, I found that he'd been there waiting all the time, with a pitcher full of his presence, ready to pour. Wanting to fill me "to the measure of the fullness of God." Just waiting for me to choose the Better Part and meet him there in the Living Room.

Living Room Intimacy, you see, is not some mystical state of being (or nonbeing) like the Hindu idea of nirvana. We need not trek to the mountains of Nepal to find it, nor go on a spirit quest like the native Americans of old. We won't find it on a shelf, in a dusty old cave, or in a museum under lights.

The Better Part is not out there somewhere. It is inside us, where Christ dwells by his Holy Spirit. Isn't that wonderful? We can't misplace the Better Part. No one can take it away from us, though unfortunately we can choose to ignore it.

Remember the painting of Christ knocking at a door? The beautiful scene hung above my grandmother's dresser for years, a gentle reminder to this little girl that Jesus longed to come into her heart. There was no latch on the outside of the wooden door where the Lord stood waiting. It could only be opened from the inside.

So it is with the door of my will. Jesus didn't force his company upon the sisters of Bethany, nor will he force it upon me. I have to let him in before we can enjoy our Living Room time together. And the door isn't always easy to open, even from the inside. But three little keys, I've discovered, can make all the difference. They are three simple truths — so simple they tend to be disregarded, but powerful enough to click open stubbornly willful doors. They have made all the difference in keeping my life centered in Christ.

What are these three little keys? They're easy to remember because they each begin with *C:*
- Consistency
- Creativity
- Conversation

Consistent Practice

As a young teenager, I read a book about Andraé Crouch, a popular gospel artist at the time. Andraé's preacher father had prayed over his twelve-year-old son's hands when their church needed a pianist, and God had answered his prayer. Andraé not only became the church pianist, but also went on to bless thousands with his music and powerful songs.

Well, that definitely inspired me. "Dear Jesus," I prayed the next afternoon as I sat down at the piano, "you know I'm not very good at this piano stuff. Would you do for me what you did for Andraé?"

I waited, but nothing happened.

Instead, the word of the Lord came to me saying . . . well, to be honest, I didn't actually hear the audible voice of God. I never have. But at that moment it was almost as if I did. Somewhere up in the region of the right side of my heart, the voice of the Lord came to me, saying:

"Practice, Joanna, practice."

Practice. I have an idea that's what God wants to whisper to our hearts when we ask for the Better Part. "You've got to invest time, darling. You need to do a little every day." If we want to be accomplished Christians, and if we want to know God in all his fullness, there is something crucial about the act of seeking Jesus on a regular, day-by-day basis.

I've learned in my own life that if I want to develop a consistent quiet time with God, I have to set aside a certain portion of my day just for him. And then I need to guard it well — even scheduling it in my Day-Timer. Because if I'm not careful, the Better Part can get shoved so far to the side of my plate that it ends up on the floor rather than feeding my soul.

It doesn't really matter *what* time of day I choose. People of faith over the centuries have had good success with a variety of times. Daniel, for instance, prayed three times a day: morning, noon, and night (Daniel 6:10). David must have been a morning person, according to Psalm 5:3: "In the morning, O LORD, you hear my voice; in the morning I lay my requests before you and wait in expectation." Jesus tended toward morning as well, according to Mark 1:35: "Very early in the morning, while it was still dark, Jesus got up, left the house and went off to a solitary place, where he prayed."

As for myself, I've fluctuated between morning and night but have finally settled for morning once again. Not only is it easier for me to find uninterrupted time then, but I've found it is a wonderful way to start the day.

But again, it's not really important *when* I choose to meet God every day. What really matters is that I show up regularly — and to be honest, that's where I've always fallen short. Because of my all-or-nothing temperament, missing a day or two of devotions was enough to throw me off track for days, even weeks. Out of sight became out of mind, and I'm ashamed to admit, there were entire months when I went without having a formal, that is, a sit-down-with-my-Bible-and-pray alone time with God.

But consistency, after all, doesn't mean perfection; it simply means refusing to give up. And that's what has saved me. Like Sidlow Baxter, I refused to give in to the possibility that I wasn't "of the spiritual sort." So with a huge amount of God's grace and a stubborn will to keep trying, I've been able to get back on track with my quiet times.

And somewhere in that dailiness, in that everyday familiarity that comes from time spent together, I have felt myself grow closer to the Lord. Steadily, consistently closer. And also, in the process, more filled with his presence. More calm and serene. More practically centered.

It's amazing what a little time-out can do for you. Especially when you spend that time with Jesus.

Some Creative Strategies

In college and the years that followed, I tried many times to read the Bible systematically, but I would inevitably give up, usually around Leviticus and Numbers. Somewhere between the laws and the begats, I'd end up falling asleep. Then I'd lose momentum. And then I'd be back to my old slapdash habits of diving here and there among my favorite passages and not really learning anything new.

But when I began using a reading guide that switched back and forth from the Old Testament to the New Testament, everything changed. The variety sparked my interest as I began to see Christ in the Old Testament and the beauty of the blood covenant in the New Testament. I could hardly wait to get back to my Bible reading each day to see what would happen next in the epic story of God's plan for humanity.

The *NIV Study Bible* my husband bought for my birthday enlivened my study time even more. I loved the contemporary language of the *New International Version*. And having everything I needed at my fingertips — a thorough concordance and cross references, as well as study notes to help when I didn't understand — kept me from getting stalled in my study.

In those two simple changeovers — switching between books of the Bible and reading a more contemporary version — I discovered a bit of the power creativity can have in our quiet times.

It is so easy to fall into habits and rituals — the ones that are imposed upon us as well as those we ourselves impose. But while the consistency of habit and the beauty of ritual can be empowering and enriching, they can also lead to dullness. *Three more chapters,* we yawn. *Then I can go to sleep* . . . And while the dullness of routine is really no excuse for abandoning our devotional times, the reality is that we stand a better chance of sticking with our quiet times when we have interest as well as will to spur us on.

There's more than one way, in other words, to enjoy a quiet time with the Lord. There's more than one approach to studying Scripture. There's more than one way to mediate and pray. The practical truth is that if we don't learn how to feed our souls so they will eat, our souls will wither and slowly die. And that may require a little variety in our spiritual diet — a little creativity in the way we approach our quiet times.

A Little Conversation

The last "C key" to the Better Part is conversation. Now that may sound a little strange to you. What does conversation have to do with quiet time?

> *Creative Quiet Times*
>
> If you've found yourself yawning during devotions — or just eager for a change — you may want to consider the following suggestions for creative intimacy with God.
> 1. *Take God out for coffee.* Find a quiet corner in a café or even McDonald's and meet with God. Take your Bible and a notebook. Grab a cup of coffee and you're set for a heart-to-heart with your very Best Friend.
> 2. *Add a spiritual classic to your devotional diet.* Though nothing should replace the Word of God, Christian books provide delicious and enriching side dishes!
> 3. *Put feet to your faith.* Take a walk with God! Praise him for his handiwork. Listen to the Bible or a sermon on tape. Pray. Your body and

spirit will appreciate the workout.

4. *Journal your journey.* Keep a spiritual diary. Record thoughts as you meditate on Scripture. Write love notes to the Lord. List prayer requests.

5. *Come before him with singing.* Add music to your devotions. Use a praise tape or sing a cappella. Read a hymn out loud.

6. *Let faith come by hearing.* Order tapes from favorite speakers or plan your prayer time around a radio speaker.

7. *Dig a little deeper.* A good Bible study will take you beyond just reading the Word. It will help you rightly divide the Word of Truth and apply it.

8. *All the King's versions.* It is important to find a Bible translation you understand for your regular devotions. But occasionally read from other versions to get a fresh perspective. Read the text out loud.

9. *Hide the Word.* Memorizing Scripture plants the Word of God deep in your heart. Then write down verses on index cards or sticky

notes and take them with you to practice.

10. *Spend a half-day in prayer.* It may seem impossible, but as you set aside a large portion of time to spend with the Lord, he will meet you there in amazing ways. You'll find a plan for a half-day of prayer in Appendix E.

As the deer pants for streams of water,
so my soul pants for you, O God.
PSALM 42:1

But our relationship with God is supposed to be an intimate, loving relationship, and what relationship can thrive without dialogue — good, honest, back-and-forth communication? We need it in marriage, and we need it in our walk with God.

A few years back I looked at my relationship with God and realized that my quiet-time communication style involved a series of monologues with very little dialogue. I'd read about what God thought. Then I'd spend a few minutes telling God what I thought. But I never allowed us to get to the point of conversation, of give-and-take discourse, of the questions and answers that bring life to a relationship.

But that changed when I began to read the Bible as God's love letter to me. I started to hear his own voice calling out to me in the pages of Scripture, and I began to respond to it from my own heart. I started a Bible-reading highlights journal in which I recorded what I felt the Lord was saying to me from his Word. (The format I used is found in Appendix D.)

Instead of the two or three chapters of Bible reading I'd tried to cram in before, I read smaller portions this time, usually one chapter. Instead of simply reading a passage, I'd meditate on it, underlining important verses as I went. Then I'd choose the verse that seemed to speak most clearly to me and respond to the verse in my journal. Sometimes I would paraphrase it into my own words. Sometimes I asked questions. But usually the verse became a prayer as I asked the Lord to apply the truth of his Word to my life and my heart.

Eventually my Bible-highlights journal became a prayer journal as well. Pouring out my heart to the Lord on paper allowed me to be honest about my struggles, my hopes, and my needs. I tried to make a point of recording answers I received as well — both the words the Lord spoke to my spirit and the answers I saw unfold in events around me. In this way my journal served as both a record of my relationship with God and my living dialogue with him. And out of that simple conversation, some amazing things began to happen.

In the first place, I wasn't just reading through the Bible; the Bible was getting through to me. It came alive as I began to study and dig deeper.

My prayer life, too, took on fresh life. No longer was I just presenting God with my wish list and some suggestions about how I thought he should handle it. I was conversing with God — both talking and listening.

No longer was I the "man" in James 1:23-24 "who looks at his face in a mirror and, after looking at himself, goes away and immediately forgets what he looks like." This newfound conversation with God wouldn't allow it! The written record sketched a pretty detailed picture of my condition — a picture hard to ignore.

As I acknowledged what I saw, I repented and applied the truth I'd found. And gradually, in the process, the Holy Spirit began changing me into the "man" of verse 25 "who looks intently into the perfect law that gives freedom, and continues to do this, not forgetting what he has heard, but doing it."

Consistency. Creativity. Conversation. I can't tell you how much these three Cs have done to help me keep my life centered in Christ. Oh, I still have a long way to go! I'm far from perfect when it comes to my spiritual diligence. But I'm far from where I used to be. I'm more stable. More centered. More steadfast. Less likely to skip my quiet times with Jesus and quicker to get back on track when I do.

Most important, my capacity for God really is bigger. I'm no longer empty, no longer dry. I know where to go to be filled, and I'm in more of a hurry to get there. More eager than ever to choose the Better Part . . . to be filled with the full measure of God, to be centered and established in Christ.

A Stable Center

Remember the Hula-Hoop girl from my birthday card? She knew the secret. She'd found her center, and so can we if we keep on choosing the Better Part on a daily basis.

In fact, we can find the kind of stability

exemplified by another set of hoops I'd like to tell you about. Another childhood toy. Perhaps you remember it. It's a contraption of metal rings called a gyroscope. *Encyclopedia Britannica* defines it as "a spinning wheel mounted in such a way that it is free to turn about any of three possible axes." It's like a supertop. Once you set it in motion, it just keeps on going, and it's very hard to knock over. In fact, if you try to push it over, it stubbornly holds its original position, continuing to spin in the same direction.

"When I was a little boy, gyroscopes fascinated me," recalls Howard E. Butt Jr. in *Renewing America's Soul*. "A gyroscope looked to me like a dancing circle: spinning freely, yet perfectly balanced and steady, held upright by some mysterious inner power."

Later, as a young adult, Howard learned that gyroscopes are more than scientific spin toys; they have numerous practical applications as well. "They stabilize our planes in turbulent weather, steady our ships as they sail through raging seas, and guide them automatically by their compasses."

What a picture of the life we are to have in Christ! As we surrender our hoops to the Lord Jesus, as we center ourselves in him, something wonderful happens. He takes those hoops and makes them dance. He turns the spinning circles of our chaotic lives into a steady, stable gyroscope mounted and held up by him alone.

He stabilizes us in the turbulence of life. He steadies us in the midst of raging seas, and he guides us by the compass of his eternal love. As we partake of the Better Part, Jesus Christ becomes the steady balance in our life of constant motion.

"The little boy in me still says: that looks like fun!" Howard writes, both of the gyroscope and the lovely application to a centered life in Christ. "And the open-eyed adult in me, looking around, whispers, 'We've never needed it more.' "9

I agree. On those crazy, loopy days when I don't feel so "hoopy," I'm learning to reach for the Lord instead of chocolate-chip sedatives. I'm learning how to leave the Kitchen and head for the Living Room where Jesus waits, because that's where I'll find everything I need and everything I want.

After all, it's not more Hula-Hoops I need to master.

What I really need is more and more of the Master himself.

8

Lessons from Lazarus

Now a man named Lazarus was sick.
. . . So the sisters sent word to Jesus,
"Lord, the one you love is sick."
JOHN 11:1,3

I love a good story. There's nothing like sipping ice tea under a shade tree and losing myself in an intriguing book on a warm summer day. I can involve myself for hours in the twists and turns of someone else's life. Suspense, mystery, romance — they are the elements of great fiction as far as I'm concerned. The obstacles and overwhelming odds make me turn pages and buy sequels.

When it comes to real life, however, I'd rather go straight to the happy ending. Let's skip the poisoned apple; I'm more interested in Prince Charming and the kiss. Happily ever after — that's the kind of story I prefer for myself.

But life rarely works like that. Most of us spend the bulk of our lives cleaning up after dwarves rather than romancing handsome princes. And, unfortunately, when dark times come and the plots of our lives thicken, we can't just flip to the back of the book to satisfy our curiosity or ease our suspense.

There's no easy way to find out how the story ends.

We just have to hang on tight as the plot line unfolds.

A Puzzling Plot

I can only imagine how Mary and Martha must have felt when their brother, Lazarus, fell ill. Everything had been going so well. Since Jesus had come to visit them, nothing had been the same. There was a new peace. A new joy. A new sense of love that permeated the whole household. The incident recorded in Luke 10:38-42 had been more than just a couple of small paragraphs. That meeting had completely rewritten the story of their lives. But now, it seemed, the plot was taking a puzzling turn.

Perhaps it all started with a fever. "A little bit of my chicken soup, a good night's sleep, and you'll feel just fine," Martha probably told her brother matter-of-factly as she spooned the tasty broth into his waiting lips. Mary probably nodded and smiled as she sat beside him with a wet cloth, cooling his brow.

"I'm sure you're right, Martha," Lazarus may have said, gratefully sinking back into his pillow and the capable ministrations of his sisters. "I'll be fine."

But as you probably already know, Lazarus wasn't.

John 11:1 doesn't go into detail about his ailment, telling us only that there was a man named Lazarus who was sick.

But through the account that follows, it's obvious Lazarus must have been a very special man. He was dearly loved — not only by his sisters, but also by Jesus. The message sent by Mary and Martha said it all: "Lord, the *one you love* is sick" (11:3, emphasis mine). Their relationship must have been exceptionally close. This wasn't a stranger. This was a friend.

So I can imagine the hope the two sisters clung to as they sent the messenger. Surely everything would be all right. The illness seemed severe, but Jesus would come. Lazarus would be made well, and their life would continue as they'd always known it.

Jesus' disciples probably assumed the same thing. After all, when the news about Lazarus came, Jesus told them specifically that "this sickness will not end in death" (11:4). "No," he added, "it is for God's glory so that God's Son may be glorified through it."

Good news, the disciples must have thought. Lazarus will live!

But God had other plans for Lazarus and his sisters. For they had a place in a story bigger and richer than Michener's, more exciting than Clancy's, more mysterious than King's and more romantic than Steele's — with more twists and dips than any novelist could ever dream up on his or her own. It's the story of God's ongoing relationship with the human race. And it's a tale the Master Storyteller has been working on ever since the dawn of creation.

The Plot Thickens

The Bible provides the basic outline. God's first draft was designed to be a perfect love story. He created a man and a woman to live in fellowship with him and with each other in fairy-tale bliss. The setting was so beautiful it defied description. And the story was sweet. Long walks in the evening. New discoveries in the daytime. No tears. No death. No sorrow.

That was God's original purpose — not only for Adam and Eve, but for you and me as well. Then a serpent slipped in, and sin spoiled Paradise. Disobedience destroyed God's manuscript and tossed the man and the woman out of Eden. The story was over, or so it seemed.

But instead of writing a cruel conclusion, Satan's attempt to interrupt God's epic tale served only as an introduction. For "the moment the forbidden fruit touched the lips of Eve," Max Lucado says, "the shadow of a cross appeared on the horizon."[1] With the fall of man, God began unfolding the greatest story of all — his incredible plan of redemption.

And so the saga continues, right down to this very day. Good and evil still war for the human soul. The conflict between love and hate remains the central theme. What Satan intends for evil, God still turns for good.

But go ahead and flip the pages.

You'll see this story has a happy ending. An incredible out-of-this-world happy ending! A glorious finale complete with trumpets and fanfare and an old-fashioned camp meeting in the sky!

But in the in-between part — well, that's where you and I come in. For though we already know the ending, we don't get to skip ahead to the end — at least not yet. And that, I believe, is because God has a lot he wants to teach us as the story unfolds. For tucked among the twists and turns of the everyday plot are valuable lessons about who God is and how he works and how we fit into the tale.

Lessons like the ones Mary and Martha learned the day they feared their brother's story had ended and all hope was gone.

A Greater Glory

I've always loved dot-to-dot puzzles. Looking at the dots, I have a sense of what the picture will eventually look like. But that's not the way things always work in God's scheme of things, as Mary and Martha found out that tragic day in Bethany. What they learned from painful experience was the first of the lessons we can learn from the story of Lazarus:

- **God's will does not always proceed in a straight line.**

That means I will not always see a clear connection between point A and point B. I won't always see the pattern in what happens to me. I won't always understand the plan.

One reason for this is that God is weaving together a greater glory than just my own. As Paul explains in Romans 8:28, "We know that in all things God works for the good of those who love him, who have been called according to his purpose." It is God's purposes, not mine, that must prevail. He is concerned not only with the individual need, but with the corporate need as well.

God wraps up my good with your good and the good of both of us with the good of others. The plot lines of our individual stories weave together to form his master plan. Nothing is wasted. Nothing is left out. There are no dead ends or red herrings; every story line is given his greatest attention, his diligent care. Your story matters to Jesus, just as the individual stories of Mary, Martha, and Lazarus mattered to him. But he always has the big picture in mind as he handles the stories of our lives. He knows the beginning from the end, and he operates accordingly.

So don't be surprised if your personal plot takes a couple of twists now and then. Don't get upset when point A doesn't automatically lead to point B. There are no detours in God's story line, not really. Just complications that he's more than able to resolve.

Satan does his best to foul things up, but God just counters his devilish ploys with moves of his own. I can only imagine what it looks like in the spiritual realms when he does. "Take that!" I can hear Satan chortle as he pencils in a diabolical plot change. "Okay," God says, "I think I will." Then with a smile that brightens the ages, God takes Satan's worst and transforms it into our best. And with each jog and twist, our story grows clearer and richer and more divine. The Author of our salvation really does know what he's doing, even when we can't figure it out.

When God gave Joseph a dream of the moon and stars bowing down to him, Joseph assumed that great things were in store for him. He didn't expect a side trip to Egypt. But God's plan was far greater than anything young Joseph could have imagined. He used those years of slavery and prison to shape a man who would eventually save not only his family and Israel but the entire known world from starvation.

When King Darius was forced to throw Daniel into the lions' den, I'm sure Daniel must have wondered if he was about to meet his Maker as kitty chow. He had no idea his miraculous rescue would serve as a catalyst for the conversion of a nation. But God had a plan.

God always has a plan. But it may not follow human logic. In fact, it may often seem to go directly against what we believe about God.

When Bad Things Happen

"The hardest problem I have to handle as a Christian," pastor and author Ray C. Stedman once said, "is what to do when God does not do what I have been taught to expect him to do; when God gets out of line and does not act the way I think he ought. What do I do about that?"[2]

These are the hard questions we must wrestle with in the story of Lazarus. Why would Jesus allow such sorrow to come to a family who loved him so much? Why would he withhold his power to heal when he'd healed so often before?

These aren't easy subjects to understand. They're not easy realities to endure — and some of you reading this book have endured more tragedy and pain than I can even imagine. Some of you have lost children. Some of you are facing a diagnosis you've always dreaded. Some of you have experienced a broken marriage and are facing life alone.

Why? There are no easy answers. The fact is, we may not know the purpose behind our pain until we see Jesus face to face. Even then, we aren't guaranteed any explanations. We are given only a promise: "He will wipe every tear from their eyes. There will be no more death or mourning or crying or pain, for the old order of things has passed away" (Revelation 21:4).

Because we live in this world, trapped in the old order of things, tragedy will touch our lives. That's simply a fact — for Christians and non-Christians alike. We will all lose loved ones. We will all eventually die. Romans 8:28 is often distorted to mean "only good things will happen to those who love God." But Paul meant just the opposite. In the very next paragraph he spells out the kinds of "things" we can expect in this world:

> Who shall separate us from the love of Christ? Shall trouble or hardship or persecution or famine or nakedness or danger or sword? . . . For I am convinced that neither death nor life, neither angels nor demons, neither the present nor the future, nor any powers, neither height nor depth, nor anything else in all creation, will be able to separate us from the love of God that is in Christ Jesus our Lord. (Romans 8:35, 38-39)

Trials are real. Bad things happen — to good people and bad people alike. And we who are Christians don't escape life, Paul says. We overcome life: "In all these things we are more than conquerors through him who loved us" (8:37).

This promise anchors our all-too-shaky world to his unshakeable kingdom.

And so do the lessons of Lazarus. For while life may shake, rattle, and roll, this rock-solid truth from John 11:5 remains: "Jesus *loved* Martha and her sister and Lazarus."

Love. That's a dependable anchor. Go ahead. Put your name in the blank: "Jesus loves _____."

The love Christ has for you is a love you can cling to, for it will hold you. Though we may not understand God's methods, that doesn't change the fact of God's love.

Even when it seems to tarry.

When God's Love Tarries

Common sense seems to dictate that Jesus would drop whatever he was doing when he heard Lazarus was sick and travel immediately to Bethany. Instead, when the bad news came, "he stayed where he was two more days" (John 11:6).

In retrospect, we can see God's purposes in this delay. After all, we have the gospel account. We know that everything turned out all right.

But what did Mary and Martha think at the time? What did the disciples think?

And what about my life — and yours? What do we do when God doesn't act or move the way we think he should?

If we're paying attention in those times, we may understand better the second lesson the story of Lazarus has to teach us:

- **God's love sometimes tarries for our good and his glory.**

As human beings, we tend to want rational reasons for everything. The Jews of Jesus' time were especially interested in the whys and what-fors of life. That's why, when they encountered a man who had been born blind, the disciples immediately wanted to know what had gone wrong. "Rabbi," they asked Jesus, "who sinned, this man or his parents, that he was born blind?" (John 9:2).

A reasonable question. After all, the religious teachers of the day had developed the principle that "there is no death without sin, and there is no suffering without iniquity." It followed, then, that where there was affliction there had to be sin. Perhaps the man had done wrong in the womb or in a preexistent state. Perhaps the man deserved his blindness. Or perhaps he was the innocent victim of his parents' sin.

The religious elite as well as common folk were big on cause and effect, much as we are today. We want explanations. We want to know why.

With one short sentence, Jesus ripped through their reasoning and shredded their shame-based philosophies. "Neither this man nor his parents sinned," Jesus answered in verse 3, "but this happened so that the work of God might be displayed in his life."

What hope must have sprung up in the blind man's heart as he heard Jesus speak those words. It wasn't his fault! He wasn't the victim of bad parenting or bad karma. God had a plan!

With spit and plain dirt, Jesus made a mud compress and placed it on the man's eyes, telling him to go and wash in the Pool of Siloam. The man was healed, and his neighbors were amazed. The Sanhedrin tried to discount the miracle, but out of one man's tragedy came another divine triumph.

Because of a fallen world, a man was born blind. But because of that man, Jesus Christ was glorified.

We are not pawns on some celestial chessboard, expendable and unimportant. We are cherished and highly loved. "Are not five sparrows sold for two pennies?" Jesus reminds us gently in Luke 12:6-7. "Yet not one of them is forgotten by God. . . . Don't be afraid; you are worth much more than many sparrows."

While we may never fully understand

why God's love sometimes lingers, we can rest assured that God's love is always at work. He may not move according to our schedule, but he is right on time for what is best. And he has our ultimate good forever in mind.

Trusting God's Character

The third lesson of Lazarus underscores this hope:

- **God's ways are not our ways, but his character is still dependable.**

In other words, we don't need to fret, even when it looks like hope is dead. We might not be able to see the end of the story. But we can trust the Storyteller.

Martha and Mary, while they were sitting at Lazarus's deathbed waiting for Jesus to arrive, had nothing to hang on to except what they knew about the character of Jesus. But what they knew was enough to sustain them. They knew Jesus loved their brother. They knew Jesus had the power to heal. They knew Jesus would know what to do. Even though they must have struggled with fear and doubt, I believe they had the underlying assurance that Jesus would eventually make everything all right.

If you are struggling to hang on in the midst of your difficult circumstances, let me remind you to go back to what you know about God. Open the Bible and find scriptures to cling to — scriptures that reveal the heart and faithfulness of God. Remind yourself that God is your strength. That he is your source of comfort. That he won't let you fall. That he loves you passionately and only wants the best for you.

"We only trust people we know," says Martha Tennison, a popular women's conference speaker. "If you're struggling to trust God, it may be because you don't really know God."

Martha Tennison has experienced this truth firsthand. On the trip home from a weekend at an amusement park, the bus that held sixty-seven members of her church youth group was hit head-on by a drunk driver. Twenty-four teenagers and three adults died in the inferno that resulted from a punctured gas tank. In the hours that followed, Martha and her pastor husband had to tell all the families that the children and the mates they loved were gone. The pain was nearly unbearable. Time and time again Martha found herself going to the Word, calling out to the God she knew was faithful.

"You find out what you really believe in the darkest hours," Martha says. "You find out that the God you *know* is the God you can hold on to."[3]

Even when his stories don't unfold the way we think they should.

God's Grammar Lessons

My background in grammar is spotty to say the least. My seventh-grade English teacher was a lovely woman, but her heart wasn't in choosing correct pronouns or tying up dangling participles. So instead of analyzing sentences and conjugating verbs, we spent our afternoons painting with watercolors and baking soufflés. Really.

Until the end of each quarter, that is, when it seemed necessary to hand out a grade for English rather than home ec. Then our teacher would tape a large strip of butcher paper around the room with 150 grammar questions printed neatly in Magic Marker. It was an open-book test. She encouraged us to peek inside our pristine, nearly-never-opened English books for the answers. There was no drilling to see if we'd learned anything, just information transferred from the book to our college-ruled paper.

We all got impressive grades. But it wasn't until high school that I learned what a preposition was for. Or that you should never end a sentence with one.

It's taken me even longer to learn the rules in God's school of grammar.

You didn't know God taught grammar? Well, he does. Everything we need to know is spelled out in his Word, which is good, because this course involves an open-book test as well. But this Teacher doesn't wait until the end of the quarter to print out the questions and tack them up around the room. Instead, God allows us to face them every day. The questions come out of our lives. The answers are found in him and his Word.

I wonder what Mary and Martha felt when they finally received word from Jesus. They'd been waiting for days. But instead of the Master, the only person they saw walking up their path was an out-of-breath courier with a message that must have rung hollow in their ears: "This sickness will not end in death."

It's hard to hope when hope is dead. It's hard to believe God's promises when your brother's body is lying in your living room.

However, God's ways are not our ways. His plots often don't take the direction we think they should. And even his grammar is not our grammar. For it is against this backdrop of despair that we find God's grammar rule number one. Listen carefully. There will be a test.

- *God's Grammar Rule #1: Never put a period where God puts a comma.*

Too often, according to Ray Stedman, we interpret God's delays as God's denials. But the story of Lazarus tells us that "a delay in answer is not a sign of God's indifference or his failure to hear. It is a sign of his love. The delay will help us. It will make us stronger."[4]

Jesus could have spoken the word and made Lazarus well. He did it with the Roman centurion's servant (Matthew 8:5-13). He did it for a Syrophoenician woman's daughter (Mark 7:24-30). Without physically being present, Jesus healed with just a word. He could have done that with Lazarus — as Mary and Martha well knew.

But God's ways are not our ways, and his timing rarely coincides with our own. While God is never late, I've found he's rarely early. That is why we must trust his schedule as well as his character.

CeCe Winans writes in her book *On a Positive Note*:

> Faith is about how you live your life in the meantime, how you make decisions when you don't know for sure what's next. What you do with yourself between the last time you heard from God and the next time you hear from God is the ongoing challenge of a life of faith.[5]

Waiting four days may have made Jesus late for a healing, but it made him right on time for a resurrection. So never put a period where God puts a comma. Just when you think the sentence is over, the most important part may be yet to come.

Simon Peter learned God's second rule of grammar the hard way. The disciple with the foot-shaped mouth meant well, but when Jesus rebuked him, Peter got the message loud and clear.

- *God's Grammar Rule #2: Don't put a comma where God puts a period.*

Throughout the Gospels, Jesus had spoken of his death. In Matthew 16:21 the Bible tells us that "Jesus began to explain to his disciples that he must go to Jerusalem and suffer many things at the hands of the elders, chief priests and teachers of the law, and that he must be killed and on the third day be raised to life."

But Peter wouldn't hear of it. He took his Master aside and began to rebuke him. "Never, Lord!" he said in verse 22. "This shall never happen to you!"

Peter probably thought he was being valiant, protecting and correcting the Lord. He must have felt pretty good about himself . . . until Jesus rebuked Peter's rebuke.

"Get behind me, Satan!" Jesus told Peter in verse 23. "You are a stumbling block to me; you do not have in mind the things of God, but the things of men."

Ouch. It's not every day the Son of God calls you "Satan," and when he does, it has to hurt. But if you are trying to put a comma where God intends a period, don't be surprised when Jesus pops your pretty bubbles. Because when you attempt to breathe life into something God intends to die, you become a stumbling block to Christ.

There are times in every life when God writes the end to a chapter, when he asks us to say good-bye to something or someone who has been important to us. It might be a spouse, a parent, or friend. It might be a job we've loved, a city we've enjoyed, a prejudice or an assumption that we've always thought was true.

Endings, in a sense, are inevitable. Dead ends, failed possibilities, and brick walls will disappoint us all. And when those endings come, we can fight them as Peter advised Jesus. Or we can accept them as Jesus did, as coming from the Father's hand.

Laura Barker Snow writes beautifully about these times:

My child, I have a message for you today; let me whisper it in your ear, that it may gild with glory any storm clouds which may arise, and smooth

Relinquishing Control

Do you ever find yourself clinging to the pencil, refusing to let God write on the pages of your life? I've discovered that the Lord is infinitely kind and patient in his dealings with us. He will show us how to relinquish our rights for his best. If you're struggling in this area, maybe these steps will help you:

1. *Ask God to make you willing.* Sometimes this is the necessary first step. If you just can't muster up the willingness to surrender control to God, then pray first for a change of attitude.

2. *Recognize you have an adversary.* The last thing Satan wants is for you to totally surrender your life to God. Pray for the wisdom and strength not to listen to his lies.

3. *Let go one piece at a time.* Sometimes we cling to control because we fear we'll be asked to make drastic changes we're not ready for. But God, in his kindness, takes us at a pace we can handle. If we simply obey what he asks of us at the moment, he'll lead us to the next step when we're ready.

I have lost all things. I consider them rubbish, that I may gain Christ and be found in him.
PHILIPPIANS 3:8-9

the rough places upon which you may have to tread. It is short, only five words, but let them sink into your inmost soul; use them as a pillow upon which to rest your weary head. . . . This thing is from ME.[6]

And that, of course, brings us back to the fundamental truth behind all God's grammar lessons. The Father knows best.

His periods may not be our periods. His commas may not be our commas. His ways may not be our ways. But God is the One telling the story, and we can trust him to take the tale in the right direction. We can have faith that everything really will turn out all right.

And it is that very faith that takes us to the next lesson Lazarus's story has to teach us.

Developing Faith

The house in Bethany was most likely filled with people following Lazarus's death. Jewish faith considered expressing sympathy a sacred duty. Mourning was so important to the Jews that an entire industry had grown up around it. If the deceased hadn't enough friends to mourn, the family would hire wailers to make sure the dead departed properly. The louder the better.

But Mary and Martha didn't have to hire anybody when Lazarus died. They had mourners aplenty, according to John 11. Friends and family flocked in to support the sisters in their grief, even from out of town (verse 19).

This means Martha once again had a houseful of company when Jesus finally arrived in Bethany. But when someone brought the news that Jesus was coming, it was Martha, not Mary, who ran to meet him. The guests, the duties, all the distractions — nothing mattered but seeing Jesus.

She met him somewhere on the road into Bethany, and with all the anguished honesty of deep sorrow, Martha poured out her grief. "Lord," she cried, "if you had been here, my brother would not have died."

Her response was natural and heartfelt. But then Martha added something I find remarkable, something that revealed just how much she had changed since the last time they'd met. "But I know," she continued, "that even now God will give you whatever you ask"(verse 22).

No longer do we see a woman trying to manipulate God. Instead of trying to rewrite the story of her brother's death — instead of putting a comma where there was a period or a period where there could be a comma — Martha was placing the quill of their lives in Jesus' hands.

Do whatever you want, she was saying. Punctuate as you please. Thy will be done.

It is that kind of surrender and that kind of resolve that sets in motion the miraculous. I can almost see the glory on Jesus' face as he declared his purpose to Martha that day on the road outside her home. "I am the resurrection and the life. He who believes in me will live, even though he dies; and whoever lives and believes in me will never die. Do you believe this?" (John 11:25-26).

How precious Martha's response must have sounded in Jesus' ears. "Yes, Lord," she told him, "I believe that you are the Christ, the Son of God, who was to come into the world."

I believe. Could there be two sweeter sounding words? In Martha's great declaration of faith and the miraculous events that followed it, we find the fourth lesson from the story of Lazarus:

- **God's plan is released when we believe and obey.**

This is one of the most exciting lessons of all, because it means that God's story, in a sense, is interactive. We are an integral part of the writing process. Our choices play a part in the unfolding of the plot. Just as Adam and Eve's disobedience blocked God's purpose, our obedience releases his plan.

Faith and obedience go hand in hand. It takes faith to choose obedience, and if you're like me, it takes obedience to choose faith when you're quaking with fear. But when God speaks a promise to our hearts, we can take him at his word. That's what Martha did. And as she did, faith arose to help her take the next step: to obey him when he spoke, even when what he told her to do seemed completely impractical.

Resurrection Power

By the time Jesus came to Bethany, Lazarus had been dead and buried for four days. The time span was significant to the Jews. "Many Jews believed the soul

262

remained near the body for three days after death in the hope of returning to it. If this idea was in the minds of these people, they obviously thought all hope was gone — Lazarus was irrevocably dead."[7]

For centuries, the two primary groups of Jewish religious leaders, the Sadducees and Pharisees, had argued about the afterlife. The Sadducees said there was no resurrection, no future life, no hell nor heaven. Life on earth was all there was. (That's why they were "sad you see."[8]) The Pharisees, on the other hand, believed there was a future for the dead. They believed in the immortality of the soul and in reward and retribution after death.

But neither sect understood the concept of resurrection. Certainly not the type of resurrection they were about to witness.

I can only imagine what went through everyone's mind when Jesus asked for the stone to be taken away. We all chuckle at the *King James*'s translation of Martha's response, "Lord, . . . he stinketh!" She only dared to speak what everyone else was thinking. There was a dead body behind that stone — a rotting one at that. "Grody hody," as my son used to say. Yuck.

Martha wasn't getting the picture. No one was. Why on earth did Jesus want to open the grave of a man who had been dead four days? To pay his last respects?

You see, Martha had faith for *what could have been:* "If you had been here, my brother would not have died" (John 11:21).

Martha had faith for *what would be:* "I know he will rise again in the resurrection at the last day" (11:24).

What Martha needed was faith for *what was happening now:* "Did I not tell you that if you believed, you would see the glory of God?" Jesus asked her in verse 40.[9]

It is the same question Jesus asks of us today: "Will you believe?" Martha's response of faith was quick, her obedience certain. "So they took away the stone," verse 41 tells us. And the rest is history. Incredible, life-changing, never-to-be-looked-at-the-same kind of history.

For when Jesus stood outside the tomb and said, "Lazarus, come out!" hell trembled. In a matter of weeks, death's grip on humanity — past, present, and future — would be completely broken. The dark shadowland of death would be filled with glorious light. And never again would we read the story of eternal life the same way again.

The final lesson from the story of Lazarus still echoes today:

- **The "end" is never the end; it is only the beginning.**

When Jesus came late to Bethany, his lateness was an act of love. A gift of perspective. A foreshadowing meant as a mercy, not only for Mary, Martha, and Lazarus, but for his disciples and for you and me.

Jesus knew we would struggle with the concept of resurrection. He knew we would have doubts when his tomb turned up empty. He knew there would be conspiracy theories and chat rooms jammed with people wanting to debate the likelihood of the dead coming back to life. So the Author of our faith, our great storytelling God, prefaced his Son's death with an act that would foreshadow the resurrection. When Jesus raised Lazarus from the dead, he put to death Satan's lie that the end is the end.

The truth of Lazarus and the secret of the resurrection is this: If Jesus Christ can turn death into life, sorrow into gladness, suffering into triumph — then nothing truly bad can ever touch our lives again. Not really. Unfortunate things may happen. Difficulties may come. But it all becomes fodder for a greater work, a more glorious glory.

Philip Yancey points to the cross and the empty tomb as turning points in the scriptural view of suffering: "When New Testament writers speak of hard times, they express none of the indignation that characterized Job, the prophets, and many of the psalmists. They offer no real explanation for suffering, but keep pointing to two events — the death and resurrection of Jesus."[10]

As a result of Christ's work on the cross, Yancey says, "The three-day pattern — tragedy, darkness, triumph — became for New Testament writers a template that can be applied to all our times of testing."[11]

Looking back, in fact, we can see that pattern all through God's story. Joseph experienced it. So did Job, though he didn't understand it. The disciples felt it. So did our Lord. *Tragedy* may come. So will the *darkness*. But *triumph* is waiting just around the corner.

That's the lesson that Lazarus's resurrection hinted at — that's the truth Jesus' resurrection would triumphantly prove.

It may be Friday, suggested Lazarus's empty tomb.

But Sunday's comin'.

An Empty Shell

Philip wasn't like the other children at church. Though he was a pleasant, happy boy, he struggled with things that came easily to other kids. He looked different, too, and everyone knew it was because he had Down syndrome. His Sunday school teacher worked hard to get the third grade class to play together, but Philip's disability made it difficult for him to fit in.

Easter was just around the corner, and the teacher had a wonderful idea for his class. He gathered the big plastic eggs that pantyhose used to come in and gave one to each child. Then, together, they went outside into a beautiful spring day.

"I want each of you to find something that reminds you of Easter — of new life," the teacher explained. "Put it in the egg, and when we get inside we'll share what we found."

The search was glorious. It was confusing. It was wild. The boys and girls ran all over the church grounds gathering their symbols until finally, breathlessly, the eight-year-olds were ready to return inside.

They put their eggs on the table, then one by one the teacher began to open them. The children stood around the table watching.

He opened one, and there was a flower. Everybody oohed and aahed.

He opened another and found a butterfly. "Beautiful," the girls all said.

He opened another and out fell a rock. The kids laughed. "A rock?" But the boy who'd found it said, "I knew you would all get flowers and leaves and stuff, so I got a rock cause I wanted to be different. That's new life to me." The kids laughed again.

But when the teacher opened the next egg, the group fell silent. "There's nothing there!" said one child. "That's stupid," said another. "Somebody didn't do it right."

Just then the teacher felt a tug on his shirt and turned to see Philip standing beside him. "It's mine," Philip said. "It's mine."

The children said, "You don't ever do things right, Philip. There's nothing there!"

"I did so," Philip said. "I did do it right. It's empty. *The tomb is empty!*"

There was another silence. A very deep, unlike-eight-year-olds kind of silence. And at that moment a miracle happened. Philip became a part of that third-grade Sunday school class. They took him in. He was set free from the tomb of his differentness. From then on, Philip was their friend.

Three months later, Philip died. His family had known since the time he was born that he wouldn't live out a full life span. An infection that most children would have quickly shrugged off took the life out of his body.

The day of the funeral, the church was filled with people mourning Philip's death. But it was the sight of nine third graders walking down the aisle with their Sunday school teacher that brought tears to most eyes.

The children didn't bring flowers. Instead, they marched right up to the altar, and placed on it an empty egg — an empty, old, discarded pantyhose egg.[12]

The God Who Weeps with Us

We will all die. Lazarus eventually did. Little Philip did. You and I will.

But never forget: The end is not the end. It is only the beginning. When we belong to Jesus, we simply leave our empty shells behind and go to glory. "Where, O death, is your victory?" Paul writes to remind us in 1 Corinthians 15:55.

"Where, O death, is your sting?"

And yet death *does* sting, even when we know better. It hurts to leave behind the people we love. It hurts to be left behind. We will all encounter many more hurts on our journey toward the grave. Sometimes the story of our lives seems like one painful episode after another.

And Jesus knew that.

Even though Jesus knew Lazarus was about to be raised from the dead, he understood Mary and Martha's pain. He did more than understand it. He felt it too. John 11:35 tells us, "Jesus wept." The word for *wept* denotes a deep sorrow with great emotion.

Because Jesus loved this family from Bethany, he wept, and he weeps with us as well. Though Jesus knows our triumphant outcomes, though he sees the joyful ending just around the bend, he still gets down in the middle of our sorrow and holds us close, mingling his tears with our own.

And that, I believe, is the essence of the story God writes throughout our lives.

Jesus Understands

"Jesus wept" is famous as the shortest verse in the Bible, but to me the real power of that two-word passage from the story of Lazarus is the reassurance that Jesus understands what life is like for us. He doesn't ask anything of us that he wasn't willing to do himself, and he promises to be with us in all we have to go through. For example:

- *Jesus knew temptation:* "He was in the desert forty days, being tempted by Satan" (Mark 1:13).

- *Jesus knew poverty:* "Foxes have holes and birds of the air have nests, but the Son of Man has no place to lay his head" (Matthew 8:20).

- *Jesus knew frustration:* "He scattered the coins of the money changers and overturned their tables. . . . 'Get these out of here! How dare you turn my Father's house into a market!'" (John 2:15-16).

- *Jesus knew weariness:* "Jesus, tired as he was from the journey, sat down by the well" (John 4:6).

- *Jesus knew disappointment:* "O Jerusalem, Jerusalem . . . how often I have longed to gather your children together, as a hen gathers her chicks, . . . but you were not willing" (Luke 13:34).

- *Jesus knew rejection:* "From this

time many of his disciples turned back and no longer followed him" (John 6:66).

- *Jesus knew sorrow:* "My soul is overwhelmed with sorrow to the point of death" (Matthew 26:38).
- *Jesus knew ridicule:* "Again and again they struck him . . . and spit on him. Falling on their knees, they paid [mocking] homage to him" (Mark 15:19).
- *Jesus knew loneliness:* "My God, my God, why have you forsaken me?" (Matthew 27:46).

For we do not have a high priest who is unable to sympathize with our weaknesses, but we have one who has been tempted in every way, just as we are — yet was without sin.
HEBREWS 4:15

Today we suffer. Today we don't understand. But someday, in that eternal Tomorrow, that same Savior who weeps with us will wipe every tear from our eyes. He'll unbind our graveclothes of earthly flesh, and we'll be set free. Someday all the scattered, broken pieces will fall into place, and we will suddenly understand the hand of God has been upon us all the time. All the tragedy — all the darkness — will instantly be swallowed up by triumph.

What a perfect ending to our imperfect stories!

That's the love of our Master Storyteller God.

9

Martha's Teachable Heart

If you hold to my teaching,
you are really my disciples.
Then you will know the truth,
and the truth will set you free.
JOHN 8:31-32

"No previous experience required. We will train you," the advertisement said. It read like a help-wanted ad for the night shift at McDonald's. Except this ad appeared on the pages of one of America's leading business journals.

After decades of dog-eat-dog capitalism, it seems, Fortune 500 companies are beginning to look for a new breed of worker. While degrees remain important, many businesses are looking for more personal qualities in their personnel. "How do you interact with others?" they ask. "Are you a team player or a maverick?"

Bottom line: Are you teachable?

Companies are ignoring glowing résumés, bypassing corporate headhunters, and going straight to college campuses to recruit their workforce. Why? "We spend more time and money 'untraining' people than we would training them in the first place," said one executive I heard on a talk show. "We don't need know-it-alls; we need people who are willing to learn."

A Teachable Heart

If Jesus would have taken out a classified in the *Jerusalem Post* at the start of his ministry two thousand years ago, I think it would have read much the same as that business ad. "No previous experience required. We will train." Jesus wasn't as interested in finding capable people as he was in finding available people. He was looking for teachable hearts.

Perhaps that's why Jesus said, "Let the little children come to me, and do not hinder them, for the kingdom of God belongs to such as these" (Matthew 19:14). Children learn quickly — mainly because they don't have preconceived ideas that keep them from hearing something new and receiving it.

Perhaps that's why Jesus called a group of ragtag men to come alongside him instead of a bunch of religious muckety-mucks. The minds of the educated scribes and Pharisees of Israel were loaded with false perceptions and man-made agendas; it would have taken years to reprogram their thinking to God's way of thinking. So Jesus chose men without résumés, without formal education, with no previous evangelical work experience.

To the rest of the world, they seemed unimpressive. Unwashed, untaught, and sometimes uncouth. But Jesus saw in them exactly what he needed — followers with the potential for transformation.

Unfortunately, though we all applaud the thought of transformation, most of us don't appreciate the process that gets us there. To be transformed means we have to change, and change too often hurts. But as Paul W. Powell writes, "God is more concerned about our character than our comfort. His goal is not to pamper us physically but to perfect us spiritually."[1]

I believe that's why Jesus chose to confront Martha's attitude after her little tantrum about help in the kitchen back in Luke 10. There was more at stake in the incident than met the eye. In Martha's outburst, Christ could see a fault line that ran deep down the woman's psyche, down to where her identity lay. Martha thought she had value because she was productive. Jesus wanted her to learn she had value simply because she was his.

I'm sure Martha's feelings must have smarted at Jesus' rebuke. After all, no one enjoys the exposure of his or her blunders. I wouldn't be surprised if there was a moment when Martha was tempted to pack up her bruised ego and stomp out of the room. She knew when she wasn't being appreciated. Let them cook their own dinner! Then they'd see how hard she'd slaved.

But instead, Martha stuck around and heard Jesus out. And if we want to be his disciples, we must be willing to do the same. Even when his words cross our will.

Are You Teachable?

Consider the following statements to give you an idea of your teachability quotient. Answer (U) for Usually; (S) for Sometimes; and (R) for Rarely.

	U	S	R
1. I feel comfortable asking for advice.			
2. I easily admit when I'm wrong.			
3. I enjoy reading for information rather than escape.			
4. I'm able to receive criticism without being hurt.			
5. I enjoy listening to other people's thoughts and opinions without feeling the need to express my own.			
6. When I read something in the Bible, I automatically think of ways to apply it.			
7. I enjoy church and Bible classes and usually take notes.			
8. I'm able to disagree with someone without feeling like I have to debate the issue.			
9. I'm willing to look at all sides of a situation before I form an opinion.			
10. I'd rather be righteous than always have to be "right."			

Give yourself 3 points for each U answer, 2 points for each S, and 0 points for every R. Then add the numbers. If you scored 24-30 points, you are well on your way to a teachable heart. If you scored 15-23, keep at it! You are definitely trainable. If you scored 0-14, you may need to make your teachability quotient a matter of prayer, because you'll find a teachable heart is one of life's greatest treasures.

Take firm hold of instruction,
do not let go;
keep her, for she is your life.
PROVERBS 4:13 (NKJV)

Cross My Heart

My mind was in turmoil as I took the kids to school that cold winter morning several years ago. Angry clouds crowded the sky above as I fought my way through the unplowed side streets. Yesterday's slush had hardened into large, icy ruts that caused my van to lurch from side to side. I had to struggle to keep hold of the steering wheel. But the real struggle that morning was inside me.

What a picture of my life, I thought, peering through the frosty windshield at the gray landscape. Dark. Dreary. Icy cold.

A huge misunderstanding had erupted between a dear friend and me several months before, and nothing I'd tried had mended it. I'd made a mistake and I'd apologized. Why wouldn't she forgive me? The mental ruts of the frozen circumstance tossed my emotions back and forth, ripping away my joy and peace, leaving me empty, hard, and hollow.

Jessica's sweet voice drifted from the backseat as she sang along with a popular Christian song on the radio. Her voice matched the soft twang of the singer's question, "Has Jesus ever crossed your heart?"

The words were strangely familiar. They echoed the words I'd used the day before to pronounce judgment on my friend. "Well, I guess you find out what people are really like when you cross them," I'd told my husband in a moment of anger. But now I sensed the Holy Spirit turning my own words like a spotlight on the darkness of my soul.

"What about you, Joanna?" I felt the Lord prompt softly. "What has this 'crossing' of your heart brought out in you?"

What he showed me wasn't pretty. There

were things in my life I'd left unsettled, core issues I'd refused to contemplate. But it was time to face them, and I knew it. For me, the simple fact that I was ready illustrates one of the most beautiful things I've learned about my Lord.

Jesus goes out of his way to prepare my heart to listen and learn. He waits for the moment I'm most ready to obey. And while I can still refuse him at any time, his rebuke is gentle. It woos me at the same time it disarms me, making me willing and open and ready to change.

If you haven't experienced this sweet aspect of our Savior's discipline, may I suggest you spend a little more time in the Living Room? Because when you're busy in the Kitchen, the rebuke sounds harsh and demanding, just one more duty to fulfill. But when you listen from the Living Room, you hear the love in God's voice and it sounds like life for your soul.

That's where Martha found it. In the Living Room. She received the rebuke of her Savior, and we've witnessed how she changed. Instead of exalting herself against God, she humbled herself, and she found the truth of King Solomon's words: "Open rebuke is better than secret love. Faithful are the wounds of a friend"

(Proverbs 27:5-6, KJV).

Especially when that friend is Jesus.

To Learn or Not to Learn

"Mom?" John Michael's eyes were dark and serious. A brilliant child (of course!), my twelve-year-old had a mind that was constantly moving, exploring, and — occasionally — mixing up words.

"Yes, Michael?" I asked.

"I was just wondering. People who are really poor . . .," he began slowly. "They're like in puberty, right?"

Well, as you might imagine, I gently corrected his mistake, and then we had a meaningful talk about the plight of starving people around the world.

Okay, so that's what I should have done.

Instead, I burst out laughing. "Puberty!?" I howled, trying to keep my voice down. "You mean poverty?"

"Yeah. That." He looked at me. "What did I say?"

I explained the difference between the two words to my son, and we both had a good chuckle. In fact, we discovered a code word for his impending adolescence. "I think I've got a pimple," he said a few

282

days later as he inspected a small white bump on his chin in the bathroom mirror.

"Cool, Michael." It was his first bona fide blemish. I patted his back and congratulated him. "You're finally entering poverty."

Teachable moments. Those times in life when truth pops up (pardon the pun), offering us a chance to grow. To learn or not to learn, that is the question. For when we are corrected, rebuked, or chastened, we have a choice. We can receive it, or we can refuse it.

John Michael could have been offended by my disregard for his feelings over his vocabulary mistake. He could have marched out the door. But he chose to receive my instruction with good humor, and in receiving it, he opened the door for a mother-son discussion on a topic not easily talked about.

As for me, I got a much-needed lesson in not taking myself so seriously. Michael has taught me how to laugh and learn from my mistakes instead of trying to hide from them.

The point is, we all get confused sometimes. Most of us are quick to admit we're not perfect — as long as we don't have to talk specifics. But when someone points out a flaw in our lives, we're not nearly as calm. And unlike my good-natured son, we're not all that likely to laugh off the criticism either. Instead, we go all stiff and huffy. Or we go ballistic, shooting off our mouths in an attempt to shoot down their theories. "That is simply not true," we say, listing the reasons. When that doesn't work, we go on the offensive, listing their faults. "Get the log out of your own eye, Paul Bunyan!" we shout, then run for cover.

But Martha, to her eternal credit, didn't do that when Jesus corrected her that day in the living room. Or at least I don't think she did.

When he observed, "You are worried and upset about many things. . . . Mary has chosen what is better, and it will not be taken away from her," there's no rebuttal recorded from Martha. No sputtering reply. In fact, the entire incident ends with the words of Jesus' rebuke.

The Bible doesn't tell us how Martha responded that day. But I'm convinced Martha received the rebuke of Jesus humbly and learned from it. I believe that Martha had a teachable heart — for nothing else could explain her mysterious transformation into the Martha of John 11 and 12.

In these two chapters we see a woman

completely different from the one we last met in Luke 10:38-42. Oh, she was still pushy, a bit impatient, and too practical for her own good. But as we have seen, there was also a tender vulnerability that wasn't there before. A new faith. A new kind of intimacy with Jesus that only comes when we receive and apply correction from God.

We've already mentioned Martha's transformation in "Lessons from Lazarus." But I'd like to focus on the changes we see in John 11, for they paint a picture of a woman changed by a teachable heart. First, Martha left a house filled with guests and hurried to meet Jesus. This was a woman who used to be obsessed about entertaining. What would make her leave a house full of company?

Making that even stranger is the fact that Martha was most likely the firstborn. She was accustomed to being the strong one. She'd held the family together before, and in the middle of this overwhelming grief, surely she would feel the need to hold it together again. But when Jesus arrived in Bethany, instead of holding down the fort, Martha threw aside her obligations and ran outside to meet her Master.

"Lord," Martha said to Jesus in John 11:21, "if you had been here, my brother would not have died." Her words dripped with grief and confusion. Mary would echo her pain moments later, using the exact same words. But only Martha had something additional to say. Without break, without pause, she added, "But I know that even now God will give you whatever you ask."

Faith. That's what was different. Instead of whining like a child, demanding that Jesus do things her way, Martha proclaimed her belief that Jesus could do whatever was needed. Gone was Martha's contentious "Tell her!" She wasn't ordering Jesus around this time. Instead, she humbly gave Jesus the authority and the room to decide what was best.

It was to this open, teachable heart that Jesus revealed himself in all his glory: "I am the resurrection and the life. He who believes in me will live, even though he dies. . . . Do you believe this?" Jesus asked Martha in John 11:25-26.

"Yes, Lord," she replied, "I believe that you are the Christ, the Son of God, who was to come into the world" (11:27).

Scholars call this declaration one of the most incredible statements of faith in Scripture, for it cuts to the very essence of who Jesus was and is. And this insightful proclamation came not from contemplative, sensitive Mary, but from organized, duty-bound — but teachable — Martha.

No longer blinded by doubt and self-interest, Martha was a woman whose eyes were open. She knew who Jesus was — not just a good man or a fascinating teacher, but the very Son of God. She proclaimed him the Christ, her Messiah.

But beyond Martha's theological understanding, I find in verse 28 the sweetest change of all: "And after she had said this, she went back and called her sister Mary aside. 'The Teacher is here,' she said, 'and is asking for you.'"

Wait a minute! What happened to the sibling rivalry we saw in Luke 10? Gone now is the resentment. Gone is any form of competition. Martha could feel not only for herself, but also for her sister. And this time, instead of shooing Mary away from the feet of Jesus, Martha pointed her there.

Clearly, this was not the same woman we saw before in that Bethany home. The anxious, demanding Queen of Everything is gone. And in her place is a woman with a transformed heart. It's the kind of transformed heart we all desire but spend most of our lives wondering how to achieve.

I think we get a new heart from the Lord the same way Martha did — by being

teachable. And being teachable, in essence, involves three things:
- being willing to listen
- acting on what we hear
- responding to discipline

Do You Have Ears?

"Hear, O Israel: The LORD our God, the LORD is one." Every morning for thousands of years, pious Jews have recited Deuteronomy 6:4. The verse opens the *Shema*, their main confession of faith, which instructs the Jewish people to: "Love the LORD your God with all your heart and with all your soul and with all your strength" (6:5).

Shema. The actual Hebrew word means "hear thou." And that's a word for us as well. The Scripture contains great truth. Powerful, life-changing words. If we're willing to *shema* — if we're willing to hear.

Unfortunately, it seems God's people have always been hard of hearing. Perhaps it's hereditary. Again and again, in the Old Testament we read about God's attempts to communicate with his wayward, hearing-impaired children:

So I told you, but you would not listen. You rebelled against the LORD's command and in your arrogance you marched up into the hill country. (Deuteronomy 1:43)

Although the LORD sent prophets to the people to bring them back to him, and though they testified against them, they would not listen. (2 Chronicles 24:19)

For many years you were patient with them. By your Spirit you admonished them through your prophets. Yet they paid no attention. (Nehemiah 9:30)

It's not hard to see a pattern here. Almost from the beginning of time, God's people have thwarted the Lord's transforming work by refusing to listen. By tuning him out. We do the same thing when we refuse to pay attention to the voice of his Spirit in our lives.

Sometimes the refusal to hear is deliberate; we don't want to face what we think God might have to say. Sometimes I think it's almost subconscious; we live in a state of denial because we just can't handle any demands the Lord might want to make.

How Does God Talk to You?

While we know God speaks clearly to us through the Bible, many of us are uncertain how to hear God's voice in our spirit. "How does God speak to you?" someone asked author and speaker Carole Mayhall. I have found her answer immensely practical and helpful:

For me, He speaks by a distinct impression in my heart. He's never spoken to me aloud, but sometimes the thought that He puts in my soul is so vivid that He might as well have! Many times it is just a thought or an idea that flashes into my mind and I know it is from Him. . . .

Sometimes a thought pops into my mind — a thought so different from what I was thinking, or so creative I never would have thought of it, or opposite to what I *wanted* God to say to me. When that happens — and it lines up with God's Word — I know I've heard His voice in a distinctive way. . . .

I pray frequently that I'll hear His voice more often and more clearly.

> When I don't, I know He hasn't stopped speaking; rather, I have stopped listening.[2]
>
> *My sheep listen to my voice;*
> *I know them, and they follow me.*
> JOHN 10:27

Sometimes we conveniently let God's voice be drowned out by the confusion of our daily existence; we avoid listening to him by being too busy to read the Bible or pray. It's almost like we're stubborn children who cover their ears and stomp their feet and hum loudly just to keep from hearing what their parents are trying to tell them.

Regardless of how we do it, the ultimate result is the same. When we refuse to listen to the Lord, we shut him out. We refuse him the opportunity to teach us, to transform our lives, and to work through us to transform the world.

Surely that's why Jesus put such a premium on listening. Over and over, Jesus' clarion call punctuates the Gospels, echoing the words of the *Shema*: "He who has ears, let him hear." And eight times in Revelation, Jesus instructs his Bride, the Church, to listen: "Let him hear what the

Spirit says to the churches."

And make no mistake, the Lord still speaks today. Through the Scriptures. Through our circumstances. In our heart, by the voice of the Holy Spirit. We can hear him if we give up our rebellion and our denial. We can hear his voice, and when we hearken to him, he will teach us.

We who have ears . . . let us listen and hear.

Doing What Jesus Says

Just hearing God's Word isn't enough, of course. The Bible makes that abundantly clear. God's transforming power in our lives is unleashed when we not only listen, but also *act* on what we've heard.

In fact, in our very refusal to apply God's truth to our lives, we may actually keep ourselves from hearing his voice in the future. Sin actually stops up our spiritual ears the same way excess wax plugs up our physical ones. When that happens, we may appear to hear, nodding and saying yes, yet have absolutely no comprehension. People with spiritually stopped-up ears are "always learning," Paul writes in 2 Timothy 3:7, "but never able to acknowledge the truth."

The sad fact is, we can grow so accustomed to God's voice that it no longer moves us. We can become like the people God warned us about through his prophet in Ezekiel 33:31-32:

> My people come to you, as they
> usually do, and sit before you to listen
> to your words, but they do not put
> them into practice. With their mouths
> they express devotion, but their hearts
> are greedy for unjust gain. Indeed, to
> them you are nothing more than one
> who sings love songs with a beautiful
> voice and plays an instrument well, for
> they hear your words but do not put
> them into practice.

Sounds frighteningly familiar, doesn't it? So do the pointed words of James, the brother of Jesus, "Do not merely listen to the word, and so deceive yourselves. Do what it says" (James 1:22).

I've already said quite a lot about obedience in this book, mainly because I believe obedience is an essential ingredient in intimacy with God and the key to having a Mary heart. And obedience is exactly what we're talking about here. Either we take

Jesus' words to heart and *change,* or we listen but disregard them. And to disregard the voice of God is worse than not listening at all. Especially if we say we love him.

When my children refuse to listen, I find myself wanting to quote the words Jesus used in John 14:21: "Whoever has my commands and obeys them, he is the one who loves me." *Don't tell me you love me,* I want to say when they come begging to watch cartoons after they've already been told to clean their rooms. *Obey my commands.*

Jesus doesn't mince words with us. He cuts to the heart of what really matters in each of our lives. He puts his finger on our sore spots, the sin-infected places we try so hard to hide. He points to our cluttered bedrooms and says, "Do this and live." Because if we want to live, we're going to have to obey.

Oswald Chambers has illuminated my life in so many ways, but perhaps none as penetrating as this simple truth about the importance of obedience:

All God's revelations are sealed until they are opened to us by obedience.
. . . Obey God in the thing He shows

you, and instantly the next thing is opened up. . . . God will never reveal more truth about himself until you have obeyed what you know already.[3]

Unfortunately, it's often easier to talk about obedience than to do anything about it. We'll dissect and analyze God's truth, debate it, and philosophize about it — anything but actually let it affect our lives.

"What did Jesus really mean?" we ask each other as we ponder the hard sayings of Christ at Wednesday-night Bible study. "Surely he didn't mean we need to sell everything we have and give to the poor," we conclude, then go on to explain why we need to cut back on our mission giving until we've paid off the new Lexus.

That's an extreme example, of course. But I do think there is something deep inside each one of us that rebels against God's authority in our life. Something deep that insists on doing things our own way. That's as true now as it was when Eve bucked God in the garden, when the children of Israel ignored the prophets' warnings, and when the Jews turned Jesus over to be crucified.

And so Pilate's question to the Jews still echoes for us today: What will you do with this man? Because to know him is to hear his words and lovingly obey him, or we know him not at all.

Kathleen Norris, author of *Amazing Grace: A Vocabulary of Faith*, describes a simple exchange that impressed this reality upon her and changed her life. The women's circle in her church had asked her to conduct the Bible study session on the Antichrist, a task for which she felt distinctly inadequate. The packet of study materials provided comfort but not much practical help, declaring that even St. Augustine had given up on the subject, claiming it was beyond him.

So Kathleen went to her pastor for help. "He quickly summarized and dismissed the tendency that Christians have always had to identify the Antichrist with their personal enemies, or with those in power whom they have reason to detest. It is an easy temptation," Norris writes. "In our own century, the Antichrist has been equaled with Adolf Hitler, Joseph Stalin, Pol Pot, and given the current state of political hysteria in America, no doubt Bill and Hillary Clinton as well."

But then, Norris writes, the pastor said something so simple it would stay with her forever: " 'Each one of us acts as an

Antichrist,' he said, 'whenever we hear the gospel and do not do it.' "4

Receiving Rebuke

What happens when we refuse to listen to God and act on what he says?

The Bible is clear that God, like a loving parent, will administer the appropriate correction in our lives. "For whom the LORD loves He reproves," states Proverbs 3:12, "even as a father, the son in whom he delights" (NASB).

The level of the discipline we receive depends mostly on the level of our teachability. When my mother was small, all her father had to do was look disappointed with her and she'd be in his arms, melting with tears, begging for his forgiveness. Suffice it to say, it required a little more force on my dad's part when it came to his eldest child. I was not only well raised, I was also well "reared." And quite often, come to think of it.

Spiritually, the same is true. If we are teachable, we come around quickly to obedience. As a consequence, the level of discipline is fairly minor, sometimes even painless. But if we are unteachable, if we refuse God's rebuke, the level of discipline increases in severity, just like my "rearing" did. Not because God is ruthless, but because our hearts are rebellious. Our loving Father will do whatever it takes to break that rebellion before that rebellion breaks us. Even if it means giving us a time-out (like having to wait for something we've wanted), taking away our toys (like the new computer that just crashed), or allowing some affliction to come our way.

"Before I was afflicted I went astray," the psalmist writes, "but now I obey your word" (Psalm 119:67). Before you think God cruel, read on. This is no trembling, abused child. This is a chastened son, who like me, can look back and say to his Father with full assurance: "You are good, and what you do is good; teach me your decrees" (119:68).

Jesus was direct in his rebuke of Martha. His words were gentle, but they pierced straight to the heart of her shortcomings. And Martha paid attention. She was teachable. All it took was a tender rebuke from the one she loved. Jesus didn't have to convince her. She didn't launch into a debate. She simply accepted his words, though I'm sure they were painful to hear.

Martha knew the secret every child who

has ever been lovingly disciplined eventually learns. You shouldn't run away from your daddy. Though correction hurts and rebukes sting, at the end of the pain, there is great reward. Hebrews 12:11 tells us, "No discipline seems pleasant at the time, but painful. Later on, however, it produces a harvest of righteousness and peace for those who have been trained by it."

I, for one, am incredibly thankful for the discipline my parents gave me. Far from crying "child abuse," I call them blessed. Because of their diligence in correcting my childhood wrongs, I have much less temptation to deal with as an adult. For one thing, I'm not tempted to steal — not since my mother marched me back into Buttrey's at the age of five and made me return the candy bar I'd taken. And I don't struggle with swearing either. I swore off cursing at the first taste of Ivory soap.

And as an adult, I'm learning to welcome the discipline of the Lord in my life as well. Instead of running from his rebuke, I find myself looking forward to it. Even — dare I say it? — asking for it. The words of Psalm 23 play through my soul like a precious song: "Your rod and your staff, they comfort me."

Several years ago, a four-year-old named

Joshua Wiedenmeyer taught me a lesson about receiving discipline I will never forget. When Josh's parents, Jeff and Tammy, dropped by on vacation, Glacier National Park was high on the list of must-sees. We loaded both families into the van the next morning and set off for a day of sightseeing. The kids chattered as we pointed out various points of interest. The van climbed the "Going to the Sun" highway through pine trees and ancient cedars until we were far above the valley floor. At the summit, we spent an hour touring the visitors center and then ate lunch in the sunshine, enjoying the incredible beauty around us.

It was nearly two o'clock when we headed back down the mountain. Nap time. Poor Josh was having a tough time. He didn't like the car seat. He didn't want a cracker. Tammy tried to comfort him. She tried to distract him. But nothing worked. Finally Dad stepped in. "Josh, do you need a spanking?"

Now I've asked my kids that question several million times, but until that day, I'd never heard this particular response. Josh paused for a moment, his eyes bright with tears. Collecting his breath between sobs, he said in a small voice, "Yes, Daddy. I do."

"John, will you please pull over?" Jeff asked my husband, who complied. Jeff got out of the front seat, opened the van door and waited as Joshua climbed over several legs and into his arms. They walked a few paces off where Jeff applied loving, but firm pressure to his son's backside, then hugged him and spoke tender exhortation. They came back to the van and Joshua climbed into the backseat, catching his breath like we all do after a hard cry, but with nary a whine.

Joshua got what he needed and the rest of the trip he was fine. What a lesson. Instead of avoiding discipline, he embraced it. At four years of age, Joshua had discovered a secret many of us live a lifetime yet never learn.

"Blessed is the man you discipline, O LORD; . . . you grant him relief from days of trouble" (Psalm 94:12-13).

A Holy Makeover

Do you want to know God? Do you really desire to have an intimate, heart-to-heart relationship with him? If you do, then respond to his rebuke. Don't refuse his correction. "If you had responded to

301

my rebuke," the Lord says in Proverbs 1:23, "I would have poured out my heart to you and made my thoughts known to you." Respond to him with a teachable heart, and you'll be surprised at the holy makeover that happens in your own life.

I want that for my life. I want a holy makeover as transforming as Martha's. My deepest fear has always been that I might wake up thirty years from now and realize I haven't changed — that I still struggle with the same worthless habits, petty attitudes, and hidden sin that I did way back when.

What a terrible thing that would be. But unless I have a teachable heart, such spiritual stagnation is my destiny. Bitter and fearful, I'll be encrusted with things from the past that I should have let go of long ago. And all because I refused to be taught by my heavenly Father.

The purpose of Jesus' death on the cross wasn't to provide fire insurance or an all-expenses-paid trip to heaven. He died and rose again so we could be made new. So we wouldn't have to stay in our trespasses and sins, tangled up by our emotions, hurts, and past disappointments. He did it so we could be "transformed into his likeness," Paul says in 2 Corinthians 3:18. No longer must we hide behind a veil of shame. Instead, with "unveiled faces" we "reflect the Lord's glory . . . with ever-increasing glory, which comes from the Lord."

Don't be *conformed* to this world, Paul tells us in Romans 12, but be *transformed*. That is the result of teachability, of being open to the Lord's lessons, and when we choose transformation, we choose something magnificent. The Greek word for it is *metamorphoo*, from which we get our word *metamorphose*, meaning to be transfigured or changed. It is the same word used to describe what happened to Jesus on the Mount of Transfiguration.

Transformation. We can experience it as well.

All we have to do is be teachable.

Jesus will change us. All we have to do is lay down our old lives — and he'll make them new.

The Butterfly

Joanie Burnside glows. Brown, cropped hair frames a beaming forty-something face as wire-rimmed glasses magnify blue dancing eyes. Joanie is also a talented actress, and I had the privilege of watching her perform a monologue one Palm Sunday at Mount Hermon, a Christian conference center.

The pre-Easter service at Mount Hermon is always poignant. I inevitably go away shaken at the immensity of Christ's work on the cross. But Joanie's presentation that year reminded me of not only what Jesus did, but what he longs to do in you and me.

You see, Jesus didn't come to make bad people better. He came to transform us into something entirely new.

My words can't paint the power behind the images I saw that morning, but with Joanie's permission, I'd like to try. Imagine with me an old woman, center stage, clothed in a dark coat and carrying a dingy laundry-type bag over her shoulder. She clings tightly to an out-of-date purse. Dirty rags cover her feet. Stooped and bent over a cane, the old woman's face is twisted with suspicion, her voice sharp and brittle as she begins her story.

Listen closely. Now and then, I hear Martha speaking. Now and then, I hear me.

"I've come to tell you the story of a butterfly," the woman begins. Her only props are the clothes that she wears and a simple wooden cross that stands behind her. "She started out as all others, a lowly caterpillar, one who would have grown but never changed. Her life would have become old, ugly, and embittered had it not been for the grace of the Creator.

"*This* is what she would have become," the old woman says, pointing at her twisted, decrepit form. "Though she willed herself to change . . . she could not. Submitting to his power was her only chance.

"Here was her scarf, which covered her head, her precious brain, her above-average intelligence. The universities and degrees were hers to obtain, to flaunt and impress . . . to shrink others down to her size.

"The hair, the crown that should have been, was merely a reflection of the anxieties that riddled her life, for she was prematurely gray. She worried about everything — her future, her past, her mistakes, her dreams.

"Her teeth . . ." The old woman bites down for emphasis. "The guardians of her mouth, one of her most vicious weapons, were ever ready to bite, to cut others to the quick with sarcasm and barbs. For out of the overflow of the heart speaks the tongue. Sometimes it was as seemingly innocent as gossip, other times judgment, and at times, outright lies as she assassinated the characters of others.

"Her purse was her security, for it housed her beloved checkbook. She was born into affluence, and as long as there was money in the bank to protect her, she was safe. No one could touch her, no one could reach her. She walled herself in with material goods — none of them evil in and of themselves, but all of them evil when worshiped and adored instead of him.

"Her cane she used like a finger, to point accusingly at the sins of herself that she saw in others. It became a wonderful crutch, this overdeveloped superego, for whenever she felt bad about herself, she could easily find bad in the lives of others around her.

"Her shoes covered one of her saddest features, her feet. Those poor, beaten stubs. She had spent a lifetime wandering aimlessly. She had no purpose, no one to follow, nowhere to go. Each day meant only another twenty-four hours of hopelessness."

The woman shifts a large sack she carries on her shoulder, then points at it. "Here was her burden, the sin she bore that weighted her down, every year getting heavier and heavier. She stuffed those sins in her sack, hoping no one else would notice what was so obvious to all. Her life had become grotesque with the weight, her sins disfiguring the beauty she was meant to be.

"Lastly was her heart, a shriveled shadow of what the Creator had given her."

Pantomiming the movement, the woman takes a small, stony heart out of her chest and holds it between two fingers. "It was hard and unrelenting, not letting any love in . . . not letting any love out . . . protected from intruders by her head, her mouth, her purse, and her cane.

"Then one day this woman met some friends who had lives of sweet purity. They offered her the Living Water, and when she could bear the thirst no longer, she took a taste . . . just a taste, mind you, for she wasn't ready to really drink yet. But that taste was so sweet, and it made her thirst beyond compare. She took, and drank, and that Living Water filled her and satisfied her from her crown to her toes."

The face of the woman onstage now glows with the memory of that water and the new life she's received. Piece by piece she begins to remove the unnecessary articles of clothing that once bound her.

"The scarf was removed and her knowledge used for his glory. Her thoughts became his thoughts as she surrendered to his Spirit." The woman unties the scarf and drops it to the floor.

"The hair, once gray with concern was made new again, for the joy that was his was now hers." The woman ruffles her hair with glee.

"The mouth that had cut down others now began to build them up, to sing psalms and hymns and spiritual songs . . . to seek ways to soothe hurts rather than cause them.

"The purse became a tool, as a sheath is to a sword. It carried something of great power. Her moneys were used to advance his kingdom rather than protect her own," the woman says as she lifts the purse for all to see.

"The cane was no longer needed as her urge to judge faded in the light of his grace. She gave it to others that needed to be held up, as she sought to come alongside and bear others' burdens.

"Aaaah . . ." The woman pauses, smiling as she shakes her finger. "And her feet? At first they began to walk, then run, skip, leap, and dance with joy, for finally she had a reason to live. A Master to follow. A path that he prepared specifically for her. Such joy she'd never known.

"The burden of her sins he took," the woman says, her voice becoming stronger and younger sounding. Her posture straightens as she drapes her things over the Cross. "How, she would never really understand, other than he said that he'd died for the right to do so.

"Her heart of stone was transformed into a new, vital, living heart." With trembling hands she lifts the small, imaginary heart heavenward, receiving a large, beating one in exchange. With her face uplifted, her eyes filled with wonder, the woman pantomimes the act of placing the new heart inside her chest.

"Create in me a clean heart, O God," she whispers, "and renew a right spirit within me" (Psalm 51:10, KJV).

The words are soft, pleading, and thankful as they drift across the quiet auditorium. The moment is holy as David's prayer echoes through each one of us.

A clean heart, O God. A right spirit. Within me.

"Thank you for hearing my tale," the woman says finally. Her voice is low and tender as she unbuttons her coat. "For as you see . . . I am the butterfly."

She sheds the cloak, revealing a splendid purple leotard with flowing multicolored wings. Sparkling and shimmering in the morning light, the costume is beautiful. Exquisite.

With arms extended, the woman exits reborn. Floating, dancing, skipping. Leaving all of her earthly garments behind. Inviting each one of us to do the same.[5]

New lives for old. That's what Jesus offers. Warm hearts for cold. And all for the price of being teachable.

As I've surrendered my life to Jesus' teaching, even his rebukes, I've learned the value of God's tender discipline. It is only when we struggle to break free from the chrysalises of our lower nature that the true beauty of the new life Christ offers can truly be known.

So don't be afraid to shed the familiarity of old patterns and old clothes.

Jesus, remember, came to make all things new.

So hear him and obey. Receive his discipline.

And then . . . get ready to fly.

10

Mary's Extravagant Love

*Then Mary . . . poured it on Jesus' feet
and wiped his feet with her hair.
And the house was filled with the
fragrance of the perfume.*
JOHN 12:3

~

He looks so tired. The face she loves is lined
and drawn as she meets him at the door.
His forehead is troubled, but when he sees
her, the Master's eyes soften. He makes his
way through the crowded foyer and takes
her hands.

"Mary . . ."

"I'm glad you're here, Lord," she says.
"It's been too long." His travels have taken
him away from Jerusalem lately. Away from

the temple courts. Away from the rumored price upon his head. "I worry for you," Mary whispers.

Jesus smiles and slowly shakes his head. "Be anxious for nothing, dear Mary. My life is in the Father's hands." His words are tender, yet intense; as though they hold hidden truth. A shiver runs down her spine as they walk toward the living room.

It's clear this visit will be nothing like the one so many months ago. Something is wrong. And yet, somehow, Mary senses something so right. It goes against logic. She can see the Master's weariness. The men are clearly worried and befuddled. And yet Mary feels a tremor within, like a single strum upon a stringed instrument. Like hope . . . or is it joy?

There is no sound, only an awaiting. As though all of heaven is standing on tiptoe listening for the song. As if all of eternity has been gathering momentum for this week . . . for this journey . . . for this Man.

A Little Perspective

No one can know what took place in Mary's heart when she met Jesus that day. However, the sweet sadness and the sense of destiny surrounding this final trip to Jerusalem seems evident. We know that Jesus had "set his face as flint" toward the Holy City. Toward certain arrest and certain death. Of all the people surrounding him, only Mary seemed to understand, for only she seemed moved to take the appropriate action.

This story found in John 12:1-8 is the last time the Bible mentions Mary, Martha, and Lazarus. (The same story, told in Matthew and Luke, doesn't mention this family by name, but the similarities of the narrative seem to indicate that those Gospel writers were speaking of the same incident.) Though religious tradition places all three at the cross, Scripture doesn't specify their presence there. It's clear, however, this family deeply loved the Lord, and he loved them. This trio from Bethany had provided something Jesus needed after leaving Nazareth three and a half years before.

They had given him a home. A family. A place to lay his head.

And for these sisters and their brother and all who loved Jesus, the mood must have been confused on that last journey to Jerusalem. According to Matthew 26:2, Jesus had told the disciples what awaited him: "The Son of Man will be handed over to be crucified." He had kept no secrets, but still the disciples seemed unable to comprehend fully what was happening.

They knew, of course, that Jesus was a wanted man. The fact had been well publicized. After raising Lazarus from the dead, he had risen quickly to the top of the religious mafia's hit list. And no wonder. Many of the Jewish community, it seemed, had had a real change of heart (John 11:45). After seeing Jesus bring their friend Lazarus back to life, they'd been convinced that Jesus was indeed something special — perhaps even the Messiah. If Jesus could do that for a *dead* man, think what he could do for someone still alive!

Temple attendance had declined as crowds flocked to hear the man from Galilee. Synagogue-growth experts were deeply concerned. Perhaps they needed to be more seeker sensitive. Perhaps they needed to focus on a feeding program — the Nazarene had had great luck with his potlucks. Clearly, they needed to do something — and fast. Everything was at risk. Especially for the religious elite.

"If we let him go on like this," the chief priests and some of the Pharisees had argued before the Jewish governing authority, the Sanhedrin (11:48), "everyone will believe in him, and then the Romans will come and take away both our place and our nation."

Loss of position. Loss of power. Loss of influence. At this point in the game, that was a risk the Jewish leaders were not prepared to take — especially not after they had worked so hard to secure just those things.

The Sanhedrin had only recently worked an uneasy truce with the Roman procurator, Pilate, and after a rocky beginning it was finally working well. When the newly appointed Pilate first paraded Roman flags bearing the emperor's image down Jerusalem's streets, the people had rioted in a frenzy against the idolatry. In the face of such opposition, Pilate had quickly retreated into a you-don't-bother-me-I-won't-bother-you understanding with the temple and its officials. The Sanhedrin had finally gotten the procurator right where they wanted him. Until Jesus showed up, that is.

"You know nothing at all!" Caiaphas, the high priest, erupted during the meeting. Like most members of the Sadducee sect, he was not known for his tact nor his kindness.[1] In his mind, he was thinking strategically, hoping to push the situation to its logical conclusion. "You do not realize that it is better for you that one man die for the people than that the whole nation perish" (11:49-50).

But it was Caiaphas who hadn't a clue. Unbeknownst to him, he had just "prophesied that Jesus would die for the Jewish nation," John writes in verses 51-52, "and not only for that nation but also for the scattered children of God, to bring them together and make them one."

So while the religious establishment plotted Jesus' downfall, God's plan to bring all humanity back to him was gathering speed. Heaven's gates began to open, ready to receive all who would come in through Jesus Christ the Son.

Eternity's song began to play. The Lamb "slain from the creation of the world" (Revelation 13:8) was about to die so you and I could know God.

Mary alone seemed to hear the echoes of that music. Only she seemed ready to respond to the extravagance of Jesus' love.

Extravagant Love

Tucking my daughter, Jessica, into bed at night is always a special treat. But of all our misty-water-colored memories, perhaps none is as sweet as that of bedtimes when she was small.

"I love you, Jessica," I'd say as I pulled her pink rosebud comforter up around her chin and smoothed her glistening blond hair as it lay upon her pillow.

"I wuv *you* more!" she'd say with a twinkle in her eye, thus beginning our favorite game. "Well, I love you most," I'd say, then kiss her on the cheek and tickle her pink-pajamaed tummy.

"Well, I wuv you the most-est," she'd announce when she'd finished giggling. Then she'd fling her arms open wide before I could, and she'd add the final words, "I wuv you the *who-o-o-le* world!"

Wow. Game over. The whole world? Now that's love. Especially for a three-year-old. Especially when you consider how much there is out there to love. Loving me the whole world meant she loved me more than ice cream. More than her favorite dolly. More than a trip to the park. More than birthday presents and her new trike. More than bubblegum and a ride on the brown-spotted fiberglass pony at Kmart. She loved me — *me* — more than all that put together.

That's extravagant love. The kind of love

that disregards everything else so it can focus on one thing alone: the object of that love. The kind of love that sacrifices everything, only wishing it had more to give. Nothing is too precious. Nothing is too exorbitant. The heart demands we give — and give all.

When Mary anointed Jesus at the banquet given in his honor, she gave her very best. In fact, she may have laid down her very future when she poured the perfume on his feet. For that jar of perfume — which Matthew and Mark describe as an alabaster jar, broken in order to be opened — may have very well held every hope and dream she'd ever had.

To be married ranked high on every Jewish maiden's wish list. Their culture, even their religion, made marriage and especially childbirth the highest form of honor. To be barren was a disgrace. But to be unmarried . . . well, that truly was a shame.

By age twelve, most young Jewish women had been promised in marriage, if they weren't already married.[2] Fathers usually arranged the unions, though the girls were given a say in the matter. Several factors were involved. One was the bride's price, the compensation paid to the bride's father by the groom. But the bride was often expected to bring something of value to the union as well.

When both sides agreed, the betrothal — the engagement part of the ceremony — was performed. An ornate document called the *ketubah* was signed by the future bride and groom, and the ceremony was sealed by a kiss. From that moment on, the couple were legally bound to wed, though the actual wedding ceremony might not take place for several years.[3] The agreement could be dissolved only by death or by divorce, the option considered by Joseph before being reassured by an angel.

As far as we know, Mary never had the opportunity to marry. Because she and Lazarus lived with Martha, it appears that their parents must have died several years before. The fact that it was called Martha's house is interesting as well, for the family estate usually went to a son. Some commentaries speculate Martha may have been married and widowed, the house an inheritance from her husband.

But what did Mary have? With no father to arrange her marriage, time was ticking away. The alabaster jar of perfume may have been a part, if not all, of Mary's dowry. Worth more than three hundred denarii, nearly a year's wages, this was no ordinary perfume. Though unromantic by name, *nard* was rare, made from the aromatic oil extracted from the root of a plant grown mainly in India.[4] It had to be imported. Mary couldn't get it over the counter at Wal-Mart. I'm not sure she would have found it at Saks Fifth Avenue. In fact, there is no perfume I know of today that can even compare in worth — approximately thirty thousand dollars a bottle.

Alabaster, on the other hand, was a common container in the Near East. The snowy gypsum shone smooth and translucent when polished. Easily carved, it formed ornate jars, boxes, vases, and flasks. Sometimes marble containers were labeled *alabastra* as well.[5] But the origin and type of the container wasn't really significant. It still isn't.

What mattered most — what matters still today — is the treasure the container holds. And the treasure Mary poured out that day was more than an expensive perfume. She was pouring out her very life in love and sacrificial service.

Unfortunately, not everyone present had Mary's kind of heart.

A View from the Dark Side

What a waste! What an extravagant, exorbitant, unnecessary display of emotion. Why a whole bottle when a few drops would have been more than adequate? Why break the jar when it could have easily been poured? And why the hair? The whole scene was messy, not at all proper or orderly. As Mary caressed the Master's feet, the perfume hung pungent in the air, her sobs the only sound breaking the stunned silence.

Why doesn't he tell her to stop? Judas thought as he watched the woman's shameful abandon. He turned away from the scene perturbed. He distrusted all forms of sentiment, anything that distracted from the cause of overthrowing the Romans and establishing the long-awaited kingdom. Following the Nazarene had been a roller coaster of emotional highs and lows for Judas, quite unsettling for a focused fellow like himself.

But Judas had hitched his wagon to a star, and he was committed to the ride no matter how rocky it got. It hadn't been easy. Certainly the Savior would establish his kingdom soon. Yet every time the crowds tried to crown Jesus king, he refused, ducking the opportunity.

Worst of all, the offerings had started to dry up. Jesus wasn't nearly as popular as before, judging by the weight of the moneybag Judas wore around his waist. It was getting more and more difficult to embezzle funds. Of course, that was such an ugly term. Judas preferred to call it "compensation for services rendered."

If something doesn't change fast, Judas thought, *I may have to consider switching careers.*

He wasn't like the rest of the disciples. The only non-Galilean of the group, this city boy from Kerioth was determined to make his mark on the world. But making a mark required money. Money he didn't have.

"Hey, Judas," one of the disciples leaned over and whispered. "How much do you think a pint of pure nard goes for these days?"

Pure nard? Judas hadn't recognized the fragrance. Why, it was worse than he'd thought. The world's most expensive perfume — someone had to say something. "Ahem . . . excuse me, Master?" he interjected. Judas pointed at the woman and her broken flask. "Why wasn't this perfume sold and the money given to the

322

poor? It was worth a year's wages." A few disciples around him murmured agreement.

"Leave her alone," Jesus replied. His eyes bored through Judas as if looking into his soul. Judas shifted uncomfortably. "It was intended that she should save this perfume for the day of my burial," Jesus continued. "You will always have the poor among you, but you will not always have me."

Judas looked to the other disciples for support. But they diverted their eyes, looking away, around, anywhere but Judas or the Master.

Now Judas swallowed as he felt things shift and solidify inside him. Instead of piercing his heart, Jesus' words had somehow cemented the deal. Suddenly everything seemed crystal clear to him. Nothing would ever change. All this talk about dying . . . there was no kingdom to come. The whole thing had been a farce.

So much for being part of a new Jewish parliament. The gig was up.

Unless . . .

A Tale of Two Followers

The story of Jesus' anointing is recounted in all four Gospels, as is that of Judas's betrayal. Whether or not Judas's thought process happened as I've speculated, the result was the same. Matthew and Mark both place Judas's dark turn of heart as happening immediately after Mary's extravagant act of love.

> Then Judas Iscariot, one of the Twelve, went to the chief priests to betray Jesus to them. They were delighted to hear this and promised to give him money. So he watched for an opportunity to hand him over. (Mark 14:10-11)

Only Matthew highlights the amount for which Judas sold Jesus — thirty pieces of silver, the exact amount prophesied four hundred years before in Zechariah 11:12-13. It was the standard price paid for a slave in Exodus 21:32 — approximately 120 denarii.

Less than half the amount of money Mary had so lavishly spilled on Jesus' feet.

Life has a way of bringing to the surface who we really are, the deep hidden motivations of our heart. "For out of the overflow of the heart the mouth speaks," Jesus said in Matthew 12:34-35. "The good man brings good things out of the good stored up in him, and the evil man brings evil things out of the evil stored up in him."

It certainly happened in Judas. But it happened in Mary as well. While the situation caused the evil dormant within Judas to rise to the surface, it was the same instance that brought something beautiful up from the depths of the maiden from Bethany.

From all appearances, Mary seems to have been contemplative by nature. And while spiritual intuitiveness made her a wonderful worshiper, it also made her susceptible to despair. Instead of running to meet Jesus after Lazarus died, if you remember, she remained in the house. Downcast and alone amid the crowd of friends, she had sunk deeper and deeper into her grief, and even the news of Jesus' coming had not been able to lift her sorrow.

But — thank God! — Jesus meets us where we are. He comes into those dark, hidden corners of our lives and, if we're willing, he shines the sweet spotlight of heaven, his precious Holy Spirit. If we allow him, he offers to clean out our personalities, tempering them through the Holy Spirit so we won't fall to the strong sides of our weaknesses and the weak sides of our strengths.

And that, as far as we can tell, is what happened to Mary. Even though she sensed, with her keen intuitiveness, the graveness of her Lord's situation, this time she did not collapse. Instead of just sitting passively and listening to the Savior, instead of being overwhelmed by grief, this time Mary responded. She gave herself in worship to the One who had given so much to her and her family.

Not so with Judas, apparently. Though Jesus knew the disciple's weaknesses, he had given Judas chance after chance in the three years they had traveled together. According to John 13:29, Jesus had even made the man treasurer of the group.

"Sometimes," William Barclay writes in *The Gospel of John*, "the best way to reclaim someone who is on the wrong path is to treat him not with suspicion but with trust; not as if we expected the worst, but as if we expected the best."[6] That's exactly what Jesus had done with Judas. But Judas had remained unchanged.

Imagine spending three years of your life

with the Messiah, yet walking away more or less the same — or even worse than when you started. Judas did just that. It can happen to any of us if we don't settle, once and for all, the question of Christ's lordship in our lives.

Until we determine whom we will serve, we run the risk of developing a Judas heart instead of a heart of sacrificial love. For whenever *our* interests conflict with *his* interests, we'll be tempted to sell Christ off as a slave to the highest bidder, rather than spend our all to anoint his feet.

Extravagant Love Versus

Tight-Fisted Love

"To know whom you worship," says Theodore Parker, "let me see you in your shop, let me hear you in your trade, let me know how you rent your houses, how you get your money, how you kept it and how you spent it."7

Jesus says basically the same thing in Matthew 6:21: "For where your treasure is, there your heart will be also."

Mary's treasure was not in her trousseau. Her hope didn't lie in what she could get from Jesus. Her joy lay in what she could *give*.

Judas, on the other hand, was after all he could *get*. That is the first difference between a love that is extravagant and a heart that is mean and tight-fisted.

Consider the following:

• *Mary had a heart of gratitude.*

Her brother had been raised from the dead. The Messiah had come, and he'd called her friend. What greater honor — what greater joy — than to give her all to the One who had given her so very much.

• *Judas had a heart of greed.*

Things weren't turning out the way he'd planned. One of Westcott's Laws of Temptations, quoted by William Barclay, is that temptation "comes through that for which we are naturally fitted."[8] Our strength can be our undoing. And Judas's strength was his ambition, his focus, and his commitment to getting ahead. It was also, of course, his greatest weakness. It caused Judas to care more about the political situation and his own bank account than the condition of his heart.

Greed is a tyrant. As women, we can fall prey to its lies as easily as men. "The leech has two daughters," Proverbs 30:15 says. " 'Give! Give!' they cry." A greedy heart is never satisfied. It never has enough.

"But godliness with contentment is great gain," Paul tells the young preacher Timothy (1 Timothy 6:6). Discontentment can creep in so easily, making us unsatisfied with what we have. It isn't long before the discontentment hardens into determination to get what we deserve, no matter the cost. But the cost is often extremely high.

"Some people, eager for money, have wandered from the faith," Paul warns Timothy in verse 10, "and pierced themselves with many griefs."

The secret to happiness lies not in getting what you want, but in wanting what you have. Judas came to his senses too late. His greed caused him to do the unimaginable — to betray a friend. To betray the Son of God. But the grief that soon replaced the greed could not heal his soul. Nor his mind. After trying to give the money back, Judas went out and hung himself, his body buried in a field bought by Jesus' blood.

Without gratefulness, we are prone to the same hardness of heart and darkness of mind that drove Judas's treachery. If we refuse to recognize the immensity of God's grace and its incredible cost on Jesus' part, sooner or later, we will take it for granted.

And once we begin to presume on God's grace, we begin to abuse God's grace — trampling it under our careless feet in a maddening rush for yet another blessing.

Without gratitude we become like the people Romans 1:21 describes: "For although they knew God, they neither glorified him as God nor gave thanks to him, but their thinking became futile and their foolish hearts were darkened." Dark minds do dark things. Look at Judas.

How sad that it is possible to *know* God but never truly *experience* God. If we want intimacy with God, we must nurture a grateful heart that glorifies Jesus.

Two Kinds of Hearts

Consider the following additional differences between the hearts of Mary and Judas. Which kind of heart do you have? Is it extravagant with gratitude or tight-fisted with greed?

- *Mary came with abandon.*
- *Judas came with an agenda.*

- *Mary heard what Jesus was saying — and she responded.*

330

• *Judas heard but did not understand.*

• *Mary held nothing back.*
• *Judas gave nothing up.*

Instead of being shamed by Mary's extravagance, Judas became critical of what she gave. His greed warped his perception. "If we find ourselves becoming critical of other people," Barclay says, "we should stop examining them, and start examining ourselves."[9]

Extravagant love is still rarely understood. "Don't you think you're going a little overboard with this 'God stuff'?" a friend may ask. "Why spend so much time in prayer? After all, God knows your heart," another may reason.

But true love always costs the giver something. Otherwise, the giving remains only a philanthropic contribution. At best, kind. At worst, self-serving. In the light of Mary's total abandon, halfway love is truly the "least" we can do.

Do we love Jesus the who-o-o-le world? Or only when it's convenient?

Extravagant Sacrifice

When a forty-nine-year-old Canadian mining executive walked into the Colombian jungle in October 1998, he went hoping to walk back out with one of his employees. Instead, he didn't walk out at all — at least, not right away.

For more than three months, Ed Leonard, a sixty-year-old driller who worked for Norbert Reinhart's drilling firm, had been held by the rebel group known as the Revolutionary Armed Forces of Colombia.

Kidnapping was, and is, big business in Colombia. In 1998 alone, more than twenty-one hundred people were abducted, though most were later released on ransom. And that's what Reinhart was hoping for. Along with a toothbrush, some books, and a camera, he reportedly stuffed one hundred thousand dollars in his knapsack to pay for Leonard's release. But there were no guarantees.

Reinhart's wife, Robin, begged him not to go. Sure, Leonard had a wife and kids, but they had two young children as well. Still, Reinhart had promised Leonard, a man he'd hired over the phone, that the job was safe. He was going to do whatever it took to get him home.

On October 6, the guerrillas took Reinhart's ransom money but demanded an exchange as well. The mining executive agreed. That afternoon on a desolate, rocky road, Norbert Reinhart met his employee for the first time.

"You must be Ed Leonard," Reinhart said, shaking the older man's hand. "Your shift is over. It's time for you to go home."

And with that he traded places with Leonard and became the rebels' captive.

The world was stunned. Some called Reinhart crazy. "Let the government and hostage professionals handle it," they said. But the negotiations had dragged on and on. When Reinhart was unexpectedly released several months later, he summed up the experience by saying, "I just did what I had to do."[10]

Extravagant sacrifice. Norbert Reinhart risked his life for the sake of his employee, not knowing what would happen to him. Though some close to the situation have pointed out less than altruistic motives, Norbert Reinhart's act is still impressive.

But Jesus laid his life down knowing full well he wouldn't walk away alive. This transaction would cost him everything, yet still he gave. And that's not just impressive;

it's revolutionary.

Jesus laid down his life for you and me. He didn't have to do it. He could have spoken the word, and ten thousand angels would have flown to his rescue. But instead, he chose not to use his own power. He humbled himself and chose the way of sacrificial death. And there was never a hint of selfishness in his sacrifice — no self-interest, not a hint of mixed motives.

Why did he do it? He did it out of love — extravagant, lavish, life-changing love.

Lavish Love

The apostle John writes in 1 John 3:1, "How great is the love the Father has lavished on us, that we should be called children of God!" What a wonderful picture — the lavish love of God. Love so wonderfully extravagant that, like a thick, rich hand cream, it must be spread around. So much love that the simple and the ordinary aren't enough.

Mary knew a little bit about that kind of love. So do a lot of Christians I know. They just give and give of themselves without seeming to tire. Compassion and service flow uninterrupted from their lives.

Sure they get weary. Sometimes they feel moody — but not for long. In fact, it seems the more they freely give, the more energized they feel.

I try to cuddle my life up close to people like that. I watch them and try to learn. Just how does Nita do all our church recordkeeping without complaining? How do Ed and Judy seem to know when people are hurting, though no one says a word? Why does Aunt Gert keep hosting the neighborhood Bible club every week? Her heart is weak, her body twisted with scoliosis, but still she loves and gives — then gives some more.

These are only a few of my heroes of faith. If you look, you'll find them all around you. They come in all shapes and sizes, ages and genders. They don't usually stick out in a crowd. Much of the time, their compassionate service is done unnoticed and unseen. But when you get up close, you'll find they have one thing in common. They know how to love — not just in word, but in deed.

That's what set Mary's love apart that day in Bethany. She not only loved Jesus; she did something about it. And what she did and how she did it point toward the secret for more fully loving God and loving people.

• *Mary loved with her whole heart.*

She didn't hold anything back. Instead, in sweet abandon, she poured everything she had into showing her love for Jesus.

Leaping into Love

Do you ever feel yourself holding back parts of your life, wondering how much you can give and still have something left? Like Mary, you feel the call to total abandonment, but surrender like that makes you afraid. If you've felt that way, you're not alone. I think every one of us comes to a crossroads in our relationship with God where we're faced with the dilemma of total or partial surrender.

I remember the day God brought me to that crossroads. For nearly a month he had been dealing with my heart, asking me to sell out to him. Jesus had been my Savior, but he wasn't yet my Lord. He was telling me it was time to surrender.

I wanted to obey, but I was so afraid. What if I said yes? What would that mean? I was a young teenager with a lot of plans and dreams. If I gave myself completely to him, would he take them all away and make me go to Africa? At the time, that was the worst fate I could imagine — or almost . . . Come to think of it, what if he made me marry a short, fat, balding man with acne on his forehead and forced us to work among the pygmies for the rest of our lives? Why, that would be even worse!

But instead of answering my questions and calming my fears, the Lord kept pressing me for a decision. "Will you give me your all?" he asked. No negotiations. No promised stock options. Total abandonment was what he demanded, and nothing less.

The dissonant workings of my spirit and flesh finally collided that summer at youth camp. I still remember the night I totally surrendered. It felt as though I was standing on a hundred-foot-high diving board with nothing but blackness beneath me. "Jump," I could hear the Lord saying. "Jump. I'll catch you."

But I couldn't see his hands. To jump meant to leap into an absolute unknown. Would he really catch me? Or would I fall, endlessly fall, as in the dreams that often haunted my nights?

I stood there shivering in the darkness, my arms clasped around all my hopes and my dreams, and I realized there was no turning back. It was all my heart or nothing. To walk away from this decision would mean, for me, walking away from God. And that I could not, would not do. So I closed my eyes and took a breath and flung myself out into the dark unknown.

"I'm yours, Lord," my heart cried. "All of me! Nothing held back."

I waited for the unending fall. I kept expecting it to come. But instead, I felt strong arms around me. Arms that built the universe. Arms that held the world. Arms so gentle, they cradled children. Arms so strong, they shouldered every burden we'd ever bear. They were the everlasting arms of Jesus. Catching me. Embracing me. Receiving me as his own.

I think I know a little of bit of what Mary must have felt that day she stood at Jesus' feet. As she held her precious ointment, she must have trembled inside. For

---

Making Jesus Your Lord

Perhaps like me, you've met Christ as Savior, you've repented of your sins, but something still seems to be missing. For me, that missing part was found when I made Jesus not only my Savior, but my Lord. Hannah Whitall Smith, in her classic book *The Christian's Secret of a Happy Life,* outlines the necessary steps:[11]

1. "Express in definite words your faith in Christ as your Saviour and acknowledge . . . He has reconciled you to God; according to 2 Cor. 5:18, 19.

2. "Definitely acknowledge God as your Father, and yourself as His redeemed and forgiven child; according to Gal. [4]:6.

3. "Definitely surrender yourself to be all the Lord's, body, soul, and spirit; and to obey Him in everything where His will is made known; according to Rom. 12:[1].

4. "Believe and continue to believe, against all seemings, that God takes possession of that which you thus abandon to Him, and that He will henceforth work in you to will and to do of His good pleasure, unless you consciously frustrate His grace; according to 2 Cor. 6:17, 18, and Phil. 2:13.

5. "Pay no attention to your feelings as a test of your relations with God, but simply attend to the state

of your will and of your faith. And count all these steps you are now taking as settled, though the enemy may make it seem otherwise. Heb. 10:22, 23.

6. "Never, under any circumstances, give way for one single moment to doubt or discouragement. Remember, that all discouragement is from the devil, and refuse to admit it; according to John 14:1, 27.

7. "Cultivate the habit of expressing your faith in definite words, and repeat often, 'I am all the Lord's and He is working in me now to will and to do of His good pleasure'; according to Heb. 13:21."

Hannah suggests we make all these things part of a daily act of our will: "And here you must rest. There is nothing more for you to do . . . you are the Lord's now."

He who began a good work in you will carry it on to completion, until the day of Christ Jesus.
PHILIPPIANS 1:6

no one gives her everything without a struggle. No one gives her all without somehow wanting to keep part of it back. Perhaps Mary had wrestled with the thought of surrender as I did. Perhaps she'd stared at the alabaster bottle in the night. *Can I? Should I? Will I?* Until she said, "Yes, Lord. I'll give my all."

So when she broke the bottle and poured the ointment, Mary didn't stop herself to count the cost or calculate how much of the ointment was actually needed. She spilled it all out. Lavishly. Extravagantly. Until her treasure ran down over Jesus' feet and soaked into the floor.

Then she did something I find disconcerting. She unbound her headpiece and wiped Jesus' feet with her hair. By that act, she laid down her glory and, in essence, stood naked before her Lord. For in that culture, no proper woman ever let her hair down in public. A woman's hair was her glory, her identity, her ultimate sign of femininity, an intimate gift meant only for her husband. But for Mary, nothing was too extravagant for Jesus; she was even willing to risk her reputation. Like a lover before her beloved, she made herself vulnerable and fragile, open for rejection or rebuke.

But neither came. Only the tender, silent approval of a Bridegroom for his bride.

Jesus watched as Mary dried his feet, and I'm sure there were tears in his eyes.

The extravagance might be misunderstood by the others, but not by the one that she loved. "She has done a beautiful thing for me," Jesus said in the face of his disciples' disapproval.

Leave her alone. She belongs to me.

Holy Kisses

Jessica and I have graduated to a new "good-night" bedtime game. It involves kisses. Multiple kisses. One on the forehead and each eyebrow. Another on the nose and each cheek. A soft peck on the lips and the chin, and then — if we can bear it — under the chin where it tickles. With giggled, whispered kisses on each ear and a great big hug to tie them all together, we say our prayers and then "good night."

I'm not sure about Jessica, but I sleep better when I know I am loved that many kisses' worth. Exorbitantly, foolishly, extravagantly loved. Covered with kisses.

Judas offered Jesus a single kiss. The kiss of betrayal. How that must have hurt the heart of God. All the time they'd spent together, all the teaching, all the love —

and then to be rejected that way. Jesus knew it was coming, of course, but even he seemed surprised by the chosen signal that night in Gethsemane. Can't you hear the pain in Luke 22:48 when Jesus asks, "Judas, are you betraying the Son of Man with a kiss?"

Unlike Judas's stingy, mocking gesture, the loving attention Mary lavished upon the Savior's feet had nothing to do with manipulation or control. When Jesus foretold his death, instead of rebuking him as Peter did — "Lord, this will never be" — Mary prepared her Savior; she made ready the way of the Lord. And instead of sinking into depression, contemplative Mary made room for the sovereign will of God as she anointed the Lover of her soul for burial.

A Test of Love

St. Augustine once preached a sermon in which he proposed a kind of self-test to see if we truly love God:

Suppose God proposed to you a deal and said, "I will give you anything you want. You can possess the whole world. Nothing will be impossible for

---

you. . . . Nothing will be a sin, nothing forbidden. You will never die, never have pain, never have anything you do not want and always have anything you do want — except for just one thing: you will never see my face."

Augustine closed with a question:

Did a chill rise in your hearts, when you heard the words, "you will never see my face"? That chill is the most precious thing in you; that is the pure love of God.[12]

What good is it for a man to gain the whole world, yet forfeit his soul?
MARK 8:36

"I tell you the truth," Jesus said in Mark 14:9, "wherever the gospel is preached throughout the world, what she has done will also be told, in memory of her."

And still the story is told — the story of a woman who loved so much she gave up just about everything. The sweet scent of Mary's extravagant sacrifice still lingers today.

We sense the precious aroma of extravagant love rising once more to heaven each time one of God's children gives his or her everything to the One who gave his all.

11

Balancing Work and Worship

*Whatever you do, work at
it with all your heart.*
COLOSSIANS 3:23

~

I love teetertotters. My sister and I used to
play for hours on an old wooden plank
clamped to a metal bar at the church camp
we attended every summer. Being older, I
was the heaviest, so I had to scoot up several inches while she sat on the very edge.
Then we were ready to go. Back and forth,
up and down, through sun-speckled July afternoons we'd teetertotter amid the pine
trees of Glacier Bible Camp. But we especially enjoyed finding that perfect spot of
synchronicity — scooting around until both

of our ends were suspended in midair. Pure, exquisite balance.

"No bumpsies!" Linda would cry whenever I'd shift my weight backward. She knew what was coming. The slightest change in the distribution of weight caused my side to plummet, making the plank hit the ground and sending my sister's little rear-endski fifty-three feet in the air.

Well, not quite. But I always tried. It was great fun.

Until my cousin Chuckie showed up, that is. He'd climb up onto the center of the teetertotter and stand with one foot on either side of the bar. Now *he* controlled which side went high, which side went low. Which side got the bumpsies.

Linda and Chuckie have always been in a cruel conspiracy against me. Growing up, they locked me out of Chuckie's bedroom every Sunday afternoon so I couldn't play Lincoln Logs. When we played hide-and-seek during the summer, I'd search for hours while they'd be inside sucking Popsicles and watching *Captain Kangaroo*. Not that I'm bitter, mind you. I just want you to understand.

So when Chuckie's I'm-so-innocent blue eyes narrowed on those July afternoons, I always knew what was coming. A bit of fancy footwork on his part, and I'd be flying through the trees screaming, hanging on to the plank with both hands, my long legs flopping in the breeze before I returned to the plank with a spine-shattering thud.

I love teetertotters.

Balancing Teetertotters

I wonder if God had teetertotters in mind when he placed Luke's story of Mary and Martha between two famous passages: the story of the Good Samaritan (Luke 10:30-37) and Christ's teaching on the Lord's Prayer (11:1-4). One deals with our relationship with people. The other deals with our relationship with God. One teaches us how to serve. The other teaches us how to pray. One breaks down the wall that divides cultures. The other breaks down the wall that divides God and humanity.

Perhaps that is why this tiny section of Scripture we first looked at is so important. In Luke's story of two women and one Savior we find the fulcrum, the pivot point of our spiritual teetertotters — the secret of balancing the practical with the spiritual, and duties with devotion. Without a fulcrum, these stories are two separate wooden planks. Both are important. Both are true. But when we place the fundamental truths of service and prayer on the pivot point of practicality — when we get down to the company's-here-and-what-do-I-do? application, the fun really begins.

I have to admit I struggle to keep that balance. We hosted a church banquet just a few months ago, and I found myself in the kitchen rather than in the worship service. I could faintly hear the speaker. He sounded dynamic. My husband even poked his head through the door and said, "You're really missing it!" But I was adamant. "These dishes have to get done," I said as I blew my wilted bangs out of my eyes. "We don't want to be here all night cleaning up."

I'm not sure at what point in the evening it hit me. Obviously, I'm a bit slow — especially when you consider I was in the middle of writing this book. But *Having a Mary Heart in a Martha World* was the last thing on my mind that night. I was flying high on Martha Stewart cruise control! The dishes gleamed, the glasses glistened, and even our mismatched cookware looked nearly new. But when everything was said and done, I realized I'd missed something special. Jesus had showed up in our midst, and I had been so busy washing dishes, I'd missed the opportunity to sit at his feet.

I'd totally forgotten everything I'd been learning about balancing work and worship.

Ouch. Bumpsies again!

Our Supreme Example

Jesus was the most balanced individual the world has ever known. In fact, that is part of why he came — to show us how to manage the tricky balance between work and worship, between what we do and what we are.

He gave us a picture of what our teeter-totter should look like in Luke 10:25-28 — just before Christ's parable of the Good Samaritan.

"What must I do to inherit eternal life?" an expert in the law asked after cornering Jesus one day (10:25). What can I do to ensure "safe passage" to heaven?

A good question to ask. But Jesus looked into the legal expert's heart and saw he was more interested in debates than in answers, more concerned about theory than practice. So Jesus turned the question around and let the "expert" give his opinion.

"What is written in the Law?" Jesus asked. "How do you read it?"

I can almost hear the lawyer's voice deepen as he gathered his robes around him and assumed the proper posture for quoting Scripture. Everyone stopped what he or she was doing. Babies quit fussing. Kids stopped chasing butterflies. For they recognized the familiar portion of the Torah as it thundered from the scholar's mouth: " 'Love the Lord your God with all your heart and with all your soul and with all your strength and with all your mind'; and, 'Love your neighbor as yourself' "(Luke 10:27).

The final sentence drifted upon the afternoon air, the expert's voice trailing off as he lifted one hand toward heaven for emphasis. Everyone was silent. The crowd waited, spellbound, their eyes shifting from the legal expert to Jesus. What would the itinerant rabbi say in the face of such learning and wisdom?

I can almost see Jesus smile and nod as he said, "You have answered correctly. Do this and you will live."

End of discussion. The expert gets an

A+. Next question?

You see, loving the Lord your God and your neighbor as yourself was and is the very thing God has always wanted us to do — it's a perfect picture of the perfectly balanced life. These two verses sum up all of the Old Testament and the New Testament combined.

God wants us to love him. Really love him.

And he wants us to love each other. Really love each other. That's how we can know we belong to him — if we have love one for another (John 13:35).

Love for God. Love for others. Worship and service. These are the two ends of our teetertotter. Though love for God comes first, the two can't be separated. One flows from the other — and back again. That's what it means to live a balanced life, a Christlike life.

But the legal expert didn't seem to get it. And if he did, he wasn't willing to give up. This rabble-rouser from Nazareth had come out of the exchange looking better than he did. So, wanting "to justify himself," the man challenged Jesus, "And who *is* my neighbor?" (Luke 10:29, emphasis mine).

Aha, the lawyer must have thought to

himself. *I've got him now.* That very question had stumped religious scholars for centuries. Of course, when you make God your exclusive property and call anyone who wasn't born a Jew a *goy* — or Gentile dog — your list of acceptable neighbors shrinks dramatically.

When you're not really interested in truth and you just want a lively conversation, Jesus is definitely the wrong person to come to. For he is Truth. And when you knock, he opens the door. When you seek, he reveals. And when you ask, sometimes you get an answer you don't want to hear. This poor old lawyer certainly did.

What he got was a bad case of the bumpsies — as Jesus brought his legalistic and superspiritual outlook thumping back down to earth with a practical picture of what loving your neighbor looks like.

Corrective Measures

Jesus is like my cousin Chuckie, only nicer. He doesn't give us bumpsies to watch us fly. He counteracts our off-kilter beliefs and lifestyles for one purpose — to bring us back into balance. But for the legal expert, Jesus' approach had to have been jarring. After all, the story Jesus told challenged some long-cherished beliefs, and it shook his Jewish sense of religious superiority, dismantling the excuses he'd used not to get involved with those lesser than himself.

The hero of the story Jesus told wasn't Moses or Joshua. He wasn't a Jew at all — not a real one anyway. He was one of those despised half-breed Samaritans who lived up north. And Jesus didn't stop there. He not only glorified the Samaritan by calling him "good," but he also made an unflattering comparison between that man's generosity and the hypocrisy of the Jews who'd walked by the bleeding, broken man on their way to Jerusalem and church.

The expert probably squirmed along with the rest of the religious elite in the crowd. Maybe the story brought to mind the ragged blind man he'd passed on the way to the debate. "Alms! Alms for the poor," he'd cried. But the religious expert was out of change, and besides, he'd given at the temple.

Jesus was hitting pretty close to home. Stepping on the toes of people for whom the sandals fit all too well.

He has a way of doing that, you know — of highlighting discrepancies we'd rather ignore. And while we may be more comfortable with our little rear-endskis planted on one end or the other, balancing our life is exactly what Jesus calls us to do.

Love the Lord your God . . . and love your neighbor as yourself.

Love God? *No problem!* some of us think. *I'm really good at the spiritual side of my walk. You might even consider me an expert. Kumbayah, my Lord, kumbayah* . . . And so there we stay, sitting on one side of our teetertotter, happy to be worshiping in the Lord's presence.

But there is more — more to this balanced Christian walk than only worship.

Love people? *Sure I do!* others of us say to ourselves as we sit on the other end of the teetertotter. *I love serving people. I'm definitely a Martha. Why just the other day* . . . And so we recite our service record and list our sacrificial accomplishments, glad to be helping the Lord.

But there is more to this balanced Christian walk than only serving.

You see, Jesus wants *all* of us to be like my cousin Chuckie (only nicer). He directs us — if I might put it this way — to get off our religious duffs and do the hard but rewarding work of balancing our Christianity, spending adequate amounts of our lives both in the Living Room and the Kitchen, worshiping and serving, loving God and loving people.

Holy Sweat — that's how Tim Hansel refers to this balance. In fact, he wrote a book with that very title. *"Holy Sweat,"* Hansel writes, "is the active melding of the spiritual and the earthy, the holy and the physical, a profound paradox that lies at the very heart of this life we call Christian."

Hansel says, "The holy is here within us, waiting to pour out of us, and . . . it's much more accessible than we ever would have thought. It's grace with blisters; it's redemption in overdrive."[1]

I like that! While I have been justified by faith alone — saved not by my works but because of Christ's sacrifice — I must partner with the Lord in the process of being sanctified, that is, being made more like him. I must allow his holiness to affect the way I live and what I do.

God provides the holy, and I provide the sweat. That's part of what it means to balance work and worship. It's what we were made for.

Though we were created for worship, first and foremost, we were also "created in Christ Jesus to do good works, which

God prepared in advance for us to do" (Ephesians 2:10). We were created for the intimate fellowship of the Lord's Prayer but also entrusted with the ministry of the Good Samaritan.

Created to say yes to the calls of both duty and devotion.

Practice Saying Yes

Remember several years ago when the take-time-for-yourself experts were instructing all us overcommitted types to go to our mirrors and practice saying no? Some of us actually did it! Tip of the tongue to the roof of the mouth, long humming "nnnn," followed by a satisfying "oh." It wasn't easy at first, but eventually we conquered it. After a while, it actually became fun.

I suppose having two toddlers gave me extra practice, but it wasn't long before that two-letter word just flowed off my lips. No . . . No, no, NO! I could say it without even thinking: *No, I'm sorry, but I'm unavailable. No, I'm sorry, but that isn't convenient.* It was so effective, no one even bothered asking anymore.

No one except God, that is.

He wasn't impressed by my self-care or

even my excuse of "family priorities." He knew my heart, and he was well aware that my no had become far too quick, a nearly thoughtless knee-jerk reaction. I was so busy protecting myself that I wasn't even stopping to consider that a request for my involvement might be part of God's call to me. So sometimes when I said no, it wasn't really to people or ministries. It was to God himself. And as I eventually discovered, you can't say no to God without suffering some major spiritual side effects.

It didn't happen all at once, but it did happen. Like the Israelites, I began to experience the spiritual consequence of prolonged self-interest: "They soon forgot His works; they did not wait for His counsel . . . [so] He gave them their request, but sent leanness into their soul" (Psalm 106:13,15, NKJV).

That's what happens, I believe, when no becomes our easy answer to anything outside our own personal agendas. Our souls grow skinny, starved, and weak. For we were created for abundant fullness, not for negative, ingrown inactivity. We were created to say an enthusiastic yes to the call of God in our lives — both his call to devotion and his call to service. Saying yes to him releases his power and his joy to our souls. It's what gives us the strength and the energy to do what he wants us to do.

At the same time, it's important to remember that saying yes to God doesn't mean saying yes to everything! When our lives are overbooked, it's easy for us to become spiritually dry and undernourished. We can barely hear God's voice above the busy noise, let alone say yes to what he is asking. In this case, we do need to learn how to say no, but only so we are able to say yes to God when he wants to give us an assignment.

"It's a great release to know that the secret to 'doing it all' is not necessarily *doing it all*," Jill Briscoe writes in her excellent book *Renewal on the Run*, "but rather discovering which part of the 'all' he has given us to do and doing all of that."2

As I've come to understand the impact that yes and no can make on my life, I've begun to look at each situation individually, even stopping to *pray* about the request before giving my answer, if you can imagine! That way, though I still have to say no sometimes, the purpose for the no is different.

Now I say no in order to say yes to God: *"No, I won't be able to be on the planning committee. The Lord is leading me to help with the nursing-home ministry."* And as I walk in this dependent obedience, I find the Lord not only blesses what I do, but he also raises up people to do the things I've had to decline. All because I've begun looking for ways to use the Y-word.

Go ahead! Practice saying it: "Y-y-y . . ." Same tongue, same roof of mouth, but instead of pointing the tongue up and inward, the tongue points up and outward — y-eh-sss! Why, it actually feels good after such a long string of downers. *Yes, I think I can help. Yes, I think it might be arranged — let me pray about it.* The effect can be absolutely euphoric! Especially when we make a conscious point of saying that yes to God.

The Rhythm of a Balanced Life

Here's something else I've discovered about balance. Being balanced is not so much a matter of staying in perfect equilibrium as it is a matter of finding the right rhythm for our lives.

You see, that pure spot of synchronicity my sister and I liked to find on the teetertotter never lasted very long. We spent a lot more time going up and down than we did hovering in the middle. In fact, that's partly what made it fun. As long as we kept ourselves going up and down, it all equaled out. We could teeter and totter to our hearts' content and still stay more or less in balance.

I've found that helpful to remember in my own life. Because, practically speaking, the balance between Living Room Intimacy and Kitchen Service more often resembles the up-and-down, back-and-forth motion of the teetertotter than it does that fleeting moment of synchronicity.

One side of my life may take predominance for a while, then the other. One day I may spend several hours in Bible study and prayer, settling softly on the side of intimacy with God, while the next day is given over to volunteering in my daughter's classroom, teetering over toward the service side. If you were to gauge those two days individually, they would appear totally out of balance. But not when you consider them together.

The same is true, I believe, of the seasons in our lives. For years, I spent most of my time chasing after two little toddlers. It was difficult to volunteer outside the home or even grab a few moments alone with

God. Now that the kids are in school, I have more time to do both. And one day, in the sad not-so-distant future, when my time will be largely my own, I may actually be able to achieve that perfect symmetry of spirit and service.

But I needn't worry too much if I don't. That's the beauty of dynamic, teetertotter balance. As long as my heart is set toward both service and worship, I don't have to feel guilty when my life seems to settle longer on one side because I know I'll eventually push off from that spot and spend some time on the other.

Planning ahead helps. If I know I'll be spending a block of time in service, such as organizing an event or taking part in a Christmas musical, then I know I need to

---

Listening to Your Soul: A Balance Checklist

Because we were created for balance, we feel the difference in our souls when our lives tilt too far in one direction or another. The imbalance will show in our attitudes, our energy level, and in the way we interact with other people. Any of the following could be an indication that you need to tilt more toward either service or devotion.[3]

> ### Signs That You May Need More Time in the Kitchen:
>
> - *Slight depression.* You feel a vague unhappiness, a sense of being down.
> - *Resentment of intrusion.* Rather than welcoming people into your life, you find yourself wishing they'd go away.
> - *Frustration over direction of life.* You feel a sense of purposelessness and sometimes wonder, "Is this all there is?"
> - *Increased self-indulgence.* You feel an itch to treat yourself with favorite foods or shopping.
> - *Apathetic attitude.* You find that very little moves you. You know your compassion level is low, but part of you just doesn't care.
> - *Low energy level.* Like the Dead Sea, you may have many inlets, but no outlets — and therefore you're growing stagnant.

build in time afterward for prayer, devotion, and adequate rest. If I know I'll be spending a block of time in concentrated worship — say a women's retreat or a week of special services — then I know I need to make sure my commitments to other people are covered and schedule in a few days of catch-up work.

But I don't need to look too far ahead. I don't have to keep a running account of hours spent in service and hours spent in worship and devotion or worry that every moment of every day is in perfect perpetual balance. What I need to do instead is submit my life to the Lord and let him help me "do the Chuckie." He'll show me how to attend to both sides of my life.

In fact, that very up-and-down rhythm can actually keep my life moving in a posi-

---

Signs That You May Need More Time in the Living Room:

- *Irritability and frustration.* You find yourself snapping at people, wound so tight you're about to "snap" yourself, and especially short-tempered with those you perceive as lazy or uncooperative.
- *Uncomfortable with quiet.* Silence makes you nervous, so you're quick to turn on the TV or the radio.
- *Low joy threshold.* It's been a long

time since you've sensed that undercurrent of joy and abundance running through your heart.

- *A sense of isolation.* You feel all alone — as if no one is there for you and no one understands.
- *Increased drivenness.* You're haunted by a sense that you must do more and more. You keep volunteering for more projects and more committees, even though you know your plate is full.
- *Sense of dryness and emptiness.* No wonder! You have many outlets and demands, but no inlets or source of strength.

Test me, O LORD, and try me, examine my
heart and my mind;
for your love is ever before me, and I walk
continually in your truth.
PSALM 26:2-3

tive direction. Our lives are meant to be dynamic, not static. Like a clock pendulum or the pump of an oil well, the rhythm actually generates energy for our lives. The truth is, we thrive on a life that is rhythmically balanced, not standing still.

Teetertotter. Up and down. Work and

worship. Love the Lord and love other people. It's the dynamic rhythm that drives a meaningful, yes-centered, balanced life.

Your rhythm of life may be different than mine — Mary and Martha certainly had different patterns. But so basic is this need for balance in our lives, the Lord has ordained certain balancing principles that apply to everyone. They provide rhythm as well as rhyme to our haphazard lives, and we ignore them to our detriment. In recent years, the Lord has been bringing two of these principles to the forefront of my heart — perhaps because these two principles are so easy to forget in our frantic culture. One is a "teeter" principle of Sabbath rest. The other is a "totter" principle of hospitality.

The Gift of Sabbath Rest

The story is told of a migrant South African tribe that regularly went on long marches. Day after day they would tramp the roads. But then, all of a sudden, they would stop walking and make camp for a couple days. When asked why they stopped, the tribe explained that they needed the time of rest so that their souls could catch up with them.

Isn't that a great concept? Letting your soul catch up. When I read this little story, it resonated deep within me. I can get to running so fast that I leave everything behind. Not just God. Not just people. I can lose my own soul as well.

I think that's why God instructed us to observe a regular period of extended rest in the middle of our busy lives. That's why he gave us a Sabbath.

In Hebrew the word *Sabbath* literally means "a ceasing of labor." It refers specifically to a day of the week set aside for rest and for worship.

The Jews have always observed the Sabbath from sundown on Fridays until sundown on Saturdays. We Christians set aside Sunday, the day of Jesus' resurrection, for our Sabbath. But the chosen day is not as important as the chosen purpose — to bring balance and perspective to our work-weary lives on a weekly basis.

"If you call the Sabbath a delight and the LORD's holy day honorable," says the prophet Isaiah, "and if you honor it by not going your own way . . . then you will find your joy in the LORD" (Isaiah 58:13-14). Unfortunately, the Sabbath is being squeezed out by our nonstop culture, and that poses a big balance problem in the lives of many Christians.

In the first place, many of us find it hard to resist the business-as-usual mentality that's become the norm. Even if we block off Sunday morning and Sunday evening for church, it's hard to resist the lure of the mall in the afternoon. We may have business meetings or other responsibilities scheduled for Sundays — ball games and recitals, to name a few. It's increasingly hard to resist the temptation to use the Sabbath as a catch-up day instead of a day of worship and rest.

Second (and partly as a result), many people find themselves in a position of having to work on the Lord's Day. They're afraid to insist on having Sundays off, fearful of losing their jobs or simply getting behind. Although, legally speaking, employers can't deny workers time off to practice their faith except in extreme circumstances, the pressure is undeniably there. (See Appendix F for some resources on what to do if you're caught in this squeeze.)

But despite all the distractions, real and imagined, I really believe that if we want balance in our lives we must set our hearts toward obeying the fourth commandment

(Exodus 20:8). The specifics of what that means for you and your family will be between you and God. But I believe that Sabbath-keeping as God ordained it must involve three things.

First, the Sabbath needs to be different, set apart; it has to contrast noticeably with the other six days. It shouldn't just be a day when we take care of errands we didn't get to on Saturday or finish paperwork we brought home on Friday.

Second, the Sabbath should be a day of devotion. It's meant to be spent in the Living Room. Kitchen duties can wait. This is a time to focus our hearts and our minds on God alone.

Finally, the Sabbath should be at least partially a family day — a time spent not only with our biological families, but also with the family of faith gathered for corporate worship and fellowship. "Let us not give up meeting together, as some are in the habit of doing," Paul wrote to the church in Hebrews 10:25, "but let us encourage one another — and all the more as you see the Day approaching."

How do these priorities translate into actual practice? Here are the Sabbath guidelines Elizabeth Stalcup and her family have decided on: "Our family attends church services on Sunday morning, no matter how tired or frazzled we feel, unless we are ill. We don't do laundry, clean house, go shopping, or cook elaborate meals. We take walks, read the Bible, visit with friends, nap, or putter in the garden."[4]

This kind of Sabbath-keeping requires a certain amount of discipline. Housework and homework must be done ahead of time. Family members may grow restless with the quiet. But those who have made Sabbath-keeping a priority testify that the balancing power of Sabbath rest is truly worth the sacrifice. After all, as Elizabeth says, "God gave us the Sabbath because He loves us."[5]

If for one reason or another, you cannot set aside Sunday as a Sabbath, may I encourage you to be creative and set aside another time each week? Some churches have midweek services or home groups, while others may offer worship services on Friday or Saturday nights. While I believe in letting the Lord's Day truly be the *Lord's* Day, I also believe that if we are sincere about seeking his face, God will help us set aside the Sabbath rest and worship we so desperately need.

I'd like to add another word of advice on

this subject — one that applies specifically to those of us who "work on Sundays" for the Lord — whether it means teaching Sunday school, playing the piano for worship, or caring for children in the nursery. Although this work doesn't prevent us from gathering with the body of Christ, it is definitely work. We may need to find a separate time for Sabbath. A time when we, too, can open our arms and take advantage of God's gift of Sabbath rest, devotion, and fellowship.

God's Gift of Hospitality

The practice of keeping the Sabbath is not the only God-ordained balancing principle that seems to be lost these days. Another one, which tilts back to the service side of the teetertotter, is the practice of hospitality. And I'm not just talking about giving dinner parties. I am talking about the practice of opening up our arms to welcome others into our lives.

"Christian women just don't have a choice about whether or not they'll be hospitable," says Rachael Crabb, author of *The Personal Touch*. "It's a biblical command. Scripture tells us that in the last days, people will be lovers of themselves. We're called to be givers instead."[6]

Over and over in the Bible, we're encouraged to show hospitality by reaching out and giving of ourselves to others, welcoming them into our lives. We are given the example of Abraham, who entertained three holy visitors without knowing who they were. Jesus exhorted us to entertain those who can't pay us back (Luke 14:12-14). Paul lists hospitality as a requirement for office in the church (1 Timothy 3:2) and encourages all of us to "practice hospitality" in Romans 12:13. Peter adds the injunction to do it "without grumbling" (1 Peter 4:9).

Ouch. That last one hits home for me. But it is the verse in Romans 12 that brings me comfort because hospitality is definitely not an area where I feel gifted or proficient. Paul's exhortation to "practice" hospitality offers me hope that I may one day improve. At the very least, I must attempt it. *Practice, Joanna, practice.*

Genetically, I should be predisposed to hospitality. Growing up, my dad was always bringing home, if I may put it so indelicately, "stray" people. Far from objecting, my mother always welcomed them with a loving heart and something to eat. In fact, for quite a while, we jokingly referred to my parents' house as "Gustafson's Home for Wayward Boys and Girls." They made hospitality look easy.

But it isn't easy — at least not always. It's something I struggle with personally — partly because I'm not a very talented housekeeper, but mostly because I'm just so busy. It's a challenge to make space in my life to bring people in. So many times I've felt like the Benedictine monk Kathleen Norris tells about in her book *Amazing Grace: A Vocabulary of Faith*.[7]

Benedictine monks, you have to understand, are experts at hospitality. Their founder, St. Benedict, made caring for strangers one of the fundamental rules of the order. "Receive visitors as you would receive Christ," he instructed. No one is to be turned away. It's been that way with the Benedictines for centuries. And yet one busy monk, when approached by a visitor with questions concerning the abbey, replied brusquely, "I don't have time for this; we're trying to run a monastery here!"

Ouch. How easy it is to get caught up in our busy lives that we forget the reason Jesus came and the purpose for which we were called.

"Practicing" Hospitality

If you're like me, hospitality doesn't come naturally. Here are a few tips from Karen Main's classic book *Open Heart — Open Home* that have helped me a lot — plus a few I've discovered on my own!

1. *Never clean before company.* Instead, try to clean on schedule and clean up as you go, so you'll always be ready for unexpected guests.

2. *Keep the emphasis on welcome, not performance.* The purpose of hospitality is to open your arms to others, not to impress them. It's better to keep things simple and warm than to go overboard.

3. *Do as much ahead of time as possible.* Plan ahead for hospitality — even cook ahead. Karen says, "Hard work indicates I'm not managing my time well, not planning or preparing ahead, doing too much, not being dependent on the Lord's strength, but on my own."

4. *Include little touches of beauty.* A few candles and a jar of daisies picked from the yard can make grilled cheese a gourmet delight. (And

they help hide the grease stain on the tablecloth as well!)

5. *Use all the help that comes your way.* When someone offers to help, say yes! Many hands make less work — and sharing the labor can be a great opportunity for fellowship.

6. *Keep records.* Karen has files of easy recipes and creative entertaining tips. Other women keep records of the guests and what was served. I've found that to-do lists organize my scattered thoughts and help me focus my energy more productively.[8]

Offer hospitality to one another without grumbling.
1 PETER 4:9

When we lived in the church parsonage, transients would come several times a week from the nearby railroad tracks searching for food or shelter. I'd be busy. They'd be scruffy or even smelly. I'm ashamed to admit that there were times I'd whisper inside, *Go away! We're trying to run a church here!*

But then, invariably, they'd say something like: "The guys at the gas station told me to come here. They said this church helped anybody."

Ouch and double ouch. As Christians, as a church, we are called to be a hospital, the very root of *hospitality*. Our lives should be a refuge for the hurting, not a country club for the comfortable.

"What good is it," James asks, "if a man claims to have faith but has no deeds?" Suppose someone is without clothes and daily food, the brother of Jesus ponders in James 2:14-17. "If one of you says to him, 'Go, I wish you well; keep warm and well fed,' but does nothing about his physical needs, *what good is it?*" (emphasis mine). James repeats the question, then concludes: "In the same way, faith by itself, if it is not accompanied by action, is dead."

Hospitality isn't an option for anyone who wants to say yes to Christ. It's part of his call to us, though it may be hard to work into our busy lives.

Leaning into Our Weakness

In my struggle with hospitality, I've discovered yet another thing about balance that's important to understand. In order to live the balanced life God desires, we may need to give more weight to the side we feel weakest in.

My sister and I would have never gotten around to actually teetertottering if I hadn't made the effort to scoot toward the middle. My "strength" would have outweighed her "weakness." I had to move toward her in order to achieve a workable balance.

The same is true of the balancing act of our lives. There are times when we have to make a concentrated effort to lean into our area of weakness, to give more weight to the area of intimacy or service that doesn't come easily for us.

That's what Martha did. She leaned away from the comfort of her Kitchen and shifted the weight of her attention toward the Living Room. Mary did the same thing when she left her place at the Lord's feet and leaned toward the active service of anointing her Lord. And I, too, am trying to learn this lesson of corrective measures, building up the weak sides of my life.

But I don't need to do it alone. Whenever I hear the sweet, convicting voice of the Holy Spirit pointing out my inconsistencies, I know he remains ready and willing to help me change. If hospitality is my weakness, he'll help me scoot toward that kind of service. When I need a little more weight on the side of Sabbath rest, he's faithful to help me lean in that direction, making me "lie down in green pastures." As I keep my eyes focused on the Lord, I'll have a passion for God and compassion for people — and the kind of balance the Lord intended for me all along.

Below the Water Line

So how do we balance work and worship? All of the things we've talked about — keeping an attitude of yes, finding a rhythm, leaning toward our weaknesses — can help keep our teetertotters balanced. But it all comes right back to the same pivotal reality that changed the lives of Mary and Martha of Bethany. It's the same reality we've returned to again and again in this book.

The secret of balancing worship and work, devotion and service, love of God and love of people is maintaining our connection to Jesus Christ. Our relationship with him is the fulcrum, the anchor, the steadying point that makes balance possible in the first place. And the deeper that relationship goes, the more stable the balance will be.

"It all begins at the water line." That's how Jeanne Mayo puts it. I've come to appreciate not only the teaching of this incredible woman, but also the way she lives her life. She accomplishes more in twenty-four hours than I do in two weeks. But in the midst of her busyness, she has made a deep commitment to balance.

It isn't easy. Besides being the wife of a pastor in Rockford, Illinois, Jeanne leads a youth group of nine hundred and superintends the church school of thirteen hundred children, not to mention a wide speaking ministry.

How does she keep a balance? I asked her not long ago. "It takes a ruthless commitment to first things first," Jeanne said. "I'm constantly having to ask the Lord to do the Psalm 139 thing on me: 'Live in my heart. Search and examine me. Know my heart.'" Then Jeanne shared a story that has become a spiritual trigger point in her life. God is faithful to bring it to mind when her life begins to slip off kilter and out of balance.

In the autumn of 1992, a man named Michael Plant commenced a solo crossing of the North Atlantic. An expert yachtsman, Plant had made the trip several times before. His brand-new sailboat, the *Coyote*, was so technologically advanced there were few like it in the world.

Plant set off alone, leaving his support team to monitor his trip by satellite and radio. Everything was going well. Even when a storm disrupted communications, no one worried much. After all, this guy was one of the best sailors and navigators to be found. His boat was equipped with state-of-the-art navigational and emergency equipment. Plant would resume radio contact when everything settled down.

But Michael Plant was never heard from again. After numerous attempts to reach him by radio, the Coast Guard sent helicopters out to look for him. They found the *Coyote* floating upside down. Its captain and sole passenger was never found.

Why? How could this happen? the experts wondered. Everyone knows that sailboats are very hard to turn over. Their deep keels and massive rudders right themselves. But as the ship was examined, the cause of the tragedy became clear. For all its technological advances and beauty, the *Coyote* didn't have enough weight beneath the water line. There wasn't enough ballast below to outweigh the fancy gadgetry above. And so it flipped over as it lost its ability to balance in the water.[9]

"Our lives will capsize as well," Jeanne Mayo concludes, "if what lies below the spiritual water line of our lives doesn't outweigh what lies above." No matter how good we may look on the surface, no matter how balanced we may seem, it's what lies below that really counts.

If we want to live a balanced life, we must concentrate on the underpinnings of that life. Jesus did. He was in constant communion with his Father. We must do the same if we hope to sail successfully through life. And we *can!* — because the cross purchased the same privilege Christ enjoyed: an intimate one-on-one relationship with God.

As we spend time in the Living Room, walking and talking with him, we fill the hulls of our lives with the rich things of God. And out of that abundance will come both a steadfastness in the midst of storms and a surplus we can share with others.

We'll be loving God and loving our neighbor. Spending time in the Lord's Prayer and playing the Good Samaritan.

381

Keeping the Sabbath. Practicing hospitality.

We'll be living in rhythm, but with a deep, solid anchor. Work will become worshipful. Worship will be a delight.

We'll be doing the "Chuckie" — and doing it with joy!

12

Having a Mary Heart in a Martha World

*To him who is able to keep you from falling
and to present you before his glorious presence
without fault and with great joy.*
JUDE 24

∾

A Mary heart. A Martha world. Can the two
parts of me ever come together? Will I ever
find the pure, exquisite joy of being centered in Christ alone? Is it really possible to
live a balanced life of Living Room Intimacy
and Kitchen Service?

Now more than ever, I believe the
answer is yes. Though I haven't "obtained
all this, or have already been made perfect," like Paul, I, too, want to "press on to
take hold of that for which Christ Jesus

took hold of me" (Philippians 3:12). I haven't arrived, but I know where I'm headed.

Wainwright House sits on Long Island Sound like the movie set of some nineteenth-century romance. Ivy trails up and over its three stories of hand-hewn rock, curling around turrets and paned windows, before creeping back down into the gardens that surround the one-hundred-year-old mansion. It was my first time on the East Coast, and staying at this beautiful estate felt like a dream come true.

Along with fourteen other participants, I sat in Wainwright's massive library listening to Elizabeth Sherrill, the best-selling author of *The Hiding Place*, teach on how to write a personal experience story for *Guideposts* magazine.

It had been an exciting fall. Not long after receiving the workshop invitation, I'd received word that WaterBrook Press was interested in publishing *Having a Mary Heart in a Martha World*. Wonderful news! Except for the fact that now I had to actually write it.

I was scared to death. Sitting in the dark-paneled room that first day, thoughts raced through my mind, criticizing and taunting me. *Who do you think you are, writing about intimacy with God?* I certainly wasn't an expert on the subject, though my heart longed to be. There were far more qualified people — of that I was sure.

"Above all . . ." — Elizabeth's voice broke through my musings as she spoke about writing in the first-person point of view — "the narrator must be the struggler."

She had my complete attention. "Rather than portraying the individual as an expert," she said, "we need to see the person grow through the story. We need to see him or her change." Something leaped inside me. Excitement. Hope.

I certainly qualified as a struggler when it came to intimacy with God. My downcast heart began to look up. Could it be that God was choosing me to write this book for the very reason I felt disqualified?

O Lord, I'm yours, I prayed silently as I scribbled down Elizabeth's words. *Take my struggles and use them for your glory. But whatever you do, please don't leave me the same. Change me. Give me a Mary heart in my Martha world.*

I had no idea how wonderful, nor how difficult, the Lord's answer to that prayer would be.

385

Lord of the Process

Don't you wish your kitchen had a replicater? You know, the kind they have on *Star Trek,* where you say, "Coffee, Colombian, two teaspoons sugar, and a sprinkle of grated Belgian chocolate" . . . and *poof,* there it is!

Unfortunately, I'm still stuck with my Proctor-Silex drip coffeemaker and this fundamental reality: It takes a process to make a product.

The diamond ring I wear on my left hand didn't just happen. Before John and I picked it out of a jeweler's window, someone mounted it in a setting of gold. Before that, someone else saw promise in a lumpy, milky stone and chiseled facets to release the beauty locked inside. Before that, a worker found that rock deep inside a mountain. And multimillennia before that moment, a trillion pounds of rock, pressure, and steam worked together to compress ordinary carbon into a shape and substance that we call a diamond.

It takes a process to get a product. The car I drive didn't suddenly appear on the dealer's showroom floor. The house I live in took four months to build — and much longer if you take into account the growing season of the trees used to build it, the mining required to form the nails, and the mixture of sand and heat used to make the glass.

Get the picture?

A product requires a process. The same is true of our Christian walk. Becoming like Jesus requires a process as well.

That simple discovery has revolutionized my life in recent years. You see, I had spent most of my thirty-seven years waiting to arrive. To be perfected.

Somewhere deep in my heart I still harbored the hope that when I *really* gave my heart to Christ, I would pop out of a Holy Ghost phone booth completely clothed in blue and red — a sweet little skirt; a long, flowing cape; and a big *S* plastered across my chest for "SUPER CHRISTIAN!" I'd be able to leap tall stumbling blocks in a single bound. I'd be faster than the fiery darts of the enemy. More powerful than all of hell's temptations.

Can't you hear the music and see the breeze ruffling my cape as I fly along?

Well, it didn't happen. In truth, I've resembled a mild-mannered, albeit female, Clark Kent more often than I've looked like any spiritual superhero. Some days it's all I can do to get out of bed. And try as I might, I've never gotten the outfit down.

You can imagine how relieved I felt when I finally got it through my head that Christianity is a process and not an event. It is a journey, not a destination.

"I thought it had been an easy thing to be a Christian," Samuel Rutherford wrote several centuries ago, "but oh, the windings, the turnings, the ups and the downs that he has led me through."[1] It is the twisting tests of life that produce character and faithfulness to God, Rutherford concludes. And I've found that true as well.

It takes a process to produce a product — and that applies to sanctified Christians as well as diamonds, automobiles, and houses. It's certainly true of having a Mary heart in a Martha world. If we want to be like Jesus, we won't be able to escape the refining process.

But we can be "confident of this," Paul writes in Philippians 1:6, "that he who began a good work in [us] will carry it on to completion until the day of Christ Jesus."

What God started on the day I surrendered my life to him, he will complete as I continually remain surrendered. It takes a process for me to become the kind of Christian I want to be — but Jesus Christ is Lord of the Process, and the process is divine.

That doesn't mean we'll always understand his methods. It is a mystery to me how God can take something as imperfect as my life and turn it into an agent for his glory. In her book *When God Shines Through*, Claire Cloninger writes about this imaginative God who takes the broken, scattered pieces of our lives and turns them into kaleidoscopes:

> For me, one of the greatest frustrations of walking through the "dailiness" of my life as a Christian is that I don't always get to see how the bits and pieces of who I am fit into the big picture of God's plan. It's tempting at times to see my life as a meal here, a meeting there, a carpool, a phone call, a sack of groceries — all disjointed fragments of mothering in particular.
>
> And yet I know I am called, as God's child, to believe by faith that they do add up. That in some way every single scrap of my life, every step and every struggle, is in the process of being fitted together into God's huge and perfect pattern for good.[2]

Claire concludes that it is those very scattered pieces that God uses to make a kaleidoscope. Instead of waiting for us to arrive, God shines the Light of Christ through the fragments we place in his hands, transforming "the disorder into beauty and symmetry," splashing the colors of our brokenness like fireworks across the sky.

Partners with Christ

Don't get the wrong idea though. This process of staying surrendered and letting Christ work in you is not as passive as that might sound.

Yes, the Lord has gone out of his way to make us his own. Yes, he died and rose again. He sent the Holy Spirit to teach and guide us. He's invested his own life to make us holy, and he'll take what we offer him and make it into something good. But we're still expected to partner in the process.

"When we all pull together, together, together, when we all pull together how happy we'll be." I always loved that song. Julie Olson and I would pair up in Sunday school and do the motions, our freshly pressed skirts swishing softly as we moved back and forth. Nicely. Sweetly. Not like Brian Larson and the other uncouth third-grade boys who turned the song into a wrestling match.

"For your work is my work," Julie and I'd sing, pointing at each other with a smile, while the boys thumped each other on the chest. "And our work is God's work," we'd continue, repeating the chorus, then clapping our hands to emphasize, "how happy we'll be."

It's amazing how well-behaved I used to be. Of course, it's easy to sing sweetly in Sunday school. Life, however, can be another matter.

As I've grown older, I'm ashamed to admit my song has taken on shades of uncouth boys and wrestling matches. I get confused and a little belligerent about what is my work and what is God's work. And every now and then, spiritually, I pull a Hulk Hogan: "It's your work, not my work," I thunder, thumping on heaven's door. "I'm tired of pulling together. It's your work, God!" I demand, trying to slip a full nelson around the Almighty. "It's your work!"

But when I settle down enough to listen, when I calm my heart to hear his voice, the

Savior reassures me, "Yes, your salvation is my work. It *is* finished. I did it on the cross. But now I want to partner with you in living it out."

A Life of Ease, Please

I don't know what I expected when I began. *Having a Mary Heart in a Martha World* had simmered in my heart for two years. What an incredible message: Jesus longs to know us! Every one of us. Mary and Martha alike, with all our different personalities and gifts and worship styles.

It was big. So big. Jam-packed with grace-filled implications. But when I sat down to write it, my words kept getting in the way. Chapter 2 alone had six different versions and as many different starts. It wasn't anything like the Holy Spirit–inspired free flow I'd imagined when I'd signed the contract. In fact, it strangely resembled work. Hard work.

I tried the All-Star-Wrestling prayer approach: "Hey! It's your work, God! I'm doing this for you — howsaboutta little help here?"

Silence.

I tried Job's "Where are you — and why

don't you care?" approach.

Silence again.

I even contemplated Jonah's "Forget Nineveh — I'm headed for the Bahamas" approach.

But still I heard nothing except the soft sense of his presence. The sense that he was there but waiting — waiting for me to catch on to what he wanted to teach me about the process.

Henrietta Mears has said there is only one way to learn God's lessons. "On your face, with your mouth shut."[3] That's a tall order for the verbally prolific. But that's where the Lord kept taking me. Down on my knees. In the vicinity of where Mary found Jesus that afternoon in Bethany.

Sometimes I just waited and listened. Other times I poured out my petition and complaint. But most of the time I found myself going back to my original prayer. Whenever I was stuck, whenever I'd tell God I didn't understand, the Lord would gently remind me of what I'd told him at Wainwright. "Take my struggles and use them for your glory," I'd said. "Change me. Give me a Mary heart in my Martha world."

And with those words would come a quietness, an awareness that the Lord was working. I began to realize that if I was yoked to Christ, then I could trust him to set the pace. He knew what I needed and what had to be done. I could trust him to accomplish what he'd started. My part was to partner with him. So I'd get up from prayer and go back to working . . . and waiting . . . some more.

The Testing of Our Faith

What I was experiencing, of course, isn't new. It has happened to every Christian at one time or another. It's the experience of sanctification — working hard beside Christ as he does his transforming work in us. It's the process of perseverance — keeping on keeping on, obeying in the little and the big things, doing the best we can, and then continuing to march on, trusting God to do the rest.

Perseverance isn't a lot of fun. Yet it is perseverance that allows God to take our muddled messes and turn them into miracles. He delights in transforming the black-carbon pressures of our life into diamonds of radiant beauty. But doing all that requires a process. A process that takes time. A process that is sometimes painful.

You've probably already surmised that I am a slightly odd woman. So you might not be surprised when I tell you I loved being pregnant. But I was especially excited about labor. Contractions. Lamaze breathing. The whole bit. I couldn't wait for it to begin.

"It's pain with a purpose," I'd rhapsodize to anyone who'd listen. In my mind, I could see myself in that cozy little birthing room, surrounded by my husband's tender arms,

---

The Lord Is My Pace Setter

The Lord is my pace setter . . . I shall not rush

He makes me stop for quiet intervals

He provides me with images of stillness which restore my serenity

He leads me in the way of efficiency through calmness of mind and his guidance is peace

Even though I have a great many things to accomplish each day, I will not fret, for his presence is here

His timelessness, his all importance will keep me in balance

He prepares refreshment and renewal in the midst of my activity by anointing my mind with his oils of tranquillity

---

My cup of joyous energy overflows
Truly harmony and effectiveness shall be
the fruits of my hours for I shall walk in
the Pace of my Lord and dwell in his
house for ever.

A VERSION OF THE TWENTY-THIRD
PSALM FROM JAPAN[4]

singing praise songs. "Hallelujah . . . Halle
— ooo! — jah. Wow, that was a big one!"
I'd say with a smile as John gently stroked
my brow. The nurse would come in, amazed
at my speedy progress. "You'll have that
baby any minute now, Mrs. Weaver. I've
never seen anyone handle labor as well as
you."

Suffice it to say, once again: It didn't
happen. Instead of triumphing through
glorious labor, I was rushed to an emergency C-Section. My baby was breech.
"Either this is your baby's bottom," my
doctor told me matter-of-factly, "or your
baby's head has a crack in it."

Nothing about the birthing process came
easily for me. When I finally surfaced from
the anesthetic and held my baby boy, my
eyes refused to focus. "I wish I could see
him," I mumbled as I held the little bundle
five inches from my face. Two and a half

years later, Jessica was born after fourteen hours of hard, decidedly untriumphant labor.

"Oh yeah?" I can hear you say. "Let me tell you about pain . . ."

I know, I know. My point is not to exchange birthing horror stories, but to remind you that good things rarely come easy. A few weeks following the birth of my children, after the incision healed and the searing, ripping, excruciating pain was just a not-so-distant memory, I could honestly say, as I held my babies in my arms, "It was worth it all."

And it was.

It Will Be Worth It All

That's exactly what James was trying to say in his letter to the churches scattered abroad. That's exactly the point of his amazing statement about the painful process of partnering with God in our Christian growth:

Consider it pure joy, my brothers, whenever you face trials of many kinds, because you know that the testing of your faith develops

perseverance. Perseverance must finish
its work so that you may be mature
and complete, not lacking anything.
(James 1:2-4)

Pure joy? What was this guy talking
about? The churches he addressed were
undergoing tremendous persecution. After
the death of one of the first deacons, Stephen, many Christians had fled Jerusalem
and spread throughout Judea and Samaria
(Acts 8:1), many of them joining Jewish
communities around the Mediterranean
(Acts 11:19-20). But instead of being welcomed by their Jewish kinsmen, they were
rejected and persecuted — denied protection by the Jews, exploited by the Gentiles,
robbed of possessions, hauled into court,
treated worse than slaves.[5] And it was to
these lonely, hurting outcasts that James
directed those unbelievable words: "Consider it pure joy" — or, according to the
New English Bible, "Count yourselves
supremely happy."

How nice — as Kent Hughes puts it, "a
letter of encouragement from Pastor
Whacko!"[6]

But what was James really saying to
those hurting Christians? He was telling
them to look *beyond* the painful surface of

what was happening to what God was doing in the midst of it all. He wanted them to see that the trials — the *peirasmos* — they were undergoing weren't haphazard. The testing of their faith had a purpose. Their trials were directed toward a glorious end. It would all be worth it if they would only persevere.

The Glorious Result

The trouble, of course, is that most of the time we'd rather not persevere. We all want a *test*imony, but we'd rather skip the *test* that gives us one. We all want a product. But we'd rather skip the process. As Charles Swindoll writes,

I fear our generation has come dangerously near the "I'm-getting-tired-so-let's-just-quit" mentality. And not just in the spiritual realm. Dieting is a discipline, so we stay fat. Finishing school is a hassle, so we bail out. Cultivating a close relationship is painful, so we back off. Getting a book written is demanding, so we stop short. Working through conflicts in a marriage is a tiring struggle, so we walk away. Sticking with an occupation is tough, so we start looking elsewhere. . . .

And about the time we are ready to give it up, along comes the Master, who leans over and whispers: "Now keep going; don't quit. Keep on."[7]

When it comes to our spiritual lives, a lot of us are all-or-nothing people. If we aren't automatically perfect, we just give up. When Christlike virtues like patience and kindness seem hard to come by, we abandon our character development and decide holiness is for those better equipped. But when we give up, we're giving up on our part of the partnership. Perseverance is one of our responsibilities in this process of being changed.

And what a change it will be! The rewards of perseverance James outlines for us are so much more than mere words. He tells us that the glorious result of perseverance will make us "mature and complete, not lacking in anything." The word he uses for *mature* is *telios*, which describes a dynamic maturity, a personality that has reached its full development. And when James says we'll be complete, the word *holokleros* means we'll be "entire, perfect in

400

every part." It was the word used to describe the condition of the high priest and the animal sacrifice given every year. It meant they were free of any disqualifying or disfiguring blemish.[8] Perseverance makes us ready to be the living sacrifices Paul describes in Romans 12:1 as "holy and pleasing to God."

God uses the pressure of trials to perfect our lives. He fashions facets in humble stone to reflect his glory. The last phrase in James 1:4 echoes through my heart with incredible hope. When we persevere, we become mature and complete, "not lacking anything." *Leipos medeis.* We suffer no deficiency. We have everything we need.

Of course, there will still be areas in our lives where we struggle. There will still be battles, and we'll lose a few now and then. But if we're willing to persevere in the process, one day — with Christ beside us — we'll win the war.

That's why I can tell you: Persevere, my friend! Persevere. Do you want more of God? Then don't settle for anything less. Do you want to be more like Jesus? Then persevere — press in, press on, press through!

And as you do, I promise you, you will be changed. Changed as Mary and Martha were changed.

Mary Heart — Martha World

I love the last picture we see of Mary and Martha in the Bible. John 12:1-3 sketches a portrait of two women at rest. At rest with their Savior. At rest with themselves.

Martha is still serving, but she does it with an attentive heart. Rather than barricading herself in the Kitchen, she serves in the Living Room, within the presence of her Lord. The busy servant has become a focused student as Martha drinks in his every word.

Mary may have started the evening sitting at the feet of Jesus, but rather than passively listening, she gives all that she has. She breaks open her treasure, spilling it out in prophetic ministry to Christ. With loving service, she prepares the Master for burial and the end of his sojourn on earth. The contemplative student has become an effective servant as Mary shows her love through extravagant deed.

And I, too, have been changed, in ways I never anticipated. I, too, have learned surprising lessons about what it means to have a Mary heart in a Martha world.

It hasn't been a comfortable process. To be truthful, I would have preferred a trip to a heavenly day spa. A twenty-four-hour makeover complete with body wrap, face-lift, and a new spiritual wardrobe. But God decided to do it the old-fashioned way. He decided to use life to teach me. He decided to use the process of writing this book.

"I'm bankrupt, God!" I cried one lonely, empty night. My words had dried up and, though my heart still echoed with the message, I couldn't seem to get past an invisible wall. I'd lived each chapter individually — the awful paranoia of "Lord, don't you care?"; the fearful anxiety of "you are worried about many things"; the wrenching grief of "if you had been here."

That night in the darkness, I felt completely alone.

But somewhere in all the wrestling, God met me there.

He spoke peace and direction, though I can't explain how he did it. Somehow his grace helped me live one day at a time — not in fear of the future or in regret of the past. More wondrous, more incredible, God began to heal the dichotomy of my life. He began to unite the two-sided spiritual schizophrenia that had plagued me for years.

Instead of trying in my own strength to mesh Living Room Intimacy with Kitchen Service, I started focusing on Christ alone.

Instead of fretting about what was and was not getting done, I began to surrender my days to the Lord, asking him to direct my paths. "You know what needs to be done today, Lord. Show me the 'one thing' and I'll do it."

With the surrender came a newfound peace. I was able to leave the tunnel vision of all-or-nothing thinking and just enjoy each day. Opportunities began to open all over the place. I had the privilege of leading a woman to the Lord when I took time to drop off a book. I bumped into an acquaintance at Jessica's basketball game who really needed prayer. Even my writing began to flow better.

Then, several weeks later, as I drove toward the hospital to visit one of our ailing church members, I found myself wondering, *Is this visit a Martha thing or a Mary thing?* I'd been asking the same question about this book. "All the work I'm putting in, all the writing and rewriting — is this Martha duty or Mary devotion?" I wasn't certain.

Suddenly as I drove along, in the midst of my mental eenie-meenie-miney-mo, I realized it was both! Visiting the hospital was doing the Martha Mary-ly. Writing about intimacy with God was Mary doing the Martha faithfully. In my once-divided heart, the two had become one. I no longer had to worry about my motives, whether I was acting out of duty or devotion. God had knocked down the wall and made the Living Room and Kitchen all one.

"It's both!" I cried, thumping the steering wheel, a huge smile on my face. "It's both."

I Surrender All

I can't tell you the freedom I felt that day. It was as if a giant puzzle I'd been working on for years suddenly solved itself. Joining the two parts of my heart seemed so natural, so simple. Almost embarrassingly easy.

But perhaps you've already discovered that God delights in an undivided heart. Perhaps you're already living in that place of perpetual ease before the Lord, simply serving him and loving him one day at a time. But if you aren't, if you are a struggler like me, take heart! God has a better way.

Ken Gire, in his book *Intense Moments with the Savior*, writes: "I've learned my strength is not found in how intensely I struggle . . . but in how completely I surrender."9 When we come to the end of ourselves and our abilities, when we relinquish our lives, Jesus promises to use them. Little is much when God is in it. Especially if that little something is you and me.

"Give yourself fully to God," writes Mother Teresa in *Life in the Spirit*. "He will use you to accomplish great things on the condition that you believe much more in his love than in your own weakness."10

When we surrender our lives to Jesus Christ, we release the Lord of the Process to do his work. For it is in our weakness that Christ is strong. It is in our inadequacy that we find him more than sufficient. And it is in our willingness to be broken that he brings wholeness — more wholeness and completeness than we ever dreamed possible.

This is a lifetime journey, the fruit of which we will enjoy for eternity. The fruit of which will remain long after we're gone.

Henrietta Mears is known for all she did in God's kingdom (developing a huge Sunday school, discipling leaders). "Yet amid all her doing," Jan Johnson writes in *Living a Purpose-Full Life*, "she positioned herself frequently at the feet of God — studying, listening, enjoying him."

In spite of her busy schedule, Henrietta

"opened her Bible in the sacred silence of personal fellowship with God with much the same attention as a starving man approaches a banquet." And when she died, Henrietta Mears was depicted as having "slipped through the veil between the present and the hereafter, which she had described over the years as being so very, very thin. Someone remarked, 'It was nothing new to meet her Lord alone, for she had often done so. This time she just went with him.' "[11]

Do you want that kind of Mary heart in a Martha world? I know I do.

I want to live so intimately with Jesus that when it's time to leave this world, I, too, slip through that very thin veil Henrietta Mears spoke about. From one glory-filled lifetime to another. From sitting "in his presence" to standing "face to face"!

But in order for that to happen, I need to persevere and be patient — because it takes a process to produce a product, and a process takes time. But never forget, Christ's beloved, this process is divine. God is right beside you! He is the one who's in charge. All he asks is that you partner with him and surrender to what he is doing in your life.

"Therefore we do not lose heart," Paul

writes in 2 Corinthians 4:16-17. "Though outwardly we are wasting away, yet inwardly we are being renewed day by day. For our light and momentary troubles are achieving for us an eternal glory that far outweighs them all."

From glory to glory, he's changing us.

So don't worry that you haven't arrived, my dear sister. Just don't give up on the process. Don't miss the journey.

For it will be glorious! It will be worth it all.

A Prayer for the Journey

O Christ, do not give me tasks equal
   to my powers,
but give me powers equal to my
   tasks,
for I want to be stretched by things
   too great for me.
I want to grow through the greatness
   of my tasks,
but I shall need your help for the
   growing.[12]

E. STANLEY JONES

Resources for

a Mary Heart

in a Martha World

Appendix A

Study Guide

Nothing has transformed my life like the study of God's Word. Something powerful happens when we go beyond other people's opinions and revelations and discover for ourselves what God has to say. I designed this twelve-week Bible study to help you do just that.

I recommend using a translation of the Bible that you enjoy and understand, as well as a notebook and a pen to record your answers. Before each lesson, ask the Holy Spirit to increase your understanding as you examine God's Word and then help you apply the truths you discover.

Each lesson starts with questions for individual reflection or group discussion, then moves into a study of scriptural principles. At the end of the lesson, you'll have an opportunity to write about what spoke most to you in that chapter. The stories, quotes, and sidebars within the chapters may provide further opportunities for discussion or reflection.

My prayer is that each of you will begin to experience the blessing God promises to those who look "intently into the perfect law that gives freedom . . . not forgetting what he has heard, but doing it" (James 1:25). There is a holy makeover waiting for each one of us. It is found in God's presence and within the pages of his Word. Dig in, ladies! You'll be glad you did.

Chapter One:

A Tale of Two Sisters

Questions for Discussion or Reflection

1. What preconceived ideas did you have about Mary and Martha before reading this book? Which woman do you relate to most — Mary or Martha? Explain your answer.

2. One woman told me, "My life is like a blender — and it's stuck on frappé!" What inanimate object best describes how your life currently feels?

Going Deeper

3. Read Luke 10:38-42. List at least two things you learn about Martha in this passage and at least two things you learn about Mary. How would you sum up Martha in one word? How would you sum up Mary?

4. A woman told me, "I guess I'm just a Martha and that I'll always be a Martha." Is it possible for our basic character to change, or are we destined to live our lives stuck in a predetermined nature? Explain your answer.

5. What does the Bible say in the following

verses about our potential for change?
    Ezekiel 36:26-27 ———————
    2 Corinthians 5:17 ———————
    Philippians 1:6 ———————

6. Have you seen God's work of transformation in your own life or someone else's? How did you know it was a "holy makeover" and not just a temporary "facelift"?

7. Read Matthew 11:28-30. Circle key words and meditate on these verses — really think about what Jesus is saying. Then memorize this passage phrase by phrase. Write it on an index card, and refer to it frequently, repeating it until it becomes a part of you.

8. What spoke most to you in this chapter?

Chapter Two:

"Lord, Don't You Care?"

Questions for Discussion or Reflection

1. The story of Mary and Martha stirs up memories of sibling rivalry for many of us. What battles with your siblings do you remember the most? What did you do to get your parents to notice you?

2. Read Luke 10:38-42. Have you ever

asked Martha's question, "Lord, don't you care?" What was the situation? How did God answer your question?

Going Deeper

3. All of us have felt alone — even great heroes of the faith felt this way. Read 1 Kings 19:1-18. How did the "Deadly Ds" of distraction, discouragement, and doubt attack Elijah after the great victory over the prophets of Baal in 1 Kings 18? I've completed the first one as an example:

   DISTRACTION: *Jezebel's anger made him run for his life.*

   DISCOURAGEMENT: _____

   DOUBT: _____

4. In this passage how did God minister to Elijah in the midst of his discouragement? How has God ministered to you when you felt alone and were hurting?

5. In Mark 4:35-41 the disciples echoed Martha's question: "Don't you care?" What does this portion of Scripture teach us about the difficult times in our lives? (Consider Isaiah 43:1-2.)

6. Read Psalm 103. List at least five of the many ways God shows his love for us. (If you are struggling to know the

Father's love, consider memorizing this chapter so you won't forget "all his benefits.")

7. Write Jesus a letter beginning with "Lord, I know you love me because . . . ," and list the ways he has shown his great love for you.

8. What spoke most to you in this chapter?

Chapter Three:

The Diagnosis

Questions for Discussion or Reflection

1. Martha wanted Jesus to tell Mary to help out in the kitchen, but instead of giving her what she wanted, Dr. Jesus made a diagnosis: "Martha, Martha . . . you are worried and upset about many things." If you had been Martha, how would Jesus' words have made you feel?

2. According to Dr. Edward Hallowell, over half of us are chronic worriers. Which of the ten signs of a big worrier on pages 73-74 do you struggle with? How do worry and anxiety spill over into your daily life and affect your behavior? your physical health?

Going Deeper

3. Fear not only affects us physically but spiritually. Read Luke 8:14. List three things that may choke the Word of God out of our lives. Which one do you struggle with most, and how does it choke you spiritually?

4. Look at the "Concern and Worry" diagram on page 83, and read the quote from Gary E. Gilley. What concerns are you currently facing? What worries?

5. What do the following passages tell us to do with our worries and concerns, and what will be the result?

Proverbs 3:5-6   COMMAND: _____
                  RESULT: _____

Philippians 4:6-7 COMMAND: _____
                   RESULT: _____

6. a. Rewrite Matthew 6:25-30 as if God were speaking directly to you and your current situation.
   Therefore, I tell you, __(your name)__, *do not worry about . . .*

   b. Read Matthew 6:31-34. Respond to this passage in a prayer to the Lord.
   Lord, I don't want to worry as the world does. Help me to . . .

7. According to 1 John 4:16-18, how can we respond to God's love, and what

will happen to fear when we do?

8. What spoke most to you in this chapter?

Chapter Four:

The Cure

Questions for Discussion or Reflection

1. Read the wagon and the rocks story on pages 102-107. Take a look in your wagon. Which rocks has God asked you to carry? Which rocks have you unwisely and sometimes unconsciously volunteered to carry for someone else?

2. Do you ever feel the driven, perfectionistic, spiritual Martha Stewart coming out in you? What does she look like at home? What does she look like at church?

Going Deeper

3. What do you think Jesus meant in Luke 10:38-42 when he told Martha that only one thing was needed?

4. a. Turn a few pages, to Luke 18:18-25, to another exchange Jesus had. What qualification did the rich young ruler give for entering the kingdom of God?

418

b. What was the one thing Jesus said he lacked?

c. Why do you think Christ focused on his wealth?

d. Why may the one thing God asks us to do be different from what he requires of someone else? (Consider 1 Corinthians 13:3 and Philippians 3:4-7.)

5. Perhaps like the rich young ruler you find yourself trying to perform for God, carrying more rocks in hopes of earning God's love and favor. What do the following verses say about works-based Christianity?

Galatians 3:3 _____

Titus 3:5 _____

6. What did Paul say in Philippians 3:13-14 was his "one thing"? Why was forgetting what was behind him so important for Paul? (Consider Acts 26:9-15.) What things in your past hold you back from experiencing all God has for you? Take a moment to ask the Lord to help you let go of anything that holds you back.

7. Using the guidelines on pages 116-117, sit down this week and begin "dumping rocks." But before you start, ask the Lord for wisdom (James 1:5). He loves

to give it, and he wants to set us free!

8. What spoke most to you in this chapter?

Chapter Five:

Living Room Intimacy

Questions for Discussion or Reflection

1. Someone has said that each of us is created "with a God-shaped hole" and that we will never be truly satisfied until we fill that space with him. Unfortunately many of us, as Teri described on page 142, fill up on spiritual Snicker Bars. What do you turn to instead of God when you're feeling empty?

2. I've written that intimacy with God comes through Prayer + the Word + Time. Which of these three disciplines is most difficult for you? Which comes easiest?

Going Deeper

3. We all face barriers to intimacy with God. Put a check by the one or two you struggle with most, then look up the verses next to that barrier. Circle the verse that is most meaningful to you.

———Unworthiness
   (Isaiah 41:9-10; Ephesians 2:13-14)
———Busyness
   (Psalm 90:12; Isaiah 40:29-31)
———Guilt / Shame
   (Psalm 32:5; 1 John 1:9)
———Pride
   (Psalm 10:4; James 4:6-7)
———Depression
   (Psalm 42:11; John 14:1)
———Trials / Hardships
   (Hebrews 13:6; 2 Corinthians 4:7-10)
4. Meditate on the verse you circled, then personalize it in the form of a prayer to God. Here is an example based on 1 John 1:9.

   God, thank you for the forgiveness that comes when I admit my sin rather than deny it. I'm so glad I don't have to clean up my act before I come to you. All I have to do is come. You promise to do the cleaning.

5. I've written that before we become Christians, Satan tells us we don't need a Savior. After we become Christians, he tells us we don't deserve a Savior. How have these lies affected your walk with God?

6. God longs to have fellowship with us. Read the following verses, and describe the metaphor Scripture uses to describe the intimate relationship we can have with God.

John 15:5 _____

Romans 8:15-16 _____

2 Corinthians 11:2 _____

7. Read the excerpt from "My Heart Christ's Home" (pages 149-151). How does it make you feel to think that Jesus longs to have time alone with you — to be at home in you? How could this realization turn your devotional life from a duty to a delight?

8. What spoke most to you in this chapter?

Chapter Six:

Kitchen Service

Questions for Discussion or Reflection

1. Dwight L. Moody said, "Of one hundred men, one will read the Bible; the ninety-nine will read the Christian."[1] Who was the first Christian in your life to live in such a way that you could clearly see Christ? How did this person affect your life?

2. Read the story of the little boy and the evangelist on page 197. How would you like Jesus to "stick out all over" your life — that is, what attitudes and characteristics of the Savior would you like God to develop in your life?

Going Deeper

3. Read John 13:1-17. Jesus' washing of the disciples' feet was a totally unexpected example of what true Christian love should look like. According to page 168, why was it so shocking?

4. J. Oswald Sanders said, "It is noteworthy that only once did Jesus say that he was leaving his disciples an example, and that was when he washed their feet."[2] In what unexpected ways could we wash the feet of those around us?

5. Place one (or more) of the following letters beside each verse that follows. In this passage Jesus ministered (a) as he went *on his way;* (b) as he went *out of his way;* (c) in *all kinds of ways.*

_____ Mark 1:29-34
_____ Mark 6:30-34
_____ Mark 7:31-35

6. How could you practically administer Christ's love in each of these ways? I've

completed the first one as an example.

As I go on my way: *I thank the school crossing guard for keeping my kids safe.*

As I go out of my way: ————————

In all kinds of ways: ————————

7. Read Acts 3:1-10. What can we learn from this passage about how to actively show God's love to those around us?

8. What spoke most to you in this chapter?

Chapter Seven:

The Better Part

Questions for Discussion or Reflection

1. Read the "hoopy birthday" story on pages 201-203. Name the Hula-Hoop responsibilities you have in your life. Which one is the most difficult to keep in motion?

2. Consider Wilbur Rees's thought-provoking words:

   I would like to buy $3 worth of God, please, not enough to explode my soul or disturb my sleep, but just enough to equal a cup of warm milk or a snooze in the sunshine. I don't want enough of Him to make me love a black man or pick beets with a migrant. I want ecstasy, not transformation; I want the warmth of the womb, not a new birth. I want a pound of the Eternal in a paper sack. I would like to buy $3 worth of God, please.[3]

In all honesty, how much of God do you want? What keeps you from wanting more?

Going Deeper

3. We live with so much less than God intended us to have. Ask God to illuminate your understanding as you read Paul's prayer for believers in Ephesians 3:16-19. Then list three truths from this passage you'd like God to make real in your life.

4. How does Matthew 6:33 relate to Stephen Covey's "First Things First" principle (page 209) — that is, putting in the big rocks first? Give an example of a time you found this principle true in your life.

5. Read on pages 216-220 about Sidlow Baxter's personal struggle to develop a devotional time. How important is our will in this process of seeking God? How important are our emotions?

6. Explain how the following Bible

characters chose to put God first despite overwhelming emotions or circumstances.

David (2 Samuel 12:13-23) ————

Daniel (Daniel 6:3-10) ————

Jesus (Matthew 26:36-39) ————

7. Use the "Journal the Journey" outline in Appendix D and the instructions on page 231 to meditate on and write about one of the following passages.

Psalm 139 Romans 8   Ephesians 4

Isaiah 55   1 Corinthians 13 James 1

8. What spoke most to you in this chapter?

Chapter Eight:

Lessons from Lazarus

Questions for Discussion or Reflection

1. What is your favorite kind of story and why?

Romance   Mystery   Biography

Adventure   Sci-Fi   Fantasy

2. Which of the following lessons from Lazarus have you found most true in your life? Explain the circumstances involved and what you learned.
   - God's will does not always proceed in a straight line.

- God's love sometimes tarries for our good and his glory.
- God's ways are not our ways, but his character is still dependable.
- God's plan is released when we believe and obey.
- The "end" is never the end; it is only the beginning.

Going Deeper

3. Read John 11:1-6. Circle key words, and think about this family's situation and Jesus' response. When you face difficulties, which of these verses might comfort you most and why?

4. Because time and space confine us, we can't always see what is really happening. What do the following verses say about this in-between time in which we find ourselves?

   John 16:33 _____

   Hebrews 11:13-16 _____

   James 1:2-4 _____

5. Martha Tennison says, "We only trust people we know. If you're struggling to trust God, it may be because you don't really know God."[4] We come to know God better through his Word. What do the following verses reveal about our heavenly Father?

Psalm 27:1 "The Lord is ———————————."

Psalm 34:18 "The Lord is ———————————."

Psalm 100:5 "The Lord is ———————————."

Psalm 145:8 "The Lord is ———————————."

6. Look up the word *trust* in a concordance. Find two phrases that speak to you, and write out the corresponding verses.

7. Laura Barker Snow writes about the difficult times we all face and how we need to view such times through the sovereignty and goodness of God, to live as if God is saying:

My child, I have a message for you today; let me whisper it in your ear, that it may gild with glory any storm clouds which may arise, and smooth the rough places upon which you may have to tread. It is short, only five words, but let them sink into your inmost soul; use them as a pillow upon which to rest your weary head. . . . This thing is from ME.[5]

How would your life be different if you could receive these words as truth and

428

not only truth but as evidence of God's love in your life?

8. What spoke most to you in this chapter?

Chapter Nine:

Martha's Teachable Heart

Questions for Discussion or Reflection

1. Which of the following best describes the kind of student you were in school?
Intellectual
Absent-Though-Present
Teacher's Pet
Procrastinator
Party Animal
High Achiever
What did you like most about school? What did you like least? How have you carried these likes and dislikes into adulthood?

2. Think of someone you consider teachable. What character qualities make you view him or her that way?

Going Deeper

3. Fill out the "Are You Teachable?" questionnaire on page 278. What did you discover about yourself?

4. We have to accept the diagnosis if we're ever going to experience the cure. I believe Martha did just that. Read Luke 10:38-42. Now read John 11:17-28. What differences do you see in Martha in these two stories?

5. Read Hebrews 12:5-11, and then list four reasons why God disciplines us and four results of that discipline.

REASONS

_____
_____
_____
_____

RESULTS

_____
_____
_____
_____

6. The Bible is filled with if-then propositions. *If* we will . . . , *then* God will . . . What do the following verses promise us if we obey? I've filled out the first verse for you.

Joshua 1:8   If . . .   *I meditate on God's Word and do it,* then . . . *I will be prosperous and successful.*

430

John 8:31-32 If . . . _____

then . . . _____

James 1:25 If . . . _____

then . . . _____

7. God is willing to forgive and change us — even at our very worst. Consider the prayer David prayed in Psalm 51:10-12 after his murderous, adulterous affair with Bathsheba. Rewrite this cry for transformation in your own words. Then read it aloud to the Lord.

8. What spoke most to you in this chapter?

Chapter Ten:

Mary's Extravagant Love

Questions for Discussion or Reflection

1. Describe a time you expressed love and concern for others and were misunderstood. How did it make you feel? Did you pull back or press in closer?

2. Consider the differences between Mary's and Judas's love for Christ:

MARY . . .
- had a heart of gratitude
- came with abandon
- heard what Jesus said

431

and responded
- held nothing back

JUDAS . . .
- had a heart of greed
- came with an agenda
- heard but did not
  understand
- gave nothing up

Which aspect of Mary's love comes easiest to you? Which aspect is the most difficult for you?

Going Deeper

3. Read John 12:1-11. What was Judas's response to Mary's extravagant love? What did John say was the motivation behind his response?

4. Read Matthew 16:21-23. What was Peter's response to Jesus' explanation that he must die? What did Jesus say was the motivation behind his response?

5. Read another account of Mary's anointing Jesus in Mark 14:6-9. Finish the following four statements Jesus made about her extravagant love.

"She has done a —————— thing to me."

"She did what she ————————."

"She poured perfume . . . to prepare for my ————————————."

432

"Wherever the gospel is preached . . . what she has ———————— will also be told." Meditate on one of these statements. Ask the Lord to show you practical ways you could love him more beautifully and sacrificially.

6. Matthew and Mark both place Judas's dark change of heart as happening immediately after Mary's extravagant act of love. According to the following verses, why are greed and the love of money so dangerous?

   Matthew 6:24 ————————————

   1 Timothy 6:9-10 ————————————

   James 4:1-4 ————————————

7. Mary loved extravagantly because she had experienced firsthand the extravagant love of God. Read 1 John 3:1 and Romans 8:31-39. Write a love letter back to God, expressing your gratitude for his lavish love and extravagant grace.

8. What spoke most to you in this chapter?

Chapter Eleven:

Balancing Work

and Worship

Questions for Discussion or Reflection

1. What does your teetertotter look like when it comes to balancing work and worship? Draw a line to show which way it tends to tilt (if it does).

Work   Λ   Worship

Pivot Point

2. Read the "Listening to Your Soul" checklist on pages 362-363. According to the checklist, do you need to spend more time in the Living Room or the Kitchen? What are some practical ways you could lean into your weak side to bring balance to your Christian life?

Going Deeper

3. On one side of the teetertotter we find the importance of loving people. Read the story of the Good Samaritan in Luke 10:25-37. Describe how the Samaritan fulfilled the following statements:
   He took NOTICE ————————
   He took ACTION ————————
   He took RESPONSIBILITY ————
   Which of these three qualities comes

easiest to you? Which is the hardest for you?

4. On the other side of Mary and Martha's story we find Christ's teaching on prayer. What does Luke 11:1-13 show about our part in prayer and God's promised response?

OUR PART

_____

_____

_____

_____

GOD'S RESPONSE

_____

_____

_____

_____

5. According to the following verses, why is it dangerous to spend all our time on one end of the teetertotter?
Matthew 7:21-23 _____
James 2:14-17 _____
1 John 3:16-18 _____

6. We all need time to let our souls catch up. From Isaiah 58:13-14, list three ways we can "keep the Sabbath" and also three blessings we will receive from honoring the "Lord's holy day."

7. According to the following verses, what

blessings do we receive from hospitality?

Isaiah 58:6-8 ————————————

Matthew 25:34-36 ————————

Hebrews 13:2 ————————————

8. What spoke most to you from this chapter?

Chapter Twelve:

Having a Mary Heart

in a Martha World

Questions for Discussion or Reflection

1. Have you ever heard a great Christian testimony and wished you could have the faith of that person or live as he or she has lived? What was the process that gave them the product?

2. When you face difficulties in life, which approach do you usually take? Explain.

The All-Star Wrestling Approach: "God! I'm doing this for you — howsaboutta little help here?"

The Job Approach: "Where are you — and why don't you care?"

The Jonah Approach: "Forget Nineveh — I'm headed for the Bahamas."

Going Deeper

3. Read John 12:1-3. Knowing what you now know about these sisters, what two things could you surmise about Martha and about Mary from this passage? How would you sum up Martha in one word? How would you sum up Mary? How does this differ from the way you described them in the study for chapter 1 (question 3)?

4. Read the following verses. Describe the process God uses and the purpose he intends.

Deuteronomy 8:2

    PROCESS _____

    PURPOSE _____

Romans 8:28-29

    PROCESS _____

    PURPOSE _____

2 Corinthians 4:17

    PROCESS _____

    PURPOSE _____

5. How do we partner in this process, according to Philippians 2:12-13?

    We do . . .

    God does . . .

6. Read Philippians 1:6 and Hebrews 10:35-36, then look up the following words in the dictionary, and write their definitions.

Confident:

Persevere:

Complete:

Which of these words mean the most to you right now and why?

7. Read Philippians 3:12-14. Circle key words, and then rewrite this passage in your own words. Read it aloud as a prayer, a declaration of faith, and/or a personal mission statement. Ask God to keep it ever before you as you run the race for the prize.

8. What spoke most to you from this chapter?

Appendix B

Resources for Living Room Intimacy

Devotions

Everyday Light by Selwyn Hughes. Nashville: Broadman & Holman, 1998.

Experiencing God (workbook) by Henry T. Blackaby and Claude V. King. Nashville: LifeWay Press, 1995.

My Utmost for His Highest by Oswald Chambers. 1935. Reprint, Uhrichsville, Ohio: Barbour & Co., *n.d.* Updated version: Grand Rapids, Mich.: Discovery House, 1992.

OverJoyed by Women of Faith (various authors). Grand Rapids, Mich.: Zondervan, 1999.

Shaping a Woman's Soul by Judith Couchman. Grand Rapids, Mich.: Zondervan, 1996.

Springs in the Valley by L. B. Cowman.

Grand Rapids, Mich.: Zondervan, 1996.

Streams in the Desert by L. B. Cowman.
Grand Rapids, Mich.: Zondervan,
1996.

We Brake for Joy by Women of Faith (various authors). Grand Rapids, Mich.:
Zondervan, 1999.

Windows of the Soul by Ken Gire. Grand
Rapids, Mich.: Zondervan, 1996.

Christian Classics

Adventures in Prayer by Catherine Marshall. Grand Rapids, Mich.: Chosen
Books, 1996.

Beyond Ourselves by Catherine Marshall.
Grand Rapids, Mich.: Revell, 1994.

The Christian's Secret of a Happy Life by
Hannah Whitall Smith. Nashville:
Thomas Nelson, 1999.

Hinds' Feet on High Places by Hannah
Hurnard. Uhrichsville, Ohio: Barbour &
Co., 1998.

In His Steps by Charles M. Sheldon.
Tulsa, Okla.: Honor Books, 1998.

Mere Christianity by C. S. Lewis. New
York: Simon & Schuster, 1996.

The Practice of the Presence of God by
Brother Lawrence. Nashville: Thomas
Nelson, 1999.

The Screwtape Letters by C. S. Lewis. New York: Simon & Schuster, 1996.

With Christ in the School of Prayer by Andrew Murray. North Brunswick, N.J.: Bridge-Logos, 1999.

Quiet Time Music

Instrumental Praise series produced by Don Marsh. Brentwood, Tenn.: Brentwood Music, 1999.

Instruments of Praise series produced by Tom Brooks. Mobile, Ala.: Fairhope Records (a division of Integrity Music), 1998.

My Utmost for His Highest series by various artists. Nashville: Word Music, 1993.

Simplicity series produced by Trammell Starks. Portland, Oreg.: Pamplin Music, 1997.

Appendix C

Resources for Kitchen Service

Service

Designing a Woman's Life by Judith Couchman. Sisters, Oreg.: Multnomah, 1995. A separate Bible study and workbook are also available.

Improving Your Serve by Charles Swindoll. Dallas: Word, 1997.

Living a Purpose-Full Life by Jan Johnson. Colorado Springs, Colo.: WaterBrook Press, 1999.

Roaring Lambs by Bob Briner. Grand Rapids, Mich.: Zondervan, 1995.

Women of a Generous Spirit by Lois Mowday Rabey. Colorado Springs, Colo.: WaterBrook Press, 1998.

Hospitality

Creative Counterpart by Linda Dillow. Nashville: Nelson, 1992.

The Joy of Hospitality by Barbara Ball and Vonette Bright. Orlando: New Life Publications, 1996.

Open Heart — Open Home by Karen Burton Mains. Wheaton, Ill.: Mainstay Church Resources, 1998.

The Personal Touch by Rachael Crabb. Colorado Springs, Colo.: NavPress, 1991.

Things Happen When Women Care: Hospitality and Friendship in Today's Busy World by Emilie Barnes. Eugene, Oreg.: Harvest House, 1990.

Home-Keeping

Decorating on a Shoestring by Gwen Ellis and JoAnn Jannsen. Nashville: Broadman & Holman, 1999.

The Hidden Art of Homemaking by Edith Shaeffer. Wheaton, Ill.: Tyndale House, 1985.

Living a Beautiful Life: 500 Ways by Alexandria Stoddard. New York: Random House, 1996.

Once-a-Month Cooking by Mimi Wilson and Mary Beth Lagerborg. Nashville: Broadman & Holman, 1999.

Welcome Home by Emilie Barnes. Eugene, Oreg.: Harvest House, 1997.

Organization

Confessions of an Organized Homemaker by Deniece Schofield. Cincinnati, Ohio: S & W Publications, 1994.

Disciplines of a Beautiful Woman by Anne Ortlund. Nashville: Word, 1984.

Emilie's Creative Home Organizer by Emilie Barnes. Eugene, Oreg.: Harvest House, 1995.

The Messie's Manual by Sandra Felton. Grand Rapids, Mich.: Revell, 1983.

When You Live with a Messie by Sandra Felton. Grand Rapids, Mich.: Revell, 1994.

Appendix D

Journal the Journey

While many people keep journals of daily events and feelings, a Bible reading highlights journal records what God is saying to us through his Word and our response to him. Here is the format that I've found works well for me.

Date _____ What I read today

_____

Best thing I marked today: *Reference:*

_____

Thought: _____

_____

_____

How it impressed me: _____

_____

_____

_____

_____

_____

_____

_____

_____

_____

_____

This Bible reading highlights format is used in the Navigator's 2:7 Discipleship Course, with seven days on one page.[6] But I've also used spiral notebooks and bound lined journals (available at stationery stores) when I've wanted more space to write. You can even draw up your own form and have it photocopied.

Appendix E

A Simple Plan for a Half-Day of Prayer

"God's acquaintance is not made hurriedly," says E. M. Bounds. "He does not bestow His gifts on the casual or hasty comer and goer. To be much alone with God is the secret of knowing Him and of influence with Him."[7]

Something powerful happens when we set apart a block of time to seek God's face intensively. Here are a few guidelines for a half-day of prayer that I've adapted from the Navigators:

1. *Find a place free from distractions.* I've found it helpful to go away for my extended prayer times. A friend's vacant house, a church or Christian conference center, or even a motel room will do.

2. *Take along your Bible, a notebook, a pen or pencil.* You may also want a

447

devotional, hymnal, a prayer list, memory verses, and your weekly schedule. Wear comfortable clothes and bring a sack lunch.

3. *Stay awake and alert.* Get adequate rest the night before. Change positions frequently. Sit awhile, walk around — vary your position to keep from growing dull or sleepy.

4. *Try a variety of approaches.* Read the Scriptures awhile, pray awhile, plan or organize awhile, and so on. You might divide the time into three parts: (a) wait on the Lord, (b) pray for others, and (c) pray for yourself.

5. *Pray aloud* in a whisper or soft voice. Sometimes thinking aloud also helps.

6. *Make a worry list.* Things often come to mind during prayer. Instead of trying to ignore them, write them down. Prayerfully prioritize them into a to-do list. Ask God to show you how to accomplish what needs to be done.[8]

Appendix F

Christian Rights in the Workplace

Religious discrimination — including requiring Christians to work on the Sabbath — has long been forbidden under Title VII of the 1964 Civil Rights Act. The following information is taken from *Christian Rights in the Workplace: What the Law Says About Religion at Work*, a booklet published by the American Center for Law and Justice.

Employers must accommodate requests by employees for absence on their Sabbath or other religious holidays. An affirmative duty arises under Title VII for the employer to make a good faith effort to arrange the employee's schedule to allow the employee to have Sabbaths off. The employer will be in violation of Title VII if they have "made no real effort"

449

or have taken a "don't care" attitude. . . . (p. 9)

The employer's affirmative duty to attempt to accommodate the employee's request for time off is not limited if the employee asks for more than one accommodation . . . [i.e.,] time off in view of two sincerely held religious beliefs. . . . (p. 9)

The same rule applies where an employee's religious beliefs prevent him from working on Sundays, *and* prevent him from asking someone else to engage in this prohibited activity for him. Merely allowing the employee to swap shifts with someone does not constitute reasonable accommodation in this instance. . . . (p. 9)

There are very few times when employers can require employees to violate their religious beliefs, or refuse to allow the employee to practice his religious beliefs at work. . . . In order to successfully assert this defense, courts require that the employer demonstrate attempted accommodation before claiming undue hardship.

Employers must also be able to show evidence of undue hardship that is more than mere speculation. (p. 13)[9]

For a more thorough discussion of "undue hardship" and our rights as Christians in the workplace, you can request the ACLJ booklet by writing:

The American Center for Law
    and Justice
P.O. Box 64429
Virginia Beach, VA 23467-4429

Notes

Chapter One

1. Vera Lee, *Something Old, Something New* (Naperville: Ill.: Sourcebooks, Inc., 1994), 102-3.
2. Excerpted in *Growing Strong in God's Family*, The 2:7 Series (Colorado Springs, Colo.: NavPress, 1987), 20.
3. Miriam Neff and Debra Klingsporn, *Shattering Our Assumptions* (Minneapolis: Bethany, 1996), 194.
4. Taken from *A New Beginning*, copyright 1995 by Stonecroft, Inc. Used by permission. To read more, go to www.stonecroft.org and click on "A New Beginning."

Chapter Two

1. Dutch Sheets, *The River of God* (Ventura, Calif.: Gospel Light, 1998), 195.
2. A version of this story first appeared as Joanna Weaver, "Out in the Cold,"

HomeLife 54, no. 6 (March 2000): 20-2.

Chapter Three

1. Joel Gregory, *Growing Pains of the Soul* (Dallas: Word, 1987), 31.
2. Edward Hallowell, *Worry: Controlling It and Using It Wisely* (New York: Pantheon, 1997), xi.
3. Adapted from Hallowell, *Worry*, 79-83.
4. "An Average Person's Anxiety Is Focused on . . ." quoted in John Underhill and Jack Lewis, comp., Bible Study Foundation Illustration Database, Bible Study Foundation Web site (*www.Bible.org*).
5. See Archibald D. Hart, *Overcoming Anxiety* (Dallas: Word, 1989).
6. Tony Evans, *No More Excuses* (Wheaton, Ill.: Crossway Books, 1996), 223.
7. Sheila Walsh, *Bring Back the Joy* (Grand Rapids, Mich.: Zondervan, 1998), 53.
8. Hallowell, *Worry*, 70.
9. Anne Driscoll interview with Dr. Edward Hallowell, "What, Me Worry?" *On Air Dateline NBC*, 4 November 1999, at the Website:

http://MSNBC.MSN.com/news/
210941.asp, 3.

10. Gary E. Gilley, "Think on These
Things" newsletter 4, no. 2 (February
1998).

11. Oswald Chambers, *My Utmost for His
Highest* (1935; reprint, Uhrichsville,
Ohio: Barbour, *n.d.*), 135.

12. Corrie Ten Boom, quoted in *Moments
— Someone Special* (Minneapolis:
Heartland Samplers, 1997), n.p.

13. Selwyn Hughes, *Every Day Light*
(Nashville: Broadman & Holman,
1998), day 1.

14. Bill and Kathy Peel, *Discover Your
Destiny* (Colorado Springs, Colo.:
NavPress, 1997), 202.

15. Quoted in Chambers, *My Utmost for
His Highest*, 30.

16. Joseph M. Scriven, "What a Friend
We Have in Jesus," *The Hymnal for
Worship & Celebration* (Waco, Tex.:
Word Music, 1986), 435.

Chapter Four

1. Adapted from a story by Rosemarie
Kowalski. Used by permission.

2. Bernard R. Youngman, *The Lands and
Peoples of the Living Bible* (New York:

Hawthorn, 1959), 213.

3. Youngman, *Lands and Peoples*, 213-4.
4. G. Ernest Wright, ed., *Great People of the Bible and How They Lived* (Pleasantville, N.Y.: Reader's Digest Association, 1974), 324-5.
5. William Barclay, *The Gospel of John*, vol. 1, rev. ed., *The Daily Study Bible* series (Philadelphia: Westminster, 1975), 248.
6. Charles H. Spurgeon, *Morning and Evening* (Nashville: Nelson, 1994), January 24, Evening.

Chapter Five

1. Robert J. Morgan, *On This Day* (Nashville: Nelson, 1997), January 5.
2. Philip Yancey, *What's So Amazing About Grace?* (Grand Rapids, Mich.: Zondervan, 1997), 97.
3. Anne Wilson Schaef, *LAUGH! I Thought I'd Die If I Didn't* (New York: Ballantine Books, 1990), May 27.
4. Kent Hughes, *Liberating Ministry from the Success Syndrome* (Wheaton, Ill.: Tyndale, 1988), 139.
5. Excerpted in *The Growing Disciple*, The 2:7 Series, Course 1 (Colorado Springs, Colo.: NavPress, 1987), 69-73.

6. Adapted from Emilie Barnes, *The Spirit of Loveliness* (Eugene, Oreg.: Harvest House, 1992), 109-10.
7. From an e-mail interview with Robin Jones Gunn, 30 January 2000.
8. Excerpt from Gwen Shamblin, "Love the Lord with All Your Mind," Week 2 of *Weigh Down Workshop: Exodus Out of Egypt* video series, Weigh Down Workshop, Inc., 1997. For more information call 1-800-844-5208.
9. Max Lucado, *The Great House of God* (Dallas: Word, 1997), 4.
10. Matthew Henry, *Matthew Henry's Commentary on the Whole Bible*, vol. 4 (New York: Revell, n.d.), 153.
11. Confirmed in a telephone conversation with Eugene Peterson, 29 January 2000.
12. Adapted from quotation in Henry Blackaby, *Experiencing God* (Nashville: LifeWay Press, 1990), 34.
13. Hughes, *Liberating Your Ministry*, 72-3.

Chapter Six

1. Taped sermon and interview with Dr. Donald Argue, Billings, Montana, March 1999.

2. William Barclay, *The Gospel of John*, rev. ed., vol. 2 (Philadelphia: Westminster, 1975), 138-9.

3. J. Oswald Sanders, *Discipleship Journal* 76 (July-August 1993): 39.

4. Quoted in Mother Teresa, *In My Own Words* (New York: Random House, 1996), 100.

5. Quoted in Philip Yancey, *What's So Amazing About Grace?* (Grand Rapids, Mich.: Zondervan, 1997), 262.

6. Brother Lawrence, *The Practice of the Presence of God* (Virginia Beach, Va.: CBN University Press, 1978), 10.

7. Charles Grierson, "Martha," *Dictionary of the Bible*, ed. James Hastings (New York: Scribner, 1909), 588.

8. Brother Lawrence, *The Practice of the Presence*, 22.

9. C. S. Lewis, "The Efficacy of Prayer," *The World's Last Night* (New York: Harcourt Brace Jovanovich, 1960), 9.

10. Henry Blackaby, *Experiencing God* (Nashville: LifeWay Press, 1990), 13-5.

11. Blackaby, *Experiencing God*, 13-5.

12. Linda Andersen, "Love Adds a Little Chocolate," in Medard Laz, *Love Adds a Little Chocolate: One Hundred Stories to Brighten Your Day* (New

York: Warner, 1998), 15. Reissued as *Love Adds the Chocolate* (Colorado Springs, Colo.: WaterBrook, 2000).

13. First quotation from Daphne Kingsma, *Weddings from the Heart* (New York: MJF Books, 1995), 111. Second quotation from Mother Teresa, *In My Own Words*, 33.

14. Kenneth C. Kinghorn, *Discovering Your Spiritual Gifts* (Grand Rapids, Mich.: Zondervan, 1984); C. Peter Wagner, *Finding Your Spiritual Gifts: Wagner-Modified Houts Spiritual Gifts Questionnaire* (Ventura, Calif.: Regal, 1995).

15. Jack B. Hoey Jr., "Breaking the Unplowed Ground," *Discipleship Journal* 39 (May-June 1987): 4.

16. John Milton, "When I Consider How My Light Is Spent," *Norton Anthology of English Literature*, vol. 1, rev. ed. (New York: W. W. Norton, 1968), 1015.

17. Jan Johnson, *Living a Purpose-Full Life* (Colorado Springs, Colo.: WaterBrook, 1999), 151-3.

18. John Ortberg, *Love Beyond Reason* (Grand Rapids, Mich.: Zondervan, 1998), 11-14,18.

19. Yancey, *What's So Amazing About Grace?* 258-9.

Chapter Seven

1. See Janet Holm McHenry, *PrayerWalk: Becoming a Woman of Prayer, Strength, and Discipline* (Colorado Springs, Colo.: WaterBrook, 2001).
2. Quoted in Dennis Rainey, *Planting Seeds, Pulling Weeds* (San Bernardino, Calif.: Here's Life, 1989), 114.
3. Selwyn Hughes, *Everyday Light* (Nashville: Broadman & Holman, 1998), day 1.
4. Robert Robinson, "Come Thou Fount of Every Blessing," *The Hymnal for Worship & Celebration* (Waco, Tex.: Word Music, 1986), 2.
5. Adapted from Stephen R. Covey, *First Things First* (New York: Simon & Schuster, 1994), 88-9.
6. Wilbur Rees, "$3.00 Worth of God," quoted in Tim Hansel, *When I Relax I Feel Guilty* (Elgin, Ill.: David C. Cook, 1979), 49.
7. Cynthia Heald, "Becoming a Friend of God," *Discipleship Journal* 54 (November-December 1989): 22.
8. From J. Sidlow Baxter's personal correspondence, 8 September 1987, as quoted in Kent Hughes, *Liberating*

Ministry from the Success Syndrome (Wheaton, Ill.: Tyndale, 1987), 78-81.

9. Howard E. Butt Jr., *Renewing America's Soul: A Spiritual Psychology for Home, Work, and Nation* (New York: Continuum, 1996), 232-3.

Chapter Eight

1. Max Lucado, *God Came Near* (Portland, Oreg.: Multnomah, 1987), 79.
2. Ray C. Stedman, "God's Strange Ways," sermon given 9 September 1984 at Peninsula Bible Church, Palo Alto, California.
3. Martha Tennison in a sermon given 25 September 1999 in Billings, Montana.
4. Stedman, "God's Strange Ways."
5. CeCe Winans, *On a Positive Note* (New York: Pocket Books, 1999), 207.
6. Quoted in L. B. Cowman, *Streams in the Desert* (Grand Rapids, Mich.: Zondervan, 1996), 35.
7. *NIV Study Bible: New International Version* (Grand Rapids, Mich.: Zondervan, 1985), text note on John 12.

8. My editor wants you to know she disavows all responsibility for this extremely corny (but very effective) memory device.
9. Tennison, a sermon given 25 September 1999.
10. Philip Yancey, *Disappointment with God* (Grand Rapids, Mich.: Zondervan, 1988), 211.
11. Yancey, *Disappointment with God*, 211.
12. Adapted from Harry Pritchett Jr., *Leadership* (Summer 1985), quoted in Charles Swindoll, *Tales of a Tardy Oxcart* (Nashville: Word, 1998), 491-2.

Chapter Nine

1. Quoted in *Daybreak Quotes* (Wheaton, Ill.: Tyndale, 1991), n.p.
2. Carol Mayhall, "Listening to God," in Judith Couchman, ed., *One Holy Passion* (Colorado Springs, Colo.: WaterBrook, 1998), 109-11.
3. Oswald Chambers, *My Utmost for His Highest* (1935; reprint, Uhrichsville, Ohio: Barbour, *n.d.*), 210.
4. Kathleen Norris, *Amazing Grace: A Vocabulary of Faith* (New York: Riverhead Books, 1998), 14-5.

5. Adapted with permission from author Joanie Burnside.

Chapter Ten

1. Josephus said that Sadducees "in their [conversation] with their peers are as rude as to aliens." *NIV Study Bible: New International Version* (Grand Rapids, Mich.: Zondervan, 1985), text note on John 11:49.
2. James B. Pritchard, ed., *Everyday Life in Bible Times* (Washington, D.C.: National Geographic Society, 1977), 305.
3. Charles Panati, *Sacred Origins of the Profound* (New York: Penguin, 1996), 323.
4. *NIV Study Bible*, text note on Mark 14:3.
5. Ruth V. Wright and Robert L. Chadbourne, *Gems and Minerals of the Bible* (New York: Harper & Row, 1970), 6.
6. William Barclay, *The Gospel of John*, rev. ed., vol. 2 (Philadelphia: Westminster, 1975), 111.
7. Theodore Parker, quoted in Cora Lee Pless, "How Do We Return?" *God's Abundance: 365 Days to a Simpler Life*

(Lancaster, Pa.: Starburst, 1997),
Dec. 27.

8. Quoted in Barclay, *The Gospel of John*, 2:111.

9. Barclay, *The Gospel of John*, 2:112.

10. Tom Fennell Timmins, "Homecoming for a Hero," *Maclean's*, 25 January 1999, 26.

11. Hannah Whitall Smith, *The Christian's Secret of a Happy Life* (Nashville: Nelson, 1999), 45-6.

12. Peter Kreeft, *Three Philosophies of Life* (San Francisco: Ignatius Press, 1989), 94-5.

Chapter Eleven

1. Tim Hansel, *Holy Sweat* (Waco, Tex.: Word, 1987), 12.

2. Jill Briscoe, *Renewal on the Run* (Wheaton, Ill.: Harold Shaw, 1992), 109.

3. Note that some of these symptoms could indicate a physical or emotional imbalance as well as a spiritual one. If they are persistent or severe, you might consider seeing a doctor as well as praying for God's direction in balancing your life.

4. Elizabeth Moll Stalcup, "Seizing the

Sabbath," *Virtue*, August-September 1998, 26-7.

5. Stalcup, "Seizing the Sabbath," 26-7.
6. Interview with Jane Johnson Struck, "Hospitality on the Run," *Today's Christian Woman*, January-February 1992, 58-9.
7. Kathleen Norris, *Amazing Grace: A Vocabulary of Faith* (New York: Riverhead Books, 1998), 265-6.
8. Adapted from Karen Mains, *Open Heart — Open Home* (Elgin, Ill.: David C. Cook, 1976), 171-6.
9. William Plummer, "Taken by the Sea," *People*, 14 December 1992, 59-61.

Chapter Twelve

1. Quoted in Howard L. Rice, *Reformed Spirituality* (Louisville, Ky.: Westminster/John Knox, 1991), 179.
2. Claire Cloninger, *When God Shines Through* (Dallas, Tex.: Word, 1994), 132.
3. Henrietta Mears, *What the Bible's All About* (Ventura, Calif.: Regal, 1983), 84.
4. Quoted in Mother Teresa, *Life in the Spirit* (San Francisco: Harper & Row,

1983), 76-7.

5. Kent Hughes, *James: Faith That Works* (Wheaton, Ill.: Crossway Books, 1991), 17.

6. Hughes, *James*, 17.

7. Charles Swindoll, *Growing Strong in the Seasons of Life* (Portland, Oreg.: Multnomah, 1983), 47-9.

8. William Barclay, *The Letters of James and Peter*, rev. ed. (Louisville, Ky.: Westminster/John Knox Press, 1976), 44.

9. Ken Gire, *Intense Moments with the Savior* (Grand Rapids, Mich.: Zondervan, 1985), 86.

10. Mother Teresa, *Life in the Spirit*, 24.

11. Jan Johnson, *Living a Purpose-Full Life* (Colorado Springs, Colo.: WaterBrook, 1999), 95.

12. Quoted in *Daybreak Quotes* (Wheaton, Ill.: Inspirations, Tyndale House, 1991), n.p.

Appendices

1. Quoted in Philip Yancey, *What's So Amazing About Grace?* (Grand Rapids, Mich.: Zondervan, 1997), 262.

2. J. Oswald Sanders, *Discipleship Journal* 76 (July-August 1993): 39.

3. Wilbur Rees, "$3.00 Worth of God," quoted in Tim Hansel, *When I Relax I Feel Guilty* (Elgin, Ill.: David C. Cook, 1979), 49.

3. Wilbur Rees, "$3.00 Worth of God," quoted in Tim Hansel, *When I Relax I Feel Guilty* (Elgin, Ill.: David C. Cook, 1979), 49.

4. Martha Tennison in a sermon given 25 September 1999 in Billings, Montana.

5. Quoted in L. B. Cowman, *Streams in the Desert* (Grand Rapids, Mich.: Zondervan, 1996), 35.

6. Format adapted from *The Growing Disciple*, The 2:7 Series, Course 1 (Colorado Springs, Colo.: NavPress, 1987), n.p.

7. Quoted in *The Growing Disciple*, 77.

8. Adapted from *The Growing Disciple*, 84-5.

9. *Christian Rights in the Workplace: What the Law Says About Religion at Work* (Virginia Beach, Va.: The American Center for Law and Justice, 1997), 9,13.

Dear Reader,

After writing this book, I have a new appreciation for the disciple John's final statement in his gospel: "Jesus did many other things as well. If every one of them were written down, I suppose that even the whole world would not have room for the books that would be written" (John 21:25). If John could walk away from his gospel knowing he hadn't said it all, then I must be willing to let the Holy Spirit take over where I've left off. After all, only he can lead you into all truth. My words are but an empty shadow of the glorious things God desires to do in you.

May the Lord take this simple story of two sisters and use this ink and paper, these words, as a doorway to bring you into a deeper relationship with him than you've ever known. Remember, it is a lifetime process and a work of the Holy Spirit — not something we have to conjure up on our own. Isn't that good news!

God, himself, desires to write a love

letter upon your heart, a letter "known and read by everybody" (2 Corinthians 3:2). I'd love to hear about the story God is writing in you. While I may not be able to answer every letter, I'd consider it a privilege to pray for you. You can reach me at:

Joanna Weaver
P.O. Box 755
Whitefish, Montana 59937
joannaweaver@hotmail.com

God's richest blessings to you, my dear sister and friend!

Joanna

I thank my God every time I remember you. In all my prayers for all of you, I always pray with joy . . . being confident of this, that he who began a good work in you will carry it on to completion until the day of Christ Jesus.
Philippians 1:3-6

Additional copyright information:

All Scripture quotations, unless otherwise indicated, are taken from the *Holy Bible, New International Version*®. NIV®. Copyright © 1973, 1978, 1984 by International Bible Society. Used by permission of Zondervan Publishing House. All rights reserved. Scripture quotations marked (NRSV) are taken from the *New Revised Standard Version* of the Bible copyright © 1989 by the Division of Christian Education of the National Council of the Churches of Christ in the USA. Used by permission. All rights reserved. Scripture quotations marked (NKJV) are taken from the *New King James Version*. Copyright © 1982 by Thomas Nelson, Inc. Used by permission. All rights reserved. Scripture quotations marked (AMP) are taken from the *Amplified Bible*, Old Testament. Copyright © 1965, 1987 by The Zondervan Corporation. The Amplified New Testament, copyright © 1954, 1958, 1987 by The Lockman Foundation. Used by permission. Scripture quotations marked (Phillips) are taken from the *New Testament in Modern English, Revised Edition* © 1958 by J. B. Phillips. Scripture quotations marked (NASB) are taken from the *New American Standard Bible*®. © Copyright The Lockman Foundation 1960, 1962, 1963, 1968, 1971, 1972, 1973, 1975, 1977. Scripture quotations marked (RSV) are taken from *The Revised Standard Version of the Bible*, copyright © 1946, 1952, and 1971 by the Division of Christian Education, of the National Council of the Churches of Christ in the USA. Used by permission. Scripture quotations marked (KJV) are taken from the *King James Version*. Scripture quotations marked (NEB) are taken from the *New English Bible*. Copyright © 1961, 1970 by the Delegates of the Oxford University Press and the Syndics of the Cambridge University Press.

About the Author

Joanna Weaver is an author, pastor's wife, and mother of two. Her articles have appeared in such publications as *Focus on the Family*, *Guideposts*, and *HomeLife*. She is also the award-winning author of the wedding gift book, *With This Ring*. Joanna lives with her family in Whitefish, Montana.